D1797373

BUGLE & YARRINGTON

BUGLE & YARRINGTON

By
JAMES JAMES

BLUE MARK BOOKS

First published in Great Britain by
Blue Mark Books Limited in 2015

www.bluemarkbooks.com

© James James 2015

The moral rights of the author have been asserted

This is a work of fiction. All characters in this publication
are fictitious and any resemblance to real persons
either living or dead is purely coincidental

A catalogue record for this book is
available from the British Library

ISBN 978-1-910369-01-2

Blue Mark Books Limited supports the Forest Stewardship Council®. The
FSC® promotes the responsible management of the world's forests.
All our books carrying the FSC® logo are printed on FSC®-certified paper

MIX
Paper from
responsible sources
FSC® C013604

Typeset in Minion Pro by Blue Mark Books Limited

Printed and bound by CPI Group (UK) Ltd, CR0 4YY

For my Parents

CHAPTER 1

Back To Work

The Christmas that had just been and gone had fallen on a Monday, so only three days off were required for ten consecutive days away from the office. Splendid! But on the first Tuesday in January, I found myself walking back to the magnificent offices of Bugle & Yarrington, the hallowed Mayfair law firm, and my employer.

I live in Marylebone and walk to Mayfair every morning, setting off at about nine-thirty and arriving ten minutes later. I take the same route, buy *The Times* from the same shop, from the same man (paying weekly, to speed collection up by about thirty seconds) and exchange smiles with the same gorgeous girl who walks in the opposite direction to me. It has been months now, and we still haven't said a word to each other. I am, however, in no doubt that she rather likes the look of me.

This particular morning was cold and wet and I was rapidly becoming both. But, I thought to myself, it could be worse: I could be on the tube with a hangover, or have malaria. It could indeed be worse, but I felt pretty grim. Having not been to work for ten days, my recollection of the legal cases left behind before Christmas was somewhat less than lucid, but a quick look through my filing cabinets would doubtless serve me with some semblance of an idea as to what was going on last year.

But that morning I wished I was anywhere but approaching Oxford Street on my transition from Marylebone to Mayfair. The only thought that cheered me up was that I'd shortly be coming to the stretch of road where I would see my unnamed beauty and a bit of pavement flirting would doubtless ensue.

And thus my mind wandered in deep anticipation of this morning's encounter with her until I reached Oxford Street, whereupon my attentions turned to the twice-daily joy of dodging taxis and buses relentlessly ploughing along from east to west and west to east. My route forces me to cross the great shopping street at a place where no pedestrian crossing exists, which doesn't in fact make the slightest difference, because my patience is such that waiting for the green man is a complete impracticality. After years of practice, my spatial awareness regarding the size and speed of London buses is excellent (although careful re-calculation was required after the demise of the Routemaster) and I can step between them seamlessly. This morning's great crossing of Oxford Street was timed to the second, and resulted in me successfully passing just in front of two buses going in opposite directions. Having just made the pavement before the second bus would have hit me, I couldn't possibly have been expected to notice the carton of milk that some fool had dropped in the gutter until the bus had run over it, bursting the carton open and spraying me from head to toe in cow juice.

Bugger.

The year had begun in a catastrophic manner.

I ignored the laughs from three irksome, spotty school kids and walked on to escape the busyness of Oxford Street. Having walked a few paces further, my natural optimism rose: it could have been worse; it was only milk, and any number of more unpleasant substances could have been covering my suit. And then to my relief I saw the large glass-windowed shop front of my dry cleaner where the memory of dropping off a suit to be cleaned just before Christmas popped happily to mind.

Never before had the pleasure of stepping into the dry cleaner's shop been so great. Usually I feel a sense of being robbed: why does it cost so much to have my pinstripes cleaned, when they don't even smell nice afterwards? I sometimes wonder if they do actually clean them, or whether they spray suits with *essence of dry cleaners* before pressing the trousers and hanging them on a cheap wire hanger in a plastic bag ready for collection.

The nice Polish girl collected my ticket and gave me my suit.

'Do you mind if I give you the suit I'm wearing?' I asked.

'No. Is fine.'

I don't think she expected me to disrobe in front of her, but there was little choice, and off came my jacket, swiftly followed by my trousers. With hindsight, my choice of underwear would not have been my most hideous boxers given to me by my mother several years ago. They were bright green. Bright lime green. And adorned with yellow bananas wearing sunglasses. My sense of justice led me to hope that whoever designed them had been forced to model them personally and very publicly for their sins against pants. The poor Polish girl didn't know where to put her eyes and feverishly tapped the till. But I knew she was checking me out.

I stood up and plonked my milk-soaked trousers on the counter and for some reason glanced out of the window.

Bugger.

There she was. My unnamed girl had actually stopped outside to view the rather unusual scene, and to add to my humiliation was openly laughing at me. Not usually having the misfortune to suffer from embarrassment, I realised that the most important of my New Year's resolutions (to talk to her before the end of January) was now going to be impossible to fulfil. An alternative route to the office avoiding her would be required to save my dignity, if indeed there was any left to save. In this awkward state, the only thing I could think to do was smile stupidly at her and raise a hand to say hello. She gave me a quick wave and carried on, still smiling.

She had never waved to me before.

I arrived at the office to find that in a moment of absent-mindedness my keys had been forgotten. This wasn't such a problem getting into the office, but it did leave me with the uneasy knowledge that getting into my flat that evening might well prove tricky. But again, being forever optimistic, I told myself that I might have lost my keys, and that losing the office keys would certainly lead to an unpleasant admission of carelessness to Angela, the human resources manager whose previous employer had been the Devil.

And so to reception.

'Morning Sue, how are you?' I asked Sue, the ever-present receptionist.

'Very well, thank you. How are you?' she said automatically.

'Very well thanks,' I said automatically.

Very well thanks? No, I'm not! I'm bloody pissed off to be in the office and I'd rather be in bed with a blonde pigtailed bombshell from Sweden.

I managed to keep my thoughts to myself.

Walking on through reception, I reflected that Sue's actually very nice, but there are some mornings (usually about five a week) when getting to my desk and drinking the coffee that lies in wait is more important than anything else.

I sat down, feeling rather as if my desk belonged to someone else. The piles of files that I had gleefully left before Christmas were sitting ominously on the desk. I had told myself that I'd be refreshed after a break from the tedium of the office. Refreshed after Christmas! Refreshed?! With what? Twenty litres of red wine and two of gin, to say nothing of port and ale. My poor addled brain could not cope with the sight of the files, let alone their bewildering content.

And then she came in!

The glorious Emily!

The best-looking secretary in London, and, I'm happy to say, mine. I mentally undressed her in ten seconds flat when I interviewed her, about three years ago. Two lawyers interview each new member of staff, and thankfully when it came to my new secretary's turn, Yarrington was the other lawyer doing the interviewing. He has an exceptional eye for ladies, although even a novice would acknowledge Emily's gorgeousness. Apart from having gravity defying breasts, a pert arse and the kind of thighs you could quite happily spend all afternoon between, reading the paper, asleep, or simply in awe of the musculature and all round fine architecture, she is a damn fine secretary and a good friend.

'Morning, darling.'

'Hi, hun.'

It's all tongue in cheek, but I know she thinks I'm good looking too.

But although we appreciate each other's good looks and get along better than most married couples, there is an unspoken understanding that no amount of booze will ever make anything happen between us. Romance would destroy our brilliant friendship. We do love flirtation, though, and long may it last. We are both currently single, not having yet found anyone good enough, and our exes were both insanely jealous of our relationship; our future spouses will have to be trustful people.

Small talk about Christmas and the New Year ensured that no work was achieved before the first phone alarm of the year at around eleven. This jolted us into panicked action. It could be a colleague wanting to know some technical legal fact, another lawyer wanting to know why a reply hadn't been forthcoming since July, or worse still, a client. After a weekend, it usually took until the Thursday for my brain to properly engage; goodness knows what ten consecutive days off could do.

It was a client.

'Good morning, Mrs Ricketts!' I said gaily, to keep her happy and to announce to Emily that she (Emily) owed me a fiver. Mrs Ricketts was the last client to call last year, and as far as I was concerned, it was a fairly safe bet that she'd be the first to call this year. Mrs Ricketts was one of the Firm's first clients and has remained faithful ever since. For some reason she took rather a shine to me when I was doing her eldest son's second divorce, and now she insists that I do all her and her family's work whether it be personal, property or money related, which I enjoy because it keeps things varied for me. She's about eighty, and as sharp as a pin and a complete pain. She takes up a lot of time, and yes, time is money, but I can't charge her for talking about her grandchildren, or her dying cat, and I still ask her about both, and more, knowing that she'll take half an hour to answer each question.

'Em, Ricketts wants her will doing again,' I announced after a twenty minute phone call which could properly have been conducted in twenty seconds.

I can't remember how many times she had done it last year, but it was generally on a monthly basis. She's exceedingly rich, and has five children, only four of whom are currently beneficiaries of her estate. She now wanted to reinstate the fifth again after she'd had the best Christmas turkey she'd ever tasted, cooked by the estranged child in question, who was in fact the eldest son whose second divorce I had handled. I'm sure there are other reasons why she changes her will, but she tells me her decisions arise from these seemingly nonsensical events. Why should one of her children suddenly be entitled to several million quid for plucking a turkey well? She likes to be eccentric; I see through the supposed eccentricity, but I cannot see the truth. I should be charging her a small fortune for my time, on top of the standard charge for will alterations, but I can't.

It is simply not worth keeping Mrs Ricketts waiting, so I suggested she came in at lunch time to sign the new will, which she thought was an excellent idea: 'Good idea, good idea! The irony is, I'll probably snuff it on the way to your office and poor old – oh! you know who I mean – the one who isn't getting a bean – won't get a bean! See you soon, dear!'

Emily amended the will in about three minutes. The bill took a further two, and the standard covering letter about thirty seconds. Daylight robbery!

But this is how I earn my living: by exchanging my legal expertise for money. I am primarily a family lawyer, which means most of my time is spent divorcing clients from their unbearable other halves. Of course, my clients are always right and reasonable, and it is their spouse or partner who is the evil one; when my client is the most arrogant pig or unreasonable cow, I tell them they're normal; when my client is clearly unhinged, I say their spouse is; when my client has committed adultery I tell them it wasn't their fault; that it was the effect not the cause; the symptom not the illness; and they believe it because they want to.

Fate left me practising family law because after qualification my options were that department or another firm. Not wishing to risk the prospect of the latter where work might actually have been necessary, my mind was made. But in fact, the size of the Firm means I am able to act for my clients in other areas: I have been known to convey property, write wills, and to help my clients avoid paying tax. Shafting the government gives one excellent job satisfaction.

Divorce cases can be depressing, but occasionally there is a client who really does benefit from my services. This is the perk of my job. The amount of money some clients waste on my fees does cause me considerable concern, but it can prove to be prudent expenditure on their part: sometimes for the emotional turmoil I have spared them, and sometimes because my fees are far less than the money I have saved them. And the money saved is often of the highest import to a divorcee because every penny they receive will be one less penny for their evil ex-spouse. This is how I justify my existence.

Mrs Ricketts duly arrived ten minutes early as per usual. She gave me the usual bone-crunching handshake, and read her new will eagle-eyed from start to finish, even though I told her that only one clause had been altered. She doesn't distrust me in the least, but she's quite correctly old fashioned enough not to sign any legal document without first reading it. It amazes me how so many clients will sign papers without even reading them; I'm sure I could persuade many of my clients to sign their own death warrants.

She eventually signed it and produced, with a great show of thanks and understated generosity, but with what is obviously a huge amount of pleasure, a bottle of Moët. I pretend to be surprised but it gets harder every time; I still haven't drunk the last bottle. But I am genuinely thankful. She's a sweetheart, and as the old bird departed, I felt rather sad.

Arriving home at quarter to six, it quickly came to mind that my keys were on the wrong side of the front door. The discovery (by the persistent ringing of their doorbell) that my keyholding neighbours were out left me with but one option: to ring the gorgeous Emily.

'Good evening, madam!'

'Why hello, sir!'

'Can I come over?'

'Yes, that would be most pleasant, but you have to pay tax and the levy this evening is two bottles. My bloodstream is still unused to being alcohol free and I need to top myself up.'

I wasn't entirely sure she understood me.

'I mean can I stay?'

'Yes, that is what I understood. Did you leave your keys at home again?'

It has happened before.

CHAPTER 2

Bugle, Yarrington And I

Bugle & Yarrington ("the Firm") was founded by Frank Bugle and David Yarrington (together "the Founding Fathers") in 1977. They had been junior solicitors in another firm which was taken over. During the takeover, they were both dismissed, respected each other's legal skills, but not, so far as anyone is aware, anything else about each other, and decided to go it alone together.

Yarrington, by virtue of his superior age and having more family money to invest in the Firm, became the senior partner and has remained unchallenged in this position of ultimate authority to date.

The Founding Fathers are so entirely dissimilar that it is scarcely conceivable that they have been partners in the same firm for thirty-odd years, practising entirely different disciplines of law. Bugle was (and is) a criminal lawyer, a genius at unhooking the petty thief or accused murderer; Yarrington is a property man and does everything from huge commercial deals to the conveyance of Mrs Jones' one bedroom leasehold flat in Mile End. But in 1977 (as now), crime and property must have been an odd mixture and there cannot have been much room for cross-departmental referrals, unless Yarrington's clients were doing dodgy property deals, and Bugle was defending them.

But still, they succeeded in expanding from a two-partner, two-secretary, and two-desk firm into a fifteen-partner, ninety-employee strong legal machine.

Bugle is respected, liked, tolerated, disliked and hated in equal measures, often in equal measures by the same person, including me. He went to an average comprehensive in ordinary Home County suburbia and then to an unnamed polytechnic (there's a fiver going to the first person who discovers which one). He delights in telling clients, colleagues and anyone else caught in his line of verbal fire that his father was a dustman, which he follows with a gay but particularly untuneful rendition of the only line of *My Old Man's A Dustman* that he actually knows. This strange attempt to claim he's a council-estate-lad-done-well without actually saying so is pretty transparent to anyone who knows him, even more so to anyone who doesn't, and so fails abysmally every time. He doesn't seem to notice though.

He graduated at twenty-one, qualified at twenty-three, and started up with Yarrington (five years his senior) at twenty-five. Not bad going. Bugle took to law and making money like a frog to water. He's an immensely tall man, towering over me, and wears a variety of ostentatious chalk stripe suits like the East-End barrister's clerks do, thinking they look as suave as the barristers they serve. One gets the feeling that the suits are tailored, though, because he has such long limbs that no shop would stock such garments off the peg. His ties are tied with a Windsor knot and are always as bright as his brighter-than-pearly-white teeth which he flashes at you regularly. His shoes and cufflinks reek of expense without style, a look that he has perfected. He talks in a confident manner – rightly so in relation to legal matters – but because of his false over-friendliness, and his obviously tried and tested standard phrases that he drops into sentences, one just can't help thinking that he's a spiv, wide boy and full-time bullshitter. He, of course, has no idea he is perceived in this light.

His wife Cathy is fat and ugly and they have two fat and ugly daughters. By all accounts, including the wedding photo in Bugle's office, Cathy was a stunner and only went to seed after she dropped the first sprog. It is well known that Bugle, poor chap, has been bitter about this for years.

Bugle loves to work; he loves his job and the law. He loves his offices, he loves court and being a lawyer; this is his life. He is lost unless he is working. He is the only man I know who gets irritable just before he is leaving the office for any period, whether on Friday nights, or, the worst time, just before Christmas or a summer holiday.

Yarrington is universally liked. He is of average height for his generation and dresses impeccably: shiny Oxfords, three piece suits, double cuffs with engraved links, modern but conservative shirt and tie combinations, pocket watch and a monocle which hangs from the breast jacket pocket. The monocle is really only for show and is used in the manner of a magnifying glass when reading the exceptionally small print one invariably finds in some contracts. He has a frightfully plummy accent, and a wicked sense of humour. His dress looks slightly ridiculous to anyone who doesn't know him (you almost expect him to pick up a bowler hat as he leaves the office) but to those who do, it's just Yarrington being deliberately eccentric. He was schooled at Eton, graduated from Oxford and trained at his father's firm. He is most definitely from the establishment and regularly tells the story of how he became a lawyer.

'Well, you know, graduated from Oxford with a first. Didn't know what to do. Thought law'd be frightfully boring. Daddy was a lawyer you see. Two years travelling round Europe at Daddy's expense. Lovely. Then he told me: "Right, boy, off your good-for-nothing backside and to work!" Told him I didn't much fancy his job, or anyone else's, thank you very much, and that writing was much more my cup of tea. "Nonsense, boy! You can't make a living writing! You'd better come with me to the office tomorrow!" So I did. Couple of years later I was a qualified solicitor. Bob's your uncle!'

This is the type of thing that enrages people not of the old school, but coming from Yarrington it is simply amusing to anyone who hears it. He fails to mention that in those two years travelling around Europe he got married, learned fluent Finnish, Arabic and German and wrote two books, one on Caesar's conquest of Britain and one on the Royal Navy from 1800 to 1815, a segment of which he submitted to Cambridge and was awarded a doctorate (no red tape in those days). His mode of transport was a yacht which he sailed single-handedly (until he met his wife) from Scarborough to Murmansk, down the coast of Norway, around the Baltic, through the Channel, round the Iberian Peninsula and finally to Cairo, visiting nearly every country on both sides of the Mediterranean on the way. The story goes that he got so uproariously drunk in Cairo that he dropped a cigarette below decks and burnt the yacht so badly it had to be scrapped. But he never talks about it and there is a strange sense of mystery surrounding the event which intrigues people yet prohibits them asking him directly about it.

I think Yarrington dearly wanted to be a writer, and that the law was an inconvenience thrust upon him by his father. But he's a good lawyer and I don't think he dislikes his profession; in fact, I suspect he enjoys the small amount of social prowess that being senior partner affords him.

I never know whether or not to thank my parents for my name. Was it a spectacular lack of imagination, or a stroke of genius that they called me James James?

I am a solicitor and relative newcomer of seven years service, although that term has ensured that I have been at the Firm longer than many.

It is a curious fact that your colleagues are the people you spend the majority of your time with. You might love, be amused by, be indifferent to, dislike or hate them (or indeed strange combinations of some or all of these), but certainly you get to know them. We all get on relatively well (with some notable exceptions), perhaps because legal employment is conducive to going for a pint or two after work, an idea promulgated by me not infrequently; indeed, it might be argued that many of the Firm's employees exhibit their truest devotion to their employer by diligently taking every opportunity to keep up excellent relations with their colleagues after such a suggestion.

I trained with the Firm, which has the unfortunate effect that some of the partners still treat me as a trainee. 'Trainee' is synonymous with 'Articled Clerk', but some upstanding members of the legal community considered the latter elitist, sexist and thoroughly old-fashioned, a view so entirely incongruous with how the rest of the legal profession was perceived, that lamentably (but in all their wisdom) the Law Society spoke and the Articled Clerk officially became a thing of the past.

The trainee works with supervising solicitors, supposedly experts in their areas of law, in order to assimilate legal knowledge, procedure and general savvyness. To give them credit, some of my supervising solicitors taught me more in a week than I learnt in a year at law school, but the enduring memory of traineeship involved being paid a pittance, being shouted at, mocked, degraded, belittled and made to do hideous jobs that at the time defied belief. My traineeship taught me how to be a thoroughly unqualified plumber, electrician, carpenter, furniture remover (smartly decked out in a Savile Row suit, mind you), tea-making champion and photocopying magician; I cleaned the windows, I swept the floor and I polished up the handle on the big front door.

Training also meant moving between departments every six months, supposedly to obtain an idea of which area of law would inspire you into a lifetime of servitude to that particular discipline. All the trainees found the same. You went into your first 'seat' thinking it would be good, the second hoping it would be more interesting than the first, the third hoping it wouldn't get worse and the fourth wondering which was the least tedious.

However, such regular moves into different departments meant that I got to know everybody in the Firm. And everybody knows me. I am one of the Firm's social protagonists and as such help hold it together. I am the person who bridges the gap between lawyers and secretaries: I go to the pub with the support staff and wine and dine with the partners; I get gossip from the non-commissioned ranks, and management and strategy talk (gossip) from the top brass; I am the main channel of information about who is doing what, who is doing whom, and what is going on throughout the office; I am eloquent enough to impress the clients, criminal and otherwise, with my wit and legal knowledge (though the ice is sometimes frighteningly thin); I am Jim to the support staff, James to the lawyers, and Mr James to the clients.

CHAPTER 3

The Offices

The night after I had stayed with Emily, we arrived at the office together, me in the same shirt and tie combination as the day before, and both of us looking rather the worse for wear. There was a time when I could drink a bottle of red with food and hardly notice a thing, but, alas, that time is past and my thirty-two year old liver cannot cope any more.

Yarrington.

'Ah, morning both! Good to see you two are bright eyed and bushy tailed and ready for the New Year! Nice tie, James. I seem to remember seeing a very similar one not so very long ago!' He never misses a thing, not that anyone would have to be particularly observant to note the regularity that Emily and I crash at each other's flats. I'm sure he thinks there's something going on, but in my hungover state a witty retort was not forthcoming. Yarrington became serious as he remembered something. 'Must see you later, old chap; I'll pop up.' And with that he pottered off.

The words 'old chap' from Yarrington do not bode well: he only ever uses them he's trying pleasantly to say something that he would rather not say and that the recipient would rather not hear. His coming up to my office was worse. He never comes upstairs.

I stood at the bottom of the staircase of Number 22 and looked up. The stairs circling grandly round the huge hallway seemed to be moving in a horrid manner which made me feel quite unwell. The bright sunlight streaming in through the domed skylight hurt my eyes. Bugle claims the glass is original which if he's right must make it over two hundred years old.

Number 22 is the original Bugle & Yarrington office, which the Founding Fathers bought in 1977. Or rather Yarrington's father stumped up the vast majority of the cash. For the first decade the Firm was based on the ground floor and the other floors were let out to pay Yarrington Senior back. All kinds of people shared the building: architects, accountants, a tiny publishing house and a photographer who had a suspicious number of young lady visitors. Bugle loved teasing him about his studio being in Mayfair. The few photos that exist show the place to be a shabby and run down affair. As the Firm grew, it pushed out the other tenants one by one, and by 1997, its twentieth anniversary, Number 22 was bulging at its very seams. The next-door Number 20 was up for sale and the Firm expanded into it, redecorating both. So now Bugle & Yarrington is spread luxuriously between two large Georgian townhouses with sixteen-foot high ceilings, beautifully proportioned rooms, elegant sash windows and carpets so thick that one of Hannibal's fully laden elephants wouldn't have made a sound crossing them.

My office is in Number 22, a far superior building, with a much more satisfactory layout and a general air of correct proportionment in every room. And everything in Number 22 is of a higher quality or design: the height of the windows, the dados, the cornices, the shutters, the door handles, the fireplaces and mantelpieces, and the stairs and banisters. Some may think that these are small considerations, but I notice them, and am thankful. Maybe I should have been an architect.

Emily made me jump back to the cold reality of a Wednesday morning: 'What are you gawping up at?'

'I was musing upon the architecture of our esteemed offices,' I replied, intentionally pompously to enable her to attack me with an amusing insult.

'Let's get some coffee.'

Clearly her brain was also in neutral (it was unlike her not to insult me when set up), but her engine must have been ticking over with sufficient revolutions to find our office bearing two cups of steaming coffee.

I spent the rest of the morning getting through and dealing with the post that had been building up in the week before Christmas and during the Christmas holidays. It's a dull occupation, but in a way rather satisfactory to see the 'in' pile diminish and to watch the stack of letters dictated by me and typed by Emily's lovely slender fingers build up on her desk ready for signature (not that they are usually signed by me; Emily has perfected my signature).

Just after lunch in that horrible sleepy time between two and four in the afternoon, the door of our office flew open. Only Bugle opens doors with such tempestuous force. If the doors hadn't been so handsome, I would have hoped that one day he'd rip one clean off its hinges. The first we saw of him was his huge clenched fist (he uses his fist to open doors) followed by a Persil-white cuff tamed with red silk links. The gangly chav-striped arm followed, with the great but shapely nose and rather gormlessly smiling face soon after.

Once his whole person was standing in front of us, it seemed to take a few seconds for his jacket to settle after the flourish with which he entered.

Emily and I sat blinking.

'Emily. James. How are you?' asked Bugle, neither waiting nor caring for an answer. His usual chitchat ensued, which consisted of him making sure in his own mind that he had asked the right questions to make you feel he cared that you were a happy employee. Of course, it didn't matter if you were unhappy, just as long as he thought it looked like you thought that he looked like he cared. He then asked what he had obviously come to ask: 'Yarrington seen you yet, James?'

'No.'

'Oh! Right you are then!' and with that he turned on his heels, his jacket lifting like a cloak. He almost pulled the door off its hinges as he opened it, grinned over his shoulder by way of goodbye and departed.

I pondered.

Emily sat thinking.

'I wonder what Yarrington wants to see you about? Bugle's clearly in on it. Are you being sued?'

'Not that I'm aware of.'

The feeling of anticipated chastisement is most unpleasant, especially from Yarrington, who likes me. It reminds me of my school days when I would go to bed wondering how many times I'd get a talking to the next day, and how many of my crimes would go undetected, or best of all, how many had been detected, but for which no suspect could be found. But the current situation wouldn't result in me having to write hundreds of lines of 'I must not use carbon paper to write my lines' or an essay about the genetics of human height after writing 'You're really short' at the top of Mr Simon's blackboard so that the diminutive pedagogue had to mount a chair to rub it off. No! The punishment in law for a serious cock-up would be my job, my salary, my profession; my life as I knew it.

Still, dwelling on the horrid possibilities of Yarrington's need to see me was an occupation more fruitless than work, which thus took preference. The correspondence having been dealt with, Emily was also keen to get down to the most serious and enjoyable part of the day.

'So have you asked her yet?' she asked.

'Who?'

'Mary.'

'Who the hell is Mary?' There were a number of possible girls Emily could have asked me about, but none I remember as Mary; a name familiar to me because my less than sane great aunt bears it, that fact alone making it hard for me to date a similarly named girl.

'The girl you see on the way to work.'

'How the hell do you know her name?'

'I don't, but we talk about her so much and I can't bear calling her "the girl you see on the way to work" any more, so I thought we should christen her, until you actually have the balls to talk to her.'

I made the point that I may once have had the balls to speak to her, but that events had taken a serious turn for the worse after the milk incident, unfortunately forgetting that no-one at work yet knew about me being doused in pasteurised cow products, which then had to be explained to a highly amused Emily.

'I expect she thinks you're quite mad getting your kit off in a dry cleaners,' was Emily's most useful input on my predicament. 'It's actually quite endearing,' she added as my face fell.

'Yes, maybe to you, because you know me. You're right. She probably does think I'm mad. I'm going to have to find an alternative route to work so I don't bump into her every morning. Dealing with the embarrassment on such a regular basis will be impossible to bear.'

'No, no! Don't do that! Strike while your poker is hot and ask her out tomorrow.'

'No, I will resume my normal route to work in February thereby alleviating my embarrassment for one month.'

'A foolish choice, Jim.' Alone amongst the secretaries, Emily never called me Jim. This was a deliberate dig, but she was probably right. But still, even my self-confidence has limits.

By six o'clock, Emily had left and Yarrington still hadn't been to see me. I wanted to leave and so grabbed my jacket, slung it over my shoulder as casually as possible and descended quickly (leaving no time for thought) to his office. I knocked and entered.

He wasn't there, but Lynn, his old trout of a secretary, was. Lynn is a bitter old bat. To say that she was not in the first flush of youth would be an understatement; to say that she was handsome would be an out-and-out untruth. She's one of those people who never smiles – really, never – and as a result the haggard old harridan has very pinched up lips resembling a cat's bottom. She always wears purple. She loves it. She has purple hair, make up, jewellery, clothes, shoes, and even purple stationery: stapler, hole-punch, pens (pens and ink) but best of all were the purple paper clips. Emily told me that it is well known among females who read certain tripe-filled women's magazines that purple represents sexual frustration; I suspect the Senators of Rome would have disagreed. I don't know how Yarrington puts up with the miserable old boot on a daily basis. Depression descended on me within seconds of being in her presence.

'Yarrington around?' I asked, as chirpily as I could bring myself so to do.

'No.'

Helpful as ever, Lynn.

I paused to see if she was going furnish me with any further information.

A couple of moments later, as Lynn continued to pound her keyboard in the manner of some badly programmed robot, I concluded that further questioning would be required.

'Would you be so kind as to tell me where he is?'

'He'll be back in the office on Monday.' she said automatically as if I were an annoying client. Clearly this robot's programmer hadn't allowed for her to answer questions requiring cognitive thought. Lynn will make it as hard as possible for you to get an answer to any question you care to put to her.

'Has he gone home, then?'

'No.'

'Well, where is he?!' I started to lose my patience.

'Probably on the way to the airport.'

'Where's he going?' I asked, not knowing he was going on holiday.

'Gatwick,' replied Lynn, as unhelpfully as she could. I had now lost my patience, and anger was beginning to build up.

'Thank you, Lynn. Where's he going *after* Gatwick?'

'Home.'

!

I was now exceedingly irked. Even now knowing that Yarrington would be out of the office until Monday, Lynn's replies were so upsetting that my instinct was to find out what his plans were for the mere fact of doing so. I resolved to ask Lynn one final and all encompassing question.

'Lynn, please, in one sentence and so that I don't have to ask any further questions, just tell me what he's doing.' It was clear to any rational human being that my temper was on the verge of being lost.

'He's going to Gatwick to pick up his brother, then he's going home to spend the rest of the week with him.'

There, that wasn't too hard, was it, you frightful old carp? I'm sure she knows how angry people get with her and that she does it on purpose to amuse her purple little brain.

'Thank you, Lynn. Good night.'

'He'll be back in the office on Monday,' she repeated automatically without taking her eyes away from her keyboard.

Thus I left the office in a state of anger and niggling fear that I'd have to wait until next week to find out what it was that Yarrington wanted to talk to me about. The more I thought about it, the more my fear grew that his wrath would descend upon me on Monday morning.

CHAPTER 4

An Offer

After the excitement of finding a new way to work, successfully avoiding Mary, I spent the rest of that week worrying about what Yarrington was about. It was one of those worries that surfaced only occasionally, but still left me subconsciously knowing that something was troubling me, and when I did remember, it made my stomach turn.

The weekend came and I longed for some time in my flat. I calculated that there had been nine working days since I had last spent any conscious time there, and there was the evidence to prove it: eight shirt and tie combinations were strewn on the floor, with well over twenty socks and various other miscellaneous garments. Having restocked the fridge with life's essentials (gin, tonic and a lemon), I cleaned up; it is vital for an eligible bachelor to keep his flat tidy at all times, because if you do let things slip, Miss Stunning will ask if she can come home with you. To turn down such an offer because you left yesterday's brown Y-fronts with orange trim adorning the pillow would be heartbreaking.

But all the time, worry about Yarrington's impending chat tormented me and I never properly relaxed, so that when Monday morning finally arrived, I was almost pleased.

And so to the office, once more.

'Morning, Emily.'

'Emily?! You've never called me *that* before! Have you met a woman over the weekend?'

'No, I just keep remembering about Yarring...'

I trailed off as he came into my office.

'Morning, both! Taking my name in vain again, James? Ha! Doubtless. Good, good!'

I failed to see how taking his name in vain was good, but he carried on: 'Good weekend? Splendid.' And then in a different tone: 'James, Dining Room, now!'

Emily said nothing and I just followed him.

'Morning, old chap. Good. Well, glad I caught you early. Been meaning to chat for a while now. Sorry I didn't get round to talking to you last week.'

'That's quite all right.'

It wasn't. It was bloody unfair.

'Angela…' he began. Any mention of Angela, the human resources manager previously employed by the Devil, did not usually mean good news. She was always butting into other people's business claiming it was her job. She was just bitter that the people she managed earned more than her, bitter that she was ugly, bitter that she'd been given notice by the Devil; just bitter.

Yarrington continued, after a dramatic pause: 'Angela and the accounts team have been analysing your monthly billings for the last year.'

Shit.

Each lawyer has a list of figures: a target, the amount billed, the amount collected from those issued bills, and yearly projections and other statistics (and damned lies) based on your last six, twelve or twenty-four months. The monthly billings are scrupulously pored over by Angela, the accounts department, and the partners. Angela does it to see who she can fire for poor performance, the accounts department do it unwillingly because it is their job, and the partners do it to see if they can afford the new Bentley, or if they'll have to wait until next month.

I intentionally ignore the figures. Worrying about one's performance has always struck me as dangerous. Thinking it is my duty to stay until ten in the evening simply because I'd only achieved half my monthly billing target did not suit my way of life at all; as far as I'm concerned they pay me a reasonable wage and I put in reasonable hours. But now the years of not worrying had been brought to a sudden end, rather like being diagnosed with a terminal illness after having ignored the symptoms. This was the 'We think you'd be better suited in a different firm' or 'We're very sad but we're going to have to let you go' which translate as 'You're too lazy to work here' and 'You are not helping me buy my new Bentley'.

My heart beat like a drum. If they had decided to give me the flick already, Yarrington was just the messenger and there would be little I could to do to reverse the decision of a partner's meeting.

Yarrington started up again after another pause (was he finding this hard or did he enjoy watching me squirm?).

'We haven't done a full analysis for nearly a year now, and frankly James, we are surprised by your figures.'

Shit. Here it comes. Mitigation on my own behalf was urgently required.

'Well,' I said, 'these figures are really rather unfair...'

'Shut up, James!' butted in Yarrington.

I could tell he was using my surname.

'They really are *very* surprising. Do you realise how much you have billed in the last six months?'

No.

No idea whatsoever, but how do you tell the senior partner that?

'Tuppence ha'penny?' I said, having concluded that the only way I could have answered it was by injecting a tiny amount of humour. He was obviously not amused, but my answer did seem to calm him in another way.

'Well, slightly more than that, pleased to say. Fact is, James, you've billed...' He paused to place his monocle and peruse the figures.

Why?! Why string out my pain in these agonising moments of monocle adjustment?!

'Fact is James,' he started up again, 'you've billed more than all the junior partners. 'Course you're not up there with the Big Boys like me, Bugle, who has done very well again, and Teddy... well, perhaps Teddy isn't the best example of a high-earning partner, but you get my gist...?'

I had already begun to ignore his speech which slipped ever further from reality as my thoughts took over.

How was this possible?

Had I become so familiar with my work that I could do more in less time? Was I charging too much? Would my clients leave me because I was charging too much, or were my fees reassuringly expensive? Had they got the figures wrong? Was I going to get a pay rise? My brain was a turmoil of such questions and disbelief.

The next thing I knew, Yarrington was peering at me, rather uncomfortably as he had his monocle in place from reading the billing figures which he seemed to have forgotten about. I think he must have known what my thoughts were.

'Right! 'Spect you wonder where we're heading with this?'

Tell me you bumbling old fool! I often wonder whether Yarrington ever knows where he is heading, except at the end of the day when it is directly towards the nearest establishment that would serve him a stiff gin and tonic.

'The partners had a succession of meetings before Christmas. We've been looking at the whole Firm, not just you. Going to be a few changes here and there. Reckon we need a new partner in Property and a new solicitor in Company. Need a new partner in your department, and a new junior solicitor there too.'

Two new lawyers in my department! We were only two to begin with! But Yarrington hadn't finished: 'So, with that in mind, we thought we'd ask you to join the Partnership. What do you say to that, James?'

Yes.

Yes, a thousand times yes! Think of the money!

'Don't want an answer now, of course. Big thing. Want you to make the right choice. Take a week or two; well, a week. If you accept, you'll be starting in February. You'll also be the youngest partner *ever* at Bugle & Yarrington, except of course Bugle himself when he started out with me. How about that!'

I really was amazed. I didn't know what to say. I mumbled something about thinking about it and telling him within a week. My fears had evaporated, like I should imagine they do when studying the exam results notice board to find that not only have you passed your exams, but that there are even a few A grades listed against your name.

Yarrington could see that this offer had not been amongst my expectations and wanted, possibly on my behalf, to finish our little meeting so that I could think about it without him being there. 'Well, I'll let you think about it. Here's a letter setting out everything. One thing, though. As a partner, you'll have to pull your weight with the old training, too. So if you accept, we'll give you a trainee for six months every year; part-time training principal as it were. Have a think. Best to keep it keep it hush-hush until you decide, though. Well *done* though, James. Well done! Be bloody good to have you fully on board, so to speak. Good to have someone with their head screwed on in the right manner, too! No pressure, though.'

No, none at all, Yarrington.

And with that he shook my hand, and still wearing the monocle grinned at me warmly.

It wasn't often that he used my Christian name, or grinned like that, and it hit me profoundly. First I told myself that he was probably a good psychologist, and second I mused that if he was, he probably was genuine about wanting to have me 'on board' and that he truly liked me. Third, I thought, I must admit, I do like him.

I started back to my office, rather dazed, and bumped straight into Angela. She looked vile. She is short, skinny and has curly but lank off-brown hair, which has a tendency to stick to places it ought not, like her forehead; she is in the unfortunate position of possessing dentition that would, without any difficulty, facilitate the incising of an apple through a letterbox; her glasses are so filthy they look like they've been smeared liberally with Vaseline and left in a dusty undercroft for a few years, which is not actually an altogether impossible proposition. Here was the sour and envious creature who had no doubt been keeping my spectacular billing figures from everyone for weeks, months, who knows, maybe years!

'Morning Angela! And what a splendid morning it is too!' I said with so much sarcastic enthusiasm that she replied:

'So you've heard then?'

'Heard what?'

She narrowed her eyes.

A pause.

Could I stop the smile? One of my failings is smirking when I shouldn't, but with Angela, the process of keeping a straight face is fairly straightforward: I just think about her naked, and anything funny very soon ceases to have any amusement whatsoever.

'Oh nothing,' she said wearily, as though everyone abuses her in the same fashion. I wondered if they did.

Smirk withheld; mission successful; Angela duly and meanly dealt with for all her acts in this life, and previous ones!

I waltzed back into my office.

'Right, sweetheart, get your coat. We're off to lunch!' I told Emily.

She looked curiously at me.

'It's not even ten o'clock… God, you okay?' she asked.

'Yes, thank you! I'm bloody splendid. If you don't want lunch, then will you breakfast with me at the Ritz?'

Emily was now totally confused, and the realisation struck me that an explanation was required.

'Yarrington asked me if I'd accept partnership.'

'Oh, he asked me too yesterday, but I declined on the basis that I know bugger all about law; I suggested you might be a better choice.'

'I'm serious.'

It is a little disheartening when one's own secretary needs convincing one's not joking.

'Oh,' she said, sensing my thoughts.

A pause ensued while I stood wondering what to say as my initial enthusiasm for the Ritz had been somewhat dampened by Emily's sarcastic response to the most exciting news I had received since I got my own office. Emily, I think, was taking in the enormity of it and concluded:

'Well, congratulations!' And in her smile, I sensed an unusual hint of admiration. 'You lucky bugger! Let's go to the Ritz, then!'

So we went to the Ritz.

CHAPTER 5

The Ritz

The Ritz sounds very glamorous, but it also happens to be quite close to the office, and although never having dined there before, a number of people from the office (including me) do pop in for a drink every so often. So the prospect of breakfast there was not really as outrageous a proposition as it might first appear.

We were duly served and it was delicious, but in truth the most entertaining part was being there and knowing we were having breakfast at the Ritz when we should have been at work.

Champagne increased this pleasure.

We finished all too soon, and started for the door, reaching the main entrance hall at precisely the same time as Bugle, who was arm-in-arm with a very good-looking blonde woman half his age. They were laughing and giggling. We all saw each other at the same moment as we crossed the floor to meet in the middle of the vast vestibule.

'What are you two doing here?' asked Bugle, who from his face seemed to feel rather stupid as soon as he'd asked the question. He hadn't even greeted us or introduced the girl; the question would have been fair enough after such formalities, or indeed if Bugle had been on his own, but with this company I thought it was probably more pertinent for him to answer his own question. As in all awkward situations I simply told the truth:

'We're celebrating – Yarrington saw me this morning.'

'Ah, yes. Congratulations,' he said without meaning it.

'Thank you,' I said with as much sincerity.

And then Bugle seemed to recover from his shock and pull himself together.

'Sorry, how remiss of me. This is my... niece, Jenny. Jenny, James and Emily, from the office. James has just been offered partnership at the Firm,' he said to Jenny, 'although lunching at the Ritz is not the best way to impress the more senior partners.' Bugle always liked administering a dig, but again I got the impression that he felt foolish as soon as he'd finished his sentence.

'I was in fact breakfasting. I think it was Napoleon who said "An army marches on its stomach".' I knew this cheek would infuriate Bugle, but that he'd have to take it in good humour with his supposed niece in tow.

He grinned angrily.

'Right, well, we'd better get back,' I said merrily. 'Nice to see you in such pleasant surroundings, Frank! Nice to meet you, Jenny.'

She smiled.

'See you in the office,' said Bugle, as menacingly as he could without being rude.

'Well now!' said Emily as we crossed Piccadilly.

'Well now, indeed! Piece-on-the-side or niece-bona-fide?!'

'Do you need to ask? He was *so* guilty!' Emily can be over-dramatic, but on this occasion my inclination was that she couldn't be wrong. 'Do you think he's paying her?' she continued, her active imagination inevitably engaging over the situation.

My conclusion was that if indeed the girl was a piece-on-the-side, it was merely a question of whether he was paying her directly for services rendered, or indirectly, through expensive eating, sleeping, clothes and other female accoutrements. But she must have been pretty special for the tight-fisted Bugle to have paid for a night at the Ritz.

CHAPTER 6

Tim

That afternoon Tim asked whether I fancied a beer after work. I've always been bad at declining such offers which has the effect that everyone knows they'll have a guaranteed drinking partner (drinking Partner, soon!) if they ask me. Consequently such invitations are very regular.

Tim is a private client lawyer. We both started training with the Firm at the same time and have been good friends since day one. I dabble in wills, trusts, offshore funds and inheritance tax; Tim is the expert. When our client's needs expand into our respective areas of expertise, as happens quite often, we consult each other, offering each other friendly words of unpaid advice. The arrangement works well, with neither of us getting too worried about doing non-paid, non-billable and non-target achieving work for each other.

Tim is one of the few people from work who I see socially outside the office, but since he got married (Emily and I were his only colleagues to be invited) he has been less social which is a shame because he has an appealing sense of humour, and loves to talk about the ins and outs of office life, his eye always looking upwards at who is a threat, who is getting paid what, who is good, who is bad, who is getting hired and who is getting fired. He listens avidly to other kinds of gossip from the secretaries, usually passed to him by me, but he never joins in with them; that is a little beneath him.

He is, I suppose, a little too serious on occasion and sometimes worryingly ambitious. There are rumours afoot that he actually enjoys the law. He has a tendency to look down on me, because he thinks my approach is not as serious as perhaps it should be. But this is merely a façade: I choose to give him the impression that my day is not all hard graft and that as lawyers we're not as frightfully important as he seems to think we are. But I fear my battle will be a losing one because due to his competitive nature he does more than his fair share of hob-nobbing with the top brass. I think he fancies some egg on his own cap, too.

At five twenty-nine I was ready; he was ready at six. This is typical.

'Do you like my tie?' he asked me, first off. He knows my sartorial eye is highly accomplished, and regularly asks my opinion of his office and casual wear, which frankly are not to my taste.

'Yes,' I lied. 'Your mother?'

'Yes,' he replied, apparently not grasping my cheek. But I suppose it was obvious: not even he would have chosen such a hideous shade of lilac.

We went to The Pub. This was the pub fifty yards from the office, the pub which I have been to at least once a week for seven years, and the pub which is so familiar that I don't even know its name. It's an old fashioned English pub, but smart, because it's in Mayfair, with smart prices to keep the riff-raff out.

'So, what news at work?' I asked, keeping a poker face and analysing his equally straight face in the hope of gleaning some information regarding any promotion that may have been offered to him.

'Not much, you?' he asked, apparently doing the same.

It was clearly up to me be more direct: 'Has Yarrington been to see you since Christmas?' I asked in a subtle enough manner.

'No.'

I hoped I had been able to stifle my surprised look.

'Why do you ask?' he asked, rather suspiciously.

'Oh, he wants to see me about something. Just wondered if he was doing the rounds, or whether it was just me. I'm probably going to get a bollocking for something or other, or I'm being sued for some daft act or omission.'

But it was hopeless; Tim wouldn't break his confidence to Yarrington if he'd been asked not tell anyone about one of the secretaries consistently eating more than her fair share of the Firm's biscuit supply, let alone an offer of partnership. He was either being as secretive as expected, or he hadn't had an offer. But I had always thought Tim would reach partnership before me – he was on the face of it a better lawyer – he put in more hours, more effort and showed much more commitment to his profession, career and the Firm. He would be pretty cross, I imagined, if he discovered partnership had been offered to me and not him. In fact, even if he'd had a similar offer, he would probably have been irked that the same had been extended to me in any case.

I then decided to direct matters away from the Firm so as not to expose myself to awkward questions from Tim.

'How's the wife?' I asked. Tim usually called his wife Charlotte, 'the wife' and much to my shame, I had come to do the same. It amused him, but it made me feel rather too much like a male chauvinist pig. Indeed, Tim has the unfortunate reputation at the Firm as being just that, which is slightly unfair.

Despite his rather male humour regarding the wife, their relationship had begun romantically: he had met Charlotte at some law dinner, and amazingly had the nerve to ask her out that very evening. Even more amazingly she accepted, and a fortnight later they had been on their first of many romantic weekends in the country. They were engaged within a year and have been married eighteen months. She says it was love at first sight and I believe her. He is totally smitten too, but he likes to uphold his man's man reputation; the thought of being under Charlotte's thumb (which he is) is enough to make him green about the gills.

'She's fine. Keeping me on a short leash as always,' answered Tim. 'I had to deal with her family for three days at Christmas. Christ knows how I got through that without smoking.'

Now Tim used to smoke more than the *Flying Scotsman* on a non-stop London to Edinburgh round trip. He's pretty much given up, because Charlotte made him, but there's that childish sticking-two-fingers-up part of him that still makes him have the odd one, mostly, I think to prove that he's not totally under the thumb, and that he's still his own man, and will do as he pleases. I think Charlotte must know, but there's this kind of unspoken war going on between them, and nothing is ever said directly.

Despite being head over heels with Charlotte, her family is another matter.

Tim thinks Camden Town is too far north.

Charlotte's family live in some godforsaken part of the Midlands.

How Charlotte escaped without an accent is, Tim once told me, the sole reason he believes in miracles. The rest of the family, sadly for him, have broad accents, which troubles him no end. He once told me he liked the accents of Yorkshire, Liverpool, Newcastle and even Somerset, but that the Birmingham accent was just too much. But, he laments, you can't help with whom you fall in love.

'Did you have any luck with the ladies over Christmas?' he asked.

'No, it's a female desert outside London.'

I recounted the milk incident and the loss of Mary, who I'd never spoken to anyway.

'Better luck next time!' were his words of wisdom, followed by: 'Michelle had the most marvellous top on today – did you notice? She was pouring out of it! Marvellous breasts!' he said looking at his pint, as much to himself as me.

We continued chatting for a while, but it being Monday, and Tim wanting to get home early to avoid the wrath of Charlotte, we decided to call it a night.

CHAPTER 7

George Teddy

Of course I decided to accept the offer of partnership. I didn't think about it or the implications thereof. Yes, the liability one had to bear was greater, financially and otherwise, but the rewards were greater in both respects too. Well, financially anyway. Thinking about it, the only good thing about being a partner was the money, apart from the minor amount of kudos that went with it. Of course, for some, this kudos was all they lived for. For some, not me.

The acceptance of the offer was expressed to Bugle and Yarrington the following Monday. Bugle said curtly: 'Congratulations, glad you decided to sign on the dotted line,' with no hint of sincerity. He was clearly not totally enamoured by the idea of me becoming a partner, probably because he was thinking that I would doubtless reduce his percentage of the profits. But my billing figures didn't lie and he must have realised the potential of promoting me.

Yarrington however did seem genuinely pleased which was honestly the only thing that kept me from starting to become doubtful about the whole thing.

His 'Jolly good, James. Ha! Just think! Bet you never thought this would happen a few years ago?!' was friendly and good-humoured. He went on to say that he was genuinely pleased that I had joined the partnership and that I was just the type of chap to run the Firm after he had retired. This, I think was true, but in any event, it make me feel more responsible about the promotion, but also proud that Yarrington viewed me in such a favourable light.

Having just left Yarrington's room, I saw George Teddy, the third partner to join the Firm. Teddy had been a peer of Yarrington at Oxford, and, legend has it, was the saviour of the same in his burning and sinking yacht in Cairo. Teddy is a shipping enthusiast, and his addition to the Firm created the shipping department, rather through his love of anything nautical than his legal expertise in the area. Teddy had wanted his name added to the Firm's upon his arrival, but despite his protestations, Bugle vetoed it; there has been a slight animosity between them ever since.

When I saw Teddy, he was slowly ascending the stairs, raincoat and hat still on, heading for his lonely little office at the back of Number 22. He is the only person in the Firm who has an office to himself, largely because he is his own department and keeps himself to himself. He is there more in body than mind, and not for many hours a day even then: his output of work and dictation is minimal and his need of secretarial support is therefore lower than any other lawyer in London.

On one rare occasion when his old secretary, the aptly named Ethel (the Unready), did actually enter his room to acquire his signature to a letter, she found him flat out on floor. Fearing the worst, the panic-stricken headless-chicken-of-a-woman set off the Firm's fire alarm and we all trooped outside to find her breathlessly telling everyone that old Teddy had finally done his last shipping case, and that seeing his corpse had been quite the worst experience of her life.

The fire alarm woke the old boy up and he came grumpily outside where he witnessed dear old Ethel fainting at the sight of this ill-tempered apparition. It was this incident that caused the rather decrepit and frail-hearted old girl to finally retire, and Teddy hasn't had a full-time secretary since. He now shares Lynn with Yarrington.

Like this morning, he usually arrives at a leisurely eleven o'clock, opens his post (usually consisting of Covent Garden tickets, yachting magazines, and of course, on Thursdays, the Law Society's *Gazette*), does a couple of hours work, goes out for lunch with a client (who is usually an old friend), comes back to the office, has an afternoon snooze, writes a letter or two (usually enclosing a cheque to the Covent Garden ticket office from the Bugle & Yarrington expenses account), and then takes a quaff at one of the established Firm drinking holes, before heading down to his St James' gentleman's club to indulge in large quantities of red meat, red wine, port and cigars. He is a bachelor and will doubtless remain one. I don't know if he's ever been in love, but one imagines that if so, it would have been unrequited. His bachelorhood has caused him to rely heavily on friends; you can tell he really loves Yarrington.

I waited until Teddy had reached the top of the stairs before saying hello.

'Ah, James, boy. How's life treating you?'

'Pretty splendidly, thanks. And you?'

'With the same old sense of humour that it usually treats me with,' was his mildly cryptic answer which was really an invitation for you to ask what he meant.

'What do you mean?' I asked, enjoying indulging him.

'Just bumped into Frankly Buggerall Brains, and he tells me that not only have you been offered partnership, but that you've accepted! Jolly good show to keep *me*, the longest standing partner aside from *himself* and David Yarrington Esquire, in the loop, I must say!' And then he realised his anti-Bugle rant had appeared rather rude. 'So sorry, old boy! Congratulations!' And he meant it, shaking my hand warmly, with a twinkle in his eye not often seen.

'How did you not know?' I asked to show my concern for him. 'Did you not discuss it a partner's meeting?'

'Oh, maybe. Don't usually bother with *those*. Frightfully dull affairs. And they're always at inconvenient times when I'd much rather be at the East India Club enjoying a nice claret. Can't stand that plonk they always give us at the Firm. I've been rallying for some drinkable wine for years.'

'That sounds like a worthy cause,' said Tim who was passing us on the grand staircase of Number 22. 'Congratulations on your news!' he continued, I think pleased for me, but harbouring the thoughts made evident by his next sentence: 'Can't believe they didn't do the same to me, though,' he said, thankfully not too gloomily. 'Your figures are terrific,' he said by way of encouragement. 'How do you fix them?'

'That's enough cheek from you, my boy!' I said, smiling at Tim's joke.

'Talk to you soon, James,' said Tim, who continued on down the stairs. 'Good to see you're busy as ever, Teddy!' he added, rather unkindly.

It was sad really. Many of the staff, even Tim who is usually a polite man, treat Teddy without much respect. He is a lovely man, a real gentleman, and never says a bad word about anyone, except Bugle, whom he despises. The lack of respect stems from the fact that he really doesn't do much work, first because he isn't inclined to, and second because his reputation as a shipping lawyer is not as high as various other maritime lawyers one could mention. Indeed, some have claimed that his acceptance into the Firm as a partner is more to do with his friendship with Yarrington from undergraduate days in Oxford and the amount of money he inherited from his late father and could invest in the Firm. I think Yarrington holds him in high esteem as a friend and intellectual, but not as a lawyer, because in truth, he's lousy.

Having a shipping department with one lawyer is daft. Teddy certainly has the required academic knowledge, only arguably has the experience, but certainly does not possess the inclination or manpower at his disposal to act for big clients, so his clients remain small, as do his fees. All the partners save Yarrington complain about him; that he doesn't bring in enough money; that his department (him, and a small portion of Lynn's time) should be brought to an end. But he remains an institution. The official line is that the shipping department is necessary for some of the company clients, and there is a small element of truth to this. But in reality, the department is probably only there as an advertisement; it adds an element that clients find attractive; a niche practice that usually only much larger or specialist firms can boast.

Not even I have much of an idea what Teddy actually does. No one has ever worked with him as the department is too small to have a trainee and the senior management would never allow another lawyer to join. The shipping department will dissolve on Teddy's retirement, that we are all sure about.

CHAPTER 8

Skiing

Having both declined to go on skiing trips with our respective skiing friends because of impossible dates, Emily and I found we both rather hankered to get *on piste*. Emily had discovered that she had enough holiday left over from last year to take a week off without eating up any of this year's paltry holiday allowance. This decided it for Emily, because wasting holiday entitlement is the gravest sin an employee can commit.

'I'm taking the last week of January off to go skiing,' she announced.

'Great! I'd love to go skiing,' I said wistfully. 'Who are you going with?'

'You.'

Emily then announced she had been studying my holiday entitlement as well. It transpired that I had four days left over from last year, so that made up my mind.

So, ignoring the threat of the inevitable rumours that would spread through the office, we booked a week's skiing for the end of January.

We arrived in the Alps to find that it had been snowing for three days and that the weather forecast was for sun indefinitely. Perfect. We were greeted at the quaint little chalet – which was right on the slopes – by a charming blonde pigtailed German girl called Heidi, and taken to our room. Which had one double bed.

We exchanged smirks, but said nothing.

The Englishness in us came to the fore: I think we both thought that as an apparent couple, to complain that we didn't have the two singles as requested would look just too odd. Heidi left us to unpack, asking, 'You like the cow? I cook it for you in one hour, down the stairs.'

'Well, looks like I finally get to sleep with you!'

'Don't get any ideas James. Do you snore?' asked Emily.

'Of course not.' I replied, not certain to which part of Emily's reply my response was in answer.

On the first night I discovered that Emily snored. Quite cute little snores, and not enough to keep a bedfellow awake: the kind of snores that any man in love with her would find endearing. But snores nevertheless.

Despite my penchant for a tipple after work, for me a skiing holiday is just that. Skiing. It's not an excuse to go and get drunk after skiing. Having never been skiing with her before, my worry was that Emily's focus might be more on the *après ski* side of things. I was delighted, therefore, when it proved that she was just as anxious as me to get in as many runs as possible before the last lift. Indeed, her energy was phenomenal, and she was always chasing me back onto the slopes after lunch when my stomach was rather too full of Alpine lager, meat, chips and mayonnaise.

One lunchtime, and probably due in the main to the glorious weather, we fancifully discussed the idea of doing a ski season to escape the grey monotony (weather and otherwise) of the English winter. The idea seemed splendid until the discourse led to matters such as the cleaning of ablutionary apparatus and lack of pecuniary remuneration whereupon we reflected that despite their unromantic nature, the offices of Bugle & Yarrington must remain our place of work for the foreseeable future.

Such was Emily's enthusiasm for skiing, that by the end of each full day when we skied back to the front door of the chalet, we had little energy for anything other than a bottle, some delicious food cooked by Heidi, and then bed.

CHAPTER 9

The Worst Month

Everyone has different opinions about their favourite month of the year, but for every Englishman, February is universally acknowledged to be the worst month.

Nothing happens in February; there are no big social events, no social events at all, come to think of it, no bank holidays, and no chance of going on holiday if you have been skiing in January; the weather is amenable only to those who like frostbite and chilblains, and to those sensible species who have the metabolism for hibernation. The only good thing I can possibly say about February is that it is the shortest month, and I hesitate to mention that so as not to dilute my hatred, for this, the worst month.

However, as my eyes opened on this first of February, I realised this might prove to be the best month in a long time; this morning was my first as a partner at Bugle & Yarrington; this morning was one month from the milk incident; my pride had returned, and my embarrassment had been banished; it was the day I had decided to return to my normal route to work with the express intention of bumping into Mary, picking her up from the pavement as she swooned at the sight of me, and asking her to accompany me for a glass or two of fine wine after our respective days at work!

I leapt out of bed with a dangerous amount of enthusiasm; it normally takes twenty minutes to find the energy for this, the hardest part of each day. But my next thought was one of doubt. Had Mary had chosen another route to work after not seeing me, not flirting with me, not enjoying her walk to work for an entire month?

Not wishing to dwell on this thought, I donned one of my favourite shirt and tie combinations, best pinstripes, and polished my shoes. Just when I was leaving, I caught a glimpse of myself in the mirror by the door and had one of those 'My God! I'm gorgeous!' moments.

And thus I set off in high spirits hoping to seduce the beautiful Mary without too much embarrassment. After careful consideration,

I picked up *The Times* as normal (if she was a *Guardian* reader, at least she would know where my loyalties lay), crossed Oxford Street successfully avoiding any milk cartons and came to the stretch of road where I knew we would cross paths if we were going to.

There was no sign of her.

Reaching the end of the road, I slowed to maximise exposure time.

Still no sign of her.

I popped into a conveniently located newsagent and bought the *Guardian.*

Nothing.

I untied and retied both shoelaces.

Twice.

I put the *Guardian* in a bin: what was I thinking?

Nine thirty-nine; I was usually at my desk by now. Sadly I had to concede defeat and walk off to the office, very much deflated and subdued. This February, I decided, looked as if it was going to be no different to any other.

On arrival at the office and the inevitable 'Good morning, how are you?' from Sue the receptionist, I found myself at my desk.

Something was wrong.

Emily hadn't arrived.

There was no beautiful smile to make my Monday morning bearable.

Worse still, there was no coffee to greet me.

The phone went.

'Mrs Ricketts! How are you?'

I'm not sure if I'd ever spoken to the dear old bird before a caffeine injection.

'I'm very well, thank you, dear. How are you? I gather that you are now a partner at the Firm. Congratulations! Did you have to change the notepaper too?'

'No, I'm afraid that James James & Co. will have to wait for next year!'

'Never mind. I suppose you'll be charging me more for your time?'

'Yes, I'm afraid so.'

'Never mind. Did I tell you that my son – the one who cooked the delicious turkey – found out that you changed my will in his favour? Do you know what he did? He bought me some flowers. Very kind of him, but entirely unnecessary. I know what else I meant to tell you – Tinker' (the dying cat) 'is really on his last legs. Now I know I said that just before Christmas, but he won't even eat smoked salmon any more. And he always eats that, even when he's poorly...'

Fifteen minutes later, Mrs Ricketts had managed to tell me that she wanted to buy a house for one of her grandsons and that she wanted me to do the conveyancing. Having never been much good at remembering to tick all the boxes in leasehold conveyancing, I was eternally grateful when she told me it was a freehold house in Kent; it would probably be hideously expensive and I'd be able to charge her a considerable fee for a minimal amount of work. Then I felt awful for thinking along such mercenary lines. But then when I mused upon the fact that the government would be taking twenty times my fee in stamp duty land tax, my guilt diminished somewhat. The agent had been advised that I was acting for her, and the details would be with me within a couple of days.

'I will get onto it as soon as I have the papers, Mrs Ricketts. Bye for now,' I said just as Emily arrived.

'Morning, Mister Partner!' she beamed.

'Morning gorgeous.'

'Sorry I'm late. Rather hungover. I look awful.'

She looked beautiful.

'The most amazing thing happened last night. I got in a cab and said to the driver "take me home" and he did.'

I thought perhaps she was still on the wrong side of a couple of bottles.

'I'm not sure I understand...'

'Don't you see?! I didn't tell him *where* I lived. I only realised after I had got out to pay him. He'd remembered me from last week, and knew where I lived!'

'Getting yourself a reputation about Town, young lady?! You'd better keep an eye out for black cabs hanging around your street!'

'Quite.' It appeared she hadn't thought of that possibility.

The next morning, after donning another favourite shirt and tie combination and my second-best pinstripes (which are very passable), I found myself leaving my flat looking forward to the possibility of meeting Mary again. The chance of a sighting had increased at least fifty percent from yesterday because even when we used to see each other regularly, there were always a few times when we would miss each other. As I reached the likely spot, I told myself that today would be different and we would meet.

But alas, no sign of her.

Reaching the end of the road, I slowed to maximise exposure time.

Still no sign of her.

I popped into the conveniently located newsagent and bought *The Sun*.

Nothing.

I untied and retied both shoelaces.

Thrice.

I put *The Sun* in a bin: what *was* I thinking?

Nine forty-nine. This habit of hanging around on street corners waiting for good-looking flirts had to stop! I realised this was a ridiculous waste of time, emotional stress, money, and unread newspapers. And then I saw her.

She was arm in arm with another girl on the opposite side of the road, not twenty yards off. I would have to work quickly. I crossed the road in front of a white van which had to slow to allow me past. The driver pooped, which made both girls look at me. Mary, of course, clocked me straight away, nudged the other, exchanged subtle smiles (but not subtle enough to escape my hawk-like eyes) and then, as if starring in a romantic comedy, they simultaneously did the shampoo advert flicks of the hair. It was a beautiful moment. It meant that not only did Mary rather like the look of me, but that she had been talking to this girlfriend about me, and furthermore that said girlfriend rather liked the sound of me, and now, having had sight of me, rather liked the look of me too. From my point of view, they were both gorgeous, had long blonde hair and rather fetching knee length skirts and boots. This classic combination is designed to keep the wearer warm in these Arctic February conditions, while exposing just enough leg to get the professional male mind working; tactics which succeed with a remarkably high hit rate.

Such were my thoughts as I approached them. We were all smirking in anticipation as I made eye contact with Mary. 'Morning,' I said, unable to suppress a smile.

'Hi,' she said as if we knew each other and didn't have time to chat right at that moment. Her tone was right, of course. We didn't know each other, and in these circumstances involving a third party, I wasn't going to be the one to start a conversation, and nor was she. I moved my eyes quickly to meet her friend's just before we passed each other.

'Hi,' said the friend, as if she wished she had been the main point of flirtation. No doubt she did.

We passed. Now came the question of whether to look round or not. My subconscious answered this question with much less debate than normal. It concluded that one of them would be unlikely to look round without tacit agreement from the other, which was itself unlikely given that timing in these situations is crucial and rarely works in one's favour; and furthermore that the chances of both of them looking round were very slim indeed. I looked round to find my carefully thought out mental arguments had been entirely incorrect; I felt rather embarrassed as they both swivelled their swan-like necks in my direction and smiled. I smiled and walked on. But I was pleased to note that they had both turned their heads towards me in an outward direction away from each other.

And so to the office, in a state of good humour and triumph.

'Morning gorgeous!'

Emily did look particularly gorgeous this morning.

'Hi sweetheart! What are you so jolly about?!'

'*I* have just bumped into Mary, and her rather lovely friend, who both, I may say, seemed to take rather a shine to me!'

'Well, of course: you're bloody marvellous!'

'Why thank you. You, I may say, are also pretty damn splendid.'

'Yes, I know,' said Emily, already bored with my quipping in anticipation of wanting to know what had happened next. 'So what happened?'

I told her.

'So what are you going to do?' she asked, interrupting my story.

'Well, assuming the lovely Mary is alone tomorrow morning, I shall ask her what her name actually is, and then ask her out for a glass or two at The Vaults Wine Bar.' The Vaults was a few doors down from The Pub, and, as its name tended to suggest, was a vaulted cellar, rather rabbit-warren like, but was considerably more salubrious than The Pub for entertaining young ladies. It was particularly conducive to winter drinking as the lack of light outside was clearly not noticed underground, and it was always warm and well supplied with candles providing a romantic atmosphere. The small and clandestine individual vaults that weren't filled with wine racks off to the side of the main bar offered comfortable seats, and a very high degree of privacy. Almost all the patrons drinking in there were most likely to be conducting a romantic liaison of one type or other, and there were probably few legitimate ones. It was handy as a divorce lawyer to have such a good source of trade so close to the office. In terms of booze, one can purchase a bottle of Bugle & Yarrington plonk for eight quid, or a 1957 Margaux for just under a grand. I usually make do with the former.

CHAPTER 10

The Partners Meet

On the first Tuesday of each month there is a partners' meeting at five o'clock. I was looking forward to my first of these arcane gatherings where all the important office business is discussed. It would be my chance to obtain sensitive information about the Firm and its employees, business plans, financial details and gossip. As I thought this, I realised that sadly I wasn't a fly on the wall, or even an eavesdropper, but a responsible partner, unable to pass on confidential information gleaned from such meetings to other, more lowly members of staff in the way that had become so familiar during my professional career. It was a sad thought, but, I reflected, knowing and not being able to divulge the sordid details was better than not knowing.

And so it was that I entered the boardroom.

The boardroom, dubbed the Dining Room (it has a board table) is a magnificent chamber on the first floor of Number 22. It is a perfect rectangle; has a sixteen-foot high ceiling and enormous mahogany doors ten feet high separating it from the Ball Room (an identical room adjacent to the Dining Room used for promotional receptions and drinks parties; it doesn't have a board table). The highly polished veneer which clads these doors is so large that I have spent many a minute in meetings wondering how big the tree from which they were cut might have been, and how those eighteenth-century carpenters were able to produce such huge sheets. There is a massive and beautiful white marble mantelpiece and surround over the brick fireplace which itself is painted a rather trendy matt black. Spotlights shining down from inside the chimney light up some exquisite red flowers beneath, arranged to resemble flames. Their fiery splendour draws the eye and imagination.

Everyone filed in and took position round the board table.

Several bottles of Bugle & Yarrington plonk were sitting decorked on the table, which boded relatively well.

There were no apologies.

I looked around the room. Here we were: the top-dogs of the Firm, including Bugle and Yarrington, all sitting round the same table drinking the same old muck that the firm dishes out every time they have an excuse. Bugle and Yarrington sat at one end, with Teddy next to Yarrington for moral support. Paul, the head of the company and commercial department, and his inseparable colleague and conspirator, Martin, both with reputations for having consistently brown noses, sat next to each other and conversed quietly with an air of secrecy about them.

Margaret, the head of the family department, and as such, my immediate boss, sat next to me. She was approaching the age when she could start drawing her state pension, and was not best pleased about it. Generally I get on well with Margaret. She has never been married, and some say that her occasionally dragon-like qualities are a direct cause, or perhaps consequence, of her frustrated spinsterhood, but she's a good sort underneath that scaly skin.

The other partners sat attentively and waited for Yarrington to begin.

'Afternoon. Glad we're all here.' Said Yarrington. 'Well, first things first. Let's raise a toast to James, the newest partner at our esteemed firm!'

All round 'cheers' and 'well done, James', except Bugle, who just gulped his wine before the toast was even toasted. 'I think the family department has needed a new partner for some time, and James has proved himself more than adequately over the past few years. When Margaret retires, I think James will prove to be an excellent head of department.'

'Who on earth said I was even considering the "R" word?' asked Margaret.

'Well, Margaret, that is of course entirely up to you, but I have heard rumours you are approaching a special birthday.'

'I have no idea what you're talking about!' For a moment, Margaret carried a look of wrath and I had no doubt that she would speak to Yarrington about not abusing the privacy of her age.

'Well, anyway, I'm sure James will do a damn fine job, until Margaret wishes to call it a day.'

'Thank you,' I said.

'Right then! On with the meeting. Here's the agenda,' announced Yarrington, clearly wishing to get to The Pub as soon as possible.

The agenda was passed round and I studied it. Far from the juicy gossip about financial matters, what famous clients we had, or which secretaries were getting fired for inappropriate behaviour on their desks, there was nothing but exceedingly tedious looking topics such as water coolers, repainting the front door ('ideas for a new colour?'), overspending on the budget at the Christmas party and the vaguely interesting topic of 'new trainees'. This was what they talked about? Did we partners of Bugle & Yarrington really have to waste our evenings talking about this mundane rubbish? Apparently so, as Yarrington solemnly started with the first item.

'Water coolers. We have had numerous requests for more water coolers from various members of staff. I think probably in this day and age, water coolers, like so many new-fangled inventions are a necessarily evil with which we must endure. They are not cheap, but I do feel that keeping the staff happy is important, and if little blue tanks perched on plastic plinths make them happy, so be it. What say you all?'

'What is wrong with taps?' I felt it was a pertinent question. Now a partner, any money spent on superfluous office equipment meant less money for me. It's amazing how quickly you change your tune once on the horrible greasy slippery pole of partnership!

'Well I quite agree,' said Yarrington. 'I've been drinking this water for thirty years and I'm still kicking. But, alas, some of the employees refuse to drink tapwater.'

'But they drink kettle water from the tap.' I observed.

'Yes, but that's been boiled.' said Paul, as if he was talking to an ejit.

Knowledge from a previous academic life came flooding back: 'Yes, but boiling makes not the slightest difference in terms of the minerals one imbibes.' I said, knowing I was talking to an ejit.

'Of course it does,' was his masterfully cunning answer, designed to throw me off balance and destroy my argument in one fell swoop.

'There is no question of London water containing too many lethal bacteria or water-borne diseases. Indeed, the bacteria content in bottled waters is often much higher than in tap water. People refuse to drink tap water because they are ignorant. They believe that somehow it is impure. Boiling it may kill off a few of the bacteria, but the minerals remain and if there are no bacteria, it's only the mineral content that makes London water different from mineral water. London tap water has actually a very healthy mineral content.'

There was a stunned silence. It was as if I had been talking in

Icelandic.

'Couldn't we get some kind of intoxicating liquor dispenser?' I asked, maybe foolishly for my first partner's meeting, but I felt the tone needed lightening.

'Don't be juvenile James,' said Bugle.

'Well, since we're on the topic of booze…' said Teddy.

Everyone groaned.

'Well, don't make those noises at me,' complained Teddy, 'I've been trying to get the B & Y plonk upgraded for years, from the kind of vinegar it is now to some form of drinkable wine. You're a bunch of hypocrites: most of you agree with me privately – why can't we reach a simple decision in these damn meetings?'

'You've got my vote,' said Yarrington cheekily.

'We're lawyers, not bloody wine merchants!' barked Bugle. 'What would the client's think if they knew how much we spent on entertainment currently, let alone increasing the wine budget?'

'They wouldn't be too impressed if they had to drink the B & Y plonk at a drinks party.' I quipped.

'That's why client entertainment is kept to a minimum.'

'But think of the business we'd drum up if client events were brought to the fore of the calendar – and decent wine was served.'

'Here, here!' added Teddy.

'Gentleman,' said Yarrington, 'I hate to stop this delightful debate, but may I remind you that we are on the subject of water coolers.' I suppose as senior partner and therefore chairman he had to control us somehow.

'Well, let's just buy a couple more then?' said Bugle.

'They're not cheap. Nor is the water in them. I think careful consideration will have to be put into this. But I am worried about the state of the pipes in this building. They're probably rather aged, and some employee might try and sue us for poisoning them.'

'They're probably lead pipes, which is why we're all going slowly bonkers,' I said to Margaret.

'Do you have anything to add, James?' asked Bugle, snidely.

'I was pointing out that the pipework may be lead, which could have a detrimental effect on our health.'

'Good God, I hadn't thought about that! James, as you know so much about plumbing and the mineral content of different water, and frankly, since you're the most junior partner, you can have an investigation and report back to us at the next meeting.'

I felt like a trainee again, but I had to agree.

Yarrington then moved on to the last item on the agenda.

'We have two new trainees starting this month. As Bugle is the training partner, I'll let him talk to you about them.'

Bugle rose stuffily to his feet. 'Thank you, David. Yes, the trainees are Matthew and Thomas. David and I interviewed them both with Angela, and we feel sure you'll all agree they are a likely pair of lads. Matthew's a bright boy. He did law at Oxford, and has just passed the professional exams with a distinction.'

I remembered failing my professional exams with distinction.

'Thomas hasn't been so lucky on the educational route, but he's worked as a paralegal for some time and has some marvellous experience, which I hope we can build on. Confident little bugger, too. Paul and Martin are going to kick him into shape for his first six months; knock him around a bit and so on.' The unpleasant pair looked at each other and exchanged cruel smiles. 'And after careful consideration, we thought we'd give young Matthew – he is young, by the way – only twenty-two, I'm told – to the person we *know* will give him some excellent training, and a bit of confidence,' said Bugle, eyeing every partner in the room, before settling his eyes on me.

'And that will be you, James James!'

'Jesus Christ.'

'Don't blaspheme in front of me!' roared Bugle, 'Nor the boy, for that matter!'

'I beg your pardon.' I said humbly. 'I'm just not sure that I'm ready to take a trainee...' I stammered, '...I have only been a partner a few hours!' I knew damn well I wasn't ready to take on a trainee, especially some jumped up little Oxford grad who could probably quote more law at me than I knew existed.

'Nonsense! With your *extensive* legal knowledge, you'll be able to have him up to speed in no time!' said Bugle sarcastically.

Yarrington intervened as he saw my face show mild signs of aggravation: 'I think, James, that he needs someone like you to get him out of himself, so to speak. Show him how to be a lawyer. Quite shy, you see. That's why we thought you might like to give it go.'

'When do they start?' I asked.

'Next Monday.'

It was now Tuesday. Having been a partner for only two days, I was faced with the prospect of having a trainee in six days. The thought of someone else sharing my room with Emily upset me greatly; we liked our arrangement. My thoughts then turned to whether the only reason they had offered me partnership was to use me as a training principal; but conversely, having a trainee did mean more work could be done: at Bugle & Yarrington trainees do not have financial targets and as a result any billable time Matthew did could be billed by me.

I knew there was no option, but Yarrington's words were so much more sensible than Bugle's. I shrugged; what else could be done?

'You'll be all right, old chap!' piped up Teddy with a kind smile.

So I agreed to have a trainee forced upon me.

The meeting thus reached its conclusion and the scheduling of the next partner's meeting was established: for reasons of mutual convenience, it was postponed until to the fifteenth of March; an auspicious date indeed.

CHAPTER 11

Mary And Martha

The next morning, after noting that of late my office attire had consisted entirely of my finest and best garments, I decided that today my outfit would be deliberately less well cut than normal. After all, one must on occasion wear garments that are clearly not as well tailored as one's regular office-wear, so that colleagues notice how well one normally dresses.

I had therefore donned a frayed non-iron polysomething single cuffed shirt (which was usually reserved for cutting my sister's lawn) and a hideous tie given to me eons ago by a well-intentioned relative. I put on suit number six, my first and worst: a rather nasty affair from an unmentionable high street shop with an ill-cut jacket that's too big for my shoulders and aged trousers that had become shiny with wear, had frayed pockets, and that had always been half an inch too short.

Unfortunately I had forgotten *why* I had been wearing my top-notch habiliments.

That morning, I had been so deep in thought about the recent changes to my office life, and the changes that would be about to happen with Matthew's arrival, that it wasn't until after leaving the flat, looking rather like a middle-manager from Basingstoke, that my memory engaged.

Mary.

Bugger.

And worse still she had been sighted: twelve o'clock at one hundred yards. Mutual recognition was established instantaneously, although I did wonder how she recognised me so quickly in this somewhat dubious attire from such a range. I recognised her sexy walk and flash of leg between skirt and boot, and then her little flick of the hair and smile.

It's amazing how quickly a hundred yards turns to ten when two people are walking towards each other trying not to smile too broadly, and one at least is thinking desperately of what to say.

'Good morning!' seemed the obvious way to start, with a very deliberate slowing of the pace to let her know that my intention was to stop for a chat. To my slight surprise and joy, she also slowed – almost to a halt – and said: 'Morning. How are you? I haven't seen you for ages...'

Praise be to God! I thought. She doesn't have an Essex accent.

'I'm okay, thanks. You?' I asked, very awkwardly. Of course neither of us would have said if we hadn't have been very well.

'Yes, good, thank you.'

'Good.'

Awkward pause.

'Well... I'm James.' I said, holding out my hand. I hate shaking hands with women; it just feels wrong, but not to extend my hand in such a way might have appeared worse.

'Martha. Pleased to meet you properly,' she said, grasping my hand with just the right amount of grip and doing a little curtsy while lifting her skirt ever so slightly with her left hand. A splendid touch!

Martha. Well, an unusual name, and not, thank God, Mary. As soon as she said, it became the sexiest, most intriguing name known to me. I saw myself announcing to my friends that my other half was called Martha, and people smirking to themselves, thinking she might be a dowdy, boring girl, with librarian specs and no sex drive. And then I thought of those people's faces when introducing them to this stunning, blonde animal with a physique to rival Emily's, and how then the smirk would be on my face.

'I thought you'd been avoiding me ever since I saw you in the dry cleaners with very little on.'

'No, no, I've just been really busy at work, and I've been going in earlier than usual,' I lied, 'I've just had a promotion which has made matters worse.' I felt foolish for bragging, and then even more foolish with the realisation that I had set myself up:

'Oh, congrats. What do you do?'

She had asked me the dreaded question way too soon. I don't mind telling people that I solicit (as it were) after they know a bit about me, so that they can draw their own conclusions, but to tell people straight off that you are a lawyer, does, I find, usually cause a hiatus in the conversation. They usually think you're boring, overpaid, or an evil money-grabbing bastard, or all three. This of course derives from people's previous experiences with lawyers, and is for the main part not entirely unfair.

'I'm a lawyer.'

'Oh,' she said. My fears were confirmed. Mitigation was needed.

'I mean, I can't say I'm particularly passionate about it or anything...'

'What's wrong with being a lawyer?' she asked, apparently surprised that I was apologising for my chosen career path.

'Well, nothing.' Damn, I hate these people that think that law is such a worthy profession! 'But many people have quite justified prejudices against the legal profession. I was merely trying to get across that I'm not a boring overpaid money grabbing bastard.' Now she was laughing.

'I'm sure you're not.'

I didn't ask her what she did, because I didn't want my prejudices about whatever she did do to come to the forefront of my thoughts now, before I knew her.

And then she looked at her watch and began to uncross her legs to manoeuvre from the standing to the locomotive. This didn't bode well; she was looking for a quick exit. I had to move quickly, but she got there first:

'I'm really sorry,' she said in a way that made it totally impossible to ascertain whether in fact she was really sorry, 'but I can't be late this morning. I expect we'll bump into each other again soon – if you come in to work at the normal time, that is!'

'What are you doing tonight?' I asked.

If my cogs had engaged earlier, their grinding revolutions may have led me to the conclusion that my question was not terribly well phrased. Putting it to her in this ill-considered manner made it all too easy for her to shoot me down, which she did promptly.

'Busy, I'm afraid.'

'Tomorrow?'

'Also busy.'

I wondered whether an attempt should be made on Friday, but concluded fairly swiftly that if Wednesday and Thursday were busy, or 'busy', then so would Friday. Just as I had decided to ask if she would like to go out for a drink at some point, at her bloody convenience, she spoke.

'Sorry, I didn't mean to sound so harsh. I am busy tonight and tomorrow, but I'm free on Friday, if you wanted to ask me out then.' She had a very slight smile around the corners of her mouth. It was incredibly attractive. But more importantly she had asked me to take her out on Friday.

I wasn't sure if it constituted normal behaviour, but I liked her style.

'Would you like to come for a drink with me on Friday?' I asked, not able to control my smile, nor she hers.

'Yes, I'd be pleased to. Where shall I meet you?'

From my experience, women like men to take the lead; it was my duty to suggest somewhere, but I knew I would say:

'I don't mind.'

'Do you know the Vaults wine bar?' she asked.

Perfect! Everything beautiful Martha was doing was right.

'Very well. My office is just round the corner. I've never seen you in there...'

'I go occasionally. I'm sorry – I must dash. Look forward to Friday. Six-ish?'

'Six-ish.' I said to her back as she hurried off.

She turned round just afterwards and gave me a knee-wobbling smile.

'Bye,' I said, probably to myself.

I was elated; I had had the bottle to ask Martha out and she had accepted, even with me wearing my most horrid office outfit.

And so to the office, through reception...

'Morning, James'

'Morning Sue.'

...and into my own familiar room where Emily awaited my arrival.

'Martha said "Yes"' I said, without even a hello.

'Oh James!' said Emily.

I love it when she says this.

'Oh, Moneypenny!' I usually say back, having visions of me in a dinner jacket, concealing my Walther PPK in my shoulder holster, and imagining Emily, renamed with a humorous innuendo, taking my arm as we waltz outside to the gadget-laden Aston Martin, before skidding off to join a car-chase around Mayfair.

Emily's 'Damn it, James! You must control your over-active imagination!' brought me back to the office.

'Sorry. I was having – '

'Another bloody Bond moment. I know.' she interrupted. 'So what happened with Martha?'

'It was pretty simple really. I just saw her and asked her.'

'I *am* pleased for you. Where are you going?'

'The Vaults, six o'clock, Friday.'

'Nice work!'

'I have some incredibly distressing news, though. Last night, as you know, there was a partner's meeting. Guess who's getting a trainee, and guess who's office is going to be infiltrated by an irksome twenty-two year old hoping to be the next Lord Denning?'

'Shit. When?'

'Monday.'

'You're kidding…?'

'Sadly not.'

'How could they do this to you so soon? How could they do this to *us*? We haven't even had our own room for very long.'

'I know. It's most unfair. But it is a big room for two, I suppose. We have been lucky. I suppose they'll bring in another desk, and he'll sit in the corner there. Angela will probably try and re-arrange the layout to make him feel more welcome which really will be annoying. He's called Matthew, by the way.'

'That means we only have three days left together.'

'You make it sound like we're lovers in a story with a tragic end!'

'In a way we are.'

It was true, I suppose. The thought of our office containing a foreign body really did fill me with dread. But there was nothing to be done, and so I decided to work.

Shortly after, I gave up. Under such circumstances, I pick up a file and go for a wander, having quickly learned as a trainee that if you carry a file and pen around the office, no one will ask questions.

'Ah, morning James!' said Tim who was walking past my door, 'Off to waste someone else's time again?' Despite being spot on, I felt that Tim verbalising this thought was a little below the belt.

'Well, actually I was hoping to pick your brains about Mr Jones' capital gains tax, and how we can sort his affairs out post divorce.'

'Well, come into my office, then.' said Tim, clearly considering whether this was indeed a ruse for a gossip or a proper query.

After putting a few questions to Tim about the finer points of capital gains tax, Tim became visibly irked. 'James, we discussed these points on the Archer file about a fortnight ago. Don't you ever listen to anything I say?'

But thankfully I knew all the answers to my questions anyway: the capital gains tax was indeed merely an excuse to chat properly and my answer, designed at once to let Tim know exactly what information was required while making him feel foolish for misunderstanding my original question, had the desired effect: he sheepishly calmed down, gave me the answer, and after thanking him, I was able to swing the conversation round to more interesting topics.

'So, how's Charlotte?'

'Same as ever. She got rather angry with me last night for not doing the washing-up.'

'Don't women ever think about anything more important?'

'Apparently not. She's getting into doing up the flat. All she can think about is curtain material, sofas, carpets and useless and hideous junk to place on every surface in the house.' Tim's minor rant had been designed as a male complaint about the female obsession with nest building and had started off as such. However, by the time he had reached the end of the sentence his tone had changed completely and he concluded with: 'It's rather sweet actually.' And he was good enough to acknowledge with an embarrassed smile that he wasn't totally chauvinistic.

'How's your love life?' asked Tim. He asks me this regularly, and never expects an answer other than the one usually given to him – that all was quiet on the women front. But today, I paused, smiled a little, and announced:

'Well, I have a date with a rather gorgeous young lady on Friday evening.'

Tim looked visibly shocked.

'Christ! Well, congrats,' he said.

'No need to be so shocked.'

'Sorry. It's been a while, though, James! Nice tits?'

'Of course!'

'Nice legs?'

'Oh, yes!'

'Arse?'

'Pert.'

'Good work, James.'

'Thanks.'

This kind of banter had evolved between us, and was as false as the flirting between Emily and I.

'Make sure you let her know who the boss is,' said Tim, as if imparting wisdom of which the gods would have been envious. 'I did that with Charlotte. It worked for while: she let me be the boss until the first day after our honeymoon. Her words, in fact, were, "Well, darling, the honeymoon's over!". Since then she's been wearing the trousers, and I don't suppose I'll ever get them back!' He paused. 'But it's quite endearing,' he concluded, again dreaming of happy times with his wife. His love for her obviously hadn't finished its honeymoon, and I envied his relationship with Charlotte, just for a moment.

CHAPTER 12

A February Friday

After a busy couple of days catching up on undone work, Friday at the office had come to a close. It was half five, and only half an hour to go before I would be happily ensconced at The Vaults with a glass of fine red sitting opposite the beautiful Martha. Having never been good at working beyond half five, my thoughts turned from the mundane contents of files to the rather more exciting contents of Martha's skirts. Such musings soon caused it time to depart for The Vaults.

The one imperfect characteristic of the Vaults is that because there are so very many vaults, it is quite hard to ascertain quickly whether the person you are meeting is actually there, and a perusal of each individual vault is required.

I was now approaching the last unchecked one. Although the occupants of that particular vault were not yet visible, the table was, together with two drinks on it, and two pairs of hands: a male pair upon a slender female pair. I recognised the huge male hands immediately: those long bony fingers could only be Bugle's. I slowed, not wanting to show my face and catch him with someone who wasn't his wife. But in order to get to the bar, my path would have to cross the face of the vault he occupied, and recognition would be inevitable.

Had I not seen his hands, though, I wouldn't have hesitated, and thus my mind was set. Walking boldly forward, I glanced into the vault. It was indeed Bugle, with his so-called niece, Jenny, who Emily and I had bumped into in the Ritz. When he saw me, Bugle's hands jumped off Jenny's as if he'd been holding a hot jacket potato.

'Ah, James, good evening. What are you doing here?'

'Um... having a drink.'

'I didn't know you drank here – I thought The Pub was your choice of drinking hole.'

Bugle didn't often drink here – in fact he only ever came in on the rarest of occasions, so he no idea how many bottles of plonk I did actually get through in this hallowed establishment.

'Well, yes, I do…' I replied. 'How are you, Jenny?'

'Fine thank you.'

It was getting rather embarrassing.

'Well, I'll leave you both to get on with it.' I said.

I'm not exactly sure what 'it' was, but it had the effect of making them both look exceptionally uncomfortable, which hadn't been my intention but was telling enough.

The bar, thankfully, was far enough away from Bugle's vault not to afford me a view inside and I relaxed again. Whilst waiting impatiently to be served, that odd sensation which arrives quite unannounced informing you that someone is watching you came over me. I turned round and there was Martha, walking slowly across the main area towards me. She looked stunning. She was wearing a beautiful knee-length electric blue silk coat, embroidered with oriental flowers. The pattern led my eye down to a flash of leg. Her blonde hair fell freely over her shoulders, and the last thing I noticed was her enchanting smile, which made my heart jump.

'You look beautiful,' I said, because it was true. I then felt rather embarrassed.

'Thank you.'

'I love your coat,' I said, thinking that the next thing I said must not be a compliment.

'Thank you. It's from my favourite boutique, Juicy Lucy's, in Chelsea. I get all my clothes from there. It's not cheap, but everything's hand made and it's *such* good quality, and you never ever meet anyone wearing the same thing as you.'

'Yes, that must be nice. So, a drink?'

'It's a miserable evening – I think I need a glass of red to warm me up!'

'They do really good mulled wine, but it does make your teeth go purple.'

'Just a glass of red please. I can't have purple teeth on the first date!'

She ordered a bottle of her choice, with which my palate happily agreed, and we found an empty vault.

'Well, I can't believe we are sitting here like this!'

'I know, rather odd, isn't it,' she said

'Yes, but in a good way.'

We started chatting, and the conversation flowed naturally from favourite drinking holes to favourite drinks, and then to favourite eateries and favourite food, and then to her favourite boutique: Juicy Lucy's in Chelsea. She explained (again) how everything was hand sewn in London making it of much higher quality and endurance (despite costing six times more than it should, and going out of fashion before the wearer has had the chance to get it dry-cleaned, let alone worn it out), and how the runs were very small (so you were never in danger of meeting anyone else daft enough to pay so much for underwear where the cost could not possibly have originated from the amount of fabric used), and how Juicy Lucy herself (the owner who was indeed called Lucy and had once been juicy) had given Martha a skirt for being such a good (vain) customer. I listened, aware of the words, but interested only in Martha's lively and animated face. Thankfully talk of Juicy Lucy eventually tired even Martha, and she asked:

'So what type of law do you do?'

She had launched yet again into the subject furthest from my heart: law.

'Family: divorces mainly.'

'Oh, that must be depressing…' she commented, and then on further consideration: 'But I bet you get some good stories?!'

'Well, yes, there are some crazy people out there, and I suppose we do see some weird and wonderful things, some of which you wouldn't believe. But it's depressing to see how badly people who once loved each other – and they all did – end up treating each other. I do feel thoroughly sorry for some of my clients, but I try never to get emotionally involved with them. I expect you think I'm a cold-hearted bastard now?'

'No, I can understand that. I suppose it puts you off marriage though?'

'No, not at all. Other people's failings are not my own; I would have no hesitation marrying the girl I thought was Miss Right. And without wishing to amplify my eligibility too much, the saying "if you're going to get married, get married to a divorce lawyer" is not far wrong – we know how expensive and grim divorces can be! And you? Are you too modern for the whole marriage idea?'

'I've never really thought about it, but I suppose I would if Mr Right came along.'

It always amuses me how regularly the hypothetical 'Mr or Miss Right' comes up in conversation between two people on a date; they are in fact talking about the hypothetical Mr or Miss Right to a prospective Mr or Miss Right. If what the other says about their own hypothetical perfect partner seems alien to them, alarm bells ring; it is therefore, a good way to weed out potential problems and incompatibilities, but has the effect of making a date more like a spousal job interview.

Enough about law, I thought. Time to swing the conversation away from me, and law.

'What do you do?'

'I'm also a lawyer.'

Bugger.

I grinned at the grim irony of the situation.

My grin subsided slowly as she obviously didn't understand why I found it amusing. Then I felt slightly riled that she let me talk for so long about law without even telling me she was a lawyer. Then another horrible thought struck me: that she too could be a family lawyer. Had we spoken on the phone? Had I been fighting tooth and nail for my client at the expense of hers? My grin had now fallen from my face entirely.

'What type of law?'

'F and I.'

F and I, darling. Oh, *I* do F and I. F and fucking I.

It did please me that she didn't do family law, but F and I meant nothing to me; and the way in which she said it almost made it seem as if she knew everyone she had told was similarly flummoxed. But I got the distinct impression that if you questioned her about it, she would just laugh and say 'oh, silly me, I'm just so used to calling it that' or 'I thought everyone knew what F and I was'.

Nevertheless, if mishandled, my ignorance could prove too embarrassing.

'Oh right. Do you enjoy it?'

'Yes, I love it.'

Christ, I thought, she's one of those strange lawyers who is either lying, gets paid an awful lot so pretends to enjoy it, or worst of all, one who does actually intrinsically enjoy it.

'Why do you love it?' I asked.

She looked surprised. She looked as if she'd never even contemplated the question before, let alone the answer.

'Just the buzz of it all, I suppose. Big deals... big clients... lots of people working together for the same end... it's just exciting.'

I often wondered whether these people did actually find it exciting, or whether working for prestigious firms made them think it was exciting, or whether they just told people it was exciting because they didn't want to let on that their big powerful jobs were incredibly boring and took up every waking hour, and that they were in fact wholly miserable.

'I also work for Barry,' she said, as an afterthought.

'Great!' I said with mock enthusiasm. 'I hear Barry is a wonderful chap to work for!'

She laughed.

'Not Barry, the B.A.R.I...'

'Oh, the B.A.R.I... of course!'

'The British Association of Regulated Institutes,' she explained. What a useless title for an association: what kind of institutions were they and how were they regulated?

'Where did they get that title from: the M.O.D.A?'

She looked puzzled.

'The Ministry of Dodgy Acronyms,' I explained.

This raised a smile.

She seemed to think her explanation of Barry was sufficient, and I decided that I was on a need-to-know basis, and that I didn't need-to-know, so I didn't make any further enquiries.

'So what do you actually do, from day to day?' I hoped this would elicit some clues about what F and I was.

'Well, there's quite a few of us in my team. We're in charge of the banking side...' (Ah, banking! Could the 'F' stand for *Finance*?) '...and we do all the figures and so on.'

What does that actually mean? I thought.

'What does that actually mean?' I said.

'Well, I analyse data, and tell the other teams what it means.'

'And you enjoy that?'

I did feel a bit guilty for asking the question in that tone of voice, but I couldn't think of anything to say to get me out of the hole. Luckily she didn't seem offended: maybe she had become used to the way in which people asked her that question.

'Well, yes. I suppose it can be boring at times, but generally it's good fun. I really like the people I work with, so that makes it better. Although most of them are actually not really my friends at all.'

That made little sense. But already she had made two negative admissions: it could be boring and most of her colleagues are not her friends.

'So you must do something else apart from analyse data?'

'Well, no... but there is lots to analyse... especially in the insolvency cases.'

F and I: *Finance* and *Insolvency*? The picture was becoming as clear as I needed it to be: she did a really boring job and appeared to enjoy it. But in her defence, I postulated that the amount she must be getting paid probably made it worth it, and that if my pay was at City-boy level, I would do almost anything. It reminded me of my student days when for a whole summer my nights were spent in a factory tapping the lids of yoghurt pots with my index finger making sure all the lids were sealed correctly. When one wasn't, my finger would plunge into the yoghurt, splurging the creamy substance all over the conveyor belt which would go round and round getting gradually warmer and smellier as the electric motor heated both rubber belt and yoghurt; by morning, it stank. I concluded therefore that I mustn't judge people by their jobs, and that for a price, people will put themselves through hell.

She began to make signs that she wanted to leave, and so did I. But now came the potentially awkward game of seeing who breaks first, each fearing the other is looking for an early escape. It is only potentially awkward because I have no problem being the first to break; if someone wants to see you again, then leaving first won't stop them; if they don't, you will have saved a few quid and enjoyed an extra hour's sleep.

I made noises that it was time for me to depart, to which she agreed.

'So, would you like to go out again?' I asked with a certain amount of trepidation: despite requesting a close to the date this evening, there is always a huge part of me that wants the girl to want another, especially this girl. I had decided that Martha was the most attractive woman (apart from Emily) known to me, and I supposed two lawyers would always have common ground to explore. I now hoped for the chance to find out what made Martha tick; to find out what she loved and hated; how she worked as person, and ultimately, whether she would be my Miss Right.

But mainly I just didn't want her to say no.

And so when she said, 'I'd love to go out again.' I was pleased. We arranged to go out the following Thursday at the Vaults again, for the sake of convenience. I walked her to the tube station (she wouldn't let me pay for her cab) and we said goodbye and then stood looking at each other. She seemed happy, and I was, but I knew I couldn't keep looking at her smiling up at me like that for too much longer without doing something inappropriate, so I planted a kiss on her cheek and said goodbye again.

She turned toward the stairs leading down into the tube. At the bottom of the first flight, just before she went out of sight, she turned and gave me the sexiest, most provocative smile anyone had given me, and blew me a kiss. It almost knocked me over. She was gone.

CHAPTER 13

Saint Matthew

My spirits were high as I opened my office door on the Monday after seeing Martha and especially after finding that Emily hadn't made me a coffee. No! on my desk sat a steaming paper cup from the top-notch coffee house opposite The Pub, which was in fact called The Coffee House. The marvellous girl had actually purchased me a coffee! I wondered who she had spent last night with. And then got rather jealous. And then she came in.

'Morning sexy,' I said in an unusually forward greeting.

'Morning, James.' she said, rather quietly.

'Morning, James?! What kind of greeting is that?! I thought you were in a good mood, having bought me a coffee!'

'I didn't buy you the coffee.'

Emily then looked rather concerned and nodded her head in the direction of the corner of the room behind me.

I turned.

'Jesus Christ!' I exclaimed.

There, in the corner, sitting silently at a desk which had previously not been there, was a boy. Well, young man. Just about young man, anyway.

'What on earth are you doing there, being all silent?!'

'James,' interrupted Emily, 'this is Matthew.'

This was the prodigal law student from Oxford. My first trainee! I had seen his curriculum vitae. It was an impressive document, notable for the high occurrences of the letter 'A', and the word 'Distinction'. For his young age, he had achieved a lot academically, but I was pleased to note he had only one degree. What really worried me was the lack of interests or sport. Even the most naïve applicant enjoys socialising, sport and reading (or in plain English: getting totally pissed, watching the snooker world championships on television on a weekday afternoon when supposedly ill, and flicking through the atextual pages of *Hello*). Everyone embellishes their extra-curricular activities, because a prospective employer cannot prove that you are lying. Having said that, it is known that not many employers actually check your academic results either; certainly Bugle & Yarrington have no idea about my less than perfect legal examination results.

I soon realised the poor boy didn't know how to answer my question. I tried again.

'Well, good morning! I'm James.'

'Good morning,' he said sheepishly holding out a hand which when shook had all the characteristics of a squid.

'Sorry for the surprised greeting – I had rather forgotten you were joining today – usually the new trainees start properly on Wednesdays after two days of inductions and so on. You know, fire drills and all that rubbish.'

'I suppose fire regulations must be complied with by law.' he replied. God help us!

'Well, yes, anyway… I suppose you have met Emily?'

'Yes.'

'She's my secretary, and a damn good one. She's also gorgeous, as you may have noticed.' The boy by this time was sitting down. He went scarlet and made the nervous but humorously ill-timed act of crossing his legs.

'Thank you very much for the coffee. It's really quite unnecessary.'

'My pleasure,' he said, rather smarmily.

I really hoped he wouldn't buy me any more coffee; I would feel obliged to him. It would also leave him wide open to rumours of him trying to please his principal a little too much.

'I'm sure you've heard that you are my first trainee, so this will be as much a learning experience for you as it will me.'

'No, I didn't know.' He didn't look too impressed.

'Ah, well. Never mind. I was a trainee not so long ago, so I know what it's like. On day one, you have no clue about anything, and everything is foreign. You will find within a week that everything you learnt at law school was a waste of time, and that it's actually a lot easier and more tedious than you have probably been led to believe.'

A sceptical look crossed dear Matthew's face. The poor boy had probably been brainwashed, like most law students since the days of Empire, to believe that the job is fascinating all day long; that one's intellect will be challenged every minute in some high-brow debate or point of complex law; that one will be at the cutting edge of watching new laws being made – perhaps even contributing to the making of new laws; that one will spend one's days heroically fighting to proudly uphold the word of English law in our civilised and just England, whose law we have been so proud of since time immemorial; that one will be fighting for the good of one's fellow Englishmen, and, most importantly of all, for that single most important principle to an Englishman: justice!

'Right. Well, we must get going. Can you fill in the Form E on the Jones file?'

'I can certainly try,' replied Matthew enthusiastically. 'What's a Form E?'

My point exactly.

'A Form E lists the assets of a client for Ancillary Relief.'

'What's Ancillary Relief?'

I wondered if he was beginning to understand what I meant by everything being foreign.

'What happens to the money after the client gets divorced. The Form E contains details about the entire financial status of one's client: it has details of properties, chattels, shares, bank accounts and other intangible assets, details about debts, children and pensions. All the information regarding Mr Jones' assets are on the file, so you just have to go through the form and fill in the blanks. Mr Jones is very wealthy, with lots of assets, so it'll be a good one for you start with. If you can do that one well, you'll be able to do anyone's. Print it out when you've finished and we'll go through it.'

He set to, but with an air of superiority as if the task was a little beneath him.

Shortly after, Angela came in with another young man who I presumed was the other new trainee, Thomas.

'Morning James,' said Angela.

She looked vile as usual, and Thomas wisely looked to be keeping his distance, a mild look of disgust on his face as he watched her. Today, Angela's glasses had slipped down her nose, and she kept tipping her head up and down looking alternately over and through the thick greasy lenses as if trying to work out which image was clearer. Still the thought of cleaning them seemed to elude her. I wondered if she could actually see my face, or whether she knew it was me simply because I was sitting at my desk.

'Morning, I'm Tom,' said Thomas, without any introduction from Angela. Bugle was right: he was indeed a confident trainee.

'James James,' I said, standing to shake his hand, which was significantly less clammy and much stronger than Matthew's. 'This is my secretary Emily, and this is your fellow trainee, Matthew.'

After the greetings had been concluded, Angela announced she was taking the new trainees off for their inductions, and that Matthew would be busy for the rest of the day and tomorrow with her. 'Good luck,' I said which raised a smile from Tom and a timid glance from Matthew. I don't think Angela had cleaned her ears out that month and she appeared to ignore the comment. And, after once more peering over her glasses with squinted eyes, she took her leave, trainees following.

Matthew arrived back in my office on Wednesday morning. Emily and he were already there when I arrived and there was a steaming Coffee House coffee on my desk.

'Morning all! Thanks for the coffee, Matthew.'

'My pleasure.'

Oh, Lord! Was this to happen every morning?

'It's really very kind of you, but please don't buy me any more coffees. You'll be broke in six months!'

'James, Mrs Green will be here in half an hour.' Emily reminded me.

'Thanks, Emily. Right, Matthew,' I said, turning to him, 'Mrs Frances Green is a new client. I have presumed two things from her name: firstly, from her Christian name that she is likely to be of an older generation, and secondly, that as a "Mrs" she will want a divorce. But as you will constantly see, it is unwise to make any presumptions in the legal profession. You'll be told this on so many occasions during your training that you will wish the word "presume" didn't exist, so I thought I may as well get in there, quick sharp, to be the first to tell you!' I smiled in an attempt to make my preamble light-hearted, but Matthew looked as if he was just being patronised. 'Well, anyway, meetings with clients are one of the best ways for you to learn the law, and how to deal with clients. You can come and see what happens, and it'd be really useful if you could take notes, too. In the meantime, please could you get on with the Jones Form E.' He clearly hadn't banished his air of superiority as he reluctantly opened the file.

Half an hour later Sue phoned to announce that Mrs Frances Green was in reception. I told Matthew to grab a notebook and note down everything that was said. He followed me out to reception to find a respectable-looking middle-aged woman waiting for us.

'Mrs Green?'

'Yes, Frances, please.'

'Good morning. I'm James James, which can be confusing, but I assure you I am the only James and the only Mr James in the office, so if you ask for "James", you can't go wrong!'

She smiled back as I shook her hand.

'This is my trainee, Matthew. Would you mind if he sat in on our meeting to take a few notes for me?' She didn't mind at all, but I watched as her initial smile of pleasure turned to a look of horror as she shook his cold, clammy and cephalopodic hand.

We adjourned to the Dining Room and made ourselves comfortable round the board table; but in truth it was only Frances and I who appeared comfortable; Matthew sat there like a stiff in an open coffin waiting for its picture to be taken.

'Now, Frances, how can I be of assistance?'

'I want a divorce.'

'Well, I do profess to know something about that. Perhaps you could tell me a bit about yourself, your marriage and your present circumstances, to give me an overall picture?'

'Yes, of course. Shall I start at the beginning? I married Trevor twenty-five years and nine days ago. He's a doctor, and I was in medical research until we had Martin and Georgie – Georgina – who are now twenty and nineteen – when I became a full time mum. I've never worked since – I tried when Martin was about ten, but it proved too difficult getting back into research after such a long gap. I only wanted to do it for myself though. Trevor is a consultant neurologist and earns a lot, so money has never been an issue. Both kids are at university. Martin – much to my disgust – and present company excluded, of course – is doing law, and Georgie has just started medicine.'

'I'd be disgusted if my kids became lawyers,' I said. 'In fact, my mother is from a long line of medics and she almost disowned me when I finally decided on law!' I could already see Frances Green had her head screwed on correctly, and had a good sense of humour. The job becomes infinitely more satisfactory when one has sensible clients.

'Wise woman,' she said, glancing at Matthew, thinking, I fancy, that his sole ambition was to be a lawyer, and that she might have upset him. The same thought crossed my mind.

'Anyway,' she continued, 'I thought all was well with the marriage.

It has I suppose been a little different since the kids left home, but we've been enjoying time to ourselves a bit more. Trevor only works four days a week now, so we have time for long weekends and so on. Well, we used to have time for that, anyway. We had a lovely silver wedding, only nine days ago... but it... well, now of course, it seems like a lifetime ago... I discovered the day after that the bastard had been fucking a nurse at work!'

It was odd hearing a well-spoken woman use that language. But she hadn't finished.

'That bitch... that bloody slut! is young enough to be his bloody daughter! He just wanted to get his end away with a nubile young thing with no wrinkles and no saggy bits! Sorry,' she said, beginning to calm down a bit, 'I'm over the shock now. I've come to terms with the situation and grieved. Now thinking about it just makes me angry!'

And with that she broke down.

The box of tissues was located and handed to her. I never knew whether this was a good move; to have tissues in readiness for emotional clients was really a necessity, but I always thought it looked like they were there because we expected clients to break down. No-one had ever made a comment about this though. I suppose they were just relieved that they had something to blow into and wipe the tears away with.

'Is this the box of snot-rags you hand to all your over-emotional, under-sexed female clients?' she sniffed.

'Well yes, as a matter as fact of it is.' No point lying, under the circumstances.

'You could have bought man sized ones!' She was calming down now. 'I'm sorry. I suppose I'm not over him yet. Until last week, I loved him dearly.'

'It's quite all right. I'm surprised you have come to see me so soon. Most people still get emotional months down the line.'

'Not me. I'll have a toy-boy within a month.'

Then she broke down again.

When she had calmed down, we went through a good deal more detail regarding her circumstances. As a family lawyer you do have to ask comprehensive questions about your client so as to get the best outcome for them, while not failing to disclose anything to the court. By the end of a divorce case the lawyer knows pretty much everything there is to know about a client in terms of money and relationships. After forty minutes of questions with Frances, I knew the basics about her, and she wanted to know how to divorce her not-so-beloved Trevor.

'In this country, the court will only grant a divorce if you can show that the marriage has broken down irretrievably. There are five ways of evidencing this.' I explained. 'The first three involve time periods of separation of between two and five years and are thus irrelevant to your case: I'm afraid nine days isn't quite long enough in the eyes of the law.

'The "unreasonable behaviour" ground is probably the most common. Unreasonable behaviour is not what the judge, or indeed the man on the Clapham omnibus finds unreasonable, it is what *you* find unreasonable. For example, one client's marriage ended when his wife brought him a cup of tea and put it on his antique desk. When he picked it up to drink, he discovered that yet again the mug had a wet bottom, and yet another piece of furniture was ruined with a tea-ring. It was just the straw that broke that particular camel's back. One lady couldn't put up with her husband's constant flatulence in bed. She filed for divorce but during the divorce proceedings it came to light that he had been diagnosed with irritable bowel syndrome, and because there was a medical term for it, she welcomed him back into the matrimonial bed where he presumably carried on happily farting away. Only a year later she divorced him because she discovered he'd never in fact seen a doctor and lied about the diagnosis. He always thought he should have divorced her for having an unreasonable opinion of unreasonable behaviour.

'The final, and I believe most relevant in your case, is adultery, which technically means any form of physical penetration with a party outside the marriage.'

'I'd like to physically penetrate his skull with an ice-axe, but I suppose that would constitute murder.'

'Probably. You might be able to claim manslaughter and use the defences of insanity and diminished responsibility, but as your lawyer my advice would be that it'd be unlikely that a jury would find in your favour and therefore not to proceed upon that course of action. You would get a wonderful sense of revenge, but life imprisonment would probably not be worth it. There are moral issues here as well, but I'm not qualified in that type of thing. Could you make an appointment to see your vicar?'

She was smiling.

'I'm an atheist. I don't give a damn about murdering either of them. Satan can have me! But I will heed your advice; I'm not so sure that prison would suit me.'

I glanced at Matthew. I fancied there was tiny smile about him. I hoped there was: after all, this was about as good as my job could be. Having a client who didn't mind a joke was a blessing. This woman had just had her life turned upside down, and her bastard doctor of a husband had, in the most clichéd of ways, been having it away with a nurse. To advise her, as her lawyer, not to do away with said nurse by the misuse of mountaineering equipment tickled me pink. Here was a lady made of sterner stuff than most.

'So in your case you could go for unreasonable behaviour or adultery.'

'Adultery. Sounds more juicy.'

'Right you are. I'll write to your husband to confirm in writing that you have instructed me in your divorce proceedings; do you know if he's instructed solicitors?'

'His solicitors are Alfred Pennington & Co so I suppose he'll use them if they have a good divorce lawyer?'

Ali P & Co (as they are known to the employees of my firm) is a good firm just down the road. They do a lot of property work, and often act for the other party in many of our own client's property deals. Their family department is small but well regarded and headed by the formidable Cressida Smyth-Jones, whose very name strikes fear into many experienced family lawyers. Darling Cressida is a hard-nosed middle-aged spinster who always believes her client is right and who cannot, under any circumstances, take, or indeed make, a joke. I have acted against her on the other side of several divorces and with Frances as my client, I was looking forward to this latest opportunity for having some fun with her.

'They do indeed have a good divorce lawyer in the form of an aptly-named Miss Cressida Smyth-Jones. She will be acting for your husband if he does use that firm. If she is his solicitor, he doesn't know what he's in for! Before you go, I must tell you about the boring admin matters. We charge by the hour and Matthew's hourly rate is obviously considerably lower than mine. I'll get him to assist where possible to keep our fees to a minimum. I usually bill monthly, depending on the amount of work done.'

'So what do I get for your hourly fee?' she asked, with mock scepticism.

I hate it when clients ask that. But Frances Green was ripe for a light-hearted answer.

'My wisdom.'

'You must be very wise for your age.'

'I am indeed. Did you want a serious answer?' I asked, partly to buy some time to think of one.

'No thanks.'

'Marvellous!' I said, and meant it.

We returned to my office after the meeting to find Emily bending down getting a file out of the filing cabinet. I caught Matthew checking out her pert bottom. It was a splendid sight and the thought crossed my mind that perhaps I had grown too used to Emily's perfect figure and that I didn't appreciate it as once I had.

'Hi guys,' she said, 'how was Frances?'

'Husband is a doctor with a particular penchant for nurses' knickers. She's only just found out.'

'Oh, no! I hope she's coping,' said Emily, always concerned for our clients.

'She's a bit tearful, but it was only a few days ago and I think she's a strong lady. She's a bit of a hoot. I think we'll have some fun with her.'

'Good. Coffee, sweetheart?' asked Emily, forgetting for a moment that Matthew was there. Matthew and I both looked at her, and then me at him, with a look telling him that Emily would never call him sweetheart. Getting used to another man in the room was clearly going to be hard for both of us.

'Thanks, darling,' I answered.

'Matthew?'

'No, thanks Miss Lewis; I tend to find that coffee unnecessarily accelerates my heart rate.'

Was every question to be met with such sober replies? Was everything to be taken so seriously? Matthew seriously needed to relax; he'd be dead of a heart attack by forty if he kept up this ultra-serious stance, with or without coffee. Emily and I exchanged exasperated glances before she tried to make light of Matthew's most recent blunder by asking him to call her Emily. I'm not sure how Matthew had found out that Emily was Miss Lewis; I'd forgotten that my long-legged, short-skirted secretary even had a surname!

CHAPTER 14

Sloane Ranger

At last it was the end of Thursday and time again to meet Martha. Between busy times during the week, most of my spare thoughts had been about her. I kept seeing flashes of her smile in my imagination, and it made my heart jump every time. I had been looking forward to finding out all about her.

We arrived at the door of The Vaults simultaneously, and I ushered her down the stairs, following as she took my lead. We crossed the main vault to the bar and stood looking at each other, she smiling amorously at me; we still hadn't said a word.

'Hello, you.' She said, in a particularly sexy manner.

'Good evening,' I said, actually rather embarrassedly, which surprised me. 'A bottle of red?'

'Sure.'

We ordered a bottle, found a vault and sat down. There was no sign of Bugle this time, thank God.

'You look amazing; I love your top.' I said, without thinking. She did look stunning, but I knew that any comment about her clothes had inevitable repercussions on the conversation front:

'It's from Juicy's. It's new in this week. I was a bit concerned about the colour. Do you think it would be better in pink or salmon?'

The one she was wearing was salmony-pink.

'Which one is that?' I asked, not unreasonably.

She looked at me as if I was totally stupid.

'The *pink* one, obviously.'

Obviously.

'I'm not sure it matters. It's what in it that matters, and that looks pretty damn good to me!'

I thought that this flattering interjection might sway her away from sartorial talk, but alas I was mistaken:

'Yes, but I'm just not sure if this pink goes with my skin tone; I think the salmon might suit me better.'

Now I am a man who likes to dress well, but to discuss my clothes at this early stage of a relationship with a potential partner was simply not on. No, my approach was far more refined, and involved arriving knowing I looked good, but not commenting upon myself; should any compliments come my way, an understated answer would be given. Talking actively about one's clothes makes one less attractive.

I had never heard a single person talk about her clothes, or the way she looked, or whether salmon or pink suited her bloody skin tone as much as Martha. She did look fabulous. She must have spent a prodigious sum of money and time on the various outfits she had worn in my company. But why didn't she leave it that? If she hadn't talked about them so much, it would have been easier to appreciate her sense of style, and acknowledge that all her stitches were of the highest quality. I may even have paid her a compliment or two. Now she was boring me.

'So what do you do when you're not shopping at Juicy's?' I asked, wincing because I'd said 'Juicy's' too.

'I like shopping at other places too, and socialising... Oh, I go to the gym too.'

She certainly did go to the gym, I thought, while the other half of my brain wondered whether there were any signs of intellectual power to match the undoubtedly fine physical specimen.

'You look fit. What do you train on?' she asked, apparently thinking that gyms interested me, and that I might know what torturous machines are located within such establishments.

'I've just been skiing which keeps me fit for a week a year.'

'Oh, lovely! I've always wanted to go skiing. Who did you go with?'

'Emily, kind of my best girl friend.'

'Oh. How do you know her?'

'She's my secretary.'

Without knowing Emily this may have seemed odd, but of course her role as my secretary came secondary to her role as my best girl friend.

'She's cute, then?' asked Martha.

'Yes, she is actually,' I said, without thinking about what reaction this might have on the seemingly confident Martha. Regret immediately struck me as a slightly disenchanted look began to manifest itself upon her face.

'So you've never been skiing?' I asked, in a hurried attempt to move onto less icy ground.

'No,' she said.

It's not often that I cannot think of anything to say.

Thankfully she did: 'So, where's the most beautiful place you've ever seen?'

This was more like it: a proper question leading to the possibilities of an interesting discussion. I gave her some examples of my favourite places to go in the world and at home, and she gave me hers, which were generally compatible in terms of booking holidays together.

The conversation flowed a little more easily from this point on, possibly because the alcohol was relaxing us, and by the time she announced that she ought to be making a move, I had concluded that another attempt at courtship would definitely be worthwhile.

'Well, do you fancy meeting up again?' I asked.

'Sure. What are you doing on Sunday night?'

I thought that it was an odd day to ask me out, but I was free: 'Nothing... but shall we exchange numbers just in case?'

'Yes, good idea.'

'What's yours?' I asked.

'You'd better have my home number... 0208...'

I didn't hear the rest of the number. It's frightening when you hear an outer London code. This girl could live anywhere; dollar signs light up in her eyes like a Las Vegas fruit machine: the dollars of travel expenses going to meet her in some ghastly suburb. No, this would not do; I had to break it to her:

'I should point out that I don't do long distance relationships.'

I was only half joking, and deep down was quite serious about it – my hatred for travelling across London is why I live in the middle – but the problem was that my own wit had made me smirk. She clearly thought my comment had been a joke and began to laugh.

The situation was hopeless; I had to ascertain how hopeless:

'Well, where *do* you live?' I asked.

'Becontree.'

I obviously looked bewildered.

'Just north of Parsloe's Park...'

Silence. She tried again:

'Near Mayesbrook Park?'

No. I wondered whether this place was in fact inside the M25.

'Well, its kind of north of Dagenham...'

Dagenham! Ye Gods!

'Ah, I know where Dagenham is,' I said, my geographical knowledge finally coming to the fore. Is it nice?' I asked foolishly, but not knowing else to say.

'No, but it's cheap.'

I concluded this would be her answer as she said it and wondered if she spent less at Juicy Lucy's whether she could have lived at a more salubrious address.

'Here it is,' she said, handing me her number on a personal card, 'Give me a ring if you have any difficulties, otherwise, I'll look forward to seeing you on Sunday.'

Again I walked her to the tube, and this time she even took my arm as we walked. I did not, however, offer her another taxi, and I thanked God that she hadn't taken me up on my last offer. How much was a taxi to Dagenham?

We got to the tube, and again she smiled up me. I kissed her cheek, as before, but this time her hand caught my neck so I couldn't withdraw and she kissed my lips, ever so softly, and withdrew; she disappeared into the bowels of the tube system leaving me alone; but the magic of that kiss kept me smiling to myself all the way home.

'How did it go last night?' asked Emily the next morning.

'Not terribly well,' I said, with my tongue half in my cheek.

'Why?'

'I found out she lived in Becontree.'

'*Where?*'

'Exactly. She tells me it's in London but eventually I found it on page seven-hundred and one of the Outer London and Wilderness Regions A-Z... Oh, I don't know Em, she keeps talking about this boutique in Chelsea where she buys all her gear. She's beginning to bore me about it – she doesn't seem to understand I'm not a girl. Maybe she hasn't had a boyfriend for a while. I know it's harsh, but we've only had two dates, and it has featured heavily in both of them.'

'She's probably just nervous,' said Emily encouragingly, and I wanted to believe her.

'So are you seeing her again?' she asked.

'Yes, on Sunday.'

'But Sunday is Saint Valentine's Day,' said Emily.

CHAPTER 15

Valentine's Day

It was indeed approaching that most dreaded day of the year for the single Londoner: Saint Bloody Valentine's Day. Who was Saint Valentine anyway? I have images of the smug little git plucking his harp happily in heaven knowing he's plucked more birds in a week than a turkey farmer has in a lifetime of Decembers.

Now this year I had three problems, all in the form of women.

The first problem was Emily and she was inexorably linked to the second: Martha. Emily and I had made a pact last Valentine's Day that if we were ever single we would go out with each other. Furthermore, as it looked like we would both be single, we had discussed where to go out just before I had asked Martha out for the first time, and now we had a table booked. My relationship with Martha was at an early stage and Valentine's Day came at inappropriate juncture that put unnecessary pressure on the proceedings. At once, perhaps unwisely, I decided that this little problem must be nipped in the bud and that Martha must be contacted as soon as soon as possible to break it to her that I was seeing Emily on the Big Day, and that seeing her would not be possible. This news did not receive the calm and reasoned response I had hoped for. ('Well, James, I'm not altogether happy about you going off with your secretary. I mean that's so clichéd; couldn't you find someone else to have a bit of fun with?'). However, after further explanation regarding my relationship with Emily, Martha seemed to have calmed down and apologised for her little outburst. But it did not bode well for things to come.

Just as I had finished pacifying Martha on the phone it rang again and the third problem presented itself in the form of my darling sister Sarah. She had previously asked me if I could baby-sit my only nephew, the troublesome five-year-old Ben, while she and my brother-in-law Michael went out for a romantic meal, and now she wanted an answer.

'Well, normally I would...'

This is true; I have done it for the past three years.

'But…?' she paused and then asked, 'have you got a date?'

'Not exactly.'

'Not exactly…? Oh, I see! You're going out with Emily?'

'You know me too well.'

She did. Just like my bloody mother. It was infuriating.

'You always go out with Emily! Can't you put her off?'

'No, we made a pact last year. Come on Sarah, you know how funny girls get over this type of thing. I did promise her.'

'Well, since you always go out with her for dinner, and we never go out for dinner, why don't you two come over here, look after Ben, and enjoy the house in our absence?'

I know my sister better than she knows herself; my cunning plan had worked a treat. Her house is beautiful. Spending an evening there without her and Michael, and with Emily, with an Aga to cook on, a huge quantity of quality booze at our disposal, and a seriously comfortable bed only a flight of stairs away, meant that the evening would be perfect.

'I'll see what Emily says and get back to you.'

'Please, James?'

'I'll see what I can do, but I'm not making any promises,' I said, to make it look like I was going out of my way to help her. And then the final flourish: 'And you'll owe me one!'

'Yes, okay, I'll owe you one,' she said, with a put-on tone of exasperation.

Damn, I'm wonderfully evil!

A phone call to Emily would now be required to make sure she was happy with the plan (she was) and the evening was set up. The booked restaurant table was cancelled, with the joyous knowledge that we would haven't to sit opposite each other in a restaurant full of tables of two, their occupants all sitting opposite each other: some at an early stage in the relationship, kissing each other far more often than is appropriate for an eating establishment; some trying desperately to look happy; some trying desperately to think of something to say; and perhaps one or two couples looking fondly at each other and holding hands.

All three Valentine's Day problems had been sorted, although there was a slight niggling fear that Martha wasn't entirely happy with the plan. I didn't entirely blame her, but we had only just started seeing each other, and to take things too quickly is always unwise; my strong-willed conclusion was that if she was not willing to wait a few days, or weeks, then she wouldn't be worth it all.

I phoned my sister back and said that a reluctant Emily and I would arrive on Sunday evening to look after Ben. Sarah, knowing that she owed me one, asked if we wanted to come to Sunday lunch and spend the afternoon there. She is a wonderful cook, and not having any other particular plans, and having confirmed the idea with Emily, we accepted gratefully.

Upon our arrival, Sarah opened the door opened and Ben peeped around it as it opened.

'Hello Ben.'

'Hello Uncle James.' I can never get used to being called Uncle James. 'Is she your girlfriend?' he asked, looking up at Emily.

Cheeky little bugger.

'No she's my secretary. '

'What's a sextree?'

'Good question!'

'James, don't confuse him,' said Sarah, 'You know Emily, Ben. Don't you remember when James and she took you ice-skating? She helps James at work,' she explained.

Ben looked bewildered at the beauty of Emily and hid behind his mother's skirt, before scampering on all fours upstairs like a monkey.

The adults went through to the drawing room, Emily letting out a rather sensual, 'Oh..!' as she walked in.

Michael asked if she was okay.

'I'm very happy to see you have finally put it up!'

Emily was a damn good painter. She had given Michael and Sarah a painting for Christmas fourteen months ago and had been most upset on her last visit to Sarah's in November when it was still sitting under the stairs. It now had pride of place over the fireplace. Emily's artistic aspirations extended beyond the amateur; she was a frustrated artist and had entered the world of the secretary quite by chance – her father had been a lawyer and had arranged her a temporary position for her to earn a bit of extra cash. Now, several years on, she relied on the cash totally, and her art had necessarily suffered. I always hoped that some gallery or other would see her talent, but it hadn't happened yet, and each year that went by made it look increasingly unlikely to happen.

'James, there's some Champagne in the fridge. Could you do the honours?'

'Of course!'

I brought two bottles of bubbly in and poured them.

'There's only four glasses.' I noted.

'There are only four of us.'

'Ben still too young for a tipple?'

'Yes, and don't go leaving your glass on anything low enough for him to get hold of. You know he'll drink anything he knows he's not meant to.'

Here was a man after my own heart.

The little fellow came in, driving a toy tractor across the carpet.

'How's the painting going?' asked Michael of Emily.

'Pretty good. I just find it so hard to find the time.'

'Any luck with exhibitions and so on?'

'No, not yet. I keep trying to put my name around, but as soon as anyone finds out I'm also a legal secretary, people lose interest at the drop of a canvas. They seem to think that unless you believe in your work a hundred percent and just paint paint paint until you manage to get a break, you haven't got a chance. The facts that you have to pay rent and eat – and drink, obviously – are, to the artistic world, irrelevant.'

'It does seem a bit daft; most of the great artists of the world had to do other jobs. Surely work is work, and painting is painting...' agreed Michael.

'Well, you know how pretentious these arty-farty types are,' I said, 'doesn't surprise me at all.'

'Ah, yes, the art expert speaks!' said Emily.

'Oh, God, yes!' said Sarah, coming in from the kitchen, 'make sure you pay close attention to everything that James says about art! He's *very* knowledgeable!'

'I'm not that much of an art heathen,' I protested, but the laughter of Michael, Sarah and Emily put an end to that admittedly tenuous argument.

'I think lunch requires some attention,' said Sarah.

'What are we having?

'Dead hen.'

'With all the trimmings?'

'Yes, James, with all the trimmings.'

My mouth started watering.

'Right, Michael, off to the kitchen with you, you have some cooking to do!' said Sarah.

'Michael's cooking?'

'Yes, he kindly offered to so that I could chat with you and Emily – usually I'm the one chained to the Aga.'

'You owe me two large favours, now Sarah.'

Michael was a lousy cook. He could turn the plumpest, juiciest, organically fed, free-range fowl into pure unadulterated carbon (in fact, knowing Sarah, the chicken was probably plump, juicy, organically fed and free-range and probably cost more than most people would spend on a thirty pound Christmas turkey).

'Oi, James, less of the cheek!' said Michael, 'I'm not that bad!'

'You bloody are.'

Sarah gave me her 'don't swear in front of the child' look, and I gave her my humble apologetic look back.

Michael shuffled unenthusiastically to the kitchen and after a few minutes chatting with Sarah and Emily, I glanced at my glass of bubbly which was on the little table next to the sofa. The once full glass was almost empty and I had only taken one sip. This could mean only one thing.

Ben had been naughty.

I heard him behind the sofa making tractor engine noises. My initial thought was that it'd be highly amusing watching a squiffy five year old, but that thought turned to horror when I thought it might make him sick. How much Champagne can a five-year old take? Should I try and hide it? What excuses could I give his mother?

'Sweetheart!' called Michael from the kitchen, 'I could use a hand just for a minute!'

'Oh, bloody hell,' said Sarah, 'can't he do anything on his own?!'

I gave her my 'don't swear in front of the child' look and she gave me her 'I'm his mother and will do as I please' look back. No justice, I thought.

Sarah departed for the kitchen to help her beloved cook.

'Ben!' I said, in an urgent whisper.

'Yes, Uncle James?'

'Did you drink my Champagne?'

'No.'

'I think you had a bit, didn't you?'

'Yes.'

'Oh, James!' said Emily. 'I can't believe you gave him booze! Sarah's going to kill you!

'I didn't – he took it himself! How are you feeling, Ben?'

He was just giggling uncontrollably on the floor.

'Do you feel sick?'

More giggles, and then he ran through to the kitchen.

A couple of seconds later, there was a wail, followed by loud crying. I jumped up and headed through. Ben was lying on the floor screaming and clutching his head. He had the unusual complaint of giggling uncontrollably and simultaneously crying.

'He ran into the door post,' explained Michael.

'How are you, sweetie?' asked Sarah hugging him on her knees.

'I'm all dizzy, Mummy,' spluttered Ben between deciding whether to laugh or cry.

'Yes, sweetie, you hit your head.'

I had my doubts as to whether to the impact had made him dizzy, or whether the dizziness had caused the impact.

'I think I can explain his behaviour,' I said nervously.

Sarah looked angrily at me.

'Would this have anything to do with Champagne, James?' she asked.

'I fear so – but it was him who was naughty, not me!' I added.

'The toddler's tipsy!' said Michael, with glee.

'Michael, it's not funny,' snapped Sarah.

But unfortunately Michael and I had already given each other the giggles.

All three men looked at each other, knowing we'd been naughty and knowing we shouldn't be finding the situation amusing, for fear of our common relation, Sarah. Of course knowing we shouldn't be laughing only made matters worse.

'Men!' said Sarah, turning to Emily for moral support.

Unfortunately, Emily too was smiling broadly at the situation.

Sarah let out noise that could only be described as exasperation, picked up her glass of bubbly and announced: 'I am going through to the drawing room with Emily. You can call me when the lunch is ready, Michael. If you need help, open a bloody cook-book!'

Emily followed on cue, but not before winking at us boys.

And so it was that until lunch was served, the boys stayed in the kitchen and the girls chatted in the drawing room. Michael and I made a pretty good effort with the lunch, and aside from a couple of minor cock-ups like him putting the bird in the oven upside down, and me dropping the sprout pan so that sprouts ran all over the floor, it was pretty good.

In the afternoon, by building a masterpiece of civil engineering and utilising every last piece of toy railway track, Ben and I upset Sarah by building the Dining Room to Kitchen Line, which she promptly tripped up over carrying a cup of tea. The cup was swept up into a dustpan by a guilty Uncle James.

By early evening, I was exhausted from having carried Ben round all afternoon. Ben was in bed with a headache after encountering his second doorframe of the day. The responsibility of his misfortune again landed on my shoulders, ironically enough because he had in fact been sitting on my shoulders; I had failed to remember that the doorways of my sister's abode hadn't been constructed at a sufficient height to allow him sitting in such a position satisfactory clearance beneath said doorway without serious consequences.

But Michael now awaited his wife to finish changing so that for once they could go and enjoy a meal out without having to worry about Ben. Well, they could try and enjoy an evening out, while worrying about me looking after Ben. Emily was also changing for the evening, though in view of the fact that we weren't going anywhere, I couldn't understand why on earth she was changing at all. Michael's shrug confirmed that he couldn't understand women either. Most importantly, this was the only time Michael could enjoy a stiff drink without accusations of acute alcoholism and thankfully he offered me one too.

We sank into the sofas with a satisfied air about us and smiled at each other as we sipped our liquor in the knowledge that our women-folk would take another half an hour to be ready. We chatted about politics and the state of the world and concluded that as in holy matrimony, the prohibition of alcohol could never be achieved without civil war. Soon after this intellectual discussion, the girls came down simultaneously, both looking splendid.

We said goodbye to Michael and Sarah, and they left declaring that we should not wait up for them. Ben was thankfully quiet all night although I did wonder if my earlier actions had caused him mild concussion or some such similar ailment which kept his normally hyperactive behaviour more subdued. This left the evening wide open for us (Emily) to cook a magnificent feast on the Aga, and for us (me) to drink my way through Michael's excellent vintages of wine. Having had a good catch-up and giggle, and having eaten and drunk our fill while even remembering to check on the seemingly unconscious Ben a few times, we decided to head upstairs to bed.

Thankfully my sister has two spare bedrooms and I wasn't forced to listen to Emily's snoring this evening. But our pact had worked; we two happy singletons had outmanoeuvred the smug Saint Valentine. I kissed her good night and made a final check on Ben. This initially caused me a slight panic because it looked like he'd stopped breathing. Nevertheless I soon discovered that his heart was still beating, and having obtained some scientific knowledge during my schooling, concluded that one cannot happen without the other, and that therefore he was merely asleep.

Very soon, I too joined him in the land of nod.

CHAPTER 16

Third Time Unlucky

I was excited to be seeing Martha. The first two dates had gone relatively well, and I had high hopes for this lucky third.

Since The Vaults seemed to be becoming our regular, we met there. Martha really was breathtakingly sexy. As I stood at the bar watching the glorious beast slink towards me across the cavernous den, I saw all the male inhabitants of the individual vaults, one by one, as Martha came into their view, swivel their heads in her direction, jaws dropping visibly, their female partners looking on jealously at the creature who had attracted the attention of their men.

'Good evening, sir!' were her first words.

'Good evening, madam!' were mine.

She grabbed my tie, and pulled my face towards her face and we kissed, briefly, but on the lips. Quite well done, I thought.

We got some wine and sat at the bar in the main vault, the little private vaults all being occupied.

'Nice coat. Is that from Juicy Lucy's?'

'Yes, how did you guess?!'

Can't think.

Having foolishly brought up Juicy Lucy's, I tried desperately to swing the conversation away from the boring boutique before Martha's love of the place, and love of talking about it took up the next half hour; a swift interjection would be required.

'Do you want to see *Die Zauberflöte*? It's on at Covent Garden soon.'

'Dee *who*?'

'The *Magic Flute*.'

'What's that?'

'What do you mean, what's that?'

'Well, what is it?' she asked, with a certain amount of awkwardness. Christ, I thought, she's not kidding.

'The opera...' I said, in a way not too make her feel too daft.

'*Opera*?' she said with some surprise, which made her look totally daft.

Then she realised she appeared totally daft, and went bright red. I averted my gaze, pretending not too notice.

'Oh, I *see*.' she said, trying to recover her blunder and failing; there was no way she could possibly recover herself.

'I've already seen it.' she announced triumphantly, assuming that this would be a failsafe answer.

'Yes, me too; I love it. Do you want to go? It's in German, and I've always wanted to see it in German.' I admit I was winding her up a little.

'German?' She asked, perplexed. 'Why would you want to watch it in German?'

I wasn't terribly sure how to answer this, but concluded that: 'That's how Herr Mozart intended it to be' would be a good answer.

'Mozart?' She blundered again, and realised she had done so. Her conclusion was: 'I'm really not into opera, to be honest.'

No shit.

'So... what have you been up to since I last saw you?' she asked, steering the conversation toward the more casual.

'Well, On Sunday I spent the day at my sister's.' I told her about the disastrous cooking of my brother-in-law and Ben drinking too much Champagne.

I smiled to myself as I remembered the combined look of shock, laughter and worry on Emily's face when she realised Ben had drunk my Champagne.

'What are you smiling about?' asked Martha.

'Just Emily.'

'Emily. *Just* Emily? It's always bloody Emily, isn't it?' she said, apparently disgusted that I had a female friend.

'Yes, I had a nice evening with her.' I wasn't stooping to her level.

'I'm glad. I had a horrible Valentine's Day. The worst one ever.'

Probably the only one she'd spent on her own, I thought. If, indeed, she had spent it on her own.

'Look, I'm sorry, but I did promise Emily that I'd spend it with her, and that was before I even met you.' Even though she was being entirely unreasonable, I didn't want to lose her quite yet.

'Yes, but having met *me*, you *could* have changed your plans. I mean, spending Valentine's Day with your secretary just because she hasn't got a boyfriend, even though you have met someone, is a bit odd, and to be honest, not the kind of behaviour I would necessarily expect.'

She was really pissing me off now.

'And after all…' she continued. I wondered what was coming and knew it was probably going to be bad.

'…She's *only* your secretary.'

That was it.

I reached for my coat.

'What are you doing?'

'I'm sorry, I don't really feel like it tonight.'

'Okay. Fine.' she said, with venom in her voice.

'Well, see you again soon,' I said, not knowing whether I actually meant it.

'Okay, bye.'

'Bye.'

I got up and walked down the bar, aware even with my back to her, that she was watching my every move.

'I can't believe you are actually going,' she said, loudly, and so that every man in the place swivelled their heads towards her. It appeared that none of them could believe I was actually going either, but she hadn't insulted their closest friend.

I knew that my actions during these few moments in The Vaults, with all eyes on me, waiting for my response, would be a turning point in our relationship. I could almost hear the wives and girlfriends, lovers and adulteresses of the head-swivelling men wishing me to leave, so they could sit smugly knowing that although Martha was perhaps more beautiful than them, there were still men above her, still men who could and would walk out without her.

I thought about all the things she was passionate about: Juicy Lucy's boutique, and… well, Juicy Lucy's boutique; I thought about her total lack of knowledge about opera and anything else not related to shopping and realised that these paled into insignificance compared to her unfounded jealously and snobbery against Emily; I realised it had been her who had jeopardised whatever relationship we might have had, and I wasn't at all sure whether she'd be able to tempt me back; if things were this difficult on the third date, what future was there?

'I can't believe you're actually going…' she had said.

My conclusions were drawn.

'Well, believe it,' I said, and left.

The next morning I decided to go to work on the new route which avoided the possibility of bumping into Martha. This irked me; she had disrupted my routine, and this new journey was not nearly as pleasant as my well-established one; I had to pick up *The Times* at a different newsagent, paying daily because I was a new customer; the architecture and streets were less grand, but most of all the situation annoyed me: why should my habits have to change for this woman?

I nevertheless arrived at the office in a fairly jovial mood. My thoughts had often been with Martha after leaving her the night before, and although the thought of losing the best looking girl in London aside from Emily was distressing, her looks really were the only distressing thing about the whole situation; my mind was made up not to miss her, or get upset that it hadn't worked out.

'How did it go last night with Martha?' asked Emily.

I knew I could make Emily dislike her in one fell swoop, and although this thought was initially malevolent, I knew that anyone who had Martha's opinion of Emily wasn't the one for me.

'Not good. She was pretty rude about the whole Valentine's Day thing. She got upset that I had been with you – because you are *only* my secretary.'

'What a bitch!' Emily looked shocked for a moment after those words had left her mouth. 'What did you say?'

'I left.'

'James, I hope you didn't bugger things up on my account?' asked Emily, genuinely concerned.

'Don't be ridiculous. Why should I have to put up with that? What would happen when inevitably she did meet you? No, it was pointless. But I don't think she could believe I just got up and left. She even said "I can't believe you're going".'

'What did you say?!'

'"Well, believe it!"'

'Oh, James!'

I had a Bond moment until Emily ruined it by announcing:

'Mrs Ricketts rang just before you got in. Please could you ring her back?'

'What did the old bat want?' I use the term 'old bat' affectionately with Mrs Ricketts.

'Will alteration.'

'I suppose it's been over a month since we did one; high time for a change!'

Emily rolled her eyes in agreement as I picked up the phone.

'Good morning, Mrs Ricketts, how are you?'

'Not bad at all, thank you James. My poor cat is not at all well, though...' And so after ten minutes of billable cat time, Mrs Ricketts finally got to the point: 'Now listen, I expect Emily told you I want to change my will again...'

This time the old bird had decided it really wasn't fair that the National Trust should have a higher percentage of her residuary estate than English Heritage after she had discovered that the latter owned Stonehenge, which she held in very high esteem. I agreed to make provision for both charities to benefit equally, she told me about a shotgun she'd bought (did the old girl still wield one?) and then we said our goodbyes.

And then just as was putting the receiver down I heard her say:

'Oh James? Are you still there?'

'Yes.'

Her timing was good. It was almost as if she had planned the afterthought.

'Oh, good! I almost forgot. I wondered if you might do me a tremendous favour?'

A request from Mrs Ricketts did not bode well; a 'tremendous favour' almost certainly meant a tremendous favour, and one that would surely be above and beyond the call of duty. I began to think about whether it would be more rude to agree to it and then decline once the particulars of the favour had been discovered, or whether to decline from the outset. I tried to avoid saying a definite 'yes' in the hope of gleaning of some further information before handing my services irrevocably to the old dear.

'Well, Mrs Ricketts, I'm quite busy at the moment. It really depends on what kind of favour you mean.'

'Just give me a straight answer, James!' she said, as if she was my mother in a bad mood. She was a cunning old fox.

Again, I thought of the most non-committed answer I could:

'Well, Mrs Ricketts, you know I should like to help if I can, but...'

'Oh, James! I'm *so* glad. I knew you'd agree. You are a good boy.'

Damnation, I thought; the old bat (in a rather less affectionate way than previously) has wangled it already!

'I expect you remember my granddaughter, Sara.'

I could visualise the Ricketts family tree that I had in Mrs Ricketts' will file; it was the only way of keeping track of who she was talking about when she was making will alterations. Sara Ursula Shepherd was the thirty year old daughter of Mrs Ricketts' youngest child, Diana, who had married Alexander Aubrey Shepherd. Diana was the only Ricketts child I hadn't met during my various legal dealings with the family, and I had certainly never met any of the Ricketts grandchildren.

'Well, I know she's Diana's eldest, but I'm not sure if I have met her.' I said to Mrs Ricketts, to move the conversation on.

'I know damn well you haven't met her!' was her reply. 'Well, anyway, she's an architect and has an important function to attend in Town – it's a ball in fact – she's collecting some architectural prize for a recent design and hasn't got anyone to go with – I expect she'll explain why, but I'll leave that to her. The long and short of it is that she needs a chaperone.'

Bugger.

It was not often that clients really annoyed me, but Mrs Ricketts had achieved what most couldn't. This was an ask too big. How could I say no? My life seemed inextricably linked to the Ricketts family and to various professional social events designed to bore even the most professional Professional socialite. And who was this Sara? Certainly none of her uncles or aunts could be described as normal, and presumably her mother Diana fitted in the with the rest of the family's eccentricity; it therefore seemed inevitable that the granddaughter of the Ricketts woman would also inherit all the mad genes of her grandmother. Why the hell did she need a chaperone? I knew Mrs Ricketts was old-fashioned, but in this day and age, surely it is acceptable to go to professional events without the need of a keeper?

But Mrs Ricketts hadn't finished.

'I understand from your pause, James, that you are trying to think of an excuse.'

She was an astute woman.

'Well,' she continued, 'I wouldn't ask unless I thought it might hold some promise for you. I hope you're not worrying about the costs of it; of course all the expenses will be paid. But I understand if you want to say "no". I just thought you and Sara would hit it off, so to speak.'

Sara and I hitting it off? Why would I hit it off with the probably insane granddaughter of the eccentric Ricketts? But she did make me feel guilty for not being more responsive. After a little consideration, I thought it might not to be too bad. It was a ball, Mrs Ricketts was paying for the whole evening, and even though it was a ball full of architects, I thought that there might just be an opportunity to meet a good-looking girl in a ball dress now that things with Martha didn't seem so rosy.

'Mrs Ricketts, I should be delighted to help your granddaughter out. I'm sure we'll get along splendidly.'

'Oh, she will be delighted!'

My mind could not be as certain: I had visions of the poor girl, who was in all probability as shy a church mouse, dreading meeting this strange lawyer at a strange ball full of her strange professional colleagues. I wondered what I had let myself in for.

'Thank you ever so much James. It's on the last day of March at the Grosvenor. I'll give her your telephone number so she can call to arrange the rest. I am thankful, James, I really am. I simply don't know how she would have coped without you.'

After all Mrs Ricketts had said, I wasn't sure if I'd be able to cope either.

All remained fairly quiet until Yarrington burst in. 'Morning, chaps!' he said, 'Seen Teddy?'

'He's not usually in at this early hour.' I said. It was only eleven o'clock.

'Early?' said Yarrington, 'Some of us have been here three hours already! Well if you see him, send him up, will you? Need to talk to him about something.'

'What?' I said, really without thinking.

'Never you mind; between old friends!' said Yarrington, 'you'll find out soon enough at the next partner's meeting, but you probably won't like it. Good day to you, sirs!' he said deliberately looking at Emily to accentuate his apparent sexism.

Emily and I looked at each other, wondering what was on the agenda for his chat to Teddy. I took our silence to mean that neither of us had any answers.

Shortly after, and very unusually, Teddy himself came into my office, with the trademark 1969 edition of *Shipping Law* tucked firmly under his arm. When not on the short book trough on his desk, the tome is usually found under his arm. So much so that I once worked out in a moment of boredom how many hours it must have rested there since 1970, the year he qualified when he had apparently purchased the volume (assuming half an hour a day it was well over three and half thousand hours). He hadn't bought a new edition since, claiming somewhat dubiously that he has an encyclopaedic memory, and remembers which paragraphs have been superseded by new pieces of law as they have come in.

However, and sometimes almost in the same breath, he also been known on numerous occasions to contradict this assertion by playing up to the antiquity of the volume, saying with relish to his colleagues, 'New Law? Doesn't trouble me. Don't let law past the sixties interfere with my life. Can't be expected to keep up to date with everything, can I?' So it becomes very difficult knowing exactly precisely how much law Teddy does in fact grasp.

'Morning Teddy,' I said, gaily.

'Morning, James,' said Teddy, 'Sue said Yarrington wanted me to see him,'

'Yes, he was looking for you earlier.'

There was a pause as Teddy seemingly made himself comfortable leaning on my filing cabinets.

'Is there anything else I can help you with?' I asked Teddy.

'I'll just wait for him here, then,' said Teddy, 'I haven't much on today anyway.'

'You can if you want, but he might be some time!' I said, clearly joking despite not laughing. Teddy didn't seem to grasp what was going on.

'Why are you sitting at Yarrington's desk?' asked Teddy, 'In fact, come to think of it, where *is* Yarrington's desk?'

Yarrington had a huge old-fashioned partner's desk, which moved with him almost six months ago when he moved out of the office I now occupied.

'Yarrington moved offices – this is my office now.'

'Oh, I see,' he said, the penny almost audibly dropping. 'James, I do beg your pardon. Where is he now?'

'Margaret's old room – the one she occupied *after* she qualified!'

'Right you are!' he said, and bumbled off.

Much as I liked Teddy, it was difficult to see how he managed to remain so behind the times. Indeed, incidents like these made me really wonder how he was still a partner. But, I concluded, with Yarrington as senior partner, that is why Bugle & Yarrington is such a glorious firm to work for: political and financial decisions are not based on sense or logic, they are based on the old-school principles of which Oxbridge college one went to, long service, trust, and whether one could bowl a googly or hit thirty-six an over.

CHAPTER 17

The Ides Of March

It was with a certain sense of foreboding that I entered the Dining Room for the partner's meeting on the fifteenth of March.

Yarrington's enigmatic words and subsequent elusion of the subject of this meeting had unnerved me.

Most were already there and after a couple of minutes all the partners, including Teddy, who I had been led to believe rarely attended partner's meetings, were present.

The minutes of the last meeting were handed round together with today's agenda. To my amazement, my request for 'some kind of intoxicating liquor dispenser' had actually been noted. It was not, however, on the agenda for this meeting.

Yarrington began.

'Well, James, have you discovered anything about the plumbing of our offices? Are we being poisoned by lead?'

A quick glance under the sink had confirmed that the pipes were indeed copper, though in colour they were a beautiful green, being encased in a thick encrustation of copper oxide. I had, of course, no idea from what metal the rest of the pipes in the building were forged.

'I have conducted an extensive research programme into the pipework of our offices and firmly conclude that the symptoms of madness consistently displayed by the employees do not emanate from lead in the water: the pipes are exclusively copper.'

'Splendid! By next month you will no doubt have discovered why the employees *are* all going mad! So, no more water coolers, then?'

'I would have to agree, given the expense of them.'

'Damn right. Damn silly things. Do we all agree?'

None of the partners disagreed, and the other points on the agenda were dealt with in a similar manner. At what we thought was the end of the meeting, Yarrington rose to his feet, no doubt to increase his gravitas as he announced something of import.

'As an addendum to the agenda, I need to talk briefly about a matter of some relevance to you all.'

He paused.

'As some of you may have gathered during your time here, I have been the senior partner for thirty years...' We all knew what was coming, and our collective hearts missed a beat. The silence of non-beating hearts was deafening. '...and so I am throwing down my sword, lowering my colours, and generally taking things easy. This sad day,' continued Yarrington in a rather Churchillian manner, 'marks the end of an era; the reign of Yarrington is over, and the reign of Bugle is about to begin! Yes, the rumours are true!' (There were none.) 'I am handing the role of senior partner to my colleague and partner of those thirty years, Mr Frank Bugle.'

Bugle looked smug.

Everyone else looked rather ill, except Teddy who just looked sad.

We all knew this day would come eventually. We all dreaded it. It was quite simple: Yarrington was liked by all because he was fair; Bugle's principles of equality and justice were on a par with those of Al Capone's bent jury, and elevating him to the position of senior partner almost certainly meant they would slip further: he would be disliked.

Yarrington's eyes darted round the room; he must have seen the looks of disappointment and exchanges of glances between the assembled partners. He tried an encouraging, 'Don't worry, I'm not leaving the Firm – I'm still going to be a full-time partner, I'm just leaving the running of the show to Frank. I just don't need the stress of it at my age,' he said, in some rather feeble attempt to explain his reasons.

'So a big toast for Frank, who probably should have had the honour some years ago!'

A muted murmur went round the room, except for the arse-kissing pair of ejits Paul and Martin, the company cads who both gave Bugle their hearty congratulations. Despite his faults, Bugle is astute and in an instant recognition of their behaviour he narrowed his eyes at Paul and Martin: no amount of kisses planted on his posterior would assist them in winning his loyalty. There were moments when I did like Bugle!

He now rose to his feet.

'Thank you, thank you,' he said.

The second one was not necessary.

'Well, it is an honour to be my own senior partner,' he said cockily, and with an annoying smirk, 'and so I will be, on a permanent basis, running these meetings, and, I suppose, the whole show. I intend to run it in the exemplary and highly successful manner that David Yarrington has done for so many years…' We all waited for the qualification, which followed all to soon: '…but over the next or month or so there will be some changes, and if you have any ideas, specific problems, concerns, or anything else *at all* bothering you, please don't hesitate to come and see me.' He flashed his unnaturally white teeth at us all. 'My door is always open, as you all know.'

Paul and Martin nodded in agreement.

Everyone else continued to look rather ill.

It was indeed the end of the era. We had enjoyed Yarrington's leadership. He displayed exactly the kind of leadership I liked, admired and respected, but most importantly of all, it was the type of leadership that really was the only way to lead me. Yarrington never told anyone what to do, never stuck his nose in unless he had to, never got angry, was never unreasonable, never to jumped to conclusions, but thought out each problem on a logical and consistent basis. Bugle not so: he was quick to jump to the wrong conclusion, quick to lose his temper, quick to lay blame on the innocent, and was forever prying into other people's problems. Worst of all, he was bossy, and liked being so.

It was indeed the end of a wise reign, I thought, and the beginning of a more dubious one. I wondered if this was how the citizens of Rome felt on the death of Marcus Aurelius. I hoped the offices of Bugle & Yarrington were not destined to descend from a kingdom of gold into one of iron and rust.

CHAPTER 18

A Reminder

The latter half of March bumbled on, my caseload with it. Mr Jones' case was reaching the preparation stages for the first court hearing where the divorcing parties try and settle financial matters in agreement with each other, the judge merely providing guidance. Despite the document not containing references to her husband's 'whore', I had managed to get Frances Green to sign her divorce petition which was issued at her request on the grounds of adultery. Mrs Ricketts phoned for advice regarding whether I thought she should be buying a new horse at this time of year given that hunts were now seemingly illegal. My answer was that she definitely should, and that it should be fast and be able to jump high gates so that any country policemen, or more likely and more seriously, any anti-hunt protestors should not be able to stop her. She thought this an eminently sensible answer. Matthew was learning fast as his curriculum vitae suggested he would, and he was now beginning to relax and not take himself so seriously. As a result, Emily and I were enjoying his company more now than when he first started. Tim was still complaining that Charlotte's prehensile digit weighed more heavily upon his head than he might have liked, and that she was more upset than him by his failure to reach partnership before me. Nevertheless, he did ask me to raise the issue at a future partners' meeting and I assured him that he should have my fullest support. Yarrington was enjoying not being the senior partner; he did not miss the responsibility of the post, although he did complain that Bugle sought his advice frequently on various administration and policy matters that arose. Bugle was enjoying the responsibility of the job, or rather the prestige of it, while relying on Yarrington's superior knowledge which thirty years experience as senior partner had given him.

Mrs Ricketts telephoned at twenty-nine minutes past five. When the phone rings at such an hour I know it should never be answered in case my evening is infringed upon by some trivial client matter. But in annoying moments of conscientiousness and before I can stop myself, I always find the receiver to my ear.

'Hello James. Knew I'd just catch you.'

'Hello Mrs Ricketts, how are you?'

'I'm losing my marbles today, but I haven't quite lost them all, and I know what day it is. The question is, do you, my boy?!'

'I certainly do, Mrs Ricketts, it's the thirty-first of March.'

'And have you anything special planned for this evening?'

There was so much potential to wind up the old bat, but my conscience kicked in and I gave her a straight answer: 'I certainly do, Mrs Ricketts, I'm taking your granddaughter out to a ball!'

'I knew you wouldn't forget, James!' She did sound pleased that I hadn't forgotten, or more to the point, that I hadn't tried to get out of it at the last minute.

'I hope you've polished your shoes, young man?'

'Yes, of course I have Mrs Ricketts.'

'Have you a proper bow-tie?'

'Yes.'

'Good, I can't stand men who use those horrid clip-on jobs. I should have sacked you as my lawyer if you'd had one of them! Frightful little things… Well, my boy, you take care of my Sara. I know she's looking forward to meeting to you.'

I thought that if she really was looking forward to meeting her grandmother's lawyer she must be stark raving bonkers, and swiftly concluded that she probably was nineteen and six to the pound.

'Speak soon, and have a good evening. And James…?'

'Yes, Mrs Ricketts?'

'Remember not to worry about money.'

'Yes, Mrs Ricketts.'

'Bye, dear!'

And she was gone.

CHAPTER 19

Sara

I arrived spot on the appointed hour at Sara's flat, which was pretty near Sarah's in South Ken, and rang the doorbell. I didn't quite know what to expect from the granddaughter of the Ricketts woman. Optimistically I hoped that her father's genes – the Shepherd genes – were more conventional than the mad Ricketts genes, and that she'd somehow got a healthy proportion of them to instil some normality into her.

The door opened.

The girl who opened the door was quite simply beautiful.

She put Martha to shame: Martha had been incredibly good-looking; here was beauty. As my pupils dilated, I took in everything I could about her – her long brown hair falling around her shoulders like breaking waves, her bright dark eyes with the slight wrinkles at each corner, the well defined cheek bones, and beautifully chiselled chin, the pert breasts, washing board stomach and magnificently trousered legs – before I realised I should speak:

'Hello, I'm James… I'm after Sara.'

'I'm Sara, good to meet you,' she said, moving away from the door and ushering me in. 'Do come in.' She took me through from the hall into the living room. 'It's so good of you to come. I was dreading this evening… I mean, not dreading going out with you…'

We smiled at each other, both waiting for the other to admit that the sensation of dread had been present in both our minds.

'Well, yes, actually I was dreading going out with you, to be quite honest… as no doubt you were with me?!' she said, hedging her bets somewhat.

'Well, I'm very fond of your grandmother, and of course it's a pleasure to be of assistance,' I said, breaking into a smile as she looked at me questioningly.

'Oh, how diplomatic of you! It's rather embarrassing. My dear grandmother probably thought she was doing me a favour hitching me up with you… not that she isn't… I mean… Oh, bugger! I'm not doing very well this evening, am I?!'

But it didn't matter; we were both laughing.

'Well, honestly I didn't know what to expect to either.'

'The whole thing arose because I was on the phone to her, explaining that I was going to this ball. She simply couldn't believe I was going to a ball on my own, and insisted that she got in touch with someone who could chaperone me, as she put it. I'm doing this as a favour to her, which is ironic, really, since you are too… I'm sorry. It's such an odd request. You must have thought I'd be as mad as my grandmother! Maybe I am!'

'I must confess I have spent some time wondering about what you might be like!'

'And me you; I was terrified that the old bird was trying to hitch me up with some balding boring banker with a good salary and marriage prospects.'

The old bird; she had called her grandmother the old bird; no one of my generation says that apart from me.

'Well, I'm not a banker, at least.'

'Thank the Lord for that! What *do* you do?'

'Solicit.'

Damnation again. Why does everyone find out what I do before they get to know me for who I am?

'Oh, right, in what field?' she asked.

'Divorce.'

'You must have a big heart, or a cold one.'

She was direct, which I liked.

'Usually people say "that must be depressing" or some such thing.'

'I suspected so, which is why I didn't.'

'So, you're an architect: you must like straight lines and drawing boards.'

'Not at all; I'm a frustrated artist; architecture is one way I tried to combine art and work, but it doesn't really work in practice. You only get paid for designing things that are functional and cheap to build: there's no scope for anything artistic in architecture.'

'I know vaguely what you mean. I'm a frustrated writer. I try and combine wit and good English into everything legal that I write, but it doesn't work. The English Courts don't look favourably on it, and the clients think you're a buffoon if you're too familiar with them in correspondence (your grandmother excepted: I can write what I like to her). There is some scope for it, mind you, which I utilise as much as possible. My job would be unimaginable otherwise. You should meet my secretary, Emily; she's a frustrated artist too.'

'Sounds like we all want other careers. But then life would be boring if we all had what we wanted... Now look, as you can see, I'm not changed – I was rather late getting back from work – so can I give you a drink, and then whiz upstairs to put my frock and woad on?'

'Sounds splendid.' I said, wondering how long it would take her to get changed.

'Great; come through.'

I followed her into the living room.

'Bubbly?' she asked, gently uncorking a bottle whose golden foil and wire cork retainer had been already been removed, and whose condensation had caused a ring on the little coffee table on which it had been standing.

'Please.' I liked her no-nonsense approach.

She handed me a flute of Champagne.

'Cheers!'

'Mmm, cheers,' she said, having already taken a sip. 'Right, I must get changed. Make yourself at home. There are some books to keep you happy. Well, they keep me happy at least... Anyway I won't be long, I promise! I'm pretty quick when I need to be.'

And with that she hopped upstairs leaving me alone in her living room, which I began to take in now the opportunity presented itself.

It was perfect.

Two large bookcases stood side-by-side, overfull, with books stuffed horizontally above the vertical ones, and on the wider shelves towards the bottom of the bookcase, piles of books standing in front the vertical books, obscuring them. I investigated the books. There was a good array of novels, ancient and modern, and books on all kinds of things: here lived a bibliophile. Two sofas occupied the middle of the room; they faced each other and there was a low table in between; I particularly liked this social arrangement because the sofas faced each other, not a television. On the opposite wall stood a late Victorian mahogany desk, no doubt a Ricketts heirloom. There were papers and paintings and paintbrushes and pens and pencils scattered all over it, and a couple of leather bound notebooks, one of which was open with handwriting on the left hand leaf. A diary? There was also a framed photo of a man with his arm around Sara, both smiling happily into the camera.

The time went quickly as I studied the various paintings on the walls, many of which had 'SS' written with a certain amount of artistic flair in the bottom corners. I refilled my glass, and then took to the sofa to peruse a couple of the books. But before I knew it, I heard Sara descending the stairs. I jumped up off the sofa, to find the Champagne had made me ever so slightly less than sober. Then in she walked. She had been beautiful in her frankly rather dull work outfit; I could not think of a word to describe her when she entered the room in a full length ball dress, her face very subtly but powerfully made up, her hair tied in the prettiest of fashions and her chest wonderfully exposed.

'You look quite beautiful.'

It was true, and I didn't feel embarrassed saying it.

'Thanks. You don't scrub up too badly yourself,' she said smiling.

We simultaneously realised she couldn't know what I looked like when I wasn't scrubbed up, and we both laughed.

'You're too kind madam. Your carriage awaits.'

CHAPTER 20

The Architects Ball

We arrived at the Grosvenor fashionably late. Said hotel was of course delightful. We had canapés and more Champagne: I find the best way to make small talk to people one has never met before is to lubricate oneself sufficiently well at the beginning of the evening.

After some time chatting with Sara and between various architects and their spouses or modern equivalents thereof, Sara and I became detached from each other: she knew a few people, and because she had won the architectural prize she seemed to be a bit of a celebrity. I was standing rather on my own feeling a little awkward and a chap about my age clocked me and wandered over.

'Good evening, you here on your own?'

'No, I'm here with Sara Shepherd.' I motioned my arm toward her.

'Oh, hello, I'm Richard – I expect you've heard of me!'

My blank expression told him not.

'Oh, right! I work with her. How odd she hasn't mentioned me; we worked on the City Tower together.'

'The City Tower?'

'The one she won the Gold Medal for.'

'Oh, I see. I don't know her terribly well.'

'Clearly. How *do* you know her?'

I thought the 'clearly' was rather rude but the immediate problem was how to answer the question I had been dreading, and no doubt the question Sara wouldn't want answered to one of her colleagues. But I didn't know a damn thing about the girl, so again I was compelled to rely on the truth: 'Her grandmother is a client of mine.'

Admittedly, this must have sounded ridiculous given that Richard had no idea what I did for a living, but he annoyed me by moving his hands in a circular motion, one over the other, asking me to explain, while simultaneously raising his eyebrows; it was the kind of kind of thing Angela would do, in her rodent-like way, knowing that she was being infuriating.

'I'm a solicitor,' I said. Here we go again, I thought: I'm a solicitor, I spend my time breaking up people's not-so happy marriages and getting paid for my troubles. 'I mainly do tax planning for Sara's grandmother,' I informed him helpfully.

'So you thought you'd chat up Sara to get a bit of the family wealth in your own back pocket, did you?'

I paused; it clearly wasn't a joke.

'As a lawyer, I'm not entitled to treat my client in such a manner, and nor would I,' I said curtly. But he had raised my heckles so I followed it up with a triumphant and final: 'Good evening, Sir!' in a slightly inebriated but wholly intentionally archaic manner, while spinning round on one heel to find a Champagne pourer.

Thankfully the call to sit down at the dinner tables came fairly quickly after my glass had been filled and I hoped a seat would enable me to stop my reeling body from causing any further embarrassment.

Everybody manoeuvred toward the seating plans pinned up at either end of the ballroom. I had some difficulty reading the seating plan, first, because by then I had become somewhat squiffy and it took me a while to work out which end of the ballroom was depicted by which end of the plan, and second, because once this feat of small-scale geographical triumph had been achieved, I couldn't find my own name. One's own name, especially if it happens to be James James, stands out on lists. Eventually I found myself named as 'Friend of Miss S Shepherd'.

What riled me further was that as I approached my table, I could see that the only free chair was between Sara and Richard. He saw me approaching the table and immediately looked round the table in a blatant attempt to ascertain if I was indeed going to be sitting next to him. When he saw I could only be sitting in the seat to his left, he caught my eye and gave me a scowl. It reminded me of school days when trying to find a seat in the dining room when none of my friends were there.

'Hello, James!' said Sara as I pulled out my chair. 'Sorry, we became rather detached... Have you met Richard?

'Yes, we've met,' said Richard and I simultaneously, and in the same tone of voice.

'Oh,' said Sara.

'Hello again!' I said again, smiling mechanically at him, 'What a pleasure to be sitting next to you!'

'Yes, indeed,' said Richard with no false enthusiasm, and turned away to talk to his other neighbour.

We didn't exchange another word all evening.

Sara's frown and enquiring expression asked me what had gone on, but I brushed it aside, and she let me.

Richard had positioned himself with his back to me so there was not even a chance of our eyes meeting. His behaviour was rude in the extreme, and I pitied Sara for having to work with such a prick. Thankfully, Sara and I were so engrossed in conversation that we hardly noticed not talking to our neighbours.

The first thing I questioned her upon was the prize she was to collect during the after-dinner speeches. She had been the winner of a competition to design a set of offices in the City, which to her utmost annoyance had been dubbed the unbelievably uninspiring City Tower, especially irksome because that name was a misnomer: it wasn't actually that big, or at eight storeys, even that high. Her design now realised, some important body of the profession had deemed it good enough for their Gold Medal. Apparently, I had heard previously from someone else, a fairly illustrious achievement, especially for someone of Sara's age.

'Well, congratulations,' I said, after her explanation.

'Thanks, but I only designed it. I feel a bit like Jørn Utzon, who designed the Opera House in Sydney. He had the inspired idea, submitted preliminary drawings, won the competition, but had no idea how to build it in practical terms, and was eventually sacked from the project.'

'You haven't been sacked.'

'No, I suppose not, but I couldn't have done it without a lot of help.'

After we had eaten, there were short speeches by the president of this professional body and the chief executive of that firm. Then Sara was given her prize by another president of a different body. There was such a lot of clapping and 'bravos!' that I wondered how modest she had been in her explanation of her winning the medal, or whether everyone was as drunk as me.

She gave a short speech thanking everyone, rather like the Oscars. It was rather grim, until she said at the end, 'I'd especially like to thank my good friend James for supporting me this evening!' And she shot me a wonderful smile.

Richard looked at me for the first time since I had sat down, a look of disgust on his face. It rather took the wind of out of my sails until the ensuing applause ceased and Sara rejoined me.

'I hate that kind of thing!' she said. She was very flushed and looked relieved that she had rejoined the safety of the table.

'Thanks for saying thanks!'

'Don't be silly,' she said, 'it was the only thing I truly meant up there! Shall we?' she said, motioning towards the door. 'I'd quite like to escape before everyone else congratulates me. I'm not terribly good at being the centre of attention, and I'm tired of the same thing being said about my design again and again.

'Yes.' I had had enough too. Sitting next to Richard for any longer would have been intolerable. It was a relief leaving the hubbub of all those architects behind, and once we'd quit the hotel, we felt truly liberated. A couple of taxis waited outside and my immediate reaction upon seeing them was that I didn't want the evening to end. Such were my thoughts when Sara said, 'I think I'd better get home.'

Smiling, but not agreeing with her decision, my mouth then proceeded to utter exactly the words my brain had told it not to: 'Yes, so should I.'

'Thank you so much for coming,' she said. 'I hope you managed to enjoy it a little bit?'

'Yes,' I said, 'It was a pleasure to meet you.'

Which was entirely true.

'I enjoyed meeting you too.'

Then she looked round at a taxi, and turning back to me smiled.

'Well, you'd better get it,' I said, and we both turned towards it, me making small, slow steps in order that the last few seconds we would spend together would be lengthened just a little.

But my mind was working so fast it couldn't string a sentence together, and by the time I'd opened the taxi door, we'd exchanged not another word.

She got in and smiled at me again.

'Bye, then,' she said.

'Bye.'

And before shutting the door, I hesitated for a moment to ask: 'Will I see you again?'

'You'd better ask my grandmother!'

And with that, the door was shut and the taxi rolled forth.

CHAPTER 21

April Fool

I arrived into the office on the first of April to find things were hotting up on the client front.

Matthew was clutching a fax, and he and Emily were sharing a joke.

'Morning all! What's going on?!'

'Morning, James. Fax here, from Mr Green's solicitors.'

'Yes?'

'"Dear Sirs,"' he read, '"Our client has instructed us that your client has, over the weekend and in our client's absence, entered the former matrimonial home and used a chainsaw to destroy and render unusable our client's bed."'

'Nice try, Matthew!' I wasn't falling for this.

He passed me the fax.

It appeared to be genuine.

'Unless Mr Green's solicitors are attempting an April fool's joke, I think it must be true,' said Matthew, and I had to agree; Cressida Smyth-Jones was not capable of instigating any sort of humour, and certainly not a prank of this nature.

I picked up the phone.

'Morning Frances, I have a fax from your husband's solicitors here saying they believe you entered the matrimonial home and destroyed your husband's bed with a chainsaw. Do you happen to know anything about this?'

'It was *our* bed'

'Your bed, then. Do I assume from your use of the past tense in reference to the bed that do you do know about the incident?'

'If I deny it in court, could I be done for perjury?'

'If you did it, then yes. To add to your husband's threat of issuing proceedings for criminal damage.'

Silence.

'Frances?'

'I deny criminal damage entirely: I'm not a bloody criminal. But yes,

I did take my brother's chainsaw to it. It was the best thing I've done in years! I think actually, it was probably the most satisfying thing I've ever done to or in that bed! Trevor should be bloody pleased that it was only the bed I cut up! I presume the fax mentioned nothing about his state of health?'

'No, as far as I am aware, your husband is in good health.'

'Ah, they haven't found his body yet!'

I always get a little nervous when clients made jokes like that. It would make it rather tricky to act for them on their murder trial.

'May I ask why you did it?'

'I hated the idea of him having rumpy-pumpy with some common little nurse on our bed!'

'Well, from what your husband's solicitor says, no-one will be using the bed for anything other than firewood!'

'Yes, I expect it'd burn rather nicely. It was oak.'

'It does make matters rather awkward though. I wrote a letter to your husband's solicitors only last week saying I hoped that we'd be able to make progress without any further acrimony.'

'I do apologise, James. I hope it hasn't put you in a difficult position.'

'Well, a little.'

'Oh, I am sorry, James,'

'Worry not! But we do have to decide how to resolve matters. Your husband's solicitors will probably carry out their threat of getting the police involved and nailing you with criminal damage, which would not be sensible.'

'Well, what do you suggest?'

'You could offer to remove the old bed and pay Trevor a reasonable sum for a new bed.'

'That seems fair enough.'

'Are you sure?' I couldn't believe she agreed to my solution so readily.

'Yes, if you think so. I don't want a criminal record, now do I?'

'No, you don't. Okay, I'll get onto it now. I know my breath will be wasted...'

'But don't do it again, right?'

'It would be wise not to. The court doesn't look favourably upon such behaviour.'

'The bloody court is meant to administer justice! If I was a bloody judge, you'd have some pretty juicy case law when I was sitting, I can tell you!'

I laughed.

'Yes, likewise! I have no doubt Frances, that you would be an excellent administrator of justice!'

'Thank you, James.'

'No problem.'

'Thank you, James. I really do mean it. You're a star. Bye for now.'

I put the phone down.

'God, I'm good!' I admitted. 'That, Matthew, is how to handle unhinged clients.'

Matthew grinned. He was beginning to see my way of thinking, which pleased me enormously. 'James, could you give me a hand with this?' he asked.

'Sure – what are you up to?' I asked, crossing the room and making myself comfortable on the corner of his desk just as Angela came in.

I say she came in; she more accurately crept in, sticking her rat-like nose round the door, her whiskers quivering as she had a good sniff around. Like a mole, I imagined she relied on her olfactory senses to find her way around the office; there was no possible way she could see through her filthy spectacles.

'Hello, Angela,' I said.

No hello from her, but instead a curt:

'Why are you sat on Matthew's desk, James?'

Here was an opportunity to wind her up.

'I'm not.'

She looked confused. Matthew was already smirking, and knew exactly where this was heading. Good lad, I thought.

'I'm *sitting* on it.'

Her confusion deepened.

It annoys me intensely when people do not realise what they have said is simply wrong; when they do not even have even a basic command of the English language.

'Get off of it, James. You shouldn't sit there.'

'No. I'm quite comfortable, thanks.' I answered, firstly because of her ghastly English, and secondly because I hate being told what to do by anyone, and most especially Angela.

'It's a health and safety risk,' she persisted. The problem was that there was no point at all in arguing with her: she would simply persist until she got her own way.

'Angela,' I said, 'I will dismount this desk, indeed I will get *off* this desk, but not because it is sensible, or more comfortable, or safer to do so, but simply to keep you happy.'

Despite my angry rearguard action, Angela looked smugly pleased to have got her own way. This annoyed me.

How is sitting on a desk a health and safety risk? I had carefully checked for staplers and pens and pins and as far as I was aware there were no such articles puncturing my bottom. I swiftly concluded that Angela's supposed health and safety concerns were in fact a power trip for her because it was the only thing she could lecture me on. I thought it best not to confuse her already overheating rodent-sized brain with these details.

'Do you want me, Angela?'

'Yes. This came by courier,' she said handing me a letter marked 'James James Esq., Private & Confidential'.

Having passed it to me, she lurked behind my shoulder waiting for me to open it.

'Thank you, Angela,' I said quite deliberately.

Thankfully she took the hint and left, scuttling from the office to find someone else to annoy. How much easier it would have been if she'd just handed me the letter and departed like any other normal person!

'What's her problem?' asked Matthew. I was overjoyed that he was developing an active dislike towards the rodent-like Angela.

Turning my attentions back to letter, I opened it and read the following:

Franklin & Co., Solicitors
1 April

Dear Mr James,

We act for Mr Archibald Peter Raef Isaac Little. Mr Little knew your late grandfather well during their university years, although from my own knowledge I do know that sadly in later life they drifted apart. I'm afraid I do know not why.

Mr Little died earlier this year and the partners of this firm are named as executors in his will. We have obtained grant of representation and the estate will be distributed shortly. We are pleased to tell you that you (as youngest grandchild of your late grandfather) have been left a considerable sum. Mr Little's will stipulates that the cheques must be collected from our offices in person by the beneficiaries.

In order to comply with Mr Little's wishes, please therefore telephone the above number to arrange a mutually convenient time for you to attend our offices.

Yours sincerely,

Mr Derek Franklin

Franklin & Co., Solicitors

'What do you think of that, Matthew?' I asked him.

He began to look excited until I asked him to consider the name of the deceased. Mr Little indeed. I had heard of other people getting similar letters, but couldn't believe anyone had been so audacious as to send one to me. It was the classic April fool letter from a probate solicitor: this prank had Tim written all over it. But he had done his homework: Matthew quickly discovered that Franklin and Company, Solicitors, were a firm specialising in probate, and furthermore that Mr Franklin did indeed work there. They were based in Dudley, Charlotte's territory in the West Midlands, but their letterhead carried a suspicious London telephone code. Further investigation showed that the number given was in fact Tim's outside direct line, and the fax number was that of his own office fax machine.

'Well what should we do?' asked Emily, in delight, knowing that the plan would involve shafting Tim for his ill-advised attempt at an April Fool's joke.

'Let's fax back!' I said.

My brain began to tick but Matthew got there first: 'What about: "Dear Sirs, thank you for your letter of today's date regarding the estate of Mr Little. I am financially very secure due to the recent death of two separate and wealthy family members, and in accordance with my right under section 142 of the Inheritance Tax Act 1984 to pass on my inheritance as a post-death variation, I nominate my close friend and colleague Mr Tim Norris of this office to be the sole and exclusive beneficiary of my share of Mr Little's estate. I believe the inheritance would have a greater impact on his life than mine."'

'Genius!' I said, somewhat surprised at my trainee's textbook knowledge of the Inheritance Tax Acts. 'Emily, did you get that?'

She had, and moments later the printer spewed out Matthew's reply which I signed and gleefully faxed to the unsuspecting Tim.

We sat in anticipated silence waiting for Tim's reply. Our patience was not tested: a couple of minutes later Tim came in, looking rather sheepish, hands in pockets, and seemingly not knowing what to say.

'Er, James, could I have a word?' he managed after several pauses and takings of breath.

I was going to try and take him for a further ride, but the collected stifled laughter of Matthew, Emily and I couldn't be contained for more than a moment and as soon I caught the glint in Emily's eye and Matthew's hand covering his smirk, we all burst out simultaneously.

Tim went bright red and commented, 'Bastards,' in a low voice before leaving hurriedly without another word.

After our laughter subsided, there was no point attempting any more work that morning, and Matthew announced:

'Just popping out for a bite to eat,' with which he left.

I sat back and considered Matthew since he'd arrived in my office only six weeks ago. He had changed dramatically from being rather shy, proper and unnecessarily fastidious into quite a fun chap. His ridiculous comments and calling colleagues Mr or Mrs or Miss had all but stopped, and he was even beginning to crack jokes himself. His handling of Tim had shown real promise. A few more injections of humour and cynicism would render my job as his first training principal complete: learning the law as a green trainee is (in my humble opinion) neither here nor there: it's all about gaining confidence and learning to deal with colleagues and clients. And in any case, learning the law from this principal would be a challenge for any trainee, given that said principal's legal knowledge was not perhaps quite as extensive as it might be. Such were my thoughts when Emily asked:

'So how was the Ricketts granddaughter?'

Because the morning had been so busy, I hadn't really thought about Sara since she'd departed the ball, leaving me on the forecourt of the Grosvenor. The question further bewildered me because during the ball I had entirely forgotten that Sara was indeed the Ricketts woman's granddaughter.

'She's very good-looking.'

'I'm sure she is, but what do you *think* of her?!' said the persistent Emily, clearly anxious not to be missing out on the latest news on my love life. I think I must have stared into the middle distance for too long, because she said, with a certain amount of surprise:

'You fancy her, don't you?!'

And I said:

'Yes, I think I do.'

CHAPTER 22

Trainee Gossip

It is certainly true that in our offices walls have ears; I have often thought about mimicking the famous poster of the train carriage: but instead of Hitler and Göring sitting behind the gossipers, the caricatures would be Bugle and Yarrington, and the caption would read: 'Careless talk costs livelihoods'.

Among the more experienced members of staff, it is common knowledge that anything anyone says in the little staff kitchen can be heard quite clearly from the photocopying room next door, but due to the acoustics, not the other way round. On this particular occasion, while still thinking about the observations that Emily had let loose regarding my feelings about Sara, I was in the photocopying room, photocopying. I soon discovered why Matthew had already taken ten minutes to make my morning coffee: he was in the kitchen gossiping with Tom, the other trainee who had started with him, and who had the misfortune of having his first seat with Paul and Martin in the company commercial department. Thomas was talking:

'They're total bastards. Paul tells me to do one thing, then Martin bollocks me for doing it the way I've just been told to do it! Neither of them explains anything, and they expect me to be able to do things straight off, word perfect. I have no idea why I'm doing some things, or what this form is for, or what that fucking order means. They make me feel stupid too, when I get things wrong, and then they laugh about it right in front of me. They really hate me, I think. I hate it, and them!' A pause. 'How are you getting on with James?'

'He's nothing like that. He's never had a trainee before, so I think he's making quite a bit of effort with me. He's always joking around – he thinks he's really funny. I suppose he is a bit. But he does explain how to do things, or Emily does, and he goes through stuff afterwards, to explain how to do it better next time. I suppose it's worth his while doing all that because he earns my fees, so if I can do certain tasks, he benefits. And we still get paid the Law Society minimum. Look at my shoes! Every time it rains I get sodden feet, but I can't afford a new pair!'

'I know! It's ridiculous! How are we meant to live? Paul told me to buy some new shirts the other day, because he said mine were common. One, I can't believe he actually has the nerve to say that, especially given his wardrobe, and two, how am I meant to buy new ones? I'm forced to be a bloody vegetarian at the moment, because I can't afford meat!'

There was a pause as the coffee was being made, and then Tom continued: 'So it seems you're lucky – you don't have to work with Paul and Martin, and you get to sit and watch Emily all day. She's so fit!'

I got rather jealous. These trainees were not supposed to talk about Emily in this manner.

'I know. She is good-looking. I love it when she bends down to get stuff out of the filing cabinets!' They both laughed and I was shocked: Matthew appeared not to be asexual after all.

'Do you reckon James is seeing her? Tim thinks he is. He stays at hers, apparently.'

'I don't know, I've been trying to work it out. I can't decide. How do you tell?'

'Hmm, stuff like when they look at each other: do they smile? Do they communicate physically without speech?'

'Yes, all the time.'

'There you have it!' said Tom. He was, I suppose, astute, but in this case, entirely wrong. I knew that people did gossip about my relationship with Emily, and I was never too bothered by it because it is the type of thing people gossip about; but when one hears that gossip first hand, it is rather more distressing than simply knowing it goes on.

'Have you heard about old Teddy?' asked Tom, on a new tack.

'Who's Teddy?'

'George Teddy, you know, the old guy who does nothing and carries that big old book around the office. He does shipping law, supposedly'

'Oh, yes. What about him?' asked Matthew.

'I heard Bugle on the phone the other night. Now Yarrington is no longer the senior partner, Bugle wants to give Teddy the boot, and he doesn't think there's anything stopping him. He said that Teddy was useless, and the only reason he's been here for that last ten years is because he's Yarrington's friend. I dunno who he was talking to.'

'I like Teddy, he seems nice.'

'Yes, he's a legend! He always cracking jokes at Bugle's expense. He shouldn't be allowed to go.'

'Well what shall we do?' said Matthew, apparently in earnest.

'What can we do? We're glorified coffee makers.'

'I suppose.'

Another generation of trainees! Nothing changes! But here were some serious allegations. Teddy should certainly not be allowed to go: he was an institution, and had been at the Firm longer than anyone save the Founding Fathers. No, he should retire when he felt like retiring. Being of the old school, he probably hadn't even contemplated that he might be ousted. He certainly hadn't contemplated his billing figures for a decade, and I didn't blame him. But the boys were right: what could anyone do about it now Bugle was senior partner? Everyone knew Teddy was legally past it: even his own secretary was someone else's full time secretary too, because he produced so little work for her.

'What are you doing this weekend?' continued their conversation. This appeared to be a safe juncture to make my entrance into the kitchen.

'Morning chaps! What are you gossiping about?' I asked.

'Oh, only our plans for the weekend,' answered Matthew, truthfully enough.

'Good. How are you getting on in your department, Tom?'

'Yes, fine thanks,' he lied.

'Good. You must be the first employee who gets on with Paul and Martin!' I said grinning, to make it clear where my loyalties lay, and to give Tom the message that even some of the partners of the Firm disliked them. 'So what's news? When I was a trainee, I knew everything about everyone in the Firm: you must have some news!'

The trainees looked at each other.

'Nothing much,' they said simultaneously.

Significant improvement would be required if they were to make it in this game.

After a couple of days and some contemplation, I decided that it was my duty to go and see Yarrington about the Teddy situation. My inclination persuading me to, I used the back stairs, rarely used by anyone, and found Tom there, crying, eyes red and blowing his nose into an already soggy handkerchief.

'Are you all right?' I asked.

Clearly not.

'What's the matter?'

'It's just Paul and Martin,' he said, tears streaming down his face as he blinked. 'They're just impossible to please. Everything I do is wrong, or crap, and if I do by some bloody miracle do something right, I don't get a word of thanks anyway. They ask me to do things and I have no idea what they're talking about. They tell me to do something and bollock me for doing it. Paul asked me just now where I was going, and when I said the loo he told me he had no desire to know that. What the fuck am I meant to say?'

'You have to stand up for yourself.'

'He hates that, and gets even more angry.'

'Yes, but eventually you'll gain his respect, and Martin's. Look, Tom. I had an awful training too. I know it can be awful: you wake up and your principal's is the first face that pops into your mind; you dread coming into work, and you feel worthless. Your confidence is destroyed. But it's only for a few months, and you'll be changing seats soon. They're bullies and all bullies are just so for a reason: just remember Paul is a bully because he's hung like a hamster and Martin because he never quite made five foot six, and things will seems better.' I had made him smile, at least. 'The truth is, when you first start training, you *are* useless,' I said smiling, 'because you have no experience of anything. But after a year, whatever departments you have been training in, you'll know a hell of lot more and be much more confident in all aspects of the job. You'll see.'

He had stopped crying now.

'Thanks, James.'

'No probs. Now you'd better go and sort your face out before anyone else catches you!' And with that we parted and I headed again for Yarrington's office.

'Afternoon Lynn. Where's Yarrington?' I said, entering his office and noting his empty chair.

'Hello, Jim. Mr Yarrington is away from his desk at the moment. Can I take a message?'

Oh Christ, I thought, here we go again.

'Yes, I can see he's not at his desk. I asked where he was.'

'He's away from his desk. Shall I give him a message?' she asked automatically, reaching for her purple message notebook.

'No, I don't want to give him a message. I just want to know where he is, and when he'll be back at his desk?'

'He's away from his desk currently. I don't believe he mentioned a time when he'd be back.'

'Thank you Lynn! Please tell him I want to see him and to ring me,' I said as sarcastically as possible and left, slamming the door and literally bumping into Yarrington as I did so.

'Sorry!' we exclaimed. I rolled my eyes at him and indicating with my thumb asked him with my eyes how he put up with Lynn.

'I've been thinking about asking her to leave for a while...' he whispered in answer. 'What can I do you for?'

'Fancy a pint tonight? I wouldn't mind a chat after work, outside the office walls, so to speak.'

'Yes, certainly. What is it James? Not too sure I like you doing this – I should be the one asking you for a chat, and making you sweat about what it might be about – not the other way round!'

'You've done that to me far too many times!' I said. 'Your turn now. Sweat until half five. See you in The Pub.'

'Cheerio.'

At half past five in The Pub, after having bought us both a pint of the finest ale in London, Yarrington asked, 'So what is on your mind, James?'

'Two things. Thomas – Tom, as he likes to be known, was in tears earlier. He was saying Paul and Martin have been up to their old tricks again: instructing him to do something and laying into him once he'd done it. The bullies have reduced the once cocky graduate into a little mouse, totally lacking in confidence.'

'Damn them! Why do they insist on treating people like this? Think they think it'll do people good – maybe they're right – doesn't seem to have done you much harm! Hard for me though, James. Don't really want to raise it with Bugle. You know what Frank's like when he gets upset. And it is true that if you mollycoddle an Article Clerk, the resulting lawyer will have the collywobbles his whole career.'

I didn't believe Yarrington's excuse. I got the impression that now Bugle was the senior partner, even Yarrington was wary of him, and it amazed me how the balance of power seemed to have shifted so quickly.

'Well, his seat is nearly finished in company commercial; he'll just have to sit it out...' concluded Yarrington.

'His seat with them is less than half complete!' I said, beginning to get annoyed with him. This I found to be an unpleasant sensation.

But Yarrington had clearly finished talking about the subject: 'I'll have a chat with Tom, and try and make him feel better. What else?'

I gave up on that topic, and continued.

'I was dropping a few eaves in the photocopying room the other day: Tom told Matthew that he heard Bugle on the phone saying that now you'd tragically resigned from the your rightful position of senior partner, Bugle was going to try and get rid of Teddy.'

'What! Are you sure?'

'That's what I heard, and I have no reason to suppose Tom would make it up – why would he? He was only talking to Matthew.'

'This is serious. Teddy won't want to leave. Know for a fact he plans to retire on his sixty-fifth Birthday and not before. God, Bugle makes me mad! Suppose he thinks Teddy isn't pulling his weight… Suppose he'd be right, but that isn't the point. Teddy is one of us. Getting rid of him simply isn't cricket.'

'Bugle doesn't like cricket.'

'How the hell does he intend to do it?' asked Yarrington, as much to himself as me.

'I suppose he just brings it up at a partner's meeting when Teddy isn't there (not too hard a prospect, I suspect) and hopes that there are enough selfish and greedy partners to pass a majority vote in favour of Teddy's dismissal.'

'Suppose you're right…' said Yarrington, trailing off into thought.

This I could not believe. Six months ago, Yarrington would have come close to dissolving the partnership with Bugle if he had suggested such a monstrous backstabbing, ball-tampering move.

'You can't let him even get close to making the suggestion, formally at least.' I said, trying to inspire Yarrington.

'No, we can't, but I'm not sure how we achieve that!' he said, almost in conclusion. 'Look, James, this is quite a difficult subject. Teddy hasn't brought much money in for years; he must be the only lawyer in London who gets paid multiples of what he earns for his firm. It's going to be tough to argue for his continuation if Bugle is serious. But thank you for letting me know. Well done! I'll cogitate upon the ramifications of Bugle's apparent proposition and perhaps we can discuss the matter anon.'

And that was all that was said about the matter.

CHAPTER 23

Daunted

The next week, after no more news about Bugle's rumoured proposals, I was on my way home after work, rather annoyed because first, I didn't really want to go home at all, second, I had failed to find a drinking partner for the evening, and third, I was having to navigate the route which avoided the possibility of bumping into Martha. My mood actually improved when a heavy April shower decide to unleash itself on all those unsuspecting Londoners on their various ways home; I had a brolly and the rainbow was magnificent against an almost black cumulonimbus.

Just as it had stopped raining and I had made the transition from Mayfair to Marylebone, I noticed the silhouette of a familiar figure against the bright wet tarmac just mounting an old-fashioned sit-up-and-beg town bicycle: it was Sara.

'Good evening!'

'James, hello! What a coincidence! This is my office,' she said nodding to a door with a rather fine architect's logo on it.

'I walk past here every day – we're about half way between my flat and my office – so it's hardly a coincidence at all!' And then, without thinking twice, or being embarrassed, I said: 'Look, I'm on my way home, but I don't want to do that at all. Let me repay you for the ball by taking you out to dinner?'

'I'd love to!' she replied. Here was a girl who just said Yes! It was refreshing.

'Splendid!' I said, and then remembering her last words to me, added, 'But I'm afraid I haven't asked your grandmother!'

'I won't tell her!' she said, beaming.

'Marylebone High Street?' It was my favourite London street and happily close to my flat.

'Sounds good. I'd better tie up the bike.'

'Why don't you leave it at mine? It's not far and we have to pass it anyway.'

She nodded in acceptance of the proposal and we set off towards my flat.

We left her bike in the communal hall shared with the offices below my flat, and ascended to it. I offered her a drink; she declined. I offered her the sofa; she accepted. And I got changed in such a hurry I didn't even bother to hang up my newest suit.

'You have a lovely collection of books.' She said as I waltzed back into my living room, fully de-suited and re-clothed.

'Thank you. I thought the same about you when you deserted me in your flat to change!'

'I had no idea you were interested in so many different things,' she said, examining my shelves with her head cocked.

'Yes, on the few nights a year that I am sober, I do enjoy a good read.'

She shot me a glance that made me realise my quip hadn't been taken as jokingly as I had meant it. Had I known her better, I may have offered her an explanation, but under the circumstances, the only thing to do was to manoeuvre the conversation away from my state of sobriety.

'I say! Since you seem to like books, and it's early, why don't we go to Daunt Books on the High Street for a quick look before we eat? It's the best bookshop in London; no, England! There are lots of places to eat just near it. Sorry, have you been before? Do you want to go?' I suddenly felt a little too eager and rather embarrassed, but she hadn't been before and she said she would love to.

It was a light, warm evening: the first of the year. I offered her my arm without thought, and she took it, seemingly with similar ease. And thus linked, and happily chatting, we made the short walk from my flat to Daunt Books. Since my first visit there several years ago, it has remained my sole provider of new books, and has supplied my shelves with many handsome and learned volumes, most of which remain unread, but which nevertheless look very intellectual, and help me to look the same. It is a beautiful Edwardian shop, the highlight of which is the long gallery towards the rear, well proportioned and appointed in oak, and lit by the commodious skylight running down its length.

We enjoyed an extensive examination of the hallowed shop, discussing the subjects of various books that caught my eye, or hers. I even managed to successfully avoid the temptation to purchase another tome, leaving for once having spent not a penny.

We went to a pricey but decent restaurant just off the High Street:

I decided that a high initial outlay might be worth it for a girl as high quality as Sara.

After a delicious meal, exceedingly quaffable wine, and lengthy discussions and anecdotes about our respective recent histories, and not so recent histories, we talked about our jobs, as one does at the beginning of any relationship, not just a romantic one. It transpired that she had designed a wonderful array of buildings, although none (yet) well known. Nevertheless, it made me feel that my job was rather mundane by comparison; at least the world would see what Sara had achieved, but she kindly pointed out that my job entailed helping people directly, which hers did not. I liked the fact that she was capable of abstract thought, a skill so sadly lacking in Martha.

'So did you enjoy the ball?' Sara suddenly asked.

'Yes, very much thank you. It was fun to meet a new crowd.' I paused. 'Except Richard, who didn't seem to take much of a shine to me. What's his problem?'

'He's always a bit off with new people. He's all right though, but I have worked with him for a few years, so I know his temperament well. He's the brother of my fiancé, Simon; that's how we met.'

Her words struck me down, almost visibly.

I didn't know what to say, and all I could manage was a feeble, 'I see.'

Her fiancé! What games had she been playing with me? Why hadn't he accompanied her to the ball? And then the whole situation became clear: I felt foolish in the extreme. Sara had been put in touch with me by her aged and slightly dotty grandmother; there had been no intention of romance on anyone's part to begin with, not even mine, but least of all those of Mrs Ricketts or Sara. How foolish I was to think Mrs Ricketts would set me up in a romantic situation with her granddaughter; how foolish of me to think Sara may have been have interested in me. Memories of the photo on her desk of her looking blissfully content in the arms of another man flooded into my head. There were a million reasons why her fiancé may not have accompanied her to the ball, and I was merely a handy chap who scrubbed up well enough to stand in. And no wonder Richard had taken a dislike to me: having little idea about my relationship with Mrs Ricketts, he couldn't possibly have known it was her who had asked me to chaperone Sara; what therefore must have he thought about Sara asking me to the ball, and what must he have thought my intentions were? I immediately forgave him for his understandably hostile behaviour and began to feel rather sorry for him. Had I known he was the brother of her fiancé, my conduct would have been quite different from the start.

And then, as if not wanting to dwell on the subject, Sara changed tack yet again, asking enthusiastically: 'Would you like to come to the *Magic Flute* with me the week after next?'

My bewilderment deepened, but because her face was so alive, and expectant, and beautiful, I said: 'I should love to.'

'It's a German production,' she said, almost more eagerly, 'I hope you don't mind but I've always wanted to see it in German!'

'No. No, I don't mind at all,' I said.

Her enthusiasm was adorable.

And that was the last proper conversation we had in the restaurant; we left soon after to take the air, albeit not that fresh, outside. Trying to consider the situation rationally, my logical mind concluded that she liked me as a friend, and was too innocent to imagine my feelings for her were becoming deeper. But still my mind was awash with emotion and confusion, and I was happy to walk in silence; so, thankfully, was she. I walked her back to my flat to pick up her bicycle, but it being late and her looking rather tired, I offered her a bed. She accepted, and since the offer of a bed had been extended, I gave her mine, it being the only one. After a glorious smile and a sexy 'Good night, James,' from her as she went from the bathroom to my bedroom dressed only in the shirt I had given her to sleep in, I wondered why I hadn't noticed her engagement ring. Unable to find an answer, I tried to sleep on the sofa.

CHAPTER 24

Further Admissions

The morning after we both overslept, me because I had been awake half the night and she because she didn't have her alarm clock. However, the sight of her going from bedroom to bathroom in my shirt perked me up remarkably quickly. We had a hasty breakfast and walked together towards our respective places of work, arriving at hers rather too quickly. She expressed concern about going to work in yesterday's clothes; I announced that I did it all the time and that it was amazing how often people didn't notice, realising only after we'd said goodbye that perhaps it wasn't the best thing to tell the girl you are after, even if she was engaged.

Once in the office, I was rather quiet, largely abstaining from banter with Matthew and Emily, and remained in this abnormally restrained mood until the phone rang and Frances Green's voice launched straight into conversation.

'James, I thought I'd pre-empt my husband, his solicitors and your fax machine.'

This could only mean that she had visited the former matrimonial home and carried out yet another crazed act of jealously and anger.

'Frances, if it's a confession you're after, I think you need to find a Roman Catholic priest. You can't bribe the Law as easily as the Church!'

'Listen, young man! No doubt I am paying for the privilege of talking to you, so you will damn well hear my confession!' she said, jokingly.

She was of course right.

'You have me there, Frances. Confess away!'

'Of course. I do find I'm usually right. Don't you worry, now: I haven't caused any damage. But do you know what Trevor has bought? A damn great big bloody Mercedes. I went over to the house to pick up the last of my chattels and there it was, with his silly personalised number plate transferred from the old one. It's "T" "R" three, "V" zero "R". Twit. I can't honestly believe I happily rode around in a vehicle displaying his own name so unashamedly on each end of it! Anyway, after his financial disclosures, I couldn't believe he had the money to buy it. I thought it was it damn unfair, and concluded that if he couldn't buy me a car, he didn't deserve to drive one either. So I made damn sure he wouldn't be able to drive it anywhere.'

Bloody hell. What has she done? My heart began to race on her account. If she had done something serious to the car, she really would be hammering nails into her own pine box.

'I have removed the spark plugs. Trevor doesn't know one end of an engine from the other. He probably doesn't even know how to get the bloody bonnet up! He's the most impractical man I've ever met!'

She paused.

'I suppose you'll have to tell his solicitors?'

'Tell them what, Frances?'

'I'm not sure I follow…'

'I have no idea what you're talking about, but I have heard that petty crime is up in your husband's neck of the woods.'

'Oh, I see,' she said. I could tell she was smiling.

'But Frances?'

'Please don't do anything like this again; it really does make my job harder, and you are likely to penalise yourself in the long run.'

'Yes, James, I understand.'

The next phone call, inevitably enough, was from Cressida Smyth-Jones. I would not now be able to make a pre-emptive strike, but at least Frances had armed me with sufficient information for a worthy counter-attack.

'Mr James?'

'Good morning, Cressida!'

'Mr James, my client now instructs me his motor-car appears to be immobile.'

'Does it appear to be immobile because it is in fact parked?'

'Mr James, obviously the car does not appear to be immobile just because it is *stationary*. My client is having trouble *making* it become mobile, which for an *automobile* is obviously troubling.'

'Oh dear. Has it been clamped?'

'I think my client would have noticed.'

I had my doubts, but I had to keep up the barrage: 'Has your client checked the petrol gauge?'

'Um… I don't know…'

By asking these simple questions I had clearly unnerved Cressida because as she knew, often the daftest explanations were the correct ones.

'Mr James, you're not answering my question.' Cressida would take more breaking than this, obviously.

'You haven't asked me a question, Cressida. You have merely stated that your client's car is immobile. I am not a mechanic…'

'Mr James!' she interrupted. 'I know damn well you are not a mechanic, and you know damn well what I am asking you even if I haven't expressly expressed my query as a question! Do you happen to know *why* my client's car has gone phut?!'

'Being somewhat of a fan of quality German automotive engineering, I do happen to know that the particular model of Mercedes that Mr Green drives does suffer from spark plug problems. May I suggest that your client checks the spark plugs?'

Of course to suggest that a brand-new Mercedes could have been suffering from a trivial problem such as this was preposterous; I don't suppose there has been a new Mercedes since about 1910 that has had spark plug problems, but I had an inkling that Cressida knew less about engines than Mr Green apparently did, and I hope to call their collected bluffs.

Neither did I let on that my interest in quality German automotive engineering extended no further than driving my 900cc D-registered VW Polo that my mother had given me when it had failed its M.O.T. several years ago.

'Thank you for your advice, Mr James. I'll let my client know.'

It had worked: my diversion regarding German vehicles had disorientated the lovely Cressida thus diverting conversation so that nothing had been admitted. Furthermore, it gave the impression that I had offered helpful unsolicited advice: Cressida Smyth-Jones, nil; James James, one.

But of course, an hour later, Cressida was on the phone again; I would have to come clean, and a swift apology seemed to me the only way to do it: 'Cressida! Good afternoon! I have my client's file open on my desk and was literally just picking up the phone to dial your number: my client has just been on the blower and I'm afraid she's playing silly buggers again; she's just admitted to tampering with the engine of your husband's car: she says that she has removed the spark plugs; how funny that I mentioned them earlier! I am very sorry about my client's conduct: I have told her in no uncertain terms that she must stop behaving like this, and I believe that she really has taken my words on board. We all want to settle matters quickly and in a civilised manner.'

I drew breath.

There was a pause as Cressida considered my speech.

'As you well know, Mr James, I was indeed telephoning you regarding the missing spark plugs which of course my client found after our last conversation. I can't work out, Mr James, who is more stupid: your client or you. But I have instructions to fight this case most vehemently and without remorse if she continues with this ridiculous behaviour.'

'Yes, of course, Cressida. I understand. Thank you for letting me know so clearly how the position stands. Speak soon no doubt.'

'No doubt,' she said wearily, 'Good bye, Mr James.'

The Cressida Smyth-Jones, James James match was now level at one all.

CHAPTER 25

The Magic Flute

Since I had last seen her, I had been trying not to think too much about Sara. But despite this, I had not been able to stop myself looking forward to the evening that now lay ahead. I was waiting on a lovely May evening outside the Royal Opera House, Sara having declined my offer to collect her from her flat. I had wondered if her fiancé had been at large.

She arrived in a taxi and she looked stunning. Her dress this evening made it seem as though the one she had worn to the architect's ball had been an outfit fit for a boring Monday in the office.

'Good evening, madam!' I said, opening the taxi door.

'Hello, sir!' she said, definitely flirting.

At that moment my eyes caught a bright flash reflected from the not insubstantial stone beautifully set on the gold band on the ring finger of her left hand. Not noticing before must have been the fault of my poor observational skills but I couldn't take this any longer and resolved to ask her this evening about her fiancé. She must have known the effect she was having on me, and I thought it jolly unfair that she could treat me in this manner.

I escorted her into the wonderfully glazed and airy bar and ordered a bottle of Champagne, together with a request that the vendor be my mortgagee for the purchase. The foreign barman didn't understand, and Sara thanked me, with a smile.

'Thanks, James, I do love a good Champagne.'

'Me too! Cheers!'

We had enjoyable chat about the architecture of Covent Garden: the present auditorium, Sara told me, was started in 1858 and is actually the third opera house, the first two having been taken by fire. She was full of intriguing information about the previous theatres and their builders, something of which I knew little.

Then I saw Teddy at the same moment as he saw me. He was with a hugely glamorous couple, upwards of sixty, who both looked magnificently Edwardian, and another equally as splendid a woman, whom he was leading by the arm. It appeared that Teddy had a lady-friend. The men wore heavy suits stitched from cloth that must have weighed several pounds per square yard, and which can only have been made before the war, probably for their fathers. In those days, sons were very sensibly made as exact replicas of their fathers to save tailoring costs, and the garments were made to last. Their shirts were starched, and beautifully white, no doubt with silver studs and removable collars. The ladies had wonderful flowing, full-length gowns, feathery fascinators and accoutrements to match: handbags, fans and jewellery.

As soon as Teddy saw me, he manoeuvred his party in our direction and introductions were made. His friends were a Major-General and his wife, and he proudly introduced the lady on his arm as Miss Pound, giving me a wink as I introduced Sara. A generation apart, we were at the opera with our respective young ladies, and this was obviously tickling the good-natured Teddy.

After a polite chat, Teddy's group headed off to chat with someone else Teddy had spotted, and Sara breathed a slight sigh of relief.

'They remind me of my grandmother and her friends! Wonderfully English and wonderfully old-fashioned, but everything has to be so proper; it's so bloody exhausting after a while!'

I agreed, but deep down, I admired Teddy's style.

The first half of the opera was magical, in part because of the music and the magnificence of the production, but in the main because I was sitting next to the most beautiful girl in the whole place. My eyes were repeatedly drawn from the stage to Sara's hands, neatly folded in her lap, and then to her face, concentrating on the music, her mouth almost showing signs of a smile during the most powerful arias. When turning towards her in a contrivance to catch her eye – which she rarely acknowledged – another enchanting trait of hers – my nose perceived the merest suggestion of her perfume. And all the while my ears caught her soft breathing between Mozart's melodies.

At half time (Sara chastised me for calling it such), we had another drink on the outside balcony overlooking Covent Garden market itself. The sky was cloudless and London seemed peaceful viewed from this angle. I knew I must ask, and that after the opera the opportunity would have passed, so I just came out with it:

'So, where is your fiancé?'

She looked down, and wore an expression of deep upset, while

uncharacteristically playing with her hands for a while. I almost
regretted asking her, but my curiosity was overwhelming, and despite
feeling sorry that she looked so uncomfortable I was impatient to know
her answer. My immediate thought and subsequent hope was that
she was annoyed with me for having asked, but only because she had
feelings for me. But would open discussion of her fiancé change our
relationship for the worse?

'Simon died.'

My stomach turned from embarrassment, or shame, or both.

'I'm so sorry. I had no idea.'

And after the initial shock of my question appeared to subside, it
became she who was anxious not to upset me.

'No, no, no! *I'm* sorry. I thought my grandmother must have told
you. You must think I'm a complete bitch.'

I said nothing.

She saw me glance at her engagement ring, obviously wondering
why she still wore it.

'I just can't bear to take it off.' She explained, fingering it with her
right hand.

Nothing more was said, though for the rest of the interval, her
downcast face and elusive eyes made it clear that she remained troubled.
I was curious to know how he had died, but my thoughts revolved
around more important questions: when did he die, and was she over
it? Was the way open for me? But most importantly and despite these
doubts, I was deeply satisfied that Sara remained an eligible spinster.

When the Queen of the Night had finished her hundred and second
curtsy, we were finally at liberty to relieve our numb backsides. We
went out, talking about how good it been, especially in German, and
once outside in the chilly night air, I decided I didn't want the night to
end quite yet.

'Shall we have a quick drink? I'm awfully thirsty.'

'No, I think I should go, if you don't mind. I'm really busy this week
and I think I should sleep.'

Damnation! My impertinent question had annoyed her, and now
she would shun me.

But I must have looked visibly crestfallen, because she said: 'I would
love to, but just not right now. Let's meet up again soon?'

I smiled in agreement.

'I should get a taxi,' she continued, 'but James...' she said placing her hand lightly on my forearm, 'I did have a lovely evening with you.'

And with that she drew me nearer with her hand and placed a kiss on my cheek, and another almost on my lips.

Then an orange-lighted taxi drove towards us, and with the hand which had been on my arm, she hailed it.

CHAPTER 26

Charlie Somers

The day after the *Magic Flute*, I arrived at the office in a buoyant mood.

It was the middle of May and the weather was becoming consistently more clement by the day. Emily's wardrobe reflected the changing weather, and her garments were becoming lighter on cloth and carried fewer stitches as each day got warmer. This particular morning she looked wonderful, and her short skirt almost made even me blush: her magnificent legs seemed to extend endlessly.

'Morning, you devilishly sexy secretary!'

'Morning, James!'

My imagination wandered for a moment: my thoughts involved clearing the files from my adequately sized desk with one sweep of the arm, placing Emily's pert behind on said desk, and...

'James! What are you thinking?!'

Damn.

Busted.

This kind of thing never happened. It was Emily: I never have such thoughts about Emily. I concluded it was the time of the year, the weather, and therefore the large expanses of flesh on show, but most importantly of all, that I was actually falling for Sara, and was experiencing some kind of frustration in light of my discovery that she was in fact an eligible and beautiful girl, albeit one wrapped in pain and grief.

'So, what is the Ricketts girl up to? Have you discovered why her mysterious fiancé is never on the scene?' asked Emily.

'Yes, he's dead.'

'Oh, shit. Sorry.'

'No need to be sorry, he wasn't my fiancé!' I said, feeling stupid as soon as the words had left my mouth. I knew what Emily had meant, but in the look that she subsequently gave me, I knew that she knew I felt foolish, and with a smile she forgave me.

'So, what happened?'

'I don't know. She didn't talk about it. She only said that he was dead.'

'Well at least she's single. Is she?'

'I think so. I hope so. She kissed me. She must be!'

'On the lips?' said Emily quickly.

'Almost. It was very erotic.'

And then Matthew arrived, curtailing our conversation.

'Morning,' he said, surveying Emily. Little bugger, I thought.

'Good morning!' we said in unison.

'So, what have we on today?' said Matthew, unusually enthusiastic for this time of the morning. The good weather must be affecting him too.

'I think I'm going to need some serious barristerial help on the Jones file. Can you ring Charlie Somers to see if he's free for a conference with the client today and also for the hearing next month? Jones wants a conference as soon as possible and I don't want to upset him – this'll be a big case – the man's loaded, and he's very good at paying my fees.'

Charlie Somers was the very first barrister I instructed and we hit it off straight away. He was about my age, and had a certain disdain and cynicism about everything legal that I couldn't help admiring. He told clients his opinion of their cases, boldly insinuating what he thought about them in the process, relying totally on his audaciousness to carry him through; a risky but finely tuned art. It made for some good conferences.

Matthew having arranged the conference with the clerks of 7 Queen's Bench Row and Jones himself, we duly arrived at Charlie's chambers late that afternoon and counsel was summoned.

'Afternoon Charlie!'

'Hallo James!' Charlie gave me his usual grin and hearty handshake.

'This is Matthew, he's my trainee.'

'Hello Matthew. Blimey! You, with a trainee, James? What has happened to the world? I suppose you want me to teach him something, since you are almost certainly incapable of imparting any legal knowledge to him, since you have none! Did you pass all your exams first time round, Matthew?'

'Yes.'

'You see?! He's already more qualified than his supervisor!' quipped Charlie. I had foolishly admitted to him on one occasion that I wasn't entirely successful in passing all my professional exams on the first taking. I had also been imprudent enough to admit that the modest improvement in my marks in the second sitting was also, alas, a modicum below the standard required by law college examiners. Thankfully on the third attempt, fortune was on my side, and I was lucky enough to pass them all by the skin of my teeth. I have since proved beyond all reasonable doubt that being a solicitor and not knowing the law is surprisingly easy: so long as you have a good barrister.

'So who have we today?' asked that very man.

'Mr Jones. He's a complete bastard.'

'Splendid! We're almost sure to win, then. I suppose he's loaded?'

'Yes.'

'Marvellous: can I get away with four hundred an hour?'

'Yes.'

'Good show.'

'Is that how all barristers decide on their fees?' asked Matthew, exceedingly boldly but obviously getting the measure of Charlie very quickly.

'Good Lord, yes! Charge the maximum one can without the client believing it's too much! Solicitors are worse though: James here charges his clients for talking about the weather!'

Philip, head clerk of 7 Queen's Bench Row, knocked and entered, announcing the arrival of our client.

'Good afternoon, Mr Jones,' I said. 'This is your counsel, Charlie Somers.'

'Hello, very pleased to meet you,' said Charlie, 'I have heard a lot about you!'

'I'd like to say likewise, but I can't,' said the snide Jones.

It was a typical case: Jones had married young, had a couple of kids, became very wealthy doing something pointless but lucrative in the city, had a number of affairs because of his fat wallet (the fatter the wallet, the fatter the man certain girls will accept) and then the wife discovers the affairs by detecting too many expensive restaurant bills and florists' invoices on her husband's bank statements, none of which she was party to, and thus files for divorce. Wife is broken hearted, husband soon realises he's too fat even for his sizeable wallet and both end up becoming old, single and lonely.

'So, Mr Somers,' asked Jones, 'will I be able to keep my house?'

'Frankly no. The court will deem your wife and children's need greater than yours. But your coffers, quite rightly for a man of your stature, are bulging at the seams,' said Charlie, glancing for a moment too long at Jones' strained shirt buttons.

The brow of the well-fed Jones knit while the brain cell not involved in the functioning of his forehead musculature considered momentarily his barrister's apparent insolent insult. The brain cell concluded a barrister couldn't possibly be so rude, and as the brows un-knit, Charlie's brain immediately began looking for the next opening. Jones meanwhile sat there looking rather smug, stroking one of his chins. 'Yes, I suppose I could just buy a penthouse somewhere. A bachelor pad for entertaining.'

'Your son will be catered for, if, as is likely, your wife gets the matrimonial home.'

'I meant for myself,' said Jones.

'Oh, I do apologise. I presumed you meant your son, him being the only bachelor involved in these proceedings,' said Charlie, a wonderfully earnest expression across his face. 'Well, what next?'

The conference went well; Jones ended up being impressed by Charlie's no-nonsense approach to the intricate details of his case, highlighting the areas where there were some arguments in his favour, but letting him know that the court's primary concern is to care for the children and wife. 'Bloody children,' was Jones' response.

Jones left, seemingly pleased with Charlie's advice, and Charlie announced:

'What an absolute bugger! I often dislike clients, but it's rare that one questions whether one should be acting for them for moral reasons. Still, one has to consider one's livelihood. I think I'll charge him five hundred an hour though, the extra hundred being a moral and ethical surcharge, so I don't have to think too carefully about whether or not I should act at all.'

'I told you he was a bastard.'

'Indeed. My brain needs cooling down, fancy a pint?'

'Definitely.'

Several pints and a steak and chips later, I ended up in bed falling into one of those troubled, drunken semi-sleeps, but safe in the knowledge that Matthew, Charlie and I had had a damn good evening.

The next morning in the office, after acknowledging the sight of another of Emily's wonderfully short skirts, but still feeling rather vague as one does the morning after the night before, Sue announced that a Mr Somers was in reception. It is very unusual for a barrister to call at a solicitor's office. They rightly like to think of themselves as the senior branch of the profession, and do not often deign to enter the offices of the lowly solicitor, despite relying on said serf for the entirety of their work. But Charlie was different, and certainly not a pompous arse. 'Send him in to my office,' I told Sue, an equally unusual thing to do: offices were for work not entertainment, the meeting rooms being meant for clients or guests. But I was certain Charlie could not be at Number 22 in a professional capacity.

The door opened and it wasn't Charlie that entered, but Matthew. He was looking decidedly ill; no doubt his young, innocent liver wasn't experienced with dealing with regular doses of large amounts of alcohol.

'Charlie's in reception,' he announced.

'I know, he's coming through I hope.'

Whereupon Sue knocked and showed Charlie in.

'Morning chaps!' said Charlie, seemingly none the worse from the previous night's booze intake. Then he noticed Emily. '...And chapess,' he added. 'So, you must be the famous Miss Emily Lewis?' he asked her.

'Yes, indeed, I am she. And you must be Charlie Somers Esquire?'

'I am he!' said Charlie, clearly enjoying the attention.

He looked at Emily in the way most men do: with admiration and slight apprehension; Emily was a confident girl, not just because of her looks, but because she could hold her own intellectually too, and she wasn't frightened of speaking her mind to anyone. I think her confident manner and general disregard of men, which was partly due to dealing so often with divorce, was why men found her cold, and sometimes aloof.

'Now,' he said, apparently thrown by Emily, 'I have completely forgotten why I stepped into your offices! Good evening, though, eh, chaps?'

'It was fun,' I agreed, and Matthew nodded his approval. 'Jones?' I asked, hoping to put his mind back on his purpose.

'Jones? Oh, fatty, yes, quite right. I had a few thoughts last night when I got home about how we should tackle this, and since I was passing your offices, I thought I'd pop in and pick up some papers.'

Charlie was the only man I knew who could think straight after consuming half a dozen pints, and the only barrister in London who would pop in to his instructing solicitor's offices to pick up papers; the latter was one of the reasons why I liked him so much. And I suspected that he had a quiet morning, and was looking for an excuse for a chat. He had his eye on the newly qualified barrister in his chambers, and Matthew having been with us last night, we had not had the opportunity of discussing said strumpet.

'James, have you got time for quick coffee?' he asked, confirming my suspicions. 'To go through what I mentioned last night...' he said, not that cryptically, which raised a slight smile from the astute Emily.

'Of course. I am a partner now, Charlie: I can do as I please!'

'Great! Now?'

'Yes, now.'

'Well, splendid to have finally met you, Miss Lewis, and I hope we'll bump into each other again very soon!'

'Yes, no doubt we will.'

And then something curious happened. Emily's lips curled at the edges while Charlie and Emily held each other's gaze for what seemed like a full minute. During this period when their eyes were locked, she nervously raised her hand to fiddle with her hair, but realising what she was doing appeared nervous, slowed her hand down, only making it more apparent she was fidgeting: her hand never reached her hair and she held it awkwardly in mid-air for a moment before lowering it again. A very slight colouration of her face rose, and she looked down to avoid any further embarrassment. Emily never looked down. These movements were subtle and perhaps perceivable only by those who knew Emily intimately, but there was little doubt in my mind that she liked this man.

'I hope so,' said Charlie, forgetting he'd already said it. 'Cheers, Matthew. See you soon. Ready James?' And with that we went for a coffee, and he talked at length about the new addition to his chambers and how he should woo her.

Once back in the office, and as soon as practically possible without appearing too keen, Emily asked, 'Why have I never met Charlie before?'

'Good question. I suppose we tend to go out after conferences when I've been at his chambers, so we go out over there. He's a good laugh.'

'Yes, he seems fun...' she trailed off. And realising that perhaps her trailing off had sounded a little too thoughtful, she quickly said: 'I'm starving. I'm popping out for lunch.' And with that she left.

In her absence, Matthew announced, 'I think she fancies Charlie.'

I began to think Matthew knew Emily too well, but had to agree with him. 'Well, they're both going to the Lincoln's Inn Garden Party on the first of June. We'll just have to wait and see what happens!'

CHAPTER 27

The Lincoln's Inn Garden Party

The annual Lincoln's Inn Garden Party was always a good evening; it was a splendid chance to strut around the beautiful and tranquil lawns of this Inn of Court, which, provided there was good weather, was one of the best venues in London for such an event.

The serenity of Lincoln's Inn always amazes me, considering it is sandwiched between the manic High Holborn and Fleet Street where throngs of suited professionals, smart secretaries, booted workmen and rucksacked tourists are constantly battling past each other, always in a hurry to get somewhere. Within the walled confines of the Inn itself, one may observe vast, empty, stone-flagged pavements, with the odd barrister's clerk pushing a trolley of files towards the Royal Courts of Justice so conveniently placed at the southern side of the Inn, or perhaps a gowned and wigged silk and his junior walking slowly round New Square, White Books under their arms, conversing deeply about their upcoming case or debriefing each other on their last hearing.

The whole place is unflustered and untroubled by the London outside.

Few from outside the legal profession enter the Inn; perhaps they think they aren't allowed; perhaps they feel too conspicuously un-legal to want to enter; perhaps they don't know how handsome the architecture is, how beautiful the lawns are, and how lovely it is to simply to walk through; perhaps some simply don't know it exists.

Despite it having rained most of that morning, it turned out to be a beautiful June day, there not being a cloud in the sky from lunchtime onwards. And being a West-End Firm, there were always a number of people from Bugle & Yarrington at the Garden Party, but this year there proved to be a particularly good turnout. The Founding Fathers and Bugle's wife were present, together with Teddy, Margaret, the head of the family department, Tim, his Charlotte and Emily. The Annual Lincoln's Inn Garden Party was always a good evening, and this one looked set to be a great one.

Upon arrival, Tim, Charlotte, Emily and I headed straight for the lawns north of New Square, beneath the west windows of the chambers of Stone Buildings.

There, dotted across the grass, stood London's finest legal brains, dressed up to the nines, drinking Champagne and talking absolute twaddle to one another; this party was amongst the topmost contenders for the legal profession's annual event that boasted the most canapés, booze, pompous twits, arrogant arses, small-talk, and bullshit. I love this kind of thing!

'It looks like quite a few people have been here some time already,' I said as we watched the beautifully turned out ladies and besuited gentlemen, 'We have some catching up to do!' Emily made me feel mildly embarrassed by touching my elbow and giving me a disapproving look. I had only been joking, I thought initially, but then realised how it might have appeared to others.

We walked up the path towards the revellers, Emily and Charlotte ahead, and Tim and I bringing up the rear. We were greeted by various very important people, some of whom were impressively weighed down by presidential pendants of the Law Society: gongs of gold held round their necks by heavy chains. Pleasantries were passed between us, and then we proceeded on to polite waiters with glasses filled with Champagne. Once armed with glasses, we were free to roam the lawns and mingle.

As soon as Emily had stepped from the paved path onto the lawn, still soft from the morning's rain, she began toppling over backwards as her heels sank into the lawn. I stepped forward to help, thrusting my glass into Tim's hand, but another, quicker gentleman had beaten me to it.

Indeed, it was the was strong arms of Charlie Somers who deftly saved Emily's modesty as her caught her from behind, one of his arms safely cradling her upper body weight around her shoulders, while the other hand made a definite and deliberate movement towards her pert posterior as the weight of that region of her anatomy plunged into his open palm. Charlie had an expression of extreme enjoyment on his face. Once both Charlie's anterior appendages had stopped Emily's fall, he cleverly propped her up again, without removing either hand until she was safely vertical again.

'It's a jolly good job I was at hand, fair maiden, to catch you as you swooned!' said the gleeful Charlie. Emily's look of horror that an unknown chap had such a good hold of one of her buttocks turned into a flirtatious smile as she turned round and realised it had been none other than Charlie who had caught her.

'Make no mistake about it, sir! I did not swoon; the plasticity of the lawn was merely too high to support my heels; but I thank you for your kind assistance,' said the equally gleeful Emily.

'My pleasure,' he said in return, and then clearly remembering who he was with, his face fell. 'This is my esteemed colleague and newest member of my chambers, Miss Felicity Warburton-Lee.'

Felicity, for a moment, clearly looked unimpressed at Charlie's firm handling of Emily's fall (and bottom), but recomposed herself admirably for a polite, 'Good evening.' Tim, Charlotte and Emily were introduced to her and she, ignoring the female presence, asked Tim and I from which chambers we were.

'I'm afraid we are lowly solicitors at the firm of Bugle & Yarrington,' I said jokingly.

She looked at us down her nose, clearly unimpressed that Charlie had friends who weren't barristers. 'I see,' was her curt answer which rather impeded the natural flow of conversation.

So this was the ice-maiden who had grabbed Charlie's attention. She was certainly a fine specimen. Emily, who knew nothing about Charlie's interest in her, and who had unusually not noticed the very slight tension in the air, immediately seemed to take a shine to her and manoeuvred over to her, asking her what type of law she practised, and how she was enjoying her early days at the Bar. This seemed to relax Felicity rather, although poor Charlie could not hide the concern on his face as they began chatting. Charlotte, naturally being drawn to the company of her own sex, joined them; the boys, naturally not wanting to get involved in female chitchat formed a circle a safe distance away.

'So what do you think?' asked Charlie, quietly.

'Charlie has his eye on her.' I explained to Tim.

'Which one?' asked Tim.

'Both, I think.' I observed.

'No, no, just Felicity!' said Charlie, his face flushing the colour of his crimson tie and matching handkerchief neatly folded in his top pocket.

Tim and I exchanged a glance, which thankfully Charlie seemed to miss.

'Well?' persisted Charlie.

'Well, she's pretty gorgeous,' I said, 'further comments to follow in the fullness of time, but I fear she may be a little aloof.'

'Quite right,' agreed Charlie, 'but it bothers me not, neither in myself nor in proud potential partners!'

My interest in the conversation took a steep decline as Tim brought up the finer legal points of an act of parliament that had thus far escaped my attention, and having no wish to have it brought to my attention at a garden party, my eyes began to survey the surrounding scene. I observed the multitude of girls tottering around in their high heels and wondered how any of them remained upright on the lawn – even my own sensibly shod feet sank a little into the argillaceous ground. After a few moments of scanning, I soon noticed Bugle and his wife Cathy talking to a group of people a little way off. Cathy could not easily be missed: she was a woman who did not hold back in culinary excesses and wore a necessarily vast aubergine-coloured jacket and skirt with a cream blouse beneath; indeed, she looked rather like an aubergine with a slice cut from it. She looked equally as bored as me, and an unmissable opportunity presented itself to me.

I excused myself from the conversation with Charlie and Tim and wandered over.

'Good evening, Cathy!' I said. We hadn't met each other that many times, but Mrs Bugle seemed a little formal. I had forgotten how ugly she was.

'Hello, James,' she said, immediately detaching herself from her husband and the rest of his group. Bugle shot me a rather angry look for being the apparent cause of his wife's quick quitting of the group.

After a refill of Champagne which necessitated moving further from Bugle, some small-talk about life in the Firm, and her congratulating me on my promotion to partner, I began to become impatient to realise my intentions of talking to her in the first place.

'Yes, I've seen a lot of Frank recently,' I said, continuing on from the topic of his recent acquisition of the post as senior partner. 'I think I saw him with a relative of yours,' I said, as inconspicuously as possible, and allowing her to continue the rest of the story.

'Oh, Jenny, yes. Our niece. Yes, she's been through a rough patch recently and Frank seems to have taken such an interest in her. It's lovely of him really – they've never been that close before.'

The apparent scandal had been innocuous; there was no gossip; Jenny was the niece despite Bugle's odd behaviour and apparent secrecy about his dealings with her. I did not pry into what unfortunate circumstances had befallen her, but was pleased that Bugle was in fact keeping his bugle in his pants.

And in any case, I couldn't ask any further questions: he was approaching us at speed, with an expression evidencing his worry that his wife stood alone with me.

'Evening James,' he said, in his usual uninterested way.

'Evening.'

'Cathy, there's someone I want you to meet. Would you mind, dear? So sorry to interrupt, James,' he continued with no hint of sincerity. 'Catch up later on in the evening, no doubt.'

'No doubt.'

And thus I found myself in the middle of the lawn, alone.

But not quite alone.

Just as I had been wondering where the rest of my party was, and which table of Champagne was closer, I saw another thirtysomething fellow, apparently in the same state of wondering what to do, and as our eyes met, my heart sank. We were close enough to chat, and he almost immediately made a step towards me, smiling in anticipation as he did so. The situation was irretrievable and the realisation that we would have to introduce ourselves and start a conversation did not fill me with enthusiasm. If it had been a foxy young lady, my emotions would have quite the opposite, but this chap made Bugle look respectable; his chalk-striped suit was more stripe than background, his tie knot was so big it made me wonder whether there was a tennis ball wrapped up inside it, and his winklepickers were so long and pointed that it was incredible that his toes did not get stuck in the lawn with every step.

His friendly, 'Hello!' made me, for a moment at least, feel rather guilty having just thought so badly of him.

'Hello, James James,' I said introducing myself.

'Um... Marcus Marcus,' he said, grinning gormlessly and extending his tiny hand.

'No, my first name is James and my surname is James.'

'Oh. Marcus Todd. Sorry. Unusual name. So what do you do?'

Take a wild guess.

'I'm a solicitor.'

'Oh, great me too!' he said with far too much enthusiasm. 'I'm with P & P. What firm are you with?'

P & P meant of course Priest and Parsons. The firm was not quite in the 'Magic Circle' of top London firms, but was nevertheless recognised as being about the best commercial outfit, paying huge salaries and expecting employees to give themselves entirely to the firm. Apparently one of the interview questions is: 'It's your sister's wedding. The firm has a big deal on over that weekend which you are needed for. What will you do?'.

'I've not heard of P & P,' I said, with the express intention of winding him up.

'Priest and Parsons,' he replied, somewhat surprised about my apparent ignorance.

'Oh, Priest and Parsons!' I said, 'Sorry, I thought you meant your firm was actually called "P & P"!'

'You didn't say who you were with?' he persisted.

'Oh, I'm with B & Y.'

'Which B & Y would that be?' he asked so as not to appear ignorant. 'I know of at least two,' he kept digging.

'Burlington & Yalland,' I said.

'Oh super! They've got a terrific reputation.'

No, you complete fuckwit, they haven't; I just made them up.

Marcus was following the rules about how to meet new lawyers to the letter and I knew his next question would be:

'What area of law do you do?'

'Family mainly.'

'Oh,' he said, taken aback by the nature of my work, which not being of a commercial nature was undoubtedly not worthy of his attention. 'I do shipping,' he said proudly.

'No doubt you come up against our reputable and fearsome partner, George Teddy,' I said, knowing that the number of lawyers against whom Teddy had entered into litigation in the last decade could almost certainly have been counted on one hand.

'No, I can't say I have,' he admitted, but it made him believe the fictitious Burlington & Yalland had a good shipping reputation.

'So I suppose your firm makes you work all hours?' I enquired.

'Yes, but it's worth it for a six-figure salary!' he gloated.

I had been talking to this stumpy city slicker for less than a minute, and already he'd dropped his grotesque salary into the picture. Quite often, anyone who is guilty of this crime is vertically challenged, probably has a severe complex about the size of other areas of his anatomy and almost certainly has no girlfriend. And so the killer question had formulated itself in my mind:

'That's great, but how do you find time for your girlfriend?'

'I don't have one,' he admitted, caught off guard by my punishing question.

I love it when that question works!

Thankfully, it had the effect required, and he seemed much less inclined to converse with me. He began to look around.

'If you need to rejoin your group, I quite understand,' I said, beginning to sow the seeds of a goodbye. 'I really must find my friends too. Splendid to meet you though, and I hope I'll bump into you anon!'

'Yes…' he said, not knowing what to say, 'Goodbye.'

And I made haste in the direction of the nearest Champagne bottle leaving him standing in the middle of the lawn, wondering again what to do.

Having recharged my glass for the nth time, I saw Margaret and Cressida Smyth-Jones heading my way and deep in conversation. This did not bode well: I would have to talk to two middle-aged and unmarried battle-axes, both highly respected family lawyers, one my immediate senior and one my adversary in the particularly difficult Frances Green case.

'Good evening, James!' said Margaret.

'Hello! Hello, Cressida! How delightful to see you!' I said, mimicking Charlie's boundless enthusiasm for social audacity.

'Good evening, Mr James,' said Cressida, as coldly as she could without being rude.

'Cressida and I were just talking about you,' said Margaret, 'she says you're quite the expert on the Mercedes engine.' And then she sighed, almost despairingly. 'Oh, dear James, I do hope you're behaving yourself?'

I generally like Margaret. She is a tough old boot, much like Cressida, but thankfully I don't have to work against her. Deep down, she has a good, dry sense of humour and can be amusing, if only subtly. However, when she treats me like a naughty schoolboy in front of the very woman who already has the high ground in the current battle between us, my estimation of her diminished somewhat. What is the point of such a comment if only to bring me down a peg or two? Cressida acknowledged the victory with a smug smile, enjoying the denigration dished out to me from my senior.

'I would never act unprofessionally; I'm afraid it's my client who isn't behaving herself,' I said, truthfully enough. 'She's a lovely woman and she's had a tough time. I think your client, Cressida, has behaved in an exceedingly ungentlemanly manner and is probably somewhat of a shit.'

Margaret drew breath at my description of Mr Green, but Cressida, thoughtfully making a slight nod in acknowledgement of the success of my firm counter-attack, then began to smile and said: 'Well, Mr James, as I'm sure you'll understand, I couldn't possibly comment.'

Margaret and I looked at each other.

Certain chemicals in the Champagne must have caused the normally formidable Cressida Smyth-Jones to have become more relaxed than her usual nature would allow, and I suspected that the bubbles of the booze had quickened the onset of this effect upon the contents of her cranial cavity to such an extent that she hadn't grasped how efficient the combination of gas and grape had been upon her; in short, she was pissed.

And I felt immediately as if I was beginning to like the darling Cressida in her current state of mind. I had never heard her crack a witticism before, especially at the cost of her own client; but best of all she had looked decidedly cheeky and had clearly enjoyed making her well considered statement.

'But Mr James,' continued Cressida, 'you had better make sure your client hasn't got access to two-stroke chainsaws or spanners for the next few weeks, or I will obtain an order to stop her going anywhere near the matrimonial home.'

'I quite understand, Cressida.'

Clearly her humour quota for the evening had been used up.

In the absence of the prospect of any further humour from either of the spinsters, I extricated myself from their presence to discover my glass again needed refilling. Why are flutes so small? Thankfully I saw Emily, Tim and Charlotte at the nearest Champagne outlet.

'Ah! There you are!' said Emily, offering me her hand. 'We're bored with this area of the lawn! Come on, let's go and see what all those people are eating!'

The four of us crossed the lawn to a large gathering of people, all happily munching canapés being handed round by waitresses. Having not eaten since lunchtime, and having quaffed a significant quantity of bubbly, we were all hungry. The problem with canapés is getting enough to satisfy one's appetite. But once you have made it clear to a couple of waitresses that you are hungry, the lovely girls are often more forthcoming, and are not, thankfully, in a position to chastise you for taking more than one nibble. And if you take only one morsel from the plate when it arrives at your circle of acquaintances, it is usually possible to pop it into your mouth and take another once everyone else has taken theirs. And thus I attempted to have my fill of delicate little tasters.

Charlotte too was digging into the delicacies with some enthusiasm. Just as she finished a tiny prawn sandwich, small enough to balance on the end of one's finger, her face changed from that of enjoyment to slight surprise.

At first, it was not evident why she was surprised, but it soon became clear that her right stiletto had began to sink visibly into the soft lawn. She stepped back with her left foot to stop the sinkage, but alas, the same thing happened with that heel too; both stilettos were rapidly losing height as they plunged into the soft mud beneath the perfect green grass. As she sank backwards, she began to loose balance and threw her arms out to try and keep her not insubstantial weight forward. She still clutched a glass of Champagne and her attempted rebalancing act had the unfortunate result of the liquid leaving its receptacle at some speed, only slowing down when it encountered Tim's face and suit jacket, he having been standing opposite her.

But throwing her arms forward was not enough to counterbalance the weight of her bulky behind falling backwards as the inexorable force of gravity played its role in bringing the manicured grass of the lawns of Lincoln's Inn and Charlotte's arse into ever-greater proximity.

Having done my usual trick of drinking too much bubbly too quickly, I found this whole sequence of events very amusing, and began laughing. Tim, who had initially not found being covered in Champagne terribly humorous, thought that the sight of his wife sprawling on her posterior on the lawns of Lincoln's Inn, with most of the West-End's top legal brass present, was hilarious. Even Emily, who had been embarrassed at her earlier fall could not suppress a smile, although admittedly it was she who went to Charlotte's aid before her husband.

'Damn you, Tim! Help me! Emily's not dressed for buggering about on the lawn either!' she exclaimed, brushing aside Emily's outstretched hand.

'Sorry, darling,' said Tim, trying not to laugh, 'I was just wiping off my soaking of Champagne.'

'Damn you, Tim! You filthy liar! You were standing there laughing at me! Shut up, James!' she said, turning on my uncontrolled fit of laughter.

Her indignation only made our giggles worse, until Tim was forced to stop himself laughing as he helped her up and inspected the damage.

'Oh, darling, you have made a mess of the lawn,' said Tim, scrutinising the flattened grass and muddy patch of lawn which had taken the full impact of Charlotte's meteoric miscarriage of balance.

'I don't give a damn about the lawn! What about my dress, you stupid idiot?! Sometimes I really do wonder why I married you!'

As Charlotte turned round to show us the damage, even I stopped laughing, for fear of her impending wrath. Only the bright green grass stains around the edge of the large muddy stain covering her entire rear-end made it clear that a much worse accident hadn't befallen the lovely Charlotte.

'I'm going to the ladies to sort this mess out. Get me another Champagne, Tim.'

'Yes, darling.'

'Emily?' ordered Charlotte over her shoulder as she set off for the loos, expecting Emily to follow her. Emily duly scurried after her, shooting us boys a mock terrified look and then smiling; but nevertheless, it seemed that Tim wasn't the only one under her bossy thumb.

Tim stood watching them cross the lawn until they disappeared around the corner of the Library. Quick as flash he whipped out a cigarette and lit it, exclaiming as he noticed me watching him: 'Quickest draw in the West-End!'

'Risky though.' I warned him.

'Nonsense! She'll be hours cleaning that mess up!'

'Mmm, you may be right there! Come on, let's get another drink.'

We manoeuvred over to a white-jacketed Champagne-pourer. I took two full glasses from the tray he held on the fingertips of one hand, while simultaneously holding out our empty glasses for a refill from the bottle he grasped in the other. He gave us a disapproving look, as if we were there simply for the Champagne.

'It's not *all* for us,' I said, 'in fact it is for our delightful women-folk, who are rapidly approaching!'

They were too, and I indicated to Tim they were approaching him from behind.

Despite still wearing the high heels, Charlotte was marching at full speed across the lawn, skirt hitched up, brows knit, hair flailing behind, looking somewhat like a glammed-up and angry Boadicea. Emily was following at a rather more lady-like pace.

'Fuck!' said Tim, a lungful of smoke exhaling with the curse.

He was about to throw the cigarette to the floor when I interjected quietly: 'No! She's too close: I fear she may have seen the smoke, you'd better give it to me.' I passed him a glass of Champagne for him to give to Charlotte and cunningly intercepted the cigarette between the customary index and middle fingers as I slid the glass into his hand. It was well done, and I wondered if the move would ever be repeated in twenty years time, at our children's eighteenth birthday parties.

'Hello, darling,' said Tim, attempting a genuine smile as his wife approached.

'Shut up, Tim. Give me your jacket.'

'Yes, darling.'

'James, why on earth are you smoking?'

I had thought my plan had been executed in an exemplary manner, but in the heat of the moment, I had failed to consider what would happen once I had managed to get the smouldering cigarette successfully from Tim.

'I always smoke with Champagne,' I said, which I thought was a stroke of genius for a moment: how would she be able to argue?

'James, I have seen you drink numerous glasses of Champagne but I have never once seen you smoke.' And with that she swung round to Tim and before he could recoil she gave him a big sniff.

'Just as I thought! Men! Damn them all! Why do they always stick up for each other?'

She gave me a look of contempt.

'Tim, I asked you to give me your jacket.'

'Yes, darling.'

It was thankfully long enough to cover the unfortunate stain.

'The next time you *dare* lie to me, it will be the last, I promise!' she spat, her face inches from Tim's. And then, totally changing tune she said, 'Well, then! Let's enjoy the evening,' and she seemed instantly to forget the unfortunate incidents which had thus far taken place.

At which point Matthew and Tom were seen approaching with Charlie and Felicity. The former pair probably didn't know anyone, and were finding it tough to bullshit to strange lawyers. I remember in my youthful days of traineeship, all those years ago, being flummoxed as to what to say to venerable old boys who had won their legal spurs before the Law of Property Act 1925 had been passed.

'I rescued these poor chaps from Reginald Raymond QC, who had collared them and was boring them to death about life before the Law of Property Act 1925!' said Charlie.

Tim introduced Charlotte to the trainees and asked if they'd met anyone interesting, with the exception of the esteemed Queen's Counsel.

'Damn right! There are so many fit girls here! It's amazing!' said Tom, flashing a smile at Charlie, who winked back.

'Good stuff,' I said. 'Any dates arranged?'

'No. As soon as they find out we're trainees they all loose interest.'

'Ah! the fickleness of women!' I said, innocently catching the eye of Felicity.

'Shut up, James!' said Emily.

'Have you seen round the whole place yet?' I asked Matthew and Tom, to change the subject, and in the absence of a reply from either of them, continued, 'Well, shall I give you a quick tour?' They quickly consented and off we went, prudently recharging our glasses before setting off into the unknown depths of Lincoln's Inn.

I took them round New Square, pointing out the wonderful array of Bentleys and commenting upon the beauty of some of the finest Georgian architecture in London. I showed them Wildy & Sons, the legal bookshop under the arch in the corner of New Square of which I have always rather liked the look, but have never actually had cause to enter. I pointed out the back entrance of the Royal Courts of Justice and that wonderful summer evening drinking hole, the Seven Stars. We walked up past Old Buildings and the chapel, and as we passed Old Square, heading for the small gate leading to Chancery Lane, we came upon Bugle kissing the lips of a girl considerably slimmer and blonder than his wife.

They both turned as they caught sight of us from the corners of their eyes.

It was Jenny!

'Christ!' said Bugle, the alcohol having made his tongue looser than it might otherwise have been.

'No need to blaspheme,' I said, the alcohol having a similar effect upon my tongue.

And then I realised there might well be need to blaspheme.

'What the hell are you all doing here?' asked Bugle, going purple.

'I was just showing the boys round the Inn,' I said, not deviating from the truth in any way.

'I, er, was – ' said Bugle in desperation, despite not having been asked anything.

Just kissing your niece?

I realised that one of my of my eyebrows was raised, waiting for a believable answer from Bugle, and also that he was aware of my facial expression, but such was my disbelief in the situation, there was nothing I could do to drop it from my face.

But this was in fact a rather serious situation, and it would probably be better to skedaddle. 'Come on, chaps,' I said to Matthew and Thomas, 'I'll show you the shortcut to Chancery Lane.' And we turned to go.

'James, a moment, if you please!' said Bugle. I quietly said to the boys that I'd meet them shortly and not to breathe a word of this to anyone. They went off tittering.

'Well, look – ' continued Bugle, trying to find his verbal footing and not enjoying my superiority, despite me having not actually said anything against him. And then he admitted the obvious: 'Look, James: I'm having a bit of a thing with Jenny.'

She smiled at me, as if she thought she was tremendously special to have Bugle's affection, and possibly out of smugness that she was seeing my boss and somehow had an advantage over me, because she had access to Bugle's heart, and no doubt, other blood-rich parts of his anatomy. I didn't give a damn about such matters, but her stupid smug smile irritated me.

'Isn't it illegal?' I asked.

I said this so that Bugle would have to admit that Jenny wasn't his niece, but she had clearly had forgotten that she was supposed to be so, because her smile fell and a look of concern replaced it: she was clearly worried about some deep, dark, and obscure law that she didn't know about. What could possibly be wrong about her relationship with Bugle? I wondered then if Bugle had been altogether candid about his marital status, and began to conclude that perhaps he had forgotten to mention Cathy and that Jenny was just cottoning on...

But then another, darker thought crossed my mind:

She was his niece!

'No of course it isn't illegal!' spat Bugle. 'Jenny isn't my niece.' The worried expression dropped from Jenny's face as the penny dropped. Bugle continued: 'I do have a niece called Jenny, who in fact I have seen a lot recently, but...' He paused. What else was there to say? 'Cathy and I haven't been happy for a long time, and one does have needs,' he explained, trying to get a sympathy vote. 'Look, James, please don't breathe a word. I'd hate to upset Cathy, despite our differences.'

This sordid affair was none of my business, and I didn't wish to make it so. What amazed me was the audacity of Bugle carrying on in this decidedly unfaithful manner, with his wife only a couple of hundred yards away.

'No, of course not.' I said, 'I'd better find the boys.'

'Thank you James,' said the guilty Bugle. 'Thanks for looking after the boys, too.'

I soon found the trainees, talking excitedly to one another about the affair of their senior partner.

'Right, stop that chatter!' I said in a moment of seriousness. 'You really mustn't say a word – to anyone – not even Emily, Matthew. It's none of our business and you know what gossip can do to marriages, and people's lives. Understood?'

'Yes, James,' they said in unison, clearly unimpressed by my stern take on the matter. But I felt it was necessary to be stern with them. They must understand how vital it was to keep this under wraps. If anyone was to find out, I didn't want it to be from us.

'Come on, then. Let's get some more bubbles!'

And thus we went back to the lawns. Dusk was just beginning to approach, and the sun had gone down. The sky was still wonderfully blue, and the light across the lawn made everyone look summery and happy. Except Yarrington, who looked rather irked as he approached.

'Evening James. Ghastly affair, this! Christ, there really are some boring gits here. Thank God for the booze. Bugle around? Gone home has he?'

'I think he's still here,' I said, 'Yes, he must be – there's Cathy.'

'Quite right! Not sure how I managed to miss her!' he beamed. 'Naughty. Shouldn't say things like that. Very unkind... Well, I'm off. Sorry not have bumped into you before. Could've done with a laugh. I did see young Charlie Somers though. He seemed to be having some difficulty trying to chat up two women at once…' Yarrington trailed off as if he'd said too much.

'Yes, I know Charlie has his eye on Emily,' I said to make him at ease once more, 'It's quite all right by me, we're not emotionally involved.'

'Just sex, then?' he asked, casually, but not being able to suppress a smile.

'No! Nor physically involved! Emily is my friend, nothing more!'

'No need to get angry, James!'

'I'm not,' I sulked.

'Well, good night, then old chap!'

And he wandered off in the direction of Margaret and Cressida who were still chatting away together.

As the skies began to darken, the lawns emptied quickly. I had a slight sense of sadness that the party was almost over. Once people started to leave there was no sense in staying; attempting to prolong the evening would only result in the last stages being anticlimactic.

Among the throngs of people migrating towards one of the exits were Charlie, Felicity, Tim, Charlotte and Emily. I joined them, whereupon Charlie, with his arm around Felicity, announced that they were going via Chambers to pick up some papers for the morning, but his wink to me made me wonder what exactly his intentions were. I hoped that Emily hadn't seen it.

I said to Felicity, 'Well, it was lovely to meet you; I'm sorry we didn't have more of an opportunity to chat,' and immediately begun to think about how daft these social events were. One turns up expectantly; but expecting what? One is well aware the whole place will be full of stuffy members of the Bar, pretentious twits from the city, and one's adversaries. Introductions are made with none of the parties having any intention to get to know one another; indeed, the first opening when it might be polite to excuse oneself is a glorious moment: it is a chance to escape the crowd whose introductions you have just completed; the hope of meeting someone new and exciting takes hold for a few seconds until one is drawn into another tedious discourse. And then at the end of the evening, having successfully avoided the people introduced at the beginning, one is forced to say goodbye to them all, saying what a shame it is that you haven't had time to chat, while breathing a huge sigh of relief that a taxi awaits. No, to enjoy the Garden Party, one must arrive and leave with well-established friends.

And thus departed Charlie and Felicity to their Chambers. Poor Emily looked miserable at the sight of them walking off, and I reached for her hand and squeezed it to try and comfort her. She gave me a sad smile in return.

We wandered off towards Chancery Lane and two taxis conveniently rolled up; the cabbies obviously knew about the garden party and that there would be lots of well-lubricated and wealthy lawyers wanting to get home to the more salubrious areas of London Town.

'I am sorry that your dress made such a close acquaintance with the lawns of Lincoln's Inn,' I said to Charlotte, having kissed her goodbye, 'I hope the mess thereby caused comes out in the wash!'

Charlotte scowled, 'Good night, James!'

'Good night, Charlotte!'

'Tim! Assist me into this taxi!'

'Yes darling,' said Tim, jumping to open the door.

And so the happy pair drove off, leaving Emily and I the second taxi, which we duly clambered into. Emily gave her address, with a nod in answer to my expression which asked if I could stay with her.

CHAPTER 28

Matters Progress

It always amazes me how something that tastes so good, and that seems so fresh and full of life and laughter can make one feel so horribly hungover the following morning. Emily and I agreed shortly after waking up that Champagne hangovers are the worst.

We had breakfast of orange juice and grapefruit, as if the goodness we believed was contained in these fruits would miraculously cure our headaches. It didn't.

Having descended the stairs from Emily's flat to her front door in a dishevelled and unshaven state, wearing yesterday's shirt, I opened the door and was blinded by the bright sunlight. Emily had wisely donned sunglasses and stepped out behind me a couple of seconds later having picked up her morning's post. She opened one letter quickly, and began smiling for the first time since the previous evening.

'What?' I asked sulkily, quite angry that she could be happy about anything in her current state.

'I have two tickets for the opening evening of the Summer Exhibition.' she announced.

'Why are you so happy about that?' I asked.

'Do you want to come?' she asked, ignoring my question.

'No, it's the kind of place where they might hang the kind of monstrosity that you might paint.'

'Shut up, James! They *are* hanging one of my paintings!'

'Congratulations!' I said, just about managing to raise a smile. But it was tremendous news: she had been entering paintings for a place in the Royal Academy of Art's Summer Exhibition since before I had known her and this was her first success. 'That's brilliant!' I continued to encourage her. 'I would suggest we go for a Champagne breakfast at the Ritz to celebrate, but perhaps we could do that tomorrow?' I gave her a congratulatory hug instead.

'Oh, I'm so pleased! I was beginning to think if I didn't get this picture in, my painting career would fail before it got off the ground.'

'No doubt this will be the catastrophic launch!' I said.

'I hope so.'

'So do I,' I agreed, squeezing her hand. 'Of course I should like to go with you.'

We stumbled through the morning, slept through the afternoon and by the time of the June partner's meeting I was in a relatively normal frame of mind.

The agenda of the meeting had only one point of discussion listed: George Teddy.

Teddy was not there.

All the other partners were.

'Right, looks as if everyone who's coming is already here,' said Bugle, 'so I will begin. No doubt you have noted the main point to be resolved in this meeting.' I wondered how it was possible to resolve a person. 'It is with regret,' continued Bugle, 'that I raise this problem.' Paul and Martin, the noxious company conspirators, smirked at each other but I mused upon the fact that I had never considered Teddy to be a problem. 'But I think we all know that Teddy's heart is no longer in the law...' This was regrettably an unarguable point. '...and that he doesn't even make enough money to cover his overheads, let alone any right he has to the partnership profit...' Again, true. '...and so, depending on what you all think, I propose to ask Teddy to consider resigning, unless of course his billing figures improve substantially in the next few months.'

We all knew this would be almost impossible for Teddy to achieve.

'I think the best way to do it is a democratic vote as to whether we think this is the best course of action,' continued Bugle.

'But what happens if you ask him and he decides against the idea?' I asked.

'Then I shall ask him to leave. So, to make it even fairer, shall we have a democratic vote upon whether we think we should have a democratic vote upon whether it is my duty for the good of the Firm to ask Teddy to consider retirement?'

There were a few nods and Bugle seized his chance: 'Right, please raise your hand if you think a democratic vote should be made upon whether I have a word to Teddy about this?'

Everyone except Yarrington and I raised their hands.

'Almost unanimous. And so we have established that a show of hands is indeed the fair way of deciding upon Teddy's future, who thinks that I should I ask him whether he will consider retirement?'

Bugle's hand went up before he had finished talking. Paul and Martin's hands went up as soon as Bugle had finished talking. And one by one the hands of the other partners began to show themselves. The order in which they went up was roughly the order in which I would place their levels of probity, but even the partners I liked and respected were agreeing: it is amazing how the thought of a slight increase in the share of the Firm's profit can decide people's minds. Even Margaret who despite her formidable persona is a kind and considerate woman, tentatively raised her arm. After a time, again only Yarrington and I sat with our arms grumpily folded like bolshy schoolboys.

'Again, the decision is almost unanimous,' said Bugle. And indeed it was: of the now sixteen partners, only two had remained faithful to Teddy, the longest standing partner aside from the Founding Fathers. 'The dissenters, of whose identity I am not surprised, will be noted for the record. If Teddy does decide to retire early,' said Bugle, as if the choice did in fact lie with Teddy, 'I will of course give him three months to wind up his affairs and current caseload, which under the circumstances, is probably eleven weeks more than he needs.'

And so, in two swift votes taken in less than five minutes, Teddy's fate was sealed.

And there apparently being no other business of import, Bugle wound up the meeting and strutted out of the Dining Room looking rather pleased with himself. A few partners could be heard mumbling about regret and what a shame it was that he had to go shortly before he retired of his own accord, but their words held no weight with me: why hadn't they voted for him, not agin?

The other partners filed out guiltily.

'I can't believe this,' I said to Yarrington, who was still sitting at the Dining Table.

'Can't you?'

'It was only a figure of speech.'

He smiled ruefully.

'Thing is, James, the case is unanswerable. He hasn't really earned anything for a few years, and we can't keep him for the hell of it.'

'I know; it just seems a shame.'

'It is. A great shame. But that's life. Chin up, old chap,' he said, and walked out sadly.

I suppose there was little else to say.

'What have we on today Emily?'

'You have a new client, at ten. A Miss Katherine Hunt; then at six of the clock we depart for the Summer Exhibition.'

'Excellent: a splendid day in the making! Do we know anything about this Miss Hunt?'

'Yes. She's called Katherine Hunt.'

At ten my phone rang and Sue told me that said client was in reception. Matthew followed me through to see a stunning thirty-something brunette look up from today's *Times*.

'Miss Hunt?'

Indeed it was. The lovely Miss Hunt.

We exchanged greetings.

'Polly Fischer...' she said, '...oh you would have known her as Polly Hubert... recommended you. She said you were a great lawyer and a fantastic support throughout the whole thing.'

Polly Hubert was a bloody nightmare. She had hired my services to remove herself from her marriage the year before, and every time she phoned me I had lost my patience with her. If she thought me supportive, then my client-pleasing bullshit must be much more satisfactory than I had previously thought. Polly had the good-fortune to marry a wealthy stockbroker (I achieved a pretty decent settlement for a three-year marriage) and then fall in love with a carpenter who had what it took to keep her nymphomaniacal sexual desires under control. I don't remember the carpenter's name as Fischer, though.

'Oh yes, Polly. How is she?'

'She's happy at the moment, I think, but I'm not sure how long it'll last.'

'She's married again?'

'Oh, yes!'

Splendid, I thought. It's not often in my line of work that one has the same client twice, but one hopes that those who cannot remain married to the same spouse may at least have a rather longer relationship with their solicitor.

Katherine Hunt, or Kate as she preferred, wanted divorce after only eleven months of marriage. She had been the girlfriend of her husband for eleven years and taking the vows of holy matrimony, like so many cases I had seen, had sunk their relationship. She was a violinist, he an investment banker. My suspicions over some form of monetary basis for the beginnings of marital unrest were confirmed when she had raised the question of becoming joint owner of his not insubstantial pad in Wimbledon and he had declined to acquiesce most vehemently. From there, things went from bad to worse as he complained that she was just after his money. He began to distance himself from her, while decreasing the distance between himself and his secretary to such an extent that she became pregnant with his child. I explained that very short marriages generally meant the parties took out what riches they brought into the marriage and that all those years of unmarried cohabitation meant nothing in the eyes of the law, but that English courts were still wife friendly and that she could expect some capital from her husband in a divorce settlement. Being devoted, Kate was inexperienced in everything other than fiddle playing, but had not as yet convinced enough critics that her talent was such that she could make a decent living from it. In fact she earned less than enough to feed herself, let alone provide housing, he having supported her financially throughout their relationship.

'The thing is,' she said, 'I'm not sure how I'll pay you.' And she leant forward putting her head in her hands and looking rather sad. 'Of course, your advice seems to have been great, and I'll use your firm again, and recommend you to others... is there some way you could try hard to keep the costs down?'

I dislike turning down clients who have been recommended to me for fear that bad press may start to circulate about my mercenary tendencies, but more importantly, I dislike turning away clients because of their financial situation; it seems grossly unfair, and Kate was in a particularly grim situation.

'I'm sure we can come to some arrangement.' I promised.

We discussed how to proceed, and I even let Matthew talk Kate through how one goes about obtaining a divorce, and the procedure thereafter.

Under the circumstances, she left a reasonably happy client and I was pleased to be able to help her with her miserable situation. As I said goodbye to Kate Hunt, my pleasure diminished somewhat as I noticed Mrs Ricketts sitting in reception.

'James!' she barked as I attempted to reach the safety of my office without her seeing me.

'Mrs Ricketts! Good afternoon!' I said. 'Have you time for a coffee?'

'Yes, I expect so, dear.'

We adjourned to a meeting room and made ourselves comfortable, steaming cups of caffeine in hand.

'Well, this is a pleasant surprise!' I said. 'May I enquire what special occasion has brought you into the office?'

'You may,' said Mrs Ricketts, with intent to be fastidious. 'I want to discuss my granddaughter with you.'

Not having spoken to Mrs Ricketts since I had met Sara, and having seen Sara twice since our initial meeting at the Architect's Ball, I had almost forgotten that she was indeed the granddaughter of the mad Ricketts woman.

'In what context?' I asked, rather concerned.

'You know damn well what context!' she said. 'Well, James, do you like my granddaughter?'

What was I to say? Admit that I found Sara beautiful? Admit that my feelings for her seemed to grow every time I saw her? Admit that I had praised a god (in whom my belief was non-existent) that she was less eccentric than her elderly relations? Admit that I was pleased her fiancé was dead?

'I like her very much,' I said, trying the most politically correct and ambiguous phrase my mind mustered at that moment.

'She's very beautiful, isn't she?' asked Mrs Ricketts, which struck me as rather below the belt.

'Rather!' I said in the old fashioned way, which I knew would amuse the old bird. 'Yes, she's lovely,' I followed up more cautiously as Mrs Ricketts' expression didn't change.

'Why haven't you taken her out recently?'

'We went to the Opera not so long ago,' I said, beginning to get nervous that Mrs Ricketts was angry about my advances on her granddaughter. But, I reflected, Mrs Ricketts and Sara had between them done all the chasing: the ball had been arranged for me; yes, I had taken Sara out for dinner, but it was spontaneous and by way of thanks for the ball; Sara had asked me to the opera, and Sara had kissed me after the opera. I had been gallant throughout and was innocent of indecent behaviour.

'Yes, yes, the opera was weeks ago!' said Mrs Ricketts. It wasn't that many weeks ago I thought. 'I was on the blower with Sara last night and she was wondering why you hadn't been in touch since.'

'Well... no reason, really... I have been very busy at work...'

'James James!' she said, which was the first time she had addressed me in such a way, 'We both know that you don't do a moment's work after half past five – not that I'm criticising you for that – I hate this busy world in which we live and you're quite right to enjoy yourself – but do not use work as an excuse! So – more to the point – are you going to ask her out in the foreseeable future?'

What did the woman want with me? Why had she entered my offices and why was she probing me so deeply about Sara? Why did she appear to be so vehemently against me having anything to do with Sara while her words strangely encouraged me to propose a further date?

'I should like to see her again,' I said, concluding that truth was the best option.

'As I thought!' said a triumphant Mrs Ricketts. 'In that case I shall have to sack you as my lawyer!' she said, with as much passion.

I regretted my previous conclusion.

'I don't see what your granddaughter has to do with my professional ability,' I protested.

'She has nothing to do with your professional ability.'

That was it. Mrs Ricketts had decided my fate, and protestations or excuses wouldn't wash with her. I could see her preparing to speak again, and I wondered what blow she would now deal to my already winded body.

'But, presumably being versed in at the least the basics of legal knowledge you will know that a solicitor cannot act for clients in whom he has a personal interest.'

'Actually, I was more interested in your granddaughter,' I said, not really caring about my choice of words.

'Exactly! And she benefits under my will and furthermore is the beneficiary of a not insubstantial trust fund to include any future spouses. You should know: you set it up! If you married her, things would not look so promising from a legal perspective! And so you see I have no option but to sack you. It is a shame, James, but more fun to be part of the Ricketts family than to serve the them on a professional basis!'

And all became clear; the mad old bat was trying to marry off her granddaughters to eligible bachelors, and what a splendid job she was doing: there were none more eligible than I! We were smiling at each other, both amused by the situation.

'Well,' I said, 'I'd better ask out Sara as soon as she is able to accompany me!'

'Yes, you had, dear.'

Mrs Ricketts decided that Tim, at my recommendation, should be her new solicitor. Then she progressed to matters of greater import such as her dying cat, who (praise be to God) was now eating smoked salmon again. Lastly, she asked how long it had been since she had reconsidered her will. She concluded that it had been long enough, and changes would be needed ere long. She left, shaking my hand, and with a wicked smile said: 'I *knew* you and Sara would get on!' and as I smiled back she shook my hand away and said, 'Well! Get on with it, man! Ring her!' and with that, she left.

CHAPTER 29

Emily's First Hanging

Shortly after, having forgotten to telephone Sara due to the excitement of the clock striking half past five, Emily and I left the office together and headed for the Summer Exhibition.

Walking past The Pub, we saw Teddy sitting in the window, shoulders hunched and looking rather glum.

'Can we invite Teddy to the Summer Exhibition?' I asked quickly.

Emily looked at me quizzically, knowing I knew something that she didn't. 'Well, my ticket only allows for two,' she said.

'I'm sure we'll get him in. Would you mind?'

She shrugged in agreement and I dived into The Pub.

'Bugle had his little chat with me this afternoon,' he said as soon as he saw me.

'I feared so. What did you say?'

'What could I say? I have three months left. It does seem rather bad form, given that I'm sixty-five in eighteen months. Loyalty to one's firm and colleagues seems to count for nothing these days. I find hard it to comprehend how even Bugle voted for my ousting; must everything be about greed and money? The worst of it is that Miss Pound – my lady friend who you met at the Opera – said she doesn't want to be associated with an old lawyer forced into retirement. Things were going so well, too.'

'Sounds like you'd be well enough without her,' I said to encourage him.

'At my age, company is hard to come by, James.'

It was hard to disagree with this, and I regretted my last comment. 'Well, Emily and I are just off to the Summer Exhibition. Do you fancy joining us? Emily wants to show off her masterpiece which they have hung!'

'No, you go. You don't want me coming,'

'Actually, I do.' I said.

'No, really, I'll be fine.'

'Are you sure?'

'Quite sure.'

We said goodbye and I turned to go, aware that Emily was waiting outside.

'James?' said Teddy.

'Yes?'

'I gather only you and Yarrington voted for me to stay. Thanks.'

His smile was warm and affectionate, and I caught a twinkle in his eye, despite his sadness. No one had ever thanked me so simply, but with so much genuine gratitude behind one tiny word, that my eyes began to well up. The words required to tell him this eluded me, but I smiled in the hope that he might understand.

'What was that about?' asked Emily when I had rejoined her outside.

'The partners decided it was time Teddy got the shove, and he found out today.'

'Bloody hell! That's awful,' she said.

'Bloody awful. Poor chap.'

'I hope you didn't decide that!' said Emily sharply.

'Yarrington and I alone dissented.'

She smiled in fondness for me.

The beauty about the location of the offices of Bugle & Yarrington is that they are well placed for after-work outings, and Emily and I soon found ourselves at the Royal Academy of Arts at Burlington House on Piccadilly. I love the courtyard surrounded by the various learned societies, one of which I frequented for the use of its library in my non-legal undergraduate days. We entered and Emily immediately set about looking for her painting, me following her like a puppy dog, but not minding knowing that previous experience in art exhibitions has told me that my eyes are particularly adept at taking in large quantities of art at once, my brain quickly dismissing most of what my eyes see as wasted canvas. As Emily searched for her painting, I took in the rest of the exhibition as we traipsed through the Central Hall, Galleries VI to II and into the Weston Room.

Eventually we found the damn thing in the Small Weston Room, crammed full of the paintings of the lesser known or unknown. Had Emily bothered to look at the index of exhibitors, she would have found the location instantly, and a perusal of the layout plan of the

Academy would have taken us straight there, but she said she enjoyed the anticipation. I suspect she knew exactly where it would be hanging anyway.

Thankfully, Emily's larger than average painting hung at eye level in the middle of one wall, and as a result, was attracting more attention than most of the paintings. Some were hung so high up, one would need to have been built as Goliath to have a chance of seeing them without a stepladder. A group of pretentious arty types were talking absolute gibberish about various paintings: how the colours juxtapose the subject matter in this painting, and how one can see into the mind of the artist and understand his feelings in that painting. But when it came to Emily's painting, the comments were more sensible, and included compliments on the style and her skill as a painter. One person even proclaimed they preferred it to any other in the room, to which there was more than one agreement.

The artist looked on with pride.

I looked on rather more dubiously: one of the more vocal critics had two paintbrushes in his top shirt pocket as if he might whip them out at any moment in order to create a masterpiece. It could only have been a pretentious affectation.

When the throng of vocal twits finally dispersed, we sidled into their place and stared at the work. It was like most of her paintings: it was true that she had undoubted talent and was capable of technical excellence, but nevertheless the end result was entirely without aesthetic pleasure.

'It's really painted very well,' I said.

'You don't have to pretend you like it, James. I'm not expecting your artistic side to suddenly come out, if you have one, which I doubt.'

'How dare you! I am well known to have one of the most critical artistic eyes in London Town!'

'Shut up James.'

We looked at the canvas adulterated with unremarkable daubs for a few moments before the room filled up again and we were obliged to move. Shuffling to one side, I overheard a fellow who looked shabby enough to be a well-renowned artist say to his companion, 'Of course it's the ones that sell on the first night that you have to watch out for; they'll be the really good artists whose work will not go unnoticed in the future.'

And then I began to take an interest in the little red spots denoting sales. There were very few – it had been open only for a matter of hours

– but from what I could discern, they were indeed on the very best of the paintings. Emily's bore no such red dot, and I thought she might be disappointed. An idea began to form in my mind, but how would I get rid of Emily for long enough to do the deed?

As soon as one group of artisans with whom Emily had been chatting discovered that she was one of the exhibiting artists, there was great excitement, followed by a great big discourse, followed by them all gazing on the wasted canvases that liberally adorned the gallery.

Despite quaffing a certain amount of bubbly from flutes nigh on nine inches tall, gobbling a selection of canapés passed round by waitresses in short skirts, and glancing at some of the country's finest contemporary art, my boredom levels had risen to an unacceptably high level, and I began to suspect that Emily was right: my artistic side was well and truly locked up somewhere beyond my reach. But she looked as if she had had enough too, and I suggested we leave, to which she instantly agreed, apparently glad to be rid of her new admirers.

We departed the exhibition, but before we quit the building, Emily said she needed the loo; here was my opportunity.

She departed in the direction of the ladies and I raced back upstairs to the exhibition, ignoring cries of 'Can I see your ticket, sir?' from the irksome youth on the door. I tried in vain to find anyone looking remotely official, and left again through the entrance door, apologising to the youth and explaining my predicament. He pointed wearily to the desk in front of the entrance emblazed with the large words 'Sales Desk'.

A bespectacled and bored-looking girl looked up at me.

'Good evening, sir. May I help?'

'Yes please. I have about one minute to buy a painting.'

'I see. Could I have the paintings number?'

Emily had the index book. I couldn't face battling through the crowds again to find the number of *Canvas Adulterated With Unremarkable Daubs* by Emily Lewis. My look must have said it all as the girl produced an index book with a somewhat tired look.

'Yes, it's Number 405,' I said finding the entry, 'I should've remembered that.'

She didn't enquire why that number stood out in my memory and instead checked her list of sales.

'I'm afraid it's been sold already, sir.'

'No, it can't have been. There was no red dot. It's by Emily Lewis.

Did you get the number right?'

'Yes, sir, I checked that number.' She said, in a slightly bored way without re-checking her list.

'Would you mind awfully re-checking?' I said, 'I really do need to buy it.'

She rolled her eyes, and scanned her list again. Her eye-rolling made me a little cross.

'As I said, Number 405 by Emily Lewis has already been sold, sir.'

'Bugger.'

She looked at me snootily.

'Thanking you,' I said, and stalked off.

Then it struck me: I should be glad some other person had bought it: first, I didn't want to spend the prohibitive amount required to secure a painting in which I found no enjoyment beholding; second, and as a result of the first, I didn't want said painting using up precious wall-space in my flat; and third, it meant someone, presumably with more knowledge of the art world than me, thought the painting had some merit.

'Where have you been?' asked Emily as I descended the stairs into the entrance hall.

'I was just seeing if your painting had been sold before we left,' I said, truthfully enough, although Emily immediately raised a suspicious look.

'I suspect I'll be collecting it at the end of the exhibition!' she laughed.

'Don't be so hard on yourself. Just because I think it's a ghastly creation doesn't necessarily mean it is. In fact, you'll be pleased to know that someone, albeit with a rather poor taste in pictures has already bought it!'

'James! You didn't?!'

It was just as well I hadn't, because I could truthfully claim: 'No! I didn't! I told you that someone with a rather poor taste in art has purchased it!'

'Are you serious?' she asked, frowning.

'Deadly. Go and ask.'

And she did; clearly I couldn't be believed. But she came back beaming.

'The woman said that was the third request to buy this evening!' she said, clearly surprised, and chuffed.

I didn't point out that the purchaser, myself and her made three.

'I wouldn't wind you up about that!' I said, 'Well done!'

And being on Piccadilly, not so far from a salubrious bar, we crossed the road and celebrated with one final and almost bankrupting glass of bubbly at the Ritz.

Next morning in the office, Emily was still in a buoyant mood when Sue rang to announce that Charlie Somers was in reception to see me.

'Morning Charlie. Your practice got so bad that you want to become a lowly solicitor?' I quipped.

'Don't be daft; once at the bar, one can never consider the possibilities of solicitation. Can we have a quick word? Man to man, as it were.'

'Certainly,' I said, ushering him through to a meeting room.

'Right. I've made a bit of a cock-up. Thing is, I seem to have a made a terrible mistake.'

'I'm not sure that my legal knowledge is superior to yours,' I said doubtfully, 'and therefore I'm not so sure if I'll be of any use.'

'No, no! It's not *legal*! I wouldn't have come to you about a *legal* matter! But you do know a thing or two about women. I'm not suggesting your knowledge or experience is as good as mine, and in fact, if I had to, I would suggest quite the opposite is true, but your knowledge of a particular woman is greater than mine, and that's what I need your advice about. You may remember at the Lincoln's Inn Garden Party that my attentions focused on a certain Felicity Warburton-Lee...'

'Yes, I do remember that, if not much else after... but I don't know her...'

'Let me finish...'

'Sorry...' I said, mocking his earnest expression.

'Yes, that's the mistake. She's a great girl. Very bright – very attractive – but the thing is, I can't stop thinking about someone else – even when I'm in bed and Flick's on top.'

'Christ! That is an awful muddle. You haven't blurted out the wrong name have you?'

'Lord no! I never blurt out names so as never to fall foul of the most elementary love-making mistake.'

'Quite right.'

'And I've got to the point where I think the only way forward is to ask out this other girl.'

'Sounds logical.'

'I've already told Flick that we can't carry on, being in the same Chambers and all.'

'Very wise. How did she take it?'

'Not too good, but it's to be expected.'

'Yes, indeed.'

'But I'm worried about asking the other one out.'

'That's not like you, Charlie.'

'No.'

The conversation was taking too long to get the crux of the matter.

'Well, for God's sake, man! Tell me who the lucky girl is!'

'Well it's not that easy...' he said, looking positively worried. 'I think you may have romantic attachments to her, but I'm sure she's interested in me.'

At this, my latent butterfly aroused itself with remarkable rapidity deep in my stomach. Charlie and I had never had this problem before. I wondered how on earth he had met Sara and I kicked myself for not ringing her yesterday to ensure my superiority in the apparent contest.

'How on earth did you meet her?' I asked, which caused some puzzlement in Charlie.

'Well, I've not *met* her, in the between-the-sheets sense!' he said, which caused me some puzzlement. 'Tim reckons I shouldn't be having this conversation with you.'

'I'm glad you are!' I said, beginning to get rather worried about the whole situation. 'Can you just tell me what's happened, and what you plan to do.'

'Well, since Lincoln's Inn, I can't get her out of my head... and I suppose I wanted to know if you'd be okay with me asking her out.'

'Well I was rather hoping of getting in there myself, I have to admit.'

'Even though she's your secretary?' said Charlie, I think genuinely surprised.

'Emily?!'

'...Yes...'

'Thank goodness for that! I thought you had met the one *I* was after!'

'You're not after Emily?'

'Christ, no!'

'Oh, that's good... You sure?'

'Yes!'

'Mind if I ask her out, then?'

'Of course not!'

'Cheers, James. Bloody hell, I was worried,' he said, the relief spreading across his face as he realised from my genuine laughter and body language that he really didn't have anything to worry about.

'Right, that's that sorted out. I thought you were talking about Sara, the architect I told you about. I thought it'd be just my luck if you'd met her too, but I did wonder how on earth you could have bumped into her.'

'You're very egotistical, James!'

'Yes, I suppose I was, just then...'

The conversation having been concluded favourably in Charlie's favour, he was now set to leave.

'Cheers, James! You've made my day!'

And with that Charlie shook my hand and departed, with much more of a bounce in his step than when he had arrived.

CHAPTER 30

Dating Games

'What did Charlie want?' asked Emily.

'Oh, just some advice.'

'From you?'

'Very funny.'

Matthew then bombarded me with questions about some work I had given him and having answered his queries, and being somewhat behind myself, I resolved to work hard until lunchtime to clear my decks.

A couple of hours later, Emily's phone rang.

'Hello? Yes… Yes…' she said, blushing, 'I'd love to! … I look forward to it … Yes … Yes … Bye …'

'What are you looking so pleased about?' I asked.

'Charlie Somers just asked me out for dinner, and I accepted.'

I noticed Matthew look up quickly, and then put his head back down, pretending to be at work and oblivious to the conversation.

'Great! He said things weren't working out with that barrister, Felicity,' I added usefully.

'I'm glad!' she smiled.

Emily looked rather too smug for my liking and I picked up the phone and dialled. It was answered quickly, catching me by surprise; in my haste, I hadn't constructed a battle plan, so I just dived in, letting everyone in the room know exactly what I was doing.

'Hi Sara, it's James … I'm well, thanks, and you? … Good … Yes, it has been a while … Busy at work … Well, do you want to have dinner sometime, sooner rather than later? … Splendid! … Yes, sounds good … See you then … Bye.'

Emily looked cross, but I knew she couldn't say anything.

'Well, I have a date with Sara, so we're both in luck!'

'Great!' she said, 'When are you doing it?'

'Friday.'

'Me too! Where are you going?'

'I'm not telling you!'

'Well, we're going to that gorgeous restaurant just off the King's Road where your sister had her last birthday, so I suggest you don't go there!' she said, which irked me tremendously because that was the very place I wanted to take Sara. I had introduced both Charlie and Emily to the place, and now they were stealing my restaurant.

It had been odd thinking that Emily and Charlie, two of my closest friends, were going out together, but those thoughts evaporated like Saharan rain when I saw Sara. She looked wonderful, and when she saw me, her smile was one of genuine joy. I knew it would remain ingrained in my memory for a long time to come. When she kissed me, almost on the lips as she had done after the *Magic Flute*, similar thoughts ran through my head.

We had gone to a restaurant of her choice on Charlotte Street in Fitzrovia, the home of many fine eateries and drinking establishments where I had spent many an hour while supposedly at lectures at the nearby College of Law. I hadn't been there for some time in an effort to forget the dark days of law school, and found myself pleasantly surprised that I was pleased to be back.

We had a very fine meal, accompanied by a quality bottle of wine and conversation which apparently flowed more easily than the wine: to my amazement the first bottle lasted until we had finished the main course, whereupon another bottle followed to ease further dialogue between us. I obtained that wonderful feeling of having drunk a lot, but having eaten so much, that the feeling of drunkenness is allayed by the food. We had talked about law, architecture, Charlie, Emily, Mrs Ricketts and the rest of her family, our respective universities and undergraduate days, and numerous other topics when there was a slight gap in the conversation. I could see Sara thinking deeply about something, and just watched her thinking: she looked perfect. But as I watched, I noticed a change in her countenance, and, although perceptible only because I had been staring at her for so long, her beauty faded by a tiny degree as a troubled look spread across her face.

'What's the matter?' I asked.

She looked up at me, smiling almost regretfully, and opened her mouth to speak.

But nothing came out.

I didn't say anything; I could see her mind at work.

She opened her mouth again, and paused, before saying, 'I feel terribly guilty about saying this... and I don't know why I'm even thinking of telling you, but it's how I feel, and I think... I *think*... you should probably know.'

She paused again, and I waited, intrigued but not worried about what she might say.

'I'm not sad Simon is dead, because I wouldn't have met you if he were alive.'

I honestly didn't know what to say.

No one had ever given me a compliment – I supposed it was a compliment – quite that deep or with such meaning before, and I felt stunned.

She was staring at me, perhaps waiting for a reaction, but all I could do was smile in acknowledgement, but also sadly for her.

Thankfully, she broke the silence.

'I'm sorry; that was quite heavy,' she said, breaking into an easier smile.

'Yes...' I agreed, still not knowing what to say.

She reached across the table with her hands, and held them open for mine. The hairs on the back of my neck stood up as I placed them in hers, and I noticed that she was no longer wearing her engagement ring.

'How did he die?'

She didn't say anything.

'Sorry, don't talk about it if you don't want to.'

'No, it's fine. He was in the Navy – in the air-sea rescue – based at Culdrose in Cornwall. Do you remember the storms last November, when all those ships went to pieces on the Lizard?' I nodded in agreement. 'He was dropped out of a helicopter and was helping the crew of that huge container ship that broke up off the Scillies. He got all the crew winched up, but the weather was so bad, the pilot couldn't keep the helicopter steady enough to get him back on board. Eventually it was running so low on fuel it had to go, and by the time the replacement helicopter got there, both the ship and he had gone.'

I had never felt so humbled; here was a greater man than I.

He had risked and given his life for others, and the odds had been against him. What had I risked for others, even with the odds in my favour?

'That must have been terrible,' I said, lamely.

'Yes, it was.'

And then, clearly wanting to lighten things up a bit, Sara let go of my hands, and leaned away from me asking, 'Shall we get a coffee?'

'Yes, splendid idea,' I said, looking around for a member of the waiting staff.

'Shall we have one at your flat? It's not far.'

'Even better!'

We paid, and I somewhat gratuitously hailed a taxi; the walk was only fifteen minutes, but under the circumstances, the requirement for speed outweighed financial considerations. Three minutes later we were ascending my stairs and three minutes after that the kettle had boiled. We collapsed on the sofa, tired after consuming too much food and drink.

The coffee soon picked us up, and we chatted merrily, draining the cafetière rapidly. I couldn't believe it when I glanced at Sara's watch and read the time as two o'clock. She saw me look and checked the time herself. And the fact that we suddenly both knew how late it was made us both sleepy at once; it is curious how the man-made divisions of time so rule our lives. But once our minds connected two in the morning with sleep, there was little we could apparently do to alleviate our sudden tiredness, and we both nodded in agreement to the unasked question of whether we should go to bed.

I went into my bedroom to collect the blanket necessary for a night on the sofa, and had just extracted it from my wardrobe, when I noticed Sara at the door. She shot me another magnificent smile and crossed the room with as much grace as lithely speed, threw the blanket to the floor and began kissing me with a surprising passion. Her momentum was such that I found myself retreating towards the bed until the back of my knees found the edge of it, whereupon we both fell into the horizontal, her on top. All feelings of tiredness vanished as adrenaline, and, no doubt, other hormones began rushing through my veins. I realised as she began to unbuckle my belt that what I had begun to long for during the course of the evening was now inevitable.

CHAPTER 31

Saturday

Waking up with Sara in my bed made me smile even before I had seen her beautiful and contented sleeping face.

When she had woken, we made love again which put a smile on my face for the rest of the day. And it was a good day. This June had been kind, and despite one or two exceptions, the run of hot and cloudless weather looked set to continue. We arose hungry, having expanded our stomachs the preceding evening, and marched straight to a café on Marylebone High Street. I felt fantastic, and wanted everyone to look at the beauty I had on my arm.

All considerations of appetite disappeared after a satisfactory English breakfast. We walked all the way up past London Zoo where we saw the curious looking emus looking curiously over their ticking electric fence. We crossed Saint Mark's Bridge over the Grand Union Canal and wandered up Primrose Hill, collapsing on a spot with a good view of London spread out to the south, and far enough away from other people to lie and kiss each other without causing offence.

The afternoon vanished in each other's arms, and we returned to civilisation after our exploration of the wilds of the park. It being a pleasant evening, we had a gin and tonic at six o'clock outside my favourite pub on Marylebone High Street. While the allure of asking Sara to stay with me that night was strong, neither of us brought it up. And I was looking forward to saying goodbye to her, despite knowing I'd feel lonely the moment she left my sight, and despite knowing I'd miss having my smiles returned by this most beautiful of creatures. Being in the company of a new lover who you want to see again is wonderful, but also tiring, and being such new lovers, and having spent twenty four hours with her, few of which were sleep, I felt the need to re-group.

After the drink we bid farewell quickly with no talk of whether to see each other again; this had been decided long before. I watched her magnificent bottom slink down the High Street away from me, and

I suddenly realised with a pang of hunger that in my clearly rather unbalanced state, my stomach had made the unprecedented mistake of failing to tell me to have lunch.

CHAPTER 32

Sunday

On Sunday morning I was rudely awoken by my telephone.

'Oh, hello, gorgeous,' I said sleepily as Emily greeted me. She had clearly been awake for longer than I.

'So how was Sara?' she asked.

'Magnificent.'

'Things going well, then?'

'Yes, very.'

'Oh, I am pleased.'

'How was Charlie?' I asked.

'Yes. Great. Really fun. He's so funny.'

'Good. Lunch?'

'Yes – normal place? – see you then. Byee!' she said, far too happily for the hour.

After what seemed like thirty seconds, but what was in fact fifty minutes, I was rudely awoken by my telephone for the second time.

'Morning!' said a bright and breezy Charlie.

'Morning, Charlie.'

'I woke you up didn't I?'

'Yes.'

'Damn, have you got someone there?'

'Not today.'

'What do you mean "not today"?'

'What do you think I mean, Charlie?'

'You got laid on Friday, then?'

'Yes.'

'You git.'

'You didn't then?'

'No.'

'I'm not surprised. Emily's very proper.'

'So what was she like?' asked the persistent Charlie.

'Magnificent.'

'Damn, it's not like you to use that word to describe a woman; she must have been on fire! Do you want to do lunch?' he asked.

'Sorry. I've got a date.'

'Ah, with your new girl?'

'No, with yours.'

Silence.

'Don't worry, Charlie!' I said. 'She is one of my best friends! We always have lunch on Sunday. Well, not always, but often.'

'Yes, I know. Sorry. Just sounded odd, that's all! Well, bugger it. If you and her are together, I'll have to phone another acquaintance!'

'Sorry Charlie.'

'No probs. Well, I'll leave you to sleep. Sounds like you need to catch up! See you on Wednesday for the hearing. Which one is it again?'

'Charlie! Haven't you read my brief? Matthew and I worked our socks off to get that to you by Friday!'

'No, I never the read brief more than twenty-four hours before the hearing. I find I can't remember a damn thing about it if I do!'

'It's the Frances Green case. Remember anything about it?'

'Ah! The angry chainsaw-wielding woman!'

'That's right.'

'You see! My memory hasn't been completely addled by booze!'

By midday I had prised myself from my bed, rather regretting having wasted the morning, and went to meet Emily at our usual Sunday lunching spot.

'Afternoon!'

We sat down and I told Emily, probably rather dreamily, about my evening and subsequent day in the park with Sara.

'You're falling for her, aren't you?'

'I think have already fallen.'

She put her hand on my arm and smiled happily for me. And then I asked her about Charlie. I had never imagined that she would be attracted to Charlie, and the way things were developing had surprised me; now I wanted some answers.

'Charlie's great. We have a good giggle together. He does make me laugh.'

'What do you talk about?'

'Oh, you know, the usual things…'

I waited.

'Oh, I can't remember, James! I haven't laughed so much for a long time, though.'

I waited again, but not expecting any further comments asked: 'So are you seeing him again?'

'Oh, yes, I expect so.'

And then Emily's face lit up, excitedly.

'What?' I asked.

'The buyer of my Summer Exhibition painting contacted me. He's the owner of a gallery somewhere in South Ken and he's hanging my painting in his new exhibition next month. He even wants to come over to my flat to see if I have a couple of other suitable pictures for the exhibition!'

'That's tremendous!'

'Yes. I was pleased to have sold the painting – I did wonder if you would turn out to be the buyer after your odd behaviour at the Exhibition – but a dealer buying it is even better!'

I smiled at her obvious enthusiasm and pride, and was happy for her.

We had a lovely lunch and happily wandered around the Marylebone High Street, window-shopping for clothes and food we didn't need, and I bought some books at Daunt to add to the pile of unread volumes on my bookshelves. Emily invited me to her flat for the afternoon – she wanted to finish a painting she thought might be suitable for the new exhibition – and she enjoyed company whilst ruining another perfectly good canvas. So to hers we went, and I collapsed on her cushions (being arty, her flat is furnished in a more bohemian manner than most) happily reading one of my recent acquisitions whilst she added a little more paint on *Canvas Adulterated By Unremarkable Daubs 2*, or whatever number of the series of paintings she had by then reached.

And so having spent a blissful Saturday with Sara, whose very name caused my heart to forget a beat, I spent Sunday afternoon contentedly with Emily, my best friend. It had been a good weekend.

CHAPTER 33

Pro Bono

On Monday morning Katherine Hunt telephoned.

'James, I'm really worried about how I'm going to be able to pay your fees.'

'I really do think you need a lawyer,' I said, for once unselfishly.

'But you are expensive.'

'Here's what we'll do. I'll take the case as far as the financial dispute resolution hearing on a pro bono basis, and depending on the outcome, we'll see how to take matters on after that.'

'Pro bono?'

'Free of charge.'

'That's so kind; I don't know how to thank you.'

'No thanks are required; it is my pleasure.'

'Well, actually, I could thank you in a small way by offering you a couple of tickets to see my quartet this Wednesday at the Wigmore Hall. Would you be interested?'

'You wouldn't happen to have four tickets would you?'

The opportunity for an outing with Sara, Charlie and Emily had presented itself.

'Yes, of course; it hasn't sold out, so the more the merrier!'

'Splendid! Thank *you* very much. I'd like to invite Charlie Somers, who is the barrister I use regularly for divorces. If you like him, we'll instruct him on your case. Don't let him chat you up, though – he has an insatiable appetite for flirting. But I hope to invite his new girlfriend too, so you should be all right!'

'Sounds entertaining! He'll get on well with Helen, our cellist. She seems to pick up a new man at each concert, whether or not there is a girlfriend present!'

'Oh dear! Thanks again, I look forward to it.'

'See you then – after the concert, probably. I hope you enjoy it.'

Four tickets duly arrived in the post on Tuesday morning, and my three guests all accepted the invitation. It had seemed like weeks since leaving Sara on Saturday evening, and my thoughts continually drifted towards my memories of her and my anticipation of seeing her again.

CHAPTER 34

Court And Quartets

Wednesday arrived: it was the day of the Wigmore Hall concert, but before that was Frances Green's financial dispute resolution, designed to bring monetary arrangements between the husband and wife to an end quickly and cheaply.

Each side comes to court with a settlement proposition – an offer for which they would be happy to settle – and the court considers how polarised they are, the lawyers arguing the merits of their client's respective cases. Whether a settlement is reached therefore depends on how reasonable, and willing to compromise the husband and wife are; it is they who must ultimately agree the settlement.

Angry, unreasonable and stubborn spouses do not agree, and failure to agree results in a final hearing where the judge decides how the assets are split. Lawyers thrive on drawn out battles: they attend two court hearings instead of one, billing their clients twice for the pleasure of their preparation and attendance; the clients spend double on legal fees, and any gain from the remnants of the marital assets directly furnishes the pockets and purses of the lawyers. The members of the judiciary who specialise in family cases adjudicate twice as many hearings, and this is good: more hearings polish their neurones and increases their knowledge of the subtle nuances of law; they must always be kept mentally busy lest their grey matter become dull and wearied. And so in reality, if the parties insist on a fight, financial matters are not resolved and one can only observe how the well-oiled English legal machine manages to perpetuate its work so magnificently.

We arrived at the Principal Registry of the Family Division on High Holborn with Matthew, in time-honoured tradition, carrying everything. These courts have a grand name, but the building is rather unpleasant, with modern, low-ceilinged courtrooms. The first person we saw was Cressida Smyth-Jones, who was with her trainee, an attractive girl whose presence made Matthew behave very oddly.

'Morning Cressida!'

'Morning, Mr James. This is my trainee, Jessica. Jessica, this is Mr James who I was telling you about, and I presume this charming fellow is your trainee, Matthew who I have heard so much about?'

I wasn't entirely sure how Cressida had heard so much about Matthew, but I introduced him nevertheless.

'Indeed, this is Matthew, the finest trainee I've ever had!'

'And, no doubt, your first?' asked the ever-astute Cressida.

The damned woman had scored thrice in quick succession.

'I hope you've sequestered your client's chainsaw, Mr James?'

'No, Cressida, that is hardly in my power! But I assure you, the only thing she has used it for since her passionate display of anger is chopping firewood.'

'Good, good. I'm sure whichever member of the judiciary we have today won't look particularly favourably on any more monkey-business.'

'I'm sure you're right, Cressida. And now, if you'll excuse me, I believe my counsel has arrived.'

'Ah! Mr Somers!' said Cressida. 'Of course! I could hardly have expected Mr James' client to be represented by anyone less fine than yourself! And you must excuse me too, gentlemen; my counsel has arrived also.'

In strode a confident Felicity Warburton-Lee.

'Christ!' said Charlie automatically as she walked up to our group.

'You know my counsel, Mr Somers?' asked Cressida.

'Intimately,' smirked Charlie, causing Felicity to blush whilst she gave Charlie a venomous look.

Cressida raised an eyebrow.

'They're in the same Chambers,' I said, stating the obvious in a feeble attempt to rectify Charlie's faux pas.

'Our clients will be here soon,' said Cressida, 'so we'd better part. For God's sake,' she continued, 'don't let on to the clients that we all know each other!'

'We don't *all* know each other,' I said.

Cressida gave Matthew a quizzical look and turned to depart, Jessica gave Matthew a smile and followed her, and Felicity pouted at Charlie and followed them both.

'What on earth was that all about?' asked Charlie when they had disappeared into the bowels of the building.

'Jessica is my girlfriend,' said Matthew.

It appeared the legal profession had become somewhat incestuous, but at least the husband had the all female legal team and the wife had the all male one; it never looked good when it was entirely boys versus girls.

A nervous Frances Green arrived, and the hearing time drew near. Before long we were in court. Charlie and Felicity put forward their respective client's settlement offers, and argued their cases. The judge didn't take kindly to my client's chainsaw antics, but was thankful she had purchased the husband a new bed after destroying the marital one. After a bit it became clear our expectations had been a little optimistic, and Felicity was doing an excellent job in convincing the judge that Trevor Green's needs in terms of financial support were much greater than we and his wife had believed them to be. By the end of the hearing, which had already been adjourned for discussion and negotiation twice, the offer of settlement that was being discussed was considerably nearer the husband's proposal than the wife's: things were going badly for us and I regretted having being so optimistic with Frances before the hearing. The day finished without a firm settlement being reached, but both parties were keen to continue negotiations in the hope to settle quickly, avoiding the cost of a prolonged argument and a final hearing.

Frances was rather down.

'I thought you said my proposal was good?' asked Frances. 'We're miles away from it now,' she said.

'I still believe your offer was good,' said Charlie. It's always better to make them more optimistic than you believe you can actually achieve, because no matter how realistic they are, the other party will have a settlement offer biased towards them. If you make yours fair to begin with, the result will be inequitable.'

'Despite the apparent shift in financial gain towards your husband, the judge clearly saw in your favour and you should be very happy with the outcome; I don't think we could have expected it go better,' I said, looking to Charlie for his obligatory agreement.

'Quite right. The negotiations over the next few days will conclude the outcome firmly in your favour,' said Charlie.

After the rather dubious outcome of the hearing, we let Frances depart alone so we could make arrangements regarding the forthcoming evening at the Wigmore Hall; it would never have done to inform the client about social arrangements between her highly professional legal team. Matthew and I set off for the office, him to drop off the papers, and me to pick up Emily. We agreed to meet shortly at a bar on St Christopher's Place to have a quick drink before the concert.

Emily and I arrived at the bar to find the not yet introduced Charlie and Sara sitting at adjacent tables, and Charlie doing all he could to attract her attentions. Thankfully, Emily was too deep in conversation with me to notice his flirtatious advances, and Sara, being remarkably attractive, had the inbuilt survivorship habit that most good-looking women have which allows them to avoid the glances of men.

As Emily and I approached, Sara and Charlie noticed us at the same time, Charlie quickly deducing his error as he noticed Sara smile at me, and communicating his apologies to me through a rare humble smile and particularly warm handshake. I acknowledged his apology with a wink, and my instant forgiveness made him relax once more. Introductions were made and we settled down.

'I'm sorry to talk shop,' said Emily, 'but before I forget, Mr Jones rang.'

Mr Jones was the wealthy city man with a particularly close relationship with his secretary, and whose final hearing was approaching in mid-July. This divorce promised to be most acrimonious, the beloved couple having by this stage developed a certain amount of hate for each other. Generally speaking, the wealthier the divorcee, the harder they fight for their share of the money; Mr Jones was especially wealthy and didn't mind paying my fees at all, as long as there was less for his wife to snatch, so I was relying on his case to contribute heavily to July's billing figures. All in all, it was a happy win-win situation.

'What did the charming fellow want?' I asked, winking at Charlie.

'He's managed to settle things with his wife. They had a meeting over the weekend.'

'You're kidding?'

'Afraid not.'

Mrs Jones had hardly spoken a word to her husband since she found him with his pants down and his secretary's skirt up. At the first hearing, she could hardly bear to be in the courtroom with him. Charlie and I had agreed that this was a profitable case that would almost certainly go all the way to final hearing. How they had sorted it out between them was a mystery and a serious blow to July's billing figures.

'Bugger,' said Charlie and I simultaneously.

'Surely it's a good thing?' asked Sara.

'Yes, for the client,' I said.

Sara clocked our trains of thought but said nothing, asking instead, 'Who won today?'

'We all did,' I said.

'Well done you. I suppose the client was pleased?'

'No, I meant all the lawyers won. Only the lawyers really win in a divorce. Each lawyer tells his own client they have taken the day, and each client goes away relatively happy in the knowledge that they did better than their spouse,' I explained.

And it's true: no one is a winner in divorce. One party may get a more favourable result: they may get a few thousand more than their spouse, or may see the kids for two extra weeks per annum, or walk away having secured possession of a precious heirloom, but they have ultimately lost, especially in lawyer's fees.

But today I had nevertheless told Frances that the result we had achieved was excellent; that Charlie, as always, had done a wonderful job; that the judge was obviously following the mainstream of the thinking of the judiciary and was wife friendly and how proper that was given the circumstances, and how husband friendly judges were usually those whose own wives had been less than faithful.

And I knew full well that Cressida, knowing her client would never speak to his wife about the court case, would have told Mr Green how well he'd done; how her Counsel had defeated Charlie's wildly optimistic arguments; that the judge was obviously bucking the trend of the modern judiciary and was thankfully very husband friendly and how lucky that had been. The psychology of the lawyers was failsafe.

'So I gather you're an artist?' Sara asked Emily, clearly unimpressed by my views on matrimonial law.

Charlie and I looked at each other, neither of us wishing to join in this conversation. We let the girls chat merrily away whilst we discussed matters of graver import such as our favourite brand of gin, how much we should charge Jones for the preparation that we had supposedly done for his case, and having enlightened Charlie about the dubious reputation of the cellist of Kate's trio, whether or not she would be attractive.

Since the girls were drinking more slowly than us due to their involved discussion about art, Charlie and I ordered another drink in order to dull any possible pain that might be caused by squeaking strings at the Wigmore Hall. Not being entirely au-fait with chamber music, or gaining a particular enjoyment from it, I have never thought that highly of the hallowed hall. I knew too that Charlie's enthusiasm was more for loud orchestras at the Albert Hall or Led Zeppelin. And on the few occasions I have visited his flat, even I have had my doubts about the blue-eyed, blonde-haired barrister as Wagnerian overtures have blasted from his speakers. Nevertheless, this was a prime opportunity to impress our lady-friends with our undoubted cultural interests, and if it proved to be awful, it'd only last an hour or two.

We arrived and settled into our seats, the girls between Charlie and I.

Sara commented on the beautiful proportions of the hall, and how the acoustics were reputedly the best in London for listening to chamber music. She said the architect had been Thomas Edward Collcut who had also designed the Savoy and Imperial College. Charlie and I listened with interest but our knowledge of physics was at best amateur; we could add little to her commentary on the best dimensions for a concert hall, apparently dependant on the frequencies of the sounds filling the room, and the reverberation time that would suit the music. We were reliably informed that reverberation times of one-and-a-half to two seconds were most suited to concert and opera halls, but that here, for Chamber music, the time would be more like a second to cater for the smaller sounds encountered.

Just as Sara drew her discourse on hertz and the volume of the room to an end, the musicians walked on stage. I hardly recognised Katherine in her long dress, but Helen the cellist did prove to be rather handsome.

'She's pretty good-looking!' said Charlie across the girls.

'Who?' asked Emily.

'The cellist,' said Charlie. 'Apparently she has difficulties keeping her legs closed, even after the concert!' said Charlie, making Emily giggle.

Just then the lady in front turned round, an angry glare in her eyes.

'That is my daughter!' she hissed.

'My dear lady!' said Charlie, 'I wasn't for a moment blaming you! That type of thing is entirely a function of genetics!' he continued. The poor woman looked relieved, then confused, and then angry, but she could not think of anything to say. Charlie had silenced her, but we were all thankful when the players finished tuning and paused to start their first piece.

I can't remember who the composer was, but he was a Russian whose first name was almost certainly Vladimir and whose surname was from the written text unpronounceable; in those cases, one's only hope of spluttering the name correctly would be to hear someone else say it first. Then the music began, and it went on for what seemed like an eternity. The dissonant, disharmonious, atonal noise reminded me of an aural version of Emily's modern paintings. After a while my bottom went numb, and the continued shifting of my posterior did nothing except annoy Sara. I clapped far too enthusiastically at the end of each piece, hoping it would be the last, only to find there was another. The hall's acoustic magnificence aside, my resounding memory of the concert was that the cacophony created by four sticks of taut horse-hair grating over sixteen strings of gut was quite ghastly.

When the last note had been screeched, the audience, me included, clapped heartily. I wondered if everyone else was relieved, but from the amount of 'bravos!' and whistling, I suspected that some people had actually enjoyed it. We left our seats as quickly as was polite and headed out into the foyer, where I was not surprised to behold Tim and Charlotte. The latter had played in a quartet herself and she liked to keep up her interest; the former was obliged to attend with his wife. Introductions between those of the six who hadn't met were made and we waited for Katherine, who soon emerged with Helen the cellist.

'Hello James,' she said, 'did you enjoy it?'

'Oh, yes, tremendous! Really well played! Well done! This is Charlie Somers, who I mentioned... and Emily and Sara...'

'This is Helen, cello virtuoso.'

'Hello!' said Charlie. 'I met your mother in the audience. Charming woman!'

'Hello,' said Helen. 'Did you enjoy it?' she enquired of Charlie.

'Yes, very much. Is it not strange that sheep's guts should hail souls out of men's bodies?!'

No one knew quite what to say to this, so Charlie continued. 'I did enjoy it, but I must admit, I believe the motifs of the second violin in the contrapuntal section at the end of the first movement could have been written more melodiously – often a problem with mid-range counterpoint – although the arpeggios of the cello simultaneous to the melody of the first violin in that section were sublime.'

Charlie paused for thought.

'I also thought the use of the major tonic chord to finish a minor piece – in which no modulation had thus far taken place – was a little demanding on the ear. Still, you played beautifully, and these are trivial points which should no doubt be directed at the composer,' concluded Charlie.

Emily looked impressed at Charlie's apparent knowledge of musical theory, and the musicians themselves looked thoroughly baffled.

'We'll have to look out for those points next time,' said Kate, recovering her position with remarkable dexterity.

Charlie, Tim and I then found ourselves detached from the group that had formed as we manoeuvred out of the way of people trying to get to door. 'I didn't know you were such a music buff,' I said to Charlie. 'I had no idea what you were talking about!'

'Oh, neither did I!' grinned Charlie. 'But neither did they! It's just like addressing a judge – if you present the argument as if you believe it to be very familiar to them, their Lordships in the Court of Appeal won't question you for fear of appearing ignorant!'

Tim and I shook our heads, smiling at Charlie's wonderful contempt for court.

'Three-line whip tonight?' I asked Tim.

'Yes,' he said, rolling his eyes. 'You know Charlotte!'

'Oh dear. Did you enjoy it as much as me?!'

Tim rolled his eyes again, but smiled.

'Look,' I continued, 'I'm going to try and get Charlie out for a drink afterwards – can you escape Charlotte's clutches?'

'I'd love to. Gasping for a fag. Should be fine. She's pretty happy with me for coming with her!'

'Splendid.'

We rejoined the rest of the group as it headed towards the door. I said my thanks to Katherine, who was anxious to leave. I supposed the life of a musician becomes quite tiring, having to work at such inconvenient times. She and Helen departed, the latter looking wistfully at Charlie as she did so, and the rest of us split up into our respective couples.

'Thank you, James. I really enjoyed it,' said Sara, 'although I suspect it wasn't your favourite?'

'No, not really,' I smiled. At least she was smiling back.

'Well, in that case it was kind of you to think of me,' she said, little knowing that I found it hard to think of anything else.

'I'd better get home, I've had a manic day.' she said, yawning.

'Thanks for coming. I'm glad you seem to get on so well with Emily. Did you have a good chat about painting?'

'Yes, I'd love to see her work.'

'I'm sure you will.'

I turned to the others. Tim, Charlotte, Charlie and Emily were all gazing down the length of Wigmore Street, apparently looking for taxis. As I caught Tim's eye, he gave me a nod, signifying that Charlotte had given him leave to join Charlie and I for a drink. One by one the women got into taxis, Tim carefully making sure Charlotte was the last, so as not to sow seeds of doubt about our plans in the minds of Emily and Sara. When Charlotte had been gallantly assisted into her cab and it had turned the corner up Wimpole Street, Tim lit a cigarette and the evening ended very satisfactorily with us three boys getting drunk.

CHAPTER 35

Settlement

The rest of June slipped by settling Frances Green's case. After the disappointing financial dispute resolution, I had made some headway after numerous calls with the fearsome Cressida. Since the revelation that Cressida's trainee Jessica was in fact Matthew's girlfriend, I had tried to get him to extract some information from behind the lines, but either he wouldn't, or young Jessica was no double agent. Frances had calmed down significantly since the opening stages of her marital breakdown, but as the negotiation reached its final stages she did insist on the rather unorthodox approach of coming into the office to direct matters from the front-line.

Frances arrived, and before I phoned Cressida, I briefed her on how I would handle the situation. And then I lifted the phone.

'Morning Cressida,' I said, Frances at my side.

'Morning Mr James,' came the wearied response.

'As you know, my client is a very reasonable woman, and her demands since we spoke yesterday are slight. I would hate to see things develop into a stalemate at this juncture; we are all trying to avoid a final hearing.'

'Knowing you, Mr James, I expect that's exactly what you are trying to force me into,' said Cressida. I was glad Frances could only hear my side of the conversation.

'You know that's not how I work, Cressida.' I rolled my eyes at Frances, who was understandably nervous.

'Well, what does your client want?'

'Twenty thousand more from the proceeds of the matrimonial home and half the savings, not a third as we said yesterday.'

'I'll take instructions,' said Cressida.

'Cressida?'

'Yes, Mr James?'

'This is my client's final offer and I am instructed that the offer will be totally withdrawn if I don't hear back by twelve.'

Silence.

My final and deadly salvo had silenced the formidable Smyth-Jones! I knew Cressida used timing to her advantage in a calculated effort to win as much for her client as possible. But this time, my deadline would thwart her; she could not possibly advise her client not to settle at this stage, and she knew it.

Eventually she said, 'Is that your instruction to me, or your client's instructions to you?'

She was quick, but she couldn't argue with my reply: 'The latter, Cressida,' I said, feigning the wearied tone she so often used with me.

'Right you are, Mr James.'

I put the phone down beaming at Frances.

'How did that go?' she asked, expectantly.

'I think we have them over a barrel. We have half an hour to find out.'

Frances and I chatted for a while. She was doing well, despite having violent dreams about destroying her husband's Mercedes. Within ten minutes, my phone rang.

'Hello Cressida! What news?'

'My client accepts your proposal.'

'Splendid. Would you like to draft the settlement agreement?'

'It'd be a pleasure.'

'Thank you, Cressida.'

'Not at all, Mr James. Goodbye.'

'Goodbye, Cressida.'

And I put the phone triumphantly.

'We have an accord.'

'Thank God,' said the relieved Frances.

The result was good, and much better than had looked likely since the hearing. But the daft thing was, we achieved almost the exact same result that had been offered by Frances right at the beginning of the whole case. The legal costs of both parties could have been totally avoided had one been less greedy, or the other less unreasonable. I don't usually point this out to clients.

'Well, Frances, it's been a pleasure.' It wasn't often that I could say this sincerely to clients, but in her case, it had. 'I wish you all the best for the future. At least this result gives you a fairly decent financial settlement, and more importantly, closure from the whole thing.'

'Yes, it does. Thank you James; I'm not sure how I would have coped without you.'

She wouldn't have coped. Maybe my fees would have been better spent on a psychiatrist, but I doubted it: legal help was the best tonic for the clients. It was designed at once to make them believe their finances were in safe hands and that they had a good chance of shafting their spouses. Adding a bit of humour, humanity and impartial advice finished off the treatment nicely.

Her sincere thanks made it worthwhile for me too.

'I'll be in touch to finish things off – you'll have to sign the agreement, but there really isn't much else to do. So I fear this may be the last time we meet on a professional basis.'

'I'm rather pleased!' she said, mockingly, but I know she was. Divorce lawyers have an odd relationship with their clients – for a few months they are the most important person in their client's life, but as soon as it's over, they don't want to know you, and the client that has been part of the lawyer's own life for so many weeks suddenly disappears. It makes me sad with clients like Frances, but on the whole I'm glad to see the back of them too.

'Well, at least I won't have any more sleepless nights wondering whether you'd be putting a sledgehammer through the bonnet of a Mercedes!' I joked back.

'You didn't lose sleep over me, did you?' she asked, at once concerned.

I laughed as I showed Frances out of my office.

'Do thank Mr Somers, too,' said Frances as we neared the wonderfully large door of Number 22. I promised so to do, and opened the door for her.

'Goodbye, then.'

'Bye,' she said, as it closed behind her.

As I walked back in past reception, Sue called out to me saying that there was a delivery for me in reception. I walked in and there stood three tall bags which looked suspiciously like they contained bottles, marked for Matthew, Emily and I. The label on my bag read: 'Don't worry, my brother is a wine merchant! Thanks again, Frances.' And the label on the bottle itself read *Dom Pérignon*, a handsome bottle of champagne indeed. By leaving them in reception, the kindly Frances had decided to give them to us, whatever the outcome might have been. I walked back into my office and put a bottle on each of Matthew's and Emily's desk, smiling.

CHAPTER 36

Three Paintings

The fourth of July saw the opening evening of the exhibition in the South Kensington gallery whose owner had bought Emily's Summer Exhibition painting. He had since been to visit her studio (or at least where she did her painting in her flat) and had taken away two more paintings to hang in his new exhibition featuring a number of other unknown, but talented artists.

After work that day, I had gone straight to Sara's flat which was near the gallery. Having taken the bottle of *Dom Pérignon* with me, we soon cracked it open in honour of Emily's new found success.

'To Emily and her painting!' I said.

'To Emily.'

'Would you like to see some of my drawings?' asked Sara.

'Not if they're anything like Emily's!' I joked.

'You're so cruel. Emily is brilliant.'

'I know she is. I just don't like them.'

'You should be kinder to her.'

'She knows I'm kidding. She knows I know nothing about art.'

Sara looked questioningly at me, but I forgave her. I nevertheless reflected that I am indeed lucky to have a friend as understanding as Emily.

'Well?' she asked, and as my blank face showed no comprehension, 'My drawings?'

'Oh, yes please.'

She looked pleased and trotted off, returning with a large portfolio full of drawings. They were different to Emily's and drawn with the exacting eye of an architect. They were mainly pencil, of buildings, nudes and other more obscure things. And they were magnificent. The detail was so astounding I asked if her she used a glass, to which her answer was yes. The best one was a pencil drawing of a dead bat she had found near her parent's house near Oxford: each tiny hair had been drawn, and the end result, if seen from arm's length could have been a photograph. But I knew this wouldn't go down well in the art world: 'painting by numbers' they'd say, or 'that is *so* last century!' meaning of course, the one before.

By the time we had finished going through them, we had drained our glasses. 'Well, Sara, you are amazing! I can't believe how good they are. We must have a toast to your drawings!'

'I'm fine, thanks. We're sure to have something at the gallery.' So I poured myself another glass and toasted her anyway.

We arrived at the gallery to find Emily and a great number of others already there. The gallery was exceedingly well organised with bubbly bearers standing dutifully at the door. I relieved one of them of three glasses, and headed towards where I could see Emily.

'Hi gorgeous!' I said as I sidled through the crowds to meet her.

She gave me a disapproving look which I assumed was because Sara was there. 'Hi Sara! How are you?'

'Well, thanks.'

'So where are they then?'

Emily led us upstairs which thankfully sounded much quieter than the ground floor and as I ascended the stairs the familiar daubs came into sight.

'Wow! They do look good in here,' I said, truthfully enough, because the paintings occupied a prime position on the largest wall in the gallery's first floor. 'Although they are still inherently ghastly.'

'Shut up James! What do you think, Sara?'

'They're fantastic. Well done for getting them in here. It's a good gallery. I hope there are some knowledgeable people here tonight.' Emily looked chuffed.

We stood around talking and the girls commented on the other paintings. A quick scan had been sufficient for my less than enquiring mind, and I began to wonder if there was anyone else to talk to while the girls seemed so engrossed discussing which type of hair they liked best in their brushes. I assumed they meant paintbrushes. Our glasses empty, I fought my way down the staircase which was now crammed with people ascending and recharged them, returning to the now packed first floor to find the girls talking about weights of paper. Emily found the hundred and forty pound best for watercolour, and without wishing to learn more, my attention drifted to a middle-aged fellow with the most splendid moustache who seemed to be surveying the scene carefully.

'Good evening, sir!' I said approaching. 'What a splendid moustache!'

'Thank you. Like the work this evening?'

'No, not much, but I'm not really into art.'

'Clearly!' he said with obvious good humour.

'Are you the proprietor?'

'Yes, I am as it happens. Hugh Daley.'

'I thought you must be. I'm James James. I'm a lawyer.'

'Oh.'

His response did seem to sum things up quite well.

'You realise you pipped me at the post at the Summer Exhibition with that picture?' I continued, not wishing to let his apparent perceptions regarding my profession destroy our otherwise entertaining conversation.

'I'm glad I did,' he replied, 'Know the artist? She's cracking.'

'She certainly is, but I'm not too keen on her paintings!'

'Lawyer, you say? James, eh? I have heard of you, I believe.'

'Emily's my best friend, and my secretary.'

'I see.' He said, looking over to her.

'That's my girlfriend she's talking to.'

At the mention of 'girlfriend' the girls looked round and advanced towards us, Emily introducing Sara.

'This is Hugh Daley; Hugh this is Sara. Hugh owns the place.'

Hugh puffed himself up like a cockerel at this, which made me smile.

'Pleased to meet you,' said Hugh, who was then dragged off by another punter wanting to quiz him on a painting.

'Hugh is great fun,' said Emily, 'and he likes my paintings!' she said, digging me in the ribs.

'Yes, he seems a jolly sort,' I said. 'Where's Charlie?'

'Oh, he couldn't come,' she said, 'he had to prepare for a big case tomorrow,' but the humour in her face vanished immediately and I knew that Charlie had never worked past six o'clock in his life when social proceedings were on offer. I wondered what had happened but she obviously didn't want to discuss it, so I was left theorising. I feared Charlie had had a change of heart in the direction of another, and my anxiety for Emily rather spoiled the rest of the evening for me.

But thankfully it didn't go on too long, and thankfully Sara elected to return home straight after, kissing me goodbye and leaving me to walk Emily to the tube.

'Fancy a chat?' I said as we passed a bench.

'Yes, I do actually,' she said, sitting down.

'What happened?'

'Oh, James! Poor Charlie! I feel awful.'

'You gave *him* the flick?'

'Yes.'

'Christ! I thought it must have been the other way round. Why?'

'I don't know, James. I really like him – I really do – he's funny, clever, a bit too silly, but in a cute way and not at all bad looking… and he makes me laugh as much as you do…'

'But…?'

'But, there's something not there between us; I just can't see us working out. I thought it'd be fairer to tell him now, rather than three or four months down the line. It's not even his fault. I think he was quite upset.'

'I wouldn't worry too much about Charlie. He'll be in love with someone else next week!' I said.

'He's a better man than that,' said Emily sternly, and somewhat to my surprise. But I took her word for it; she was an excellent judge of character and thankfully I'd never been involved romantically with Charlie.

'Are you all right?' I asked.

'Yes, just sad for him. I asked if we could still be friends, because I'd like that. I asked him if he would come tonight but he said he needed a little more time than that. I wouldn't want to lose him as a friend, or miss out on things you two do together. That would be sad.'

'I'm sure he'll get over it, and you can be friends,' I said, a little doubtfully in light of Emily's last comment. But the Charlie I knew would have another lover within the month, and all would be well. Above all, I was relieved that Emily had been the dumpor and Charlie the dumpee.

'I hope so,' concluded Emily.

I hoped so too. Charlie had left a message with me asking if I could see him the Friday after – already the last Friday in July – and it was unlike Charlie to plan so far in advance. Clearly he needed a chat too.

'How's everything going with Sara?' asked Emily.

'Splendid!'

'Still fallen for her?'

'Definitely fallen. What do you think of her?'

'I think she's great too,' she said, squeezing my arm.

'I'm glad. I couldn't handle it if you didn't like my girlfriend.'

'Shall we go? I'm all right now,' said Emily, looking far from happy, but standing up.

'Yes, if you're sure. But I'm worried about you.'

'I'm sure,' she said. 'Come on, stupid, you're worrying about nothing. As I said, I just feel sorry for Charlie.'

She pulled me up from the bench and we set off again for the tube station.

CHAPTER 37

Breakup Causes Rifts

I arrived in the office the following Monday in a splendid mood. I always find arriving at the office in such a state odd: the feeling usually dissipates a certain extent as I cross the stone-flagged floor of the hallway of Number 22. By the time I reach reception and say hello to Sue, the buoyancy has begun to obtain the qualities of lead; once in my office, Emily's chirpy smile usually keeps me going for a few minutes before the despondent mood of being a full time desk attendant kicks in, until freedom temporarily establishes itself again at half-past five.

This morning, however, instinct quickly told me that Emily was not in a good mood: when I gaily entered my office and said 'good morning' she looked up for a moment, apparently in mild humour, but upon seeing me she muttered a muted 'morning' and returned to work without further ado. Whatever vestiges of my amenable disposition that had previously remained now vanished immediately.

Her mood worsened later in the morning when I asked her what was wrong.

'Bloody hell, James, you're really annoying me today!' she said, 'I'm going to make a coffee.' And with that she left the room

'What's up with her?' I mouthed at Matthew.

'Pretty obvious,' he said.

She had seemed so in control of the Charlie situation when I had last spoken to her about it that I assumed that she was in fact in complete control. Now I understood that her break-up with Charlie might be more complicated than originally thought, and that I shouldn't have asked her in front of Matthew.

Despite my best efforts, Emily's mood did not improve much the day after, which proved conclusively that it was an ongoing problem thus far undisclosed, and therefore best left alone. Matthew was nearing the end of his six months with me, and by this stage did actually have quite a lot of his own work, so he was busy, and much to my disappointment, not really in the mood for office banter. There was only one thing for it, the pastime that instilled boredom and despondency into my bones like no other: work.

This went on for some days, the drudgery of legal proceedings getting ever more tedious without our usual jokes and interludes to partake in discourses about anything other than the work in hand. By the morning of the last Friday of July, it became so unbearable that as soon as I knew Matthew would be out of the room for some time, I decided that things must be sorted out for the good of all involved.

'What's wrong, Emily?'

'Nothing, I'm just not feeling great, that's all,' she said, elusively.

'Emily, please tell me what's wrong. I hate seeing you unhappy like this. I know you're unhappy, not just in a bad mood. Let me help? I know Charlie too, you know.'

She looked round, mildly surprised.

'Oh, it isn't your fault James. I'm sorry: I shouldn't take it out on you.' She looked miserable, and despite being in the office, I had to hug her. It was only afterwards that I considered what might have happened had anyone come in, but after this incident, Emily bounced back to her usual self fairly quickly.

Once Emily's spirit had improved, Friday afternoon slipped by much more quickly and by five o'clock Emily and Matthew had departed and as arranged I was preparing to leave for 7 Queen's Bench Row. Seconds before my departure, Purple Lynn (for some reason sitting on reception) phoned to announce that Mrs Ricketts had arrived at the office. Mrs Ricketts' habit of telephoning last thing on a Friday was tolerable, but this unannounced visit was bordering on the upsetting.

'Hello, Mrs Ricketts! How are you?' I said, waltzing into reception.

'Tip-top, thank you, James. And yourself?'

'Not too bad, as you see!'

I noticed her Barbour and wellies had something of the smell of the farmyard about them.

'Would you like a cup of tea?' Lynn asked Mrs Ricketts, knowing full-well I didn't like to be kept late on Fridays while she smiled sarcastically at me, apparently with the express intention to really piss me off.

Mrs Ricketts' answer of 'Oh, yes please!' did not bode well: she meant to stay for a lengthy chat, not simply to hand me a new codicil to her will, or law report from *The Times* about post-death variations. She kept pretty up to speed with legal developments and seemed to think that her lawyer needed her constant research and updates to take care of her affairs, which argument probably did hold some merit. She was especially concerned about events after her death, no doubt because she would not able to give me advice in person. She had even once proclaimed that if she were terminally ill, she would do her own probate from hospital, at which I didn't smile, because I knew she was deadly serious.

'Well, what can I do you for?'

'Speak English, boy!'

'I'm sorry, it's not meant to be taken seriously.'

'Well, you're a lawyer for God's sake!'

'You're my favourite client, Mrs Ricketts, and I thought the lawyer – client relationship had become more of a friendship, especially since I am no longer your lawyer!' I said, knowing the result this would have on the darling Mrs Ricketts. She smiled fondly at me, head slightly cocked and agreed:

'Quite right, James! You're the first lawyer I've trusted in my life, and probably the last, since I'll probably be ending up in a pine box before too long. Still, no point hanging around getting ancient and decrepit! No, a massive heart attack is what I'm praying for. And since I'm not entirely sure my prayers will be answered in time, I have taken matters into my own hands: I still have a proper fried breakfast every morning, and eat as much clotted cream and jam as my scone will allow!'

Sue came in with the tea tray, and Mrs Ricketts took some time getting the amount of milk correct before sipping her favourite hot beverage thoughtfully.

'Well, what is it you need to see me about?'

'I'm not happy with this fellow Tim that you've palmed me off with.'

'Mrs Ricketts, Tim's expertise in this area of law is far superior to mine.' She looked at me suspiciously. 'Really it is,' I said by way of assurance.

'Well,' she said, somewhat dubiously, 'you may be right, but he certainly hasn't the manners or sufficient knowledge of the English way of doing things, as you do. Do you know he sent me a bill for re-drafting my will?'

'I am afraid that it is customary for lawyers to bill their clients.'

'You didn't.'

'Actually I did.'

'Not often.'

'No, but you change your will fairly regularly, Mrs Ricketts, so I was able to judge when a bill was appropriate. Perhaps Tim doesn't realise how often you like to change your will. I'll have a word with him. I'm sure it's a simple misunderstanding.'

'Well, I'm not keen to pay it. It not just legal bills: I'm never keen to pay any bills, but one must, or one ends up boiling rainwater on a camping stove simply in order to have a lukewarm bath. It's outrageous!'

'As I said, I'll have a word with Tim,' hoping to conclude the matter.

'I could understand if it had been a whole new will, but the redraft was dead easy: I got a bloody parking ticket for staying too long at Stonehenge, so English Heritage were scrubbed from the will then and there! I wrote the chief executive a letter saying so, too. The way these establishments are run defies belief! Unbelievable! I'd have given that parking attendant's shins a rap with the butt of the twelve bore if I'd seen the blighter!'

Throughout Mrs Ricketts' story, I had been shaking my head slowly, combining the movement with a concerned expression across my face to show Mrs Ricketts my agreement with her. I somehow couldn't find the words to vocalise that agreement and concluded that I was glad that she had only expressed a wish to break the parking attendant's legs as opposed to the doubtless more colourful option of unleashing both barrels in his direction.

'So are you unhappy with Tim's work in any other way?'

'Oh, goodness, no! Nice chap. How are things going with Sara, anyway?' she asked, clearly bored with talking about Tim now I had promised to rectify the supposedly erroneous billing.

'Splendidly.'

'Have you fallen for her?' asked Mrs Ricketts, scrutinising my face between squinted eyes.

'I believe I have.' I replied, at which point her eyes became wide for a moment before a broad smile closed them up again.

'If she's wise, she'll have fallen for you to, my boy! Well done!'

And with that she stood up ready to leave, the true objective of her visit now accomplished.

As I opened the front door and allowed Mrs Ricketts through, I noticed a muddy and decidedly badly parked Land Rover across the road. Approaching said vehicle was a traffic warden. 'If those are your wheels, Mrs Ricketts, you'd better make haste: I fear an officer of the Council approaches, and no doubt you haven't bought a ticket!'

'Good God! Thank you James, much obliged!' with which she literally gathered her skirts and marched off shouting to the traffic warden: 'You sir! Stay where you are or I'll bloody well run you down!' The poor chap froze until she had clambered up into the Land Rover whereupon he retreated up the front steps of house opposite, out of harm's way.

The powerful engine roared, and Mrs Ricketts could be seen confidently engaging the gears. Having been driven once as her passenger, I knew she was an assured driver, and on this occasion she looked no less so. However, my suspicions that sight of the traffic warden had unnerved her were confirmed when apparently the difference between accelerator and brake became somewhat cloudy in the mind of the mad old misanthropist. This uncharacteristic confusion had the unfortunate consequence of causing the powerful Ricketts' Land Rover to lurch forward at some speed into the rear of a large black saloon which was itself propelled forwards into the red pillar box in front, causing this fine Edwardian edifice to topple from its proud perpendicular posture into a somewhat less dignified, off-horizontal attitude.

CHAPTER 38

Queen's Bench Row

As a result of Mrs Ricketts' disastrous driving, I arrived at 7 Queen's Bench Row rather late. As I sat waiting for Charlie to descend from his room, I picked up the *Financial Times* and immediately noticed it was dated Friday, thirtieth of July. This date rang a vague bell which suddenly seemed to chime as heavily as a cathedral's only three feet away as it dawned on me that a double-booking had erroneously occurred: my presence was required by Sara.

Charlie came down smiling.

'I'm so sorry, Charlie...' I said, and was about to continue when he interjected:

'But you must leave post-haste to attend Sara!'

'How on earth do you know that?'

'A charming woman from your office called Lynn phoned to say Sara had phoned the office and would like you to phone her. She wonders why you are late.'

'Shit. Women's minds operate in such an odd way. She did ask me the other day if I was free on the thirtieth, to which I answered "Yes" because I was free on the thirtieth. I knew the only evening I was busy this week was with you on Friday. How the hell was I to know Friday was also the thirtieth?!'

'I quite agree,' agreed Charlie, 'I had no idea it *was* Friday today until your Lynn phoned. I tried to explain to her that you weren't due until tomorrow night, but she was having none of it. It was only then I asked Philip, the clockwork clerk, what day of the week it was. He confirmed that it was indeed Friday. I'm afraid I rely totally on the clerks to tell me what I'm doing. When I have a week without a court hearing – like this one – I find that one hangover drifts into another, and after a couple of groggy mornings one very quickly loses count of the days!'

'Quite.' I agreed. But knowing that my departure would have to be achieved hastily, I found it my duty to ask Charlie how he was doing post-Emily. 'How are you doing? Are you coping? Have you spoken to

Emily? She seems pretty upset too...'

'Well, no need to worry! I was just about to say that things have hotted up with Felicity again. It's probably a good thing you can't go out this evening – Felicity asked me to join her on her father's yacht in the Med – I'm off tomorrow with her.'

I smiled. Emily had been forgotten and the old Charlie was back.

'Splendid! You don't waste any time! How did this happen?'

'Well, I'm not entirely sure if she knew anything about my brief attempt at wooing Emily, and once Emily had unceremoniously given me the boot, all I had to do was turn up the flirt factor with Felicity and she fell into my arms. Quite literally, in fact: I was on my way to the library in Chambers, and I saw Felicity clock me as I walked past her office. From a combination of creaking floorboards and glimpses of her reflection in the glass of the doors en route to the library, it became obvious that she was following me with the express intention of effecting a liaison in there.' Charlie grinned. 'The library is seldom used by anyone, but on occasion some law does slip through even the finest legal minds and one is forced to enter the cold and draughty room full of law reports and cases. Quickly ascertaining that none of my other learned friends were in residence researching a point of law, I headed to the law reports of the Queen's Bench Division which have the advantage of being furthest from the door.

'Shortly after I had plucked a dusty volume off the shelf, the door creaked open, and the floorboard just inside the door groaned slowly, as if Felicity had tried to enter quietly and on tiptoes. She obviously realised this approach wouldn't work as the whole damn place creaks, and having dispensed with stealth, she quickened her pace, finding the aisle where I lay in wait quite quickly. I looked up from the tome in which I had been entirely un-engrossed, and offered to help her find what she was looking for. She replied, "I just have," and promptly kissed me.'

'Blimey!'

'It was rather a passionate kiss, too. She was so enthusiastic that she pushed me back right into the QBD case reports, a number of which were dislodged from their shelves. The noise of them hitting the wooden floorboards aroused Philip whose office is directly below. He's very protective over his books, and quick as a flash he was in there too, wanting to know exactly what we had been up to. I explained carefully that I had been assisting Miss Warburton-Lee with replacing some of the volumes on the higher shelves, which pleased him. Felicity departed quickly, three unwanted QBD volumes under her arm, and I too was about to depart having replaced all the remaining volumes, when Philip said: "Miss Warburton-Lee seems to have been very thankful for your efforts with her books." She hadn't thanked me, and I conveyed my supposed lack of understanding to Philip with a look to which he replied: "She's left most of her lipstick on you!"'

We both laughed.

'Anyway, I digress! You must bugger off and see Sara and I must pack for my yachting trip with the Warburton-Lee family!'

'Yes. I must fly. How long are you going for?'

'August.'

'Bloody hell, I hope you get on with her old man!'

'Likewise! He's a judge, which doesn't bode well. I've never yet got on with one!'

We agreed to meet up in early September when Charlie returned from his yachting trip – assuming he hadn't jumped ship earlier than anticipated.

By seven o'clock I arrived in South Kensington at Sara's house, very late, but safe in the knowledge that I had an excellent excuse.

'You're an hour late,' was her greeting.

'I'm so sorry, but I do have a good reason for my unpunctuality.'

'Oh, yes?' she enquired rather too sceptically. 'Your receptionist, Lynn, I think she said, told me you were out with a certain Charlie Somers.'

She had me stumped. Of course I had actually been with Charlie: Lynn, for once, had proved helpful to someone seeking assistance from her (I queried her intent: as usual her actions towards me had proved incredibly irksome), but my admission had to come:

'Well, I did see him very briefly...'

'And that's your excuse? What was so urgent about seeing him? And don't tell me you had to deliver a brief, because for one I doubt you've ever delivered a brief in your life, and two, I know he's going away for a month as from tonight.' And she stood, arms folded, waiting for an answer. She was right of course: I could give her no answer about Charlie save the annoying truth which was that I had remembered him and forgotten her. But then I thought my sin was not even this great – I hadn't forgotten her – I knew I was seeing her on the thirtieth – I just hadn't twigged that today *was* the thirtieth. Of course, I knew in the mind of a woman, that this argument would hold no weight, so I moved on to the next.

It hurt me that she hadn't considered that there might have been another reason for my lateness, and now I played my trump card: 'Your grandmother came to see me. Afterwards, she promptly drove her Land Rover into the car in front which cannoned into a pillar box in front of that, toppling it. It took a while sorting it all out, because she had threatened a traffic warden before the collision; he unfortunately reported her threats to an officer of the Metropolitan Police who had arrived on the scene at the behest of a postman who had reported serious vandalism of one of Her Majesty's pillar boxes.'

It worked. Her expression went from one of anger to worry.

'Oh no! Is she all right?'

'Yes, physically she's fine. She was a little worried that the Land Rover's bumper had some paint chipped from it, but when I pointed out that the car in front was approximately three feet shorter than it had been a few minutes previously, and that the supposed paint chips were in fact splinters of that car's undercoat, she seemed greatly relieved. Thankfully, the pillar-box had fallen on several bags of sand that had been left by some forward-thinking highway engineers, and apart from being uprooted, had suffered no damage. The postman demonstrated that the door was in perfect working order as he collected the afternoon's post. I explained that I was her lawyer, gave my card to all involved, said she'd pay for all the damage caused (to which she tacitly acquiesced), apologised to the traffic warden and postman, and departed without further ado, all parties having been placated.'

After my explanatory speech, I was pleased to see Sara's expression change from one of worry to one of relief, but as her countenance again began to show the marks of anger, it was my turn to become worried.

'So why did you go and see Charlie, instead of coming here and only being a little bit late?'

She had me stumped again. Again, the only answer I had was the painful truth, and again I made my admission:

'Well, there was a certain confusion between conflicts of the diary between those arrangements on the thirtieth and those on the last Friday of the month.'

'You forgot.' She said. It wasn't a question.

'Well, I wouldn't go quite that far,' I said, 'it was more of a mix-up.'

'James, you forgot.'

CHAPTER 39

The Natural History Museum

Despite the rather disastrous start to the evening, Sara soon became happier when I offered to take her out for dinner instead of allowing her to cook. In the end we had a good evening, and somewhat to my surprise she agreed to accompany me to the Natural History Museum the next day, which, when I was a boy, was the only reason I ever went to South Kensington.

The next morning I woke in a state of excitement; there was an exhibition on about mass extinctions, which I knew would have to involve dinosaurs, and although a career in law offers little exposure to prehistoric beasts, there is nothing to stop one pursuing other interests at the weekends.

At the museum, the most exciting exhibit, save from the *Diplodocus* in the main hall who never fails to impress me, despite seeming to shrink in stature every time I meet him, were the complete fossilised skeletal remains of *Lystrosaurus*. I explained to Sara that this unremarkable and rather small tetrapod had been one of the few reptiles to survive the huge mass extinction at the end of the Permian, 251 million years ago, where as many as sixty percent of taxonomic families, and ninety percent of species were wiped out: a biological catastrophe on a scale unknown to humans. *Lystrosaurus* and his descendants flourished in the early Triassic and put very simply, he was therefore father to all the dinosaurs. My discourse on earth history continued until 65 million years ago, to the end of the Cretaceous, when the dinosaurs were finally knocked on the head and the rise of mammals began. That she was interested pleased me, although she did spend much of the time studying the arches and stonework of the museum itself.

After the exhibition, and not sensing a burning desire from Sara to explore the rest of the museum, I suggested we leave and do something else. She readily agreed, and at her request, we wandered down through Onslow Square and Sydney Street and began window-shopping along the King's Road. After a couple of hundred yards, I noticed a familiar name swinging on a sign above a ladies boutique: Juicy Lucy's. Memories of Martha came flooding back.

My curiosity got the better of me as we passed the window, and I slowed down in an attempt to discover how much exactly Martha was willing to pay for her clothes. Sara noticed my reduction in speed and asked if I minded if we went in.

'Not at all,' I said.

All the better for realising my purpose, I thought.

The clothes were beautiful.

'They are beautiful,' said Sara, 'but beautiful prices too.'

'Hello, James,' said Martha, on the other side of a rail.

'Hello! What are you doing here?'

Stupid question.

'Shopping, funnily enough.'

'Oh, sorry: Sara, this is Martha,' I said, by way of introduction, 'Martha, this is my girlfriend Sara.'

I saw Sara look at me sharply, but thought it best to get the important information out of the way sooner rather than later in case some calamity ensued, and to avoid a full-blown handbag fight.

Pleasantries were exchanged between the girls, Martha holding her end up well under the circumstances.

'So, have you forgiven me yet?' asked Martha.

'Yes, of course!' I said.

What else could I say?

'I'd love to chat, but I have a date with a hairdresser and must dash,' she said. 'Well, lovely to see you, James,' she continued, apparently sincerely, 'and nice to meet you, Sara.'

She left, clutching two large bags from her favourite shop.

'Who was that and why did she want to know if you have forgiven her?' asked Sara.

'She's a fellow lawyer, and it's a long story,' I said, not wishing to have to tell her.

'I have all day,' she smiled, I think innocent of jealousy.

'Well, I went out with her a couple of times, and she insulted Emily in an unacceptable manner. I told her so and walked out.'

'I see. I'll try and remember,' she said.

We left, and I realised I had still failed to ascertain the expense of the clothes.

After that rather surreal experience, which wasn't really surprising given the regularity with which Martha had professed to frequent the boutique, Sara and I had a splendid afternoon basking in the sun whilst taking tea in a King's Road café. The day ended at her flat, with a delicious plate of food, expertly cooked by me, and a large quantity of red wine.

CHAPTER 40

All Quiet On The West-One Front

July had been quiet, but August looked like it would be dead. August is always a quiet month on the divorce front: the summer holidays are well under way and everyone has already embarked on or is looking forward to their family holidays. It is only at the end of August, when people used to spending upwards of seven contented hours a day at work away from their beloved spouses have been locked together in a small hotel room (with the added inconvenience of irksome whingeing children), that they begin to question whether their vows might be changed from 'until death do us part' to 'until September'.

I had the post-summer holiday boom to look forward to in September, but for now I just had to work out how I was going to get through the month. Charlie was away for the whole of August on the Warburton-Lee yacht, Tim and Charlotte were already away and Emily had booked a painting holiday in Italy with her father, where they could both enjoy themselves whilst soaking up artistic inspiration from all around. I was rather jealous, but also wise enough not to harbour any ambition to paint, long since recognising that my artistic bent went no further than colouring in Land Registry title plans. Before long though, she too departed, and I was left alone. It was hot and sunny outside, never the weather for work, and work I did not.

Suddenly, though, Angela poked her whiskers round the door causing me to start from a pleasant post-lunch dream.

'James! You're free on Thursday, aren't you?'

'Oh, let me just check my diary… why do you ask?' I asked as casually as possible. I knew damn well I was free, but I wasn't letting on until I knew what she had in store. The problem was, she was standing right over my desk, and if I opened my diary, the first thing to greet both our eyes would be the clean white page of Thursday. Or possibly in her case, she might first see the detritus that had been building on the lenses of her glasses these last two years.

'I'm afraid I must I have left my diary in my briefcase. Can I let you know later?'

'What's that?' she asked, pushing a divorce petition off my diary with a wiry finger and looking over the top of her glasses at me suspiciously.

'Good lord!' I said, 'Well done!'

'Free!' she exclaimed, as Thursday's page opened. She stood there, gloating smugly, as if she had won a great victory. The annoying thing was, she had. 'In that case, you now have a meeting with me at eleven!'

The 'eleven' was said with a flourish.

She stood watching me.

'Can I help you with anything further, Angela? I'm very busy this afternoon.'

'No, that'll be all!' she said, still standing there for some as yet unknown reason.

I put my feet on my desk to annoy her, and ignored her by picking up the meatiest looking book on my desk and pretending to study it carefully.

'Feet!' she said, pointing at my feet.

'Hands!' I replied, waving my hands.

At first I thought Angela had simply lost her temper, but I soon realised that the bundle of papers she was carrying had launched themselves into the air and were now floating down like vast snowflakes because she had suddenly required the use of her arms to soften her landing as she was batted forth into the room by the door as Bugle burst in with his usual tempestuous force.

'Angela! Get up! What the blazes are you doing?' roared Bugle, who through his speed and strength had not apparently realised the cause of Angela's unfortunate accident.

'Sorry, Mr Bugle,' squeaked Angela, desperately collecting the papers which had distributed themselves all over the floor, and a few of which were still airborne. 'I was just trying to arrange a meeting with James about his billing figures,' she explained, for the first time.

'Damn you, Angela! I told you *I* was going to conduct those meetings! Just trying to assert your authority anyway, were you?' roared Bugle.

'I...I... thought... I think I need to leave,' stammered the unfortunate Angela, still on her knees, gazing up at Bugle in blind terror, her glasses having slipped right down her nose.

Having collected the last of her papers, Angela scuttled out, sticking to the wall to avoid the glare of Bugle, or perhaps to find the door without the use of her much impaired sense of sight.

'Stupid woman,' said Bugle when she had gone. 'She was arranging that meeting outside my authority *just* so she could abuse her apparent position of authority. Makes me mad!'

It made me mad too, though I worried that Bugle himself would now be having this meeting with me. But thankfully his hatred of Angela seemed to be occupying him for the moment, and his, 'I'll talk to you about it after the next partner's meeting,' did not have the hallmarks of anything too serious.

Then I wondered why Bugle *had* entered my office with such gusto.

'Well, can I help?' I asked helpfully.

'God, no. I merely heard Angela drivelling on just behind your door and thought I'd give her a shock whilst I was passing! Better be off – got a client waiting for me down the Old Bailey! Cheers James!'

Teddy was the main, and indeed only, topic of the August partners' meeting. Most partners were themselves on holiday, but it was noted that Teddy's billing had not improved in the last month. It had in fact remained the same as the month before: at zero. This meant he had only a month to deliver a fairly substantial bill, the odds of which were becoming longer by the day. It looked as though Teddy's fate was certain, partly because he seemed to have little intention of doing anything about it himself, and partly because he couldn't.

As the few partners who had attended filed out, Bugle took me aside.

'James, as you know, Angela has been perusing your billing figures and while you continue to earn well, we are concerned that your time recording compared to your billing is somewhat erratic and biased heavily in the favour of certain clients.'

'Well, I do work for some clients more than others,' I said.

'Yes, but you don't bill some clients as much as others! Every time you lift the phone, or write a letter, or so much think of a client, you must record time on the file. Christ! Even when you're going to the loo you must be thinking of something! If it's a client, bill the buggers! In particular, we note that a Mrs Ricketts, a Mrs Green and a Miss Hunt have been benefiting from your time without having to pay for much of it.'

Despite his draconian billing methodology, Bugle was right – these were clients who I liked and who I did not bill anything like the time I spent working for – and now the vile Angela had spotted my preferential billing I was in for it from the senior management.

I tried to explain: 'Mrs Ricketts is an old client of the firm; I act for her entire family and believe me, the firm owes her not the other way round.'

'Never heard of her,' said Bugle.

'She's not a criminal.' I replied; Bugle takes no interest in clients, save his own criminal ones.

'She may not be a criminal, but neither is she a good client.'

'She is a good client. She's one of the oldest clients of the firm…'

'She is not a good client,' interrupted Bugle. 'Good clients pay their fees; that's the beauty of them.'

'That is true. But they keep returning to the firm, and recommend other good clients, so a little leniency in the billing department is in fact good business,' I argued.

'But I gather you are conducting a relationship with the granddaughter of this Mrs Ricketts?' he persisted.

'She is now Tim's client, I said. 'But frankly, Frank, I don't think you're in any position to lecture me about who I should be having a relationship with,' I said.

The anger that flashed in Bugle's eyes scared me somewhat as he brought his head so close to mine that his mouth was next to my ear and I could no longer see his visage.

'How dare you blackmail me!' he spat, quite literally, into my ear, causing me to flinch as his saliva hit me.

As I recoiled, I could see his smug expression. He thought my flinch a sign of terror.

'Don't spit,' I said.

'Sorry.'

!

I had the upper hand.

'I wasn't blackmailing you,' I continued, which was true, 'but I think we should forget about this conversation, don't you, Frank?' I said, blackmailing him.

'Watch what you say, my boy!' he spluttered, not quite believing what I'd said. And with that he stalked off, silent and seething.

CHAPTER 41

My Faults

Sara had telephoned and asked whether I could meet her after work. I had been delighted by the structure of her sentence: she hadn't asked whether I would *like* to meet her after work, she had asked if I was *able* to, which meant she was missing me, and not only desired my company, but *needed* it. Furthermore, she chosen to meet at a bar that neither of us had frequented which pleased me because as relationships develop, new locations unknown to both parties become part of that relationship, where future meetings can be planned and looked forward to.

I was now there and entered and saw her sitting at a table with two gin and tonics.

Marvellous!

'Hi darling,' I said, which surprised me, because I hadn't used that expression for years in any other way than to casually greet Emily, but having said it, I realised that our relationship was now at the stage when I felt proud to use it in the proper way.

'You're late again,' was her greeting.

'Sorry, a bloody client rang up at half-past. They always ring up and expect you to be delighted to sort our their matrimonial problems just when the old saliva glands are working overtime in anticipation of a stiff gin!'

'Why do you always make light of your job, James? Aren't you proud of what you do? You seem to make everything into a big and not very funny joke.'

I paused, trying to think of a sensible answer, but my pause was just too long for Sara and she started talking again.

'I do like you very much, you know, but I'm just not sure if I can be with someone who doesn't take their job seriously enough.'

I laughed, not believing that her words were serious, but soon realised my mistake. In a panic, I knew I must explain myself to rid her mind of these foolish ideas.

'I make fun of it, because in truth, law is boring: one deals with the same type of thing day in, day out: often tediously dreary matters regarding the minutiae of people's lives that are indescribably uninspiring; law does not entail life or death like medicine (the only comparable exception being long prison sentences, for which I have no desire to be responsible); no one will thank you or show any form of gratitude for longer than it takes them to say "thank you" because most people come to lawyers in times of need, with no money: the last situation when one would normally willingly employ a stranger to assist with one's most personal life; my work is purely transitory: there will be nothing left to show for my hours of toil, except a dusty warehouse full of old files; as an architect, you leave behind a tangible and often handsome construction, and you should be grateful for that legacy; apart from any inherent interest that one may possess in the intricacies of English law, having a good joke at the expense of the legal system, or one's client, or other lawyers, or oneself, are the greatest pleasures a lawyer can expect from his profession. Do you understand?'

Whether she had listened, I know not, but her reaction had been pre-determined:

'We need to talk seriously,' she said, ever an indication of ill tidings.

'I thought I was.'

'It's not just the indifference with which you treat your job: you have no respect for your clients, my grandmother doubtless included; you overcharge them and think of their fees as monthly targets not their own hard-earned money which they are paying you to help them; you don't or won't try to appreciate forms of music that you haven't experienced before and prefer to insult the players and their families; you drag me round museums full of dead animals without even enquiring whether I'm remotely interested: well, James I'm not! I don't give a damn about the Premium mass extinction, or whether *Tyrannosaurus Rex* had feathers; I want to live in the here and now, and plan the future, not forever consider what has been: that's why it's called *history*, James. You drink too much; you quaff expensive Champagne as you would water without the slightest appreciation for its taste, and are continually drunk, or on the way to being drunk; I don't want to be with someone who has to be drunk to enjoy himself; your best friend is an obnoxious, womanising oaf and frankly I have no idea how he is a supposedly successful barrister; you actually *forgot* our last date because of him; but worst of all, James, you fancy your bloody secretary!'

As she had said all this, I thought of answers for all her unfair accusations: I wanted to say in return that I had respect for my clients, especially her grandmother whom I liked and cared for very much; I had just spent the best part of a month acting without charge for an unfortunate and impoverished Katherine Hunt, and had got into trouble for doing so; my fees must be looked at as monthly targets, because otherwise I'd have my crown of partner removed, and possibly my job also; I conceded that I'd never be passionate about Chamber music; she seemed to enjoy the Natural History Museum and I had hoped she appreciated that my interests extended beyond the legal; my appreciation of Champagne *is* great, and it just so happens I like appreciating it quickly; but my actions had proved to her on numerous occasions that alcohol is not an essential ingredient in having fun; to call Charlie an obnoxious, womanising oaf was hard: he wasn't the most sensible man I knew, but despite his apparent distaste for all things legal, he worked bloody hard all day, and sometimes all night, and the time he could spend away from his job was used to forget the serious and stressful court proceedings that occupied most of his life; I had already explained to her that in relation to our last date, the word 'forget' was rather hard on me, and in fact it had been more of a cock-up; finally, for the only woman in recent times to have captured my heart as quickly and completely as Sara had, it was an absurdity that she should claim that I had feelings for Emily.

But I couldn't say a damn thing. Even as my mind began to construct these thoughts into a workable argument to explain that she was wrong, it began to dawn on me that Sara must have been pondering upon my faults for some time, of which it seemed there were indeed too large a number for her to consider our futures entwined, and had now, uncompromisingly, and with no easy way of rectifying the situation, told me exactly what she thought of me.

This conclusion rendered my sails devoid of wind, my rigging in tatters. I opened my mouth a couple of times in an attempt to convey my thoughts, but each time, the realisation that my combined faults were too great for her stopped me. She realised what my confused mind was trying to do, and like one would put down an injured racehorse, said: 'I'm sorry, James, I've already made up my mind.'

I was too late: I knew, despite her flawed reasoning, that she had indeed made up her mind. Then a flash of anger rose within me, and I wanted to tell her exactly what I thought of her to hurt her in return...

but realised suddenly that her tiny faults did not matter to me; her faults didn't quite make her perfect, but they didn't make her any less attractive in my eyes. And thus my anger faded: I had no reason to be angry, and an emotionless state quickly took over as I tried to comprehend what had happened.

My comprehension remained absent when she said, 'Well, I suppose I should go. I can't really think of anything else to say.'

Neither could I, and she departed leaving me with a full gin and tonic and hers half full. I drank them and ordered two more. After a moment's consideration, my anger returned. Why hadn't she told me of her concerns before? They were only small problems that I could have changed if need be. Perhaps she thought I couldn't change. Perhaps I couldn't. Perhaps her perception of me was more accurate than my own. The gin went to my head quickly in my emotional state, and thoughts of worry, doubt and shame visited and revisited my mind, each time in a slightly different form, in a slightly less rational manner.

CHAPTER 42

Life Goes On

Somehow I managed to get home in one piece and collapse on my bed. The next morning, a Saturday, I woke up in my suit. I had managed to relieve myself of my tie which gave me a slight feeling of satisfaction: even in my addled state, I had had the forethought to remove it in case it asphyxiated me whilst sleeping: an unfortunate way to go indeed.

It gradually dawned on me what had happened the night before: Sara had dumped me and I had got very drunk, on my own.

Then to my delight I saw on my bedside table a glass of water and a packet of soluble paracetamol, also containing codeine and caffeine, next to it. Sometimes, even when totally pissed, I did have remarkable foresight. I plopped two of the huge, life-saving pills into the water and listened the glorious sound of them effervescing, knowing that as soon as they had finished, I could drink the potion and my headache would start to vanish. Some minutes later the room was again silent and the pills had fully dissolved. I tipped the magnificent cocktail of drugs down my neck and decided to wait thirty minutes for them to kick in before contemplating any further form of movement.

Sometime during that period, but not before the drugs had worked, I realised it was my birthday.

Later in the morning, having had another soluble paracetamol, a cup of tea and a shower, shave and sheet change, I felt much better. Well enough, in fact, to descend the stairs to see if I had any birthday post. A paltry pile of post greeted me. There were three cards: one was from Emily, or presumably from Emily, because the name and address was typed and the envelope had a Bugle & Yarrington frank on it; another bore the handwriting of my mother, and the last that of my sister. I didn't open them until the evening, and the messages were so pointless I wondered why they had bothered wasting three perfectly good cards, envelopes and stamps. Well, two stamps, anyway.

I spent the day moping round my flat, attempting to do chores, or read, or even do nothing, and think nothing. But every time I focused for more than a minute on anything other than Sara, her image, her words and her memory would again creep into my thoughts, causing a hitherto unknown pain in my heart. Despite once having a counter-argument for each of her criticisms, these were now forgotten and I began to believe that perhaps my character was indeed fatally flawed. If Sara, who seemed so right for me, thought I was useless in so many ways, who would fall in love with me for who I was? Maybe she was right: maybe I was a useless drunk who bored people with trips round the Natural History Museum. Maybe Charlie was an obnoxious womanising oaf. Maybe I was.

The highlight of the day was when my sister phoned to wish me happy birthday. She announced – as part of my birthday present she said – that she was pregnant and due in October. I tried to be enthusiastic as possible, and felt rather guilty for not having seen her for so long; last time she'd not even had a small bump to give her state away. Finally, she invited Sara and I to join her and Michael and Ben in Cornwall for the last week of August. I accepted gratefully, and said it'd be unlikely that Sara would be able to make it. I couldn't bear to hear her words of sympathy so soon after my misfortune. She knew something was up when she asked what I was doing for my birthday and I hesitated. To her credit, she did not probe further.

Having decided it was futile to attempt any further kind of enjoyment while this state of depression was upon me, the rest of my birthday evening consisted of me, fish and chips, and a bottle of red.

The second bottle of red made Sunday morning less pleasant than it otherwise might have been, and thus Sunday passed in a similar manner to the previous day. Whilst ironing part of my vast shirt collection on Sunday afternoon, it struck me that I had to pull myself together: I therefore decided that for the week ahead, the first without Sara, the third week in August and my last working week until September, I would work hard to gain something out of the lousy situation before joining my sister and her family in Cornwall the week after.

On Monday morning, I discovered a flaw in my plan: it was still the summer holidays, and although divorces were doubtless brewing steadily, there was a significant lack of files on my desk. The one client who did keep me busy, however, was Katherine Hunt: I spent most of the week attempting to agree a favourable settlement. Having not been married long to her partner, her legal grounds with which to fight were not strong, but her moral grounds were sound. Thankfully, her husband's solicitor obviously thought her client was a bastard, and agreed with most of my arguments, making it relatively easy for Katherine's husband to agree to at least some of our financial terms, the most important being his agreement to sell the matrimonial home. This made for a triumphant but lonely celebration on Thursday night. By Friday morning, I had even got him to agree that my firm would do the conveyancing, and having obtained the promise of a signed house transfer from him as part of the deal, I went to see Yarrington immediately to get the property sold.

'Morning James,' he beamed as I entered his office. Then his phone rang.

'Lynn, can you take it please – it looks like James has some instructions,' said Yarrington, and then, turning to me: 'I expect it's Mr Wyles. New client. Buying a house. Jittery as a paranoid meerkat and a complete fool. Rings up every day to see how things are going, despite me telling me him I'd ring him if anything did happen. He's totally stupid – works in the city – earns a bomb – God knows how.'

Then Lynn piped up, 'There's Mr Wyles on the phone, says he wants to speak to you urgently.'

'Bloody idiot,' said Yarrington, quite loud enough for Lynn's phone to have picked up the words and conveyed them to the client. 'Tell him I'm not here,' he continued, equally as loud.

'Mr Yarrington says he's not here,' said Lynn.

It was difficult to work out whether Lynn was being intentionally bloody-minded or just very stupid. But she had certainly enraged Yarrington because by this stage his colour had risen to that of a particularly brightly coloured beetroot.

'Damn you, Lynn! Now I'm going have to talk to him. Put him through. Sorry James, won't be a tick.'

Yarrington's phone rang.

'Good afternoon, Mr Wyles,' said Yarrington is his client voice. 'I'm very well – trust you are too? … Excellent … No, no! I think my secretary meant … Mr Wyles! I was in fact referring to a client who has just arrived in the office…! No, of *course* it doesn't mean I'll ignore you when you come to the office … No, I'm afraid nothing has happened since yesterday … These things do take time … It's perfectly normal … Nothing to worry about … Yes, Mr Wyles, I'll call as soon as hear anything … Yes, speak tomorrow then … Goodbye.'

Down slammed the phone.

'Bloody idiot. God, I hate clients.'

Just then, Paul, head of the company department, came in.

'Afternoon all,' he said cockily.

'What the dickens do *you* want, Paul? I'm busy here with James,' said the now impatient Yarrington.

'I just wanted you to check the bill for Abacus Ltd. I was worried that perhaps my billing figure was a little ambitious. Would you mind?'

Yarrington impatiently waved him over and grabbed the bill, eyes narrowing as he perused it. 'You've charged them fifteen hundred!' he exclaimed as his eyes reached the bottom line.

'Yes, I can always bring it down a bit if you think it's too much…'

'Nonsense! These buggers have made my life hell for nearly twenty years! No doubt you had to deal with Jones, the director? He's a real shit. James is doing his divorce. I'm amazed he found anyone stupid enough to marry him in the first place. No, no, no! Fifteen hundred, indeed! Fifteen hundred?!' he repeated, getting more irate by the second. 'These are one of the firm's oldest and wealthiest clients. The whole company is run by irksome little shits and just because they're called Abacus, doesn't mean they can count! You'll charge four grand for this one, and make sure a grand of that is billed to me, not you!'

'Right you are,' said Paul, embarrassed by something or other, and left.

'Sorry James, one of those infuriating days when one's time seems to belong to someone else. Lynn, could you be a darling and make us two cups of tea please?'

'I've just made you one, David,' she said.

'Yes, Lynn, I can see that. I'm thirsty and James doesn't have one at all. If you would be so kind…?'

Lynn levered herself out of her chair and left, grumbling something under her breath.

'Right, James. How can I help?'

'I have a client who goes by the name of Katherine Hunt…'

'The name rings a bell…'

'Through a masterful piece of negotiation, I have persuaded her husband to sell the matrimonial home to give her a largely moral payout for being a class A bastard. It's a big property.'

'Good, I like big properties. One's bill is rarely challenged.'

'Ah,' I said.

'Oh,' said Yarrington, 'Do I perceive from your reaction that this is your so-called *pro bono* case?'

'How perceptive you are!'

'I'll do it this once. Be careful though, James. I'm not the senior partner any longer, but more importantly one doesn't want to tie oneself up with the clients too much. I gather you've been seeing something of old Mrs Ricketts' granddaughter.'

The words struck me with almost a physical force; thus far I had managed not to think of her all day.

'You should be careful, James,' continued Yarrington, 'Ricketts, Hunt, I don't know.'

'Well, the Ricketts granddaughter had enough of me as of last week.'

'Good,' said Yarrington, not intentionally unkindly. 'Well, I'll do this conveyance for you, but I am going to charge a bit – it's a huge property,' he continued, looking at the particulars. 'In fact, how the hell did you wangle such a good settlement?' he asked, peering up at me.

I shrugged, for once being modest.

Yarrington looked at me with approval, and the following silence made it clear our conversation was over.

'Thank you,' I said, and left as quickly as I could, leaning against the wall as soon as the door had closed. Yarrington's words about Sara had hit me hard. Underneath my cheerful demeanour, I had an unprecedented sense of underlying sadness and regret: sadness to have lost Sara, regret that I had done so in the manner in which I had, and because I hadn't said anything once it had happened.

Normally, I would have taken Emily out for lunch to unload my problems on her, but alas! she was away, and although Matthew and I had become pretty good friends – as far as that is possible in the same office – I was not ready to confide my affairs of love to someone ten years my junior.

Such thoughts were eventually banished, and my mind turned to the present: to Friday afternoon. Having obtained Yarrington's consent to do Katherine Hunt's conveyancing for virtually nothing, her case had more or less been concluded. Despite coming to a very satisfactory outcome for her, Sunday night's resolution to work hard all week had not been entirely successful: my fifth hangover of the week was just wearing off, and despite a remorseful thought about my lack of determination, I concluded then and there that my steam had irretrievably run out. By the end of the day I was dearly glad that I could depart the office for another evening of miserable drunken solitude.

'Bye, Sue,' I said wearily as I left, walking straight into Cathy Bugle as my downcast eyes failed to spot even her vast bulk entering the hallway.

'Beg your pardon, Cathy! How are you?'

'Not unreasonable. And yourself?'

'Splendid!' I replied, feeling far from it, but not having the energy to make small talk.

'Frank in?'

'Yes, I should think so…'

'He's in his office – not to be disturbed under any circumstances,' piped up Sue from her reception desk.

'I'm his wife, for goodness sake!'

'Let me take you up to his office,' I said, never having been particularly concerned for authority, especially Bugle's.

I knocked on his door. Noises indicative of a certain amount of hurried movement emanated from within, followed by a 'Do *not* enter! There's paper *all over* the floor!'

Cathy and I looked at each other, perplexed. But I could see her begin to wonder why her husband should have to power to stop her, his wife, from entering his office. Clearly having found no satisfactory answer, she barged in, followed tentatively by me.

And there was paper all over the floor. It looked as though Bugle had swept the whole lot off his desk in one sweep.

'Are you all right, Frank? You look flustered.'

'No, I'm not all right. I've been trying sort all this out and now you're here.'

'Lovely to see you too, darling!'

Bugle just sat there, facing us from behind his large partner's desk – the closed type that has a panelled back in order that it should look elegant when it faced into the room. I wondered how many partners had owned it since its construction in what I guessed to be about a hundred and thirty years ago. My main problem was estimating the average working-life-span of a partner in late Victorian England, when cases like *Jarndyce* could keep a partner in business from his twenties until he was too old and weak and tired of the case to come to work at all. Now, after years of legal reform, cases are still as tedious, but the tedium is condensed into less time and it is possible for the lawyer to extract more in the way of remuneration from each one, facilitating earlier retirements after a more lucrative career. Such were my thoughts when I noticed a silence between the Bugles and Cathy looking at Frank very oddly.

I have no idea what inspired her to ask it, but Cathy then asked the strangest of questions: 'What on earth of have you got under your table, Frank?'

Bugle looked like a schoolboy who had just been caught throwing a paper aeroplane which had successfully hit the back of the master's head as he wrote on the blackboard.

'My feet!' he joked, forcing a smile.

But Cathy had already started moving across the room. Bugle jumped up and put his enormously long arms out in her direction, as if trying in some vain way to stop his wife's physical progress across the room to the desk. Once she had a clear view into the leg-hole under his desk, she clapped her hand to her mouth and stood staring.

Bugle stared at her.

I stared at them both.

After a lengthy pause, Cathy said: 'James! Over here, now! I want a witness!'

My eye caught Bugle's in order to obtain his assent. It was not forthcoming, but he didn't object; I therefore assumed his tacit agreement and walked over to the far side of the desk.

What we beheld was surprising.

The opening to the large leg-hole of the desk had framed – with remarkable composition – a particularly pert bottom, just about covered by the shortest of skirts. The owner of said bottom was on all fours under the desk, head into the hole, bare legs and feet out. On the floor next to the strumpet lay her particularly brief briefs and matching bra which had evidently been designed to support a substantial pair of tits.

A shapely hand on the end of a slim arm extended from deeper within the leg-hole of the desk and collected the offending undergarments, while the bottom started wiggling as its owner began to reverse out.

'Stay in there you little tart!' screamed Cathy. 'I don't want to see your face!'

The bottom stopped wiggling.

No one moved for some time.

'Goodbye, Frank,' said Cathy, and walked out.

CHAPTER 43

Cornwall

My sister Sarah, now noticeably pregnant, Michael and Ben had already had a week of their annual fortnight to Cornwall when I joined them for the second week. I arrived in Penzance after an epic railway journey from Paddington, and was thankful to find them waiting at the station.

'Where's Emily?!' demanded Ben, straight away.

'She's on holiday with her Daddy,' I said, but this did little to improve his mood.

We drove to the cottage near St Ives, on loan from one of Michael's father's friends, and Ben immediately demanded to go crabbing, which I secretly enjoy very much. Ben and I set off down the track to the sea leaving Sarah and Michael breathing large sighs of relief to have a moment's peace from their exhausting and inexhaustible son. After a while Ben was lucky and wound the orange string up to find an equally orange and fairly sizable crab on the end. The crab was placed in a bucket, and Ben wanted to know all about him: could his pincers bite your finger off? What about your arm? Why were his eyes on stalks? Why do crabs walk sideways? Does he taste nice? I answered all his questions except the last, because I had no intention of killing the crab. After gingerly picking it up from behind, Ben threw it back into the sea, much to the crab's relief. Those little stalky eyes had been filled with terror.

We went back to the cottage in time for supper and had pre-killed crab for a starter. Ben didn't like it and thought that crabs were much more amusing alive. Once he had gone to bed, Sarah, Michael and I sat up and chatted until the small hours. She asked directly what was wrong and I told her about Sara. It was good to talk about it, and although I didn't say exactly why Sara had decided she could not conceive our combined future, her kind words were comforting.

The rest of the week was spent on the beaches, cliffs and coves of the westernmost part of Cornwall. Ben was fascinated by the rockpools and their contents, and with his shrimping net we managed to find all sorts of new and wonderful creatures for him to examine. We went on cliff walks, and Ben always insisted on bringing his kite in the shape of *Pteranodon* that I had given him for his last birthday. The first time we launched it, he was inquisitive to know all about pterosaurs, the ancient flying reptiles, and I smiled ruefully as I thought of Sara's opinion of the subject. We built huge sandcastles to withstand the incoming tide and Cornish waves, and Ben pretended to be Canute in consistently vain attempts to stop the sea destroying them. Leaving Sarah to peruse the art galleries and shops of St Ives, the boys went mackerel fishing on a little boat, and caught a surprising number. Ben watched the slowly dying fish in the bottom of the boat in fascination and without remorse; I felt rather sorry for them. Michael insisted that Ben was old enough to attempt surfing, and Uncle James was appointed his teacher while his parents kept warm and dry. Being Englishmen, we braved the waters without wetsuits and after half an hour of successful surfing, ran up the beach to our waiting towels, cold and blue.

The week in Cornwall did me good: the slowness of life compared to that of London was blissful and the most important decisions that had to be made were what type of pasty to have at lunch time, or in the evenings whether to have red meat and red wine, or fish and white wine. The solitude of walking along cliffs almost alone with just the vast expanse of sea at which to gaze was liberating. While the pain of losing Sara was still always present, I was becoming numb to it; while my heart still missed a beat when I thought of her, the Cornish sea air and exercise made it stronger by the day.

CHAPTER 44

All At Sea

September arrived, and with it, Emily.

'Morning James!' she said when I arrived at the office, rushing round from her desk to embrace me.

'Morning!'

I couldn't think of any adjectives or pet names to call her, because in her post-holiday and very bronzed state she looked quite gorgeous, and even I had forgotten how spectacular she was. Despite being September, the weather was still very warm, and I was delighted to note that Emily was still using her summer wardrobe of short office skirts. All I could manage was a broad smile: I was delighted to have her back in the office after two weeks of what had seemed like an eternity without her.

'How are you?' she asked.

'Infinitely better having seen your legs!' I said, my senses finally returning.

'Shut up, James!' she said, her face showing visible signs of reddening beneath her tan.

'Good holiday?'

'Wonderful!'

'What did you get up to?'

'Swam, ate, and painted. I've put on so much weight!'

She looked lithe and fit enough to have won Wimbledon.

'I painted so much!' she enthused, 'I've enough for a whole exhibition! Well – some of them may be a bit sketchy, but then I could do a sketching exhibition!'

'Brilliant!' I said, her enthusiasm being infectious. 'Did your father enjoy himself?'

'Yes, I think so. It was odd going away with him, but lovely: I hadn't spent time with him for years. We had a number of looks in restaurants as people were trying to work out whether he was my lover or my father! He said he was flattered that people assumed he was so wealthy! How have you been? How's Sara?'

Despite having the underlying knowledge that something was troubling me, and that I wasn't happy, again, I had thus far managed to banish thoughts of Sara on that particular morning. But again, the mention of her name brought the unhappiness to the surface, and I felt a physical shock at the mention of it. I had hoped someone had already told Emily.

'She gave me the flick.'

'Oh, James! I'm sorry. Are you all right?'

I didn't need to answer.

'No, of course you're not,' she answered for me. 'I'm so very sorry. She was great.'

'She still is, that's the worst of it.'

The phone rang for the first time since we had been in. Normally the expectation would have been to hear Mrs Ricketts' voice, but since Tim was now her lawyer – a thought that distressed me now she had no reason not to be my client – my guess as to who it would be was uncertain.

'Hello, James, it's Katherine Hunt.'

'Hello, how are you?'

'Fine thanks. Thank you so much for doing such a great job with my mess. You were brilliant! I had never hoped for such a good outcome from such a lousy situation.'

'It was a pleasure.'

'I once said I didn't know how to repay you, but I hope I have a solution.'

'Yes?' I said, intrigued.

'Your firm does shipping law doesn't it?'

'Yes, our partner George Teddy is an eminent figure in the shipping world. He's got over thirty years experience,' I equivocated, not mentioning that his experience has been gained more at the helm of his yacht and from reading *Yachting Monthly* than in the courtroom.

'Fantastic. My brother John owns a large freight company, and his previous lawyers have caused several fairly big cock-ups, causing him to loose some substantial sums of money. He wants to talk to you about suing them.'

'I suppose that would be more of a professional negligence claim,' I said, doubtful whether Teddy's tenuous shipping knowledge extended into such treacherous waters.

'Yes, but he assures me he needs a shipping lawyer who understands that end of things to bring the claim successfully,' she said.

'Right, well, we must see him,' I said trying to remain positive. 'I don't suppose you know the name of the firm he wants to sue?'

'Yes, he did say. Priest and Parsons, it's called. If we're successful, he said he'd pay you for all your work with me, so I hope I may be able to repay you for all your marvellous help.'

I gulped. I had enjoyed helping Katherine, and I wanted to help her brother. I just wasn't sure whether the one-man shipping department of Bugle & Yarrington would be strong enough to take on the city giant Priest and Parsons. But I remembered Marcus Todd from the Lincoln's Inn Garden Party, the shipping lawyer who worked there, and concluded that if all their lawyers were of a similar calibre, we did indeed stand a chance. And I sorely remembered the plight of Teddy: this deal would, from the sound of it, be lucrative, and save not only his job, but also his failing relationship with the snobbish Miss Pound. Foolishly, perhaps, my mind was made up.

'Well, I'd better introduce him to Teddy, then.'

'Fantastic. Can I introduce him to you?'

'Certainly. When are you both free?'

'This afternoon.'

'Three o'clock?'

'Yes. Fantastic. See you then.'

'Tell him to bring some paperwork!' I said before she went, evidently excited that she had found her brother a lawyer.

I phoned Teddy to tell him the good news, but his phone rang and rang for so long that had he been asleep it would surely have woken him, leading me to the conclusion that he was out. I phoned Lynn, supposedly his secretary when he does produce some work, to see if she knew his whereabouts.

'Where's Teddy?'

'Out sailing. He left this morning.' said the remarkably helpful old cow.

'What! I need him at the office by three!'

'He said there was no point in even pretending to be at the office, now that the partners had almost unanimously given him the proverbial boot. He's off to the Scilly Isles.'

'Well, has he sailed?!'

'How should I know?'

'Telephone the bloody yacht club.'

'I don't know the number.'

'Yes, you do Lynn, we have rung him there before. If you can't find it, ring the operator.'

'They don't have operators now.'

'You know what I mean, Lynn.'

'James? Oh! Hello! Teddy here. At the yacht club. Lynn just caught me finishing lunch before I find my boat. You wanted me? I'm afraid I can't go for a pint this evening, I'm off to the Scilly Isles.'

'With Miss Pound?'

'No, no, she still is under the impression I'm being booted out, and she's not so keen on that at all,' he said, apparently accepting his destiny.

'Well, if you can get back to the office by three, I think I have a case big enough to keep you afloat in the office for weeks! Fancy taking on Priest and Parsons?'

'Good Lord, no! We'd have no chance! Thanks for the offer though. See you in a week!'

And he put the phone down.

'Lynn! The number of the yacht club, please?'

'I haven't got it any longer.'

'Well where is it?'

'In the bin.'

'Where is your bin, Lynn?'

'Under my desk.'

'Seeing as I'm on the telephone to your extension number, my extraordinary powers of deduction tell me that you cannot be more than three feet from your desk, unless you have installed a particularly long chord on your telephone. May I suggest, therefore, that you bend down and retrieve the number from your bin?'

'For goodness sake!' she said, as if I had asked her to walk to the yacht club personally, 'I'll have to put the receiver down to do that! Hang on!' Her phone slammed onto what must have been her desk, and there was much heavy breathing, sighing and grunting as no doubt she tried to squeeze her bosom and arms beneath to desk to retrieve the bin. I heard Yarrington in the background saying 'What on earth are you doing, woman?!' which made me wish I had been in his office to witness the incident.

'I have it!' she said triumphantly, but out of breath.

I phoned the yacht club for some minutes, but apparently the entire membership was all at sea.

'You'll have to phone Katherine and postpone the meeting. We'll try and get hold of Teddy somehow – even if it's after he's arrived on the Scilly Isles. I'm sure you'll be able to talk sense into him at some stage,' said the wise Emily. I agreed that Katherine must be phoned, but was not so sure Teddy would see sense, if, indeed, it was sense; his reaction may have been the wisest: it would be a huge undertaking to take on Priest and Parsons in a litigious claim.

So I telephoned Katherine to apologise that the meeting would have to be postponed, explaining that Teddy had been called urgently to the Scilly Isles on a site visit. She was impressed that he made so much effort for his clients. I agreed. Quite reasonably, she wanted to know when he'd be back. I said we hoped to speak to him tomorrow to confirm. The excellent service she had received from the Firm in the past, coupled with her recently acquired high estimation of Teddy paid off: the client was quite happy about the whole situation. To prevent Teddy becoming an ex-lawyer, we had twenty-four hours to locate him, bobbing around on a thirty-foot tub somewhere between Chichester and the Scilly Isles.

But by the close of play, and despite Matthew's best efforts with maritime research, short of calling the Royal Navy or coastguard and reporting Teddy for large-scale drug trafficking in an attempt to have him repatriated, there was nothing we could do to reach him. So we did what all proper lawyers do in similar situations: gave up and went home.

CHAPTER 45

The Mysteries Of Shipping Law

The next morning I arrived in the office determined to find Teddy. Matthew had already ascertained from the yacht club that Teddy's boat had a radio, but that it appeared to be off. He contacted the harbourmaster at Hugh Town on St Mary's, the largest of the Scillies where it had been established that Teddy was sailing for, and asked him to notify us if Teddy took a berth there. Then we sat down to consider what else could be done.

'Did you notice Teddy's umbrella in the brolly stand yesterday?' asked Matthew.

'Can't say I did. Why?'

'Well yesterday was baking, and there were certainly no umbrellas in the stand because Angela walked into it and knocked it over. This morning the brolly was there.'

'Are you sure it was his?'

Matthew looked at me, smiling. It was an unnecessary question: Teddy's umbrella was an ancient affair, and quite unmistakable; it had a marvellous old-fashioned curved handle, made out of some beautiful red hardwood that was probably now extinct, and had a frayed bootlace tied round it to keep it together when closed.

'Are you saying he's actually *in* the office?'

'Just a thought.'

I leapt off my chair and ran up to Teddy's office to find him calmly reading *Yachting Monthly* and sipping a coffee, which, from the boozey smell emanating from the cup, was laced with something much stronger.

'What on earth are you doing here?!' I asked, incredulously.

'What on earth do you mean?' he said, vacantly.

'We all thought you were on your boat!'

'I should be,' he said grumpily, 'but some silly bugger drove off with the wrong trailer and the wrong boat. Dennis Heath, his name is.'

My understanding of the situation was not complete, and Teddy realised this from my expression. 'I arrived at the yacht club to find my boat absent, which drew me to the conclusion that someone had half-inched it. I alerted the local constabulary and the secretary of the club. The secretary came with me to the scene of the crime and noticed that Mr Heath's boat was parked next to where mine should have been. Mr Heath had departed earlier towing a boat away behind his motor vehicle. The secretary was able to contact Mr Heath before he had gone too far. Realising his mistake, he drove back to the club, by which stage the local constabulary were on hand to arrest him. Despite his, the secretary's and my own protestations that his mistake was innocent, it was only when the identical blue covers were pulled off the boats that the officer in charge realised that Mr Heath would have to have been a raving nutcase to have driven off with my rotten shell over his polished craft, and the handcuffs were thus released. Despite her husband's criminal innocence, I fear his marital stability is far from healthy: Mrs Heath, realising I was a lawyer, and in a mood that I would not describe as balanced, asked if I handled divorces. I duly gave her my card with your number on it so expect a call from her. Patricia Heath.

'Anyway,' continued Teddy, 'by this time it was far too late to set off to the Scilly Isles, so to Mayfair I returned. Today there is a force eight, and thus you find me, in my office and frankly, rather cheesed off.'

'Yes, well you had me worried too. I want you to do this Priest and Parsons case.'

'Good God, man! I thought you were joking! You must be joking!'

'Teddy, this case could save your bacon.'

'I'd be damn fool to take them on.'

'You have three willing helpers in the form of Matthew, Emily and I,'

'You *are* serious?'

'Of course I am.'

'Thank you James, really. But I haven't done a case on this scale for years. I don't think I could cope.'

'I just thought of Miss Pound, that's all. One case. A few weeks of work. And a good client. Still, if you've made up your mind...'

At the mention of Miss Pound, Teddy stirred. 'Who is the client?' he asked.

'Hunt Shipping is a limited company,' said John Hunt, brother of

Katherine, 'We ship engines and engine components worldwide.'

Teddy, perhaps in fear of losing Miss Pound, or perhaps because he had nothing to loose, had finally come to his senses and agreed to a meeting with his new shipping client. At three o'clock the day after originally planned, a mere twenty-fours late, John Hunt had arrived. He was a well-dressed fellow and looked like his sister, in a handsome, masculine way. He had by all accounts made a great deal of money through Hunt Shipping, but had recently lost a great deal too. He began to tell us how.

The company had chartered a ship laden with a large consignment of engine parts to be exported from Japan for use in European factories. Not long after leaving Japan, the ship had developed a considerable leak and put into Hong Kong for repairs. Thankfully, none of the cargo had been damaged. Temporary repairs were carried out, but despite the ship's captain and the shipowner's own surveyor advising that the ship was not seaworthy, the advice from Priest and Parsons (who had drafted all the contractual agreements and insurance policies between the parties, and who had employed their own surveyor) was that the ship must leave in order that the cargo should reach the European factories in time for their needs.

In heavy weather on the South China Sea, the temporary repairs failed and the ship began taking on water rapidly. Thankfully, the design of the ship was such that total loss was avoided, and it put it into Singapore.

The ship's captain refused further temporary repairs, and the shipowner's surveyor agreed, stating that the cargo would have be unloaded and ship would have be properly repaired in a dry dock. Even the surveyor sent from Priest and Parsons was obliged to draw the same conclusion. Much of the cargo had by this stage been damaged by seawater, and that which wasn't would arrive too late at its destination to satisfy the contractual terms of the shipment. One of the destination factories subsequently sued Hunt Shipping successfully for breach of contract because the goods were still stuck in Singapore when they should have arrived. Priest and Parsons had drafted this contract.

John went into great detail about the drafting of the documents and kept referring to failed insurance policies, bills of lading, charterparties, time charters and other such terms peculiar to the shipping world. He discussed suing the carrier for breach of the Hague-Visby rules, whatever they might be, suing the surveyor arranged by Priest and

Parsons for negligent advice, and most importantly, suing Priest and Parsons themselves for the abysmal drafting of all the aforesaid documents and contracts.

Much of this talk went rather over my head, but I looked interested and concerned at the right places, and tried my best to keep track of events. I was mightily pleased that Teddy seemed to know exactly what was going on, and that he was even noticeably excited by the case, his eye glinting when he heard new facts from John, or when he scanned through a document or contract to find a sentence or clause in our favour. Once John had finished his story, Teddy checked some of the documents again, and concluded:

'Everything Priest and Parsons has done seems to have been a disaster, and I suspect it all originates from the negligent drafting of the initial charterparties and bills of lading. They seem to have totally failed in maintaining their duty of care, and have seemingly not acted as reasonably competent solicitors should have. If their errors directly caused your financial loss, as again it appears, their tortious liability is unguarded. This is all we have to prove! I will have to have a look in more detail of course, but if all you have told me is true, and we have the evidence, I suspect we'll have a fair trade wind behind us, and dear old Priest and Parsons will be stuck in the Doldrums!

'The most interesting thing is that their surveyor gave the go-ahead for the ship to leave Hong Kong. This *may* be because they knew damn well that if the goods didn't get to Europe within the (negligently drafted) contractual time period, Hunt Shipping could be sued, and they could be sued in turn for negligent drafting. They may have taken this gamble on purpose, and if they did – which I intend to find out very soon – it will not pay off!

'Of course, I'll need absolutely *all* the papers,' continued Teddy, 'but from those you brought today, your organisation appears to be thoroughly ship-shape and Bristol fashion, which makes my job much easier. I do like organised clients! Once I have all the paperwork and have reported fully to you, we can assess the situation. How does that sound?'

'Brilliant. Thank you!' said John, rightly impressed by Teddy's handling of the matter. 'I'll let you have the other papers by courier this afternoon. There are a few boxes of them!'

John left, apparently a good deal less worried than when he had arrived, which is always pleasing to see in a client. I began to feel that shipping litigation was the most morally acceptable type of law I'd yet come across: the firm we were would be fighting was wealthy and insured, and no individual would be financially shafted, even though the lawyers of this prestigious firm seemed to have been thoroughly negligent and had offered very expensive and lousy advice to Hunt Shipping Limited.

The initial meeting had thus been a success, and because Teddy had agreed to consider the initial stages of the case on his own, my trainee and I both returned to our office, leaving Teddy to return to his for a further perusal of John's papers.

Because of the paucity of unhappy families, Matthew and I found ourselves happily unemployed, and having congratulated him on his inspired thought about Teddy's umbrella, I gave him leave to depart early. He did not wait for me to change my mind. Emily too was not busy, and we found ourselves looking at each other across the room.

'James, you're very glum. Sara?'

My heart jumped at the sound of her name. 'Yes, I suppose. I still can't believe she said what she said. I'm also vaguely worried about this Hunt case. I did such a good job with Katherine, I'd hate for us to bugger up her brother's business! And if we win, the brother has promised to pay my fees for her case, which'll get me out of the mire with Bugle and Angela. There's a lot riding on it.'

'Well, I think you need cheering up. I don't like to see you so miserable. Dinner at mine?'

I smiled. 'There's nothing I'd rather do! But first, I have the partner's meeting so I'm afraid I can't leave early. I have to try and persuade them to keep Teddy, for the time being at least.'

'That's ok. I'll wait for you. Good luck.'

It being nearly four-thirty, I ascended once more to the Dining Room, this time for the September partner's meeting, safe in the knowledge that a good evening lay ahead.

CHAPTER 46

Retirements

The partners assembled around the dining table, as usual, and waited for Bugle to arrive, which didn't take long.

'Today we have to address some unhappy issues,' he began. Everyone looked round at each other. Bugle's admission that affairs had become unhappy meant that circumstances were almost certainly worse.

'It is with much sadness that I have to report that Margaret, who has been head of the family department for more years than I care to remember, has decided to retire.'

All eyes were immediately on her. She looked vaguely sad through her smile.

'Yes,' she said, 'I'm afraid so. It has been a long and difficult decision, made mainly because my husband is also to retire next month. Eventually he persuaded me that enjoying life outside the office was preferable to enjoying life in the office.'

I failed to see why she had needed persuasion.

Everyone offered congratulations and support, except me. I wondered how on earth I was going to cope without Margaret's advice on my cases where the law had got a little beyond me.

'But the good news,' continued Bugle, 'is that we will shall need a new head of department.'

And his eyes swung round to me.

Another promotion! This would indeed be good news: I would have Margaret's office, which had more sizeable desks and magnificently large windows overlooking the street in front: my days of looking into the courtyard at the back would be over. James James, head of the family department at Bugle & Yarrington! Maybe they'd hire a more junior lawyer to assist me. The fears about my lack of legal knowledge disappeared as I realised my word would be gospel in all things family: there would be no one to challenge me! Best of all, it would mean a higher percentage of takings from the partnership.

A wry smile curled Bugle's lips as he declared: 'We have yet to appoint that person, but the interviews have already taken place, and we have thus far narrowed it down to two candidates. Margaret and I are re-interviewing them this week, and a decision will be announced thereafter.'

Bugger.

'Sorry, James,' he added, to a few muted laughs.

It took me a while to forgive him for this doubly cruel treatment.

'I see Teddy isn't here,' said Bugle, about to broach the subject of another imminent departure, 'which is probably just as well. As you know, in June *two* votes were cast to decide what about to do about Teddy's recent performance. Again, as you know, we *almost* unanimously decided that while regretful, we would have to put it to him that his performance wasn't high enough for him to continue at the firm. I regretfully have to report, that he hasn't billed a penny since that decision,' he said, with some satisfaction, 'and therefore, I am going to ask him to resign.'

Bugle surveyed the scene. Yarrington sat silently, looking at the table, ever so slightly shaking his head. Having resigned as senior partner, there was little he could do, and in truth, had he still been senior partner, the others would have revolted against him anyway. The position was such that Teddy had no cards to play, except one. And I had to play it for him.

I stood up, my eyes almost levelling with Bugle's, who unfortunately still had the height advantage.

'James, there's nothing you can say that will stop Teddy's departure. This firm is not a bloody charity! Sit down!' said Bugle, his temper rising.

'I beg to differ.'

'This had better be good, James.'

'Teddy is not here because he's in his office working very hard. He has just been instructed by a large shipping company. It is in the matter of a negligence claim against the company's previous lawyers.'

'And may we enquire who that company's lawyers were?' he said, sarcastically as if he expected it be a sole practitioner with an office in Slough.

'Priest and Parsons.'

At this name, everyone took note: Bugle looked decidedly angrier; Yarrington looked sharply at me, asking me with his wise old eyes a hundred questions at once; and the seemingly symbiotic company pair,

Paul and Martin looked at each other and began an urgent discussion in whispers.

'Christ! I hope our professional indemnity insurance is up to date!' said Bugle, perhaps wisely, 'Perhaps we should increase the cover!' No one laughed, and I believe he felt slightly foolish that his joke fell flat.

'And who is our client?'

'Hunt Shipping Limited.'

'That wouldn't be anything to do with that recent client of yours, who you gave your services away to, would it? I see there's a conveyancing file open for her, Yarrington. No doubt you'll be charging.'

'Of course,' said Yarrington.

'And what about this case, James?' asked Bugle. 'Are you and Teddy providing your services for free? You seem to be good at that.'

'No. In fact, we already have funds on account. Substantial funds.'

My reply had angered both Bugle and Yarrington, but for polarised reasons: Bugle because he could not argue with the fact we had monies on account, and Yarrington because he was hoping for my sake that it didn't have anything to do with Katherine Hunt, who he knew would be benefiting from his hugely reduced conveyancing bill.

'What are you two talking about?' said Bugle, turning on Paul and Martin, who had continued to whisper.

'We just wanted to know why I hadn't been consulted,' said Paul, 'I deal with company matters, especially company litigation.'

'There is a lot of technical shipping law involved,' I said, oiling the wheels.

'This is ridiculous!' said Bugle.

Now Yarrington rose to his feet. 'Why is it ridiculous, Frank? The only reason Teddy is being ousted is because, admittedly, his billing of late has been awful. But we haven't supported him. Teddy must have felt outdated and unwanted for months! We haven't *tried* to get in any shipping work. Now we have, for God's sake, let's give the man a chance! Even if it's one case, it may bring in some cash. How much is the claim for, James?'

'You don't want to know. Our insurers will hit the roof.' I couldn't pretend otherwise.

'Well, then,' continued Yarrington, 'he already has money on account: let's support him, even if it is his last case!'

After Yarrington's loud and enthusiastic speech, the silence was very evident.

'Give him a month,' I said, quietly.

Bugle looked around. The change in his expression was perceptible as he acknowledged the number of nods and quiet murmurs of agreement. Only Paul and Martin looked dubious, no doubt because they fancied adding the bill for this seemingly prestigious and valuable case to their own billing figures.

'Right. Fair enough. One month,' said Bugle.

Yarrington clapped his hand on the table in excitement and sat down. I followed suit.

'On the condition that Bugle and I examine the papers first, to make sure we know what this is all about,' said Yarrington, giving his generous support to Bugle, in an attempt to appease him somewhat.

Bugle looked content at this suggestion.

CHAPTER 47

Hidden Art

As planned, Emily and I arrived at her flat and I looked round attempting to locate the numerous canvasses that she must have used in order to paint enough pictures for an entire exhibition. But my search was in vain.

'Where are all your canvasses?'

'I haven't used canvas this time,' she smiled.

'Thank God for that! Have you finally realised that the earth can provide a finite number of them, and that they shouldn't be wantonly consumed?!'

'Shut up, James.'

'Well, where are the pictures, then?'

'Hidden from your view. You've never liked a single painting of mine before. I don't want your criticism all evening!'

'I've always admired your talent, even though the end result is ghastly! Please show them to me?!'

'No! You'll have to wait and see.'

'You're being very secretive.'

'Yes. Now what do you want for dinner?'

'Ah! Now there's a question!' Emily thought that her change of conversation had been unnoticed, and that the way to my heart was through her cooking. While the latter was certainly true, the former wasn't, and although I knew there was no point in pursuing the matter, I remained intrigued as to the subject of her new paintings, and where they were hidden.

Having assisted Emily to eat most of her delicious supper while she was cooking it, and having been sternly reprimanded for doing so, we sat down to eat the remnants.

'So,' she said smiling, 'what's news?'

I told her what had been happened in her absence: of Sara's views on my character; of settling Katherine Hunt's case very satisfactorily; of my somewhat disastrous birthday; of Cornwall; and of Katherine Hunt's reappearance in the office with her brother. Unusually, she didn't have much to say about Sara, except that she didn't know how daft she had been, which was pleasant to hear: since Sara's speech my confidence had plunged to depths not witnessed since being the only boy in the senior school choir who could sing soprano. I was still deeply troubled by the affair, and having spent many hours mulling Sara's words over and over and over, had almost come to believe that she was right. I suppose Emily didn't realise how my confidence had been shaken, and I couldn't blame her for it.

She talked of her holiday in Italy and I was most envious. She had a few photographs to aid her in completing some of the uncompleted paintings. She and her father had been to Florence, down through Tuscany, had spent a night in Rome (surely a week in Rome is insufficient? I questioned, but, she explained, they were on a painting holiday) and had ended up on the Amalfi Coast.

It was splendid to have Emily back in Town, and after the most jolly evening I'd had for a while, we went to bed, me taking up position on the sofa, having been banished from the spare room because it contained the new and secret artwork.

The next morning Emily and I arrived together to find my phone already ringing and Yarrington sitting at my desk, apparently waiting for me to arrive.

'Morning, David,' I said, 'do you mind if I take that?'

'Not at all.'

I reached across the ensconced Yarrington and picked up the phone.

'This is Patricia Heath. I met your colleague whose boat my stupid husband stole. I want to divorce him.'

'I see. May I ask a few questions?' I asked.

'Certainly.'

'Has he done this before?'

'What?'

'Boat stealing... or indeed any other similar incidences of absent-mindedness?'

'No.'

'Does he beat you?'

'No... well only... no, no! He doesn't beat me.'

'Madam, may I suggest that this is a daft reason for divorce? You will lose your home, a great deal of money in my fees, and his lawyer's fees, and most importantly you will lose your husband. Forget his misdemeanour: we all have faults. Forgive him, and continue to lead a happy life together! Good day!' And down went the phone.

'Bloody hell, James, do you speak to all your clients like that?' asked Yarrington, aghast at my manner.

'No, but she needed to be told. I don't have time for daft cows like her now I'm assisting Teddy with this shipping case.'

'You *assume* you are assisting Teddy. Presumably you are waiting to get the all-clear from the senior partner?'

'I assume I have it.'

'James, you always have been rather too cavalier.'

Yarrington paused, and I felt that a reprimand would be inevitable.

'But damn you, it seems to work!' smiled Yarrington.

The compliment in place of a chastisement was wonderful!

'Bugle and I went through it with Teddy last night,' continued Yarrington, 'and agreed that he should do it. I must say, it looks rather good: I don't understand the law, but the facts of the matter seem to go strongly in our favour. We looked at the paperwork: the fees that Priest and Parsons charged that poor bugger Hunt were astronomic! If we charge at half their rate, Teddy will make his annual target. I told him to quote two-thirds of their rate. We don't want to make it look as if we're cheap! Clients like paying for good service; it makes them think they are getting a better service.'

We both smiled.

'But James, why the hell didn't you tell me about the whole thing before the meeting?' he asked, almost exasperated.

'No reason, really. I just didn't think of it,' I said truthfully.

'Oh, James!' he said, exasperated. 'When will you learn?!'

I shrugged.

'Well, good luck with it all. Keep me updated. See you anon.'

Just as I was passing the hallway of Number 22 on my way up to Teddy's office, the front door opened, and Cathy Bugle walked in. In all the recent excitement, and partly because I had to, the matter of Bugle's indiscretion had been placed well and truly to the back of mind. Poor Cathy looked miserable.

'James, just the person,' she said, spying me.

'Hello, Cathy. Let's go to a meeting room.'

'Thank you.'

'How are you doing?' I said, once our rear-ends had established themselves in the luxurious chairs.

'Not too bad, all things considered. But Frank is issuing a divorce petition soon. He already has solicitors instructed.'

'I'm so sorry, Cathy. I thought maybe you might have been able to reconcile things.'

'Don't be daft. We haven't been in love for years. Frank shows no affection for me or the girls, and hasn't done so since they were little.'

'I do think you shouldn't tell me too much: I'm in rather a tricky position.'

'Yes, I'm sorry. Well, I wondered if you could recommend a good solicitor to help me. I won't divorce him, you know. I refuse.

'You want to *fight* your divorce?'

Most divorces are fought, in a sense, but usually over who gets what, the financial matters, and of course, the children. Cathy wanted to contest the divorce itself: she wanted the court to refuse the grant of it. In nearly a decade at the Firm, I hadn't witnessed a single contested divorce, and I told her so.

'I know. But it's for the girls. I don't want to lose the Surrey house, either; my life is now that house, and my friends nearby. Frank mainly stays in London and he's got enough money to buy himself a flat. My parents are almost dead, and they'd be devastated: they love Frank.'

'Well, look, I mustn't advise you too much. I'll leave the advice to your solicitor. And I think I have just the person: Cressida Smyth-Jones, head of family at Alfred Pennington & Co. She's not cheap, but she's worth every penny: she's a great lawyer: I've been up against her a few times, and she's more than a match for me, although I have to admit, our last altercation ended in my triumph! She's a bit of a battle-axe, but that's what you need, I think.'

'Thank you, James,' she said. 'Well, I mustn't take up too much of your time, or indeed be spotted by my darling husband, so I should go. Could I leave you with this?' she said, producing an envelope marked 'Mr Bugle'.

'Certainly.'

'Good. Thanks.'

'Goodbye Cathy,' I said, as we marched through the hall at some pace to minimise the risk of unfortunate encounters. 'Take care.'

'I'll try. Bye, James.'

I marched back to my office and picked up the phone.

'Good morning, Cressida!'

'Ah, Mr James, how can I thwart you today?'

'Now now, Mrs Smyth-Jones, there's no need for that attitude! I am actually passing you some instructions: a new client! She comes with my personal recommendation.'

'Are you quite well, Mr James? Why are you not taking on this client?' she asked, immediately suspicious.

'A conflict of interest, I'm afraid.'

A pause. I think the darling Cressida was recoiling from the fact that I was passing her work, and with my personal recommendation. 'Well, thank you. Much obliged,' was all she could allow herself to say.

'It's a pleasure. I have just recommended you to the wife of my senior partner, no less. Cathy Bugle.'

Emily looked up, a stunned expression on her face. Matthew wore a knowing smile, which caused Emily to look even more perplexed.

'Ah…' said Cressida.

'Is there a problem?'

'I'm not sure if I can take her on.'

'Are *you* quite well, Cressida?' Cressida lived for divorce: she had the reputation of never declining instructions, despite adverse circumstances against her client. She knew nothing of the Bugle circumstances, as far as I was aware, which were firmly in Cathy's favour.

'Well…'

'Well…?'

'It's just that I'm rather busy at the moment. But I'm sure one of my colleagues would be delighted.'

This made no sense: Cressida loved being busy.

'Well, I'd appreciate it if you could find time. I've known her for a while and I did specifically give her your name.'

'Alfred Pennington & Co. would be delighted to act for her. I can't. I am sorry, Mr James,' she said, conclusively. There would be no arguing with her.

'Right you are,' I said, accepting defeat.

'Thank you, James. I appreciate it.'

She had called me James! Cressida was behaving very oddly indeed.

'It's a pleasure. Speak soon, no doubt.'

'No doubt. Goodbye.'

'Cathy Bugle?' asked Emily, still amazed.

Now that the divorce was public, I explained what the trainees and I had witnessed at the Lincoln's Inn Garden Party and what Cathy and I had witnessed in Bugle's office.

'Oh! How awful. Poor woman! What a way to find out. So Jenny wasn't his niece?'

'Apparently not.'

'Bastard!'

By lunchtime, I decided that Teddy had had sufficient time for a preliminary perusal at the papers, and I wanted to get going on the case fearing that my limited knowledge of shipping law would require me to do a significant quantity of my own research to aid him properly. Teddy's office was deserted. A large quantity of seemingly untouched papers marked 'Hunt' lay on the left of his desk, and the ancient tome of *Shipping Law* lay to the right.

'Lynn, where's Teddy?' I said, entering Yarrington's office.

'How should I know?'

'You're supposedly his secretary,' I replied.

'I haven't typed a letter for him for months, other than to Covent Garden to order opera tickets,' she replied.

Yarrington looked up, his monocle falling to his chest, where it dangled from the its little gold chain.

'Lynn, you're not being terribly helpful,' he said.

'Oh! I'm trying to do *your* work, David! I hate interruptions when I'm typing. I lose the flow!'

'Well, I seem to remember Teddy coming in here this morning and telling you he was off to the shops,' he continued, with a remarkable amount of patience. 'Perhaps you could have furnished James with the limited information we do have on Teddy's whereabouts.'

'Huh! James asked where he was. I don't know which shop he's in! It won't help us to find him knowing that he is shopping…'

'Shut up, Lynn,' said Yarrington, beginning to lose his patience.

'Don't you speak to me like that, David!' she said, at which point I closed the door quietly behind them, letting them sort each other out.

Teddy's whereabouts, as Lynn had said, were immaterial, but the fact that he was out shopping was most vexing. Now he had agreed to take on the case, he must work on it. But my anger faded immediately as I saw the good-natured Teddy ascending the stairs towards me, with a large parcel under each arm.

'I've been shopping!' he declared.

'I know… but I think we should get on with some work…'

'Quite right, old boy! But I thought these might help,' he said, stepping past me and depositing the parcels heavily on his desk. He unwrapped the first: it was the first volume of the latest edition of *Shipping Law*.

'Two volumes, now!' he observed. 'In my day, it was all in the one. Most of the newfangled stuff is probably superfluous, anyway, but best be sure of the law before we analyse the facts of the matter!'

'Quite right. Well, I'll let you press on. Let me know when you need a hand.'

'Will do! Cheerio… Oh, James?' he said, just before I had departed.

'Yes?'

'Thanks, James. For this case.'

The next day, Teddy said he knew how to proceed and he subsequently kept me busy all week with various research requests, many of which I passed on to Matthew. We ploughed through all the paperwork that John Hunt had given us, trying to pick up on any invalid or incorrect advice that Priest and Parsons had previously given our client. Teddy paid particular attention to the drafting of the contracts, the bills of lading and charterparties that had been so damaging to our client. I did not enjoy the work: it was painstaking with few human elements, and because Teddy was in command, it felt like being a trainee again. Being told what to do and then having to do it did not agree with me, this way of working being the preserve of larger firms, where only the most senior lawyers have control of the file, his or her minions doing the tedious donkey work and photocopying. But the September surge of divorces seemed delayed this year, and with little work of my own, I was pleased to be putting the hours in. After Katherine's case and Cornwall, my billing figures for August were almost as bad as Teddy's. More importantly, I was helping Teddy win his rightful place in the office, and we were both assisting John Hunt, whose company had been financially shafted by Priest and Parsons in a multitude of ways.

The end of the first week of September marked the end of Matthew's first training seat, and therefore his time with me. However, I was so busy helping Teddy with the shipping case, that at Matthew's request I asked the senior partner if his move to the next department might be delayed so that first Matthew could run my practice while I was assisting Teddy, and second so that he might be the first trainee at Bugle & Yarrington to be involved with a big shipping case. Bugle, despite still believing that Teddy would 'fuck it up royally' agreed, noting that the Firm has always tried to accommodate the wishes of its employees.

CHAPTER 48

Counsel's Advice

The next Monday I managed to get hold of Charlie, he finally having returned from the Warburton-Lee yacht. We agreed to meet up that evening.

'I'm going out for a drink with Charlie. Fancy joining us?' I asked Emily.

'I'm not sure it's wise...'

'Well, I think it is. If you're worried about his feelings for you, I should forget them. He's just spent nearly five weeks on holiday with Felicity.'

'I suppose,' she said, looking rather miffed that anyone could get over her so quickly.

But then another thought struck me.

'You have feelings for him?'

'No, James! You do get the wrong end of the stick sometimes.'

'Good, you'll join us then?'

'It's a kind offer,' she said, giving me an odd look, but without pausing concluded, 'but I think I'll give it a miss. I've got lots to do at home.'

'Oh.' Emily having a lot to do at home was quite unlike her. 'What do you have to do?' I asked, perhaps a little too inquisitively.

'Never you mind!'

Yet another, slightly more perturbing thought struck me, as my protective side took over. 'You haven't got a date, have you?' came out, without much thought.

'No, James. You are useless! You go and have fun with Charlie. I expect you've a lot to catch up on.'

I felt relieved that she hadn't got a date. It had been odd when she was seeing Charlie, but it didn't feel right that she should move on so soon after him. Charlie, on the other hand, was renowned for moving on; that he had found a berth on the Warburton-Lee yacht raised not an eyebrow.

The day having been spent rather tediously reading volume one of Teddy's new *Shipping Law*, I left early and headed to the Pub, where Charlie was already installed at the bar.

'Charlie!'

'James!'

'God, you look good!' I said. And he did. Five weeks of Mediterranean sun had bronzed him beautifully.

'Thank you! You're looking pretty splendid yourself, in a less brown way, but splendid nevertheless!'

'Pint?'

'Yes. I've had a lousy day with my head in a great fat law tome. We'd better work quickly and enjoy the evening to its fullest extent. So... Did you have fun? Where did you go? How Felicity's old man?'

'Terrific! We got on splendidly!'

'You mean you enjoyed the company of a member of the judiciary?'

'Yes, a novel concept I admit, but he is almost retired; his wig will be collecting dust before too long, I should think. We spent much of the time inebriated. I don't know how he brought the boat safely into harbour on so many occasions, but he said berthing a yacht is like playing billiards – easier after one bottle and a disaster after two!'

'He sounds like the right sort! And Felicity?'

'Unbelievable!'

'Does that mean you are husband and wife?'

'Christ, man! I wouldn't go that far, but we shared the same cabin, if that's what you mean!'

'Marvellous!'

'Yes, it was rather.'

'I can't believe your luck!'

'Neither can I.... We get on brilliantly,' he mused. 'I did get in trouble with her a few times though. Once, she was below deck and heard her father and I trying urgently to locate his rather fine binoculars. Our excitement evidently intrigued her and she emerged on deck to find us taking it in turns with the binoculars to examine a rather fine Italian bird sunning herself on the front of another yacht with absolutely nothing on. Splendid sight,' he said, shaking his head at the memory of it. 'Thankfully she was able to see the amusing side of it.'

'Well, that's a good thing. Jealous women are most unattractive.'

'Hmm. How's Sara?'

Even though I was now able to banish thoughts of Sara relatively

effectively, the mention of her name still affected me. My explanation
of the Sara saga had Charlie riled, and his summing up of the event was
typical: 'Stupid cow.'

'She may be so,' I said, 'but unfortunately I had totally fallen for her.
She didn't have too many discernable or even major faults – certainly
none that were intolerable – and when you meet someone like that who
has so many problems with you, it knocks you for six.'

'I felt a bit like that with Emily.'

'Yes, but you've just spent five weeks on a yacht with a gorgeous
barrister, whose father likes you!'

'Damn right! That's my point. Move on! Forget Sara. She's clearly
way too picky, or after someone who doesn't exist. She doesn't write
poems does she?'

'Not that I know of.'

'You should be careful of a woman who like poetry. There's little
chance of you matching her expectations.' If this had come from
anyone other than Charlie, I should have asked if he was speaking from
experience. 'Besides,' he continued, 'there are lots of girls who wouldn't
have problems with your so-called problems.'

'Yes, but they're not Sara.'

'Emily wouldn't.'

'I know Emily wouldn't! But she's not my bloody girlfriend!'

'No.'

Having discussed many other issues of the day, we departed, awash
with booze yet again.

'Good night with Charlie?' asked Emily.

'It was until I woke up this morning.'

'You look dreadful!'

'Thanks.'

'Oh, James, you silly boy! When will you learn? It's only Tuesday!'

Teddy produced a draft of the initial letter that he intended to send
Priest and Parsons which set out the claim and the terms under which
our client would settle. Having read it a number of times, referring
regularly to *Shipping Law* volumes one and two, it appeared to make
sense, and was in fact robust in its demands. Teddy wondered if we
should seek the opinion of a barrister before we sent it out, but both
Matthew and I had begun to get on top of the case and background law,

and were so impressed with Teddy's knowledge and understanding of the factual and legal issues, we both concurred that Counsel's advice was superfluous to needs and the letter was duly sent.

The next day we received a fax in reply, and a grumpy Teddy announced that they had refused the terms of our initial letter. After a telephone discussion with John Hunt, Teddy agreed that we should therefore issue court proceedings. By Friday, this was duly achieved, after much work, especially on the part of Emily who was effectively working as Teddy's secretary as well as mine, after we concluded that Lynn's help was in fact more of a hindrance.

The week after, already the third week of September, we spent much time taking witness statements from the employees of Hunt Shipping Limited in order to produce a convincing case at court. By this stage, my own work was getting busier, and poor Emily was working flat out. I had a word with Yarrington about Lynn's performance, or rather the lack of, but he explained that in unusual circumstances we all had to do as best we could. Nevertheless, our case was looking more and more watertight by the day, and Teddy decided that another letter offering out of court settlement should be despatched to Priest and Parsons. This had gone by mid-week, and the pressure began to subside as our work declined: we had done what we could to date, and we now waited for a reply from the other lawyers. I took the opportunity of trying to get some bodies together for a mid-week celebration, celebrating the fact we had nothing to do, but none were availing: Emily was still being coy about her evening activities, and departed as soon as she was able; Charlie was constantly 'with Felicity', whatever that meant; Matthew said that he was obliged to spend this week with his Jessica because she'd been working so hard of late he'd hardly seen her; and Tim was under Charlotte's thumb, and as a result was smoking constantly on the steps of Number 20. Even Teddy, who I had asked out a couple of times, partly to discuss the case in hand, was busy. Miss Pound's interest in him had increased substantially now that she knew he was a valued partner of the Firm again and was working on an important case.

By Friday we still hadn't heard whether Priest and Parsons would settle on our terms. The deadline was the following Wednesday, and we couldn't work out whether this less than prompt reply boded well or ill. But it looked like we'd have to sit it out over the weekend.

'Can I tempt you into having a quick one with me?' I asked Emily on Friday afternoon.

'I'd love to James, but I'm busy. But promise me you'll come out with me next Friday?'

'I most certainly will! What do you have in mind?'

'I want to take you to a gallery.'

While the thought of an art gallery on a Friday evening filled me with a certain amount of dread, there would almost certainly be free booze, and I had seen so little of Emily recently that any destination with her would probably be fun. At five twenty-five my phone rang, instilling dread into my bones. This would no doubt be the worst phone call of the week.

'An art gallery it is, then,' I said, and picked up the phone.

Emily waved as she slipped out.

The conversation that ensued was thankfully short, but worrying nevertheless, as Bugle had simply barked: 'My office, now!'

CHAPTER 49

Bugle Is Frank

I knocked on the door of Bugle's office with some trepidation; one was never quite sure what to expect when such a summons was issued, but past experience told me that things were probably far from rosy.

'Come!' he boomed.

'Hello, Frank,' I said, going in.

'James.'

'What can I do you for?' I said, gaily, fully believing it's best to be jolly on such occasions, thus making it look like one doesn't think one's head is on the block.

'Sit down.'

'Thank you.'

'This Hunt case seems to be going well?'

'I believe so.'

'Good.'

I waited for him to gather his thoughts as he fumbled with his red silk cufflinks.

'Well, frankly James, I'm glad. And I understand the whole affair was basically down to you.'

'I just pointed a few people in the right direction really.'

'I think you did more than that.' He paused again. Bugle's oratory skills weren't bad, but today he seemed to have particular difficulty addressing me. And when he finally opened his mouth, the words came very quickly: 'Well, thank you James. Despite what you may think, I'm glad old Teddy has had a renaissance, even if it is only this case. Good effort. Well done.'

'Thank you, Frank.'

'Good.'

He paused again. Was that it? Had the mighty Bugle requested my presence in order to show his gratitude? If so, it was an unprecedented move, which was, perhaps, why he was finding it so awkward.

'I understand Cathy came into the office to see you the other day.'

My head had been placed on the block.

How on earth had he found out?

'I'm so sorry Frank. She said you were petitioning for divorce.'

'Yes, I'm sorry too. But I hadn't intended to petition. Is that what she said?'

'Yes.'

'Why did she think that?'

'She didn't say.'

I was beginning to sweat. When one is waiting for the blade to descend, it's best not to engage in chat.

'And you recommended Cressida Smyth-Jones to her.'

'Yes.'

'Does that mean you think she's lousy or excellent?'

'I wouldn't recommend anyone a lousy lawyer.'

'So you think she's excellent?'

'Yes.'

'Good.'

Good?! What on earth was he talking about? His delivery had been odd since I'd arrived. His usual quick and booming voice and been replaced by a quiet and slow murmur.

He still wasn't explaining himself and the tension was becoming unbearable.

'I'm not sure I follow...' I said to elicit a response.

'We're just about to appoint her as head of the family department,' he announced.

'Fuck me,' I said, quite by accident.

'I'd rather not.' Normally he'd have clouted me for swearing, but instead he'd cracked a joke. Even more odd was that Bugle habitually finds his own jokes amusing, and this one was delivered without the hint of a smile. 'So I take it you are surprised?' he asked.

'Well, yes.' My surprise was such that my brain hadn't yet reacted to the news. A moment later, my neurones had processed the information, and immediately came back with a host of thoughts and questions: she would be superior; how would she treat me? She would know more than me; could I stoop so low as to ask her advice? Would we be working on the same files? Would be working in the same office?

'I wanted to check with you first if you thought she was good, but since you do, I shall ring her shortly. I take it you have no objection to working with her?'

'*With* her?'

'Well, since Matthew is moving on to his next seat this time next week, there'll be a space in your room. She will begin the week after: first Monday in October.'

'What about Margaret's old room? Can't she have that?' While I respected her as a lawyer, I wasn't convinced that working in such close proximity to the woman who I had taken such delight in riling on every possible occasion would be congenial for either of us.

'It's only a temporary arrangement until the secretary issue has been resolved.'

'She's not bringing her previous one?' I asked, to which Bugle looked up, evidently surprised.

'No, you'll have to share Emily. It'll only be for a couple of weeks, and then we'll have a rethink. That okay?'

The thought of sharing Emily, especially with Cressida whose workload would almost certainly be heavier than mine, did not bring me joy, but two weeks was a finite period and just about short enough to be bearable. 'I suppose it'll have to be,' I mused, a wry smile crossing my face.

'Yes, it will,' said Bugle, smiling for the first time. 'She speaks very highly of you.'

'I think that must be the other Cressida Smyth-Jones.'

Bugle's smile extended, and for a fleeting moment, I wondered if he might just be beginning to understand me.

'Right, well, that's all,' he said, resuming his normal pace of speech. 'Thanks for your advice re Cressida. I shall tell her the good news!'

'It's a pleasure.' And I got up to go.

'James?'

'Yes?'

'I gather you have been in the wars on the women front too?'

Was no subject, however personal, safe from gossip amongst colleagues?

'Yes, spot of bother. Nothing to worry about.'

'That's not what I heard, but I'm sorry to hear it.'

'Thanks.'

And again I turned to go. But just as I'd opened the door, my concern for Bugle stopped me, and I suddenly felt unable to leave without enquiring after him.

'Is everything all right, Frank?'

'No, not really. Have you a moment?'

'Of course.'

'I'm devastated about this whole thing with Cathy and Jenny.'

I had no idea what to say.

'It's so fucking difficult,' he continued, 'Cathy has shown no interest in me for some time, and I don't blame her, because I haven't shown any interest in her either. But I still love her. I think. But I can't imagine growing old with her. I can't imagine looking forward to spending retirement with her. We're just too different. She hates law. I love it. She hates London, which is why she insisted on the Surrey house. I love London and hate Surrey. Suburban bloody utopia, full of middle class families, with two, three or more cars on the driveway and two more spaces for more in the garage. They all have supposedly perfect children, who go to Oxbridge but spend most of the time between the sheets with a different lover for every day of the week, and a new drug to go with them. She loves our daughters. I do, in a way. But I do wish they were more... ambitious. I think that's the right word. They're useless. God, I sound awful, but they are. No interests, no boyfriends, no ambition. No bloody humour. Not that they had much chance from my genes, but at I least I bloody try. I know you're probably sick of hearing it, but I had to work bloody hard to get where I am now. I started with nothing, managed to scrape a degree at a ghastly polytechnic and thank God, seemed to be good at law. Now these kids are handed degrees on plates, waltz into jobs they haven't got the faintest idea about and end up hating, and still think they are hard done by. Makes me sick. Cathy hasn't been interested in sex since the word go. Jenny isn't like that. She's young, funny, clever, interesting. She had to work too, and she appreciates her position as a result. You can't stop her in bed. I love her. But I hate the thought of losing Cathy, or hurting her. Too late for that, I suppose. I hate the thought of losing Jenny, too. But I love Cathy. I think.

'Christ, James, I'm sorry. You don't want to hear all this. But...'

'Go on?'

'I don't have many people I can talk to about all this.'

'It sounds like you need a drink. Shall we go to the pub?'

'Bloody hell, yes!'

And so Frank Bugle and I went to the Pub together for the first time in our lives. He was remarkably open with me about his life and its frustrations. I felt rather useless not being able to help in any way except being able to listen, which perhaps was what he desperately wanted and needed.

CHAPTER 50

Hard Work Pays

By the next Monday afternoon, we still hadn't heard from Priest and Parsons, and we began to worry that our outlook had been over-optimistic and that their legal might and as yet unseen arsenal of evidence would destroy our case and thus blow our shipping department, such as it was, out of the water. Teddy decided to telephone them before our deadline expired the day after next.

He reported that they were waiting for Counsel's opinion on the matter, and that their barristers were two Queen's Counsels, no less. Teddy had apparently told them that we hadn't needed even the opinion of even a junior member of the bar, at which there was a stunned silence. He thought this was tremendously funny, and chuckled away to himself at the thought of it. He also thought it was good news: the fact that they had two silks on the case meant they thought they were in deep water.

Tuesday's post yielded nothing, and our worry crept back. Priest and Parsons were leaving things very close to the deadline. Perhaps their QC's had a knowledge of law far superior to that of Teddy's, which was, admittedly, not a wholly inconceivable notion. Perhaps Teddy had missed some vital piece of new legislation that would bend things in their favour, and worryingly, new legislation could mean anything post 1970. Teddy's nerves were clearly frayed: by lunchtime he smelt somewhat of whisky and cigars, a habit he usually reserved until after his evening meal. It was difficult to comfort him, he being the main authority on which we had based our case.

On Wednesday morning, Teddy and I arrived early to prepare for what we now considered to be certain calamity. He looked tired, and admitted that he hadn't slept much the night before. The whiff of liquor and strong tobacco products was already upon him and the post hadn't even arrived. He sat in reception waiting for it, trying, but failing to read *The Times*.

Everyone was now in the office. Both Bugle and Yarrington had enquired about the answer to our settlement offer, throwing further worry onto the matter.

There was little we could do, and so the inhabitants of my office ploughed through our usual work.

Then, at nearly eleven o'clock, Teddy burst in, beaming.

'James! Everyone! Listen to this,' he said brandishing a page of the distinctive Priest and Parsons letterhead. '"Dear Sirs, we hereby accept the your terms of settlement in full with the following provisos: (1) that you undertake to give us a further five working days from the date of this letter to allow us time to deliver to you the Settlement Monies (as defined in your letter of 22 September), and (2) that subject to (1) above, you withdraw all court proceedings in relation to the matter immediately and agree not to issue any further proceedings until you have received the Settlement Monies. We look forward to hearing from you. Yours faithfully, Priest and Parsons." How about that?!' he exclaimed.

'Congratulations, Teddy!' I said, rising to shake his hand.

Emily actually kissed the old boy, which caused him much embarrassment.

'Well, I'm pretty irked that it didn't go to court. My fees will be significantly less now we've reached a settlement!'

'This is true, but the result is tremendous! After all your carefully crafted correspondence to them, they must have realised they were on a losing wicket. Well done!'

He must have been proud. While in the end, the evidence in the case did appear to be firmly in our favour, the law and facts involved were highly complex, and Teddy, with much assistance from Emily, and a little from Matthew and I, had worked tremendously hard to achieve such a brilliant result in so short a time frame. The best thing about the result was that Priest and Parsons had effectively admitted liability and also that they acknowledged that if the matter had gone to court, they would have been found not to be reasonably competent solicitors. And I knew that John Hunt had promised to pay my fees in relation to his sister's unfortunate matter – a tiny fraction of the settlement sum, but important for me to prove a point to Bugle: that a little flexibility in billing certain clients can pay dividends.

'Well, thank you all: Emily, you've been the most efficient secretary I've had the pleasure of working with; James, you're useless at shipping law, but invaluable at eliciting information from people; and you can, despite your profoundly undeserved reputation, get through huge quantities of reading rather quickly; Matthew, my boy! your research has been perfect: you'll be a first-rate lawyer. Fancy doing a whole training seat with me?'

At this, Matthew looked somewhat concerned. This case, had after all, been the only one Matthew had seen Teddy work on in his whole time at the Firm.

'Well, I'm not sure it's up to me,' he said, diplomatically.

'No, I dare say that's the case. Well, the offer is there. Thank you again. Needless to say, I wouldn't have had a hope of doing this on my own. Your help has been much appreciated. Well, I must ring the client to tell him the good news, and then I suggest we all go for a very boozey lunch!'

Teddy reported that the client was extremely happy, and most satisfied with our services; he wished to retain Bugle & Yarrington as his company's lawyers, and indeed ask the Firm to act for him personally as well. Katherine Hunt phoned me, her brother obviously having had spoken to her, to congratulate us. She also asked that I send John a full bill to include all my time taken on her case, which he would duly settle.

Teddy, Emily, Matthew and I then went out for lunch which was so boozey, none of us could stay awake that afternoon, let alone do any work; but it was a welcome break after what had been, unusually for all of us, a stressful few weeks in the office. Between post-lunch snoozes, I noticed that *Shipping Law* volume two still lay on my desk. I decided to return it to Teddy, and ascended to his office.

'Hello, Teddy. I see your new self-teaching and research programme continues, despite having won the day!' I said to Teddy who was reclining in his chair, feet on desk reading October's *Yachting Monthly*.

'Quite right! Ah! Volume two of my new tome,' he said, noticing his book under my arm, 'Wouldn't believe a word of it, old chap. Simply not up to the '69 edition. There's all kinds of superfluous dross in there, probably because two volumes commands a higher price than one, and the editors are lousy. Large chunks of the recent law – which this supposedly deals with – are simply missing. I've a good mind to write to the publisher to tell them exactly what I think, and give them some pointers. I might just do it, actually.'

'Do so, you've nothing to loose!'

Teddy looked at me. I waited for his cogs to turn.

'Thank you, James. I owe you much.'

'Don't mention it. I'm glad it worked out so well.'

'Likewise. Likewise,' he said, again reclining in his chair, pondering upon a matter which he never vocalised.

I slipped out, leaving him to his thoughts.

Having told Emily that the darling Cressida would be joining us the following Monday, to which her response was rather subdued and surprisingly not surprised, we made the most of the time left without her, which time would be the last with Matthew in my office. Since the end of the Hunt shipping case, none of us had much enthusiasm for starting something else until after the weekend, when, no doubt, Cressida's rod of iron would rule. Accordingly, in the latter stages of the week, not much was achieved on the work front. I spent some time on Friday afternoon with Matthew, discussing his time with me. From the rather irksome ex-student who'd been rather too anxious to please me, he'd learnt both the law and the beginnings of how to be a lawyer remarkably quickly, especially considering he had the marked disadvantage of having me as his teacher.

'Well, Matthew,' I began, 'this is sadly your last afternoon with me. I hope you've enjoyed yourself?'

'Well, to be honest, I was dreading family law. I couldn't think of anything worse, and it's what Jessica has her heart set on – we couldn't both be family lawyers! But in fact I've really enjoyed it. Also liked the shipping case. Thanks for getting me in on it.'

'It was a pleasure. Well, Emily and I had misgivings too. We didn't want our cosy little office invaded by an oik, but it's all worked out splendidly! It'll be weird being just the two of us again – even more weird having Cressida at your desk!'

'Jessica says she's been pretty good to work with – and if she's kind to her trainee, I wouldn't worry too much,' said Matthew, trying to reassure me. Jessica was a trainee, and was probably very polite and did things by the book; Cressida's new colleague would be quite different, but not wishing to talk too much about what the future held with Cressida, I changed the subject.

'I'd love to have another trainee. You've helped me tremendously too – there's no way I could've got through so much work without you – so thank you.'

'It's been great. I'm sorry to move on, but I'm looking forward to company law.'

'Are you with Paul and Martin for your next seat?'

'Yes.'

'Good luck! Don't let them give you any grief.'

'Thanks for all your help. You've been a good teacher!' he said smiling, but apparently sincerely.

'I tried! Now bugger off home. You won't be allowed to leave early in the company department!'

I watched rather sadly as Matthew placed the last of his effects into a cardboard box. I had enjoyed teaching him, as far as my limited pedagogical skills enabled me. It had added a new dimension to my job, one beyond the normal satisfaction of helping clients: it made me more aware that what was said or done might just possibly help shape Matthew's legal life and career. I hoped that it would anyway, and thinking that it might was enough to give me a certain sense of satisfaction that my job had not thus far given me.

'Bye,' he said, his box under one arm.

'Bye, Matthew,' said Emily.

And he was gone.

'I hope he thought he gained something from us,' I said.

'You know he did,' said Emily.

And half an hour later we departed, despite my protestations, for an as yet unknown gallery where I'd have to pretend to like the pictures. But at least I was with Emily.

'So, where are we going?' I asked, once we had clambered into a taxi.

'Hugh Daley's gallery in South Ken. The one where my paintings were in July.'

'Splendid! There's an excellent public house just round the corner,' I said, 'perhaps we might elope there after you've looked at the paintings!' I had forgotten the name of Hugh Daley since my last visit, but he seemed a jolly fellow, and I vaguely looked forward to winding him up about artistic matters.

'I hope you'll look at the paintings, too James.'

'I thought you knew me better than that.'

'You might actually like them for a change, although that probably is hoping for too much.'

She did know me after all.

The taxi duly pulled up outside the gallery, which appeared to have a hideous number of people milling about inside. Thankfully in the doorway, as last time, there were two lovely looking girls each with a tray of full glasses. All was not lost. Inside, I saw the moustachioed Hugh Daley gesticulating, no doubt about the quality of his paintings.

We entered, taking a glass each.

Hugh clocked Emily immediately, and came rushing forward to greet her, ignoring me even though his way was blocked by me.

'How are you, me dear?' he asked her, kissing her on both cheeks twice.

Arty types are nearly as bad as those who choose to tread the boards.

Pleasantries were exchanged, and Emily remembered me to him.

'Ah the lawyer!' he said, 'I look forward to catching up with you later, but first I must introduce the artist to a few folk who have been admiring her paintings! Have you met Miss Emily Lewis?' he said.

'Of course I have,' I said, irked by his stupidity.

'Well, then, there's only forty-nine people left to introduce her to! Emily! Come with me!'

Emily?

She thrust a catalogue into my hand as she followed Hugh. Her name graced the cover.

Disbelief and astonishment were words that could only begin to describe my state of mind. The effect of these emotions caused a massive build up of heat in my head which caused me to inadvertently consume my whole glass of wine to assuage it. I flicked quickly through the pages of the catalogue. Emily was the sole artist exhibiting! All these people – and the gallery was very full – were here to see her work!

When I looked up, she was smiling and shaking the hands of people who had just been introduced to her by Hugh. She glanced at me, noting that I was evidently a little more than mildly bemused, and the amused expression that lit up her face made me smile back. Realising that she would be detained for a while, I decided to peruse her paintings, in the hope that one might be found that might agree with my famously eclectic taste. Having manoeuvred my way through the throngs of people, I found myself staring at the first of Emily's pictures that I had ever liked.

Emily had switched from her usual oil on canvas to watercolour, and the result was breathtaking. She had employed a loose style, which somehow looked intentionally messy when each brush stroke was studied, but now, these untidy strokes came together to form stylised but lucid and completely coherent prospects. There was a series of Florentine street scenes, the people and the light and realism of the buildings and their shadows making the pictures into something more than a snapshot of Florence. Warm, Tuscan terracottas and the blue haze in the middle distance of the one lone rural scene almost inspired me to book a flight to Italy then and there. Having taken in this transformed style of Emily's, my attention turned to the other side of the room which was becoming busier. My surprise was not great when I saw a number of her more usual *Canvas Adulterated With Unremarkable Daubs* series, over which my eyes glanced rapidly, finding instead Emily herself approaching.

'Sorry to desert you!' she said, having detached herself from her admirers.

'Don't be silly. Emily these are wonderful! This is wonderful!' I said, looking around at all her paintings and punters praising them.

'Don't tell me you like them?!'

'I do! The watercolours are wonderful! How on earth have you had time to paint all these?'

'On holiday. And since; why do you think I have been a hermit for the last month?'

'I thought you had a secret chap!'

'Silly!' she said, poking me. 'Have you been upstairs?'

I had forgotten that the gallery had an upstairs, and I followed her up to find that thankfully it was still almost empty. The contrast of less people and markedly different artwork was striking.

The first to greet my eyes was a magnificent pencil drawing of a male nude. An unannounced surge of jealously raced through me.

'Who's that? No wonder you've been busy,' I said, rather crossly, observing his beautiful musculature and fine features.

'Shut up, James. It's Antonio.'

'Oh, Antonio. That's all right then!'

'He was the son of the lady who owned the place where Dad and I stayed on the Amalfi coast. That's his wife, James,' she said, looking at the drawing to her right. 'Anna-Maria.'

The drawing of Anna-Maria was superior even to that of her husband, and she was even more beautiful than him. Or Emily had made her so. From a distance, both looked like monochrome photographs. Thinking Anna-Maria somewhat more pleasant than Antonio to examine closely, examine her I did. The detail of each pencil stroke was amazing, but it wasn't simply the quality of the drawing that made them so wonderful: her body caught the light in which Emily must have drawn her magnificently.

Emily saw me shaking my head in disbelief and smiled.

'That's my favourite,' she said, indicating with a nod of her head the huge canvas at the end of room, a wall to itself. I was immediately drawn to it, and paced a little closer.

She had used her newfound loose, but somehow exacting style. The picture was the interior of a room, the majority of which was dimly lit, but painted looking towards a large open window. Initially, my eye was led to the view through the window because it was bright: the setting sun, though itself obscured by clouds, reflected brightly off the glittering sea creating a wonderfully unusual light which Emily had utilised marvellously to conceive the rest of the picture: the grey and white of the clouds juxtaposed with the golden glistening sea were contrasted with some flowers in a box on the windowsill which provided shades of red. The reflected sunlight fell through the window to the right, warmly illuminating a this time clothed Antonio who was sitting on the windowsill reading a book. He sat with his back to the edge of the window, facing into the window. The glazed window frame was on a hinge and had been swung into the room behind him before he had taken his place on the sill, the glass reflecting the scene outside and his face to the viewer. But one could still discern details of the wall behind the reflection on the glass. Opposite him, on the left, the side of the interior of the room that was ill lit, sat Anna Maria, her back to the other window frame, also clothed, also facing towards the window and Antonio, and also reading a book.

Except that she wasn't reading a book. She had let her wrist relax – only a tiny fraction – but enough to see that her book was no longer at a natural angle for her eyes to have been following its text. Her head, the last main focal object to which my eyes had been drawn on account of the painting's chiaroscuro, was similarly at a very slightly curious angle. My eyes found hers, which despite being in deep shadow were bright and alive.

She was looking at Antonio.

'By God, Emily, it's fantastic!'

'What did you say?'

'Nothing. It's really… it's my favourite too.'

I smiled at her. I knew my eyes told her what I thought of it. She touched me on the arm. 'I'm glad you finally like something I've painted,' she said. 'It does mean a lot to me, you know, despite what you may think.'

'Well, it's certainly a cut above *Canvas Adulterated With Unremarkable Daubs.*'

'What's that?'

'The one you had in the Summer Exhibition.'

'Shut up, James!'

But the painting *was* wonderful, and I didn't know what else to say without saying too much; it was the first time any painting had profoundly affected my emotions.

CHAPTER 51

All Change Please

I arrived in the office on the first Monday of October to find it transformed: Matthew's desk had an extra table attached to it, making it nearly twice as big as it had been; two bookcases had manoeuvred themselves into the space behind the desk and were full of files and learned looking matrimonial law books; my filing cabinets had been busy reproducing over the weekend and had doubled in number; Matthew's small chair had transformed into a luxurious, leather, reclining and armed beast, and his smiling face had been replaced by that of a determined looking Cressida Smyth-Jones.

'Mr James, good morning,' said she.

'Morning, Cressida.' There was little else to say, under the circumstances.

'May I say how delighted I am to be joining your firm?' asked Cressida.

'You may say it, but may I reserve the right to disbelieve you?'

'No, you may not,' she retorted. 'I want to make myself clear, Mr James...'

'James, please...'

'Very well, James. I will make myself clear. I understand that you may find this situation rather odd – indeed it is – but despite what you may think, and despite your somewhat unorthodox way of dealing with certain matters, I want you to know that having dealt with you as an adversary on a number of occasions, you have my deepest respect as lawyer, and that I have in fact been looking forward to working with you.'

Cressida had stumped me.

'Well, thank you, Cressida.'

'I don't expect you were expecting that, and I'm not presuming that you will acquiesce, but let's give it a crack! I think we'll be sharing the same office for a couple of weeks until the Firm hires me a secretary. I think Mr Bugle will have a meeting with us this week to discuss the workings of the department. In the meantime, I'm afraid that I'm exceedingly busy with some of my old cases, and on your desk are a couple of new instructions for you because I simply haven't got time for them. Do you have capacity, or shall I send them back to Alfred Pennington?'

'You're giving me your old firm's work on day one?!'

'Yes. I surprise myself sometimes,' she said, amused.

'Well, I never turn work down.'

'Good. There are the files. There are a couple of briefing notes that set out what I know – I'm afraid you'll have to ask the clients anything else – I suggest you get them in for a meeting. And now, I'm must get down to the Principal Registry for a hearing. I don't expect to be back today, but I look forward to seeing you in the morning.'

'Morning sweetheart!' said Emily, as she entered.

'You must be Emily,' said Cressida. 'Do I understand that you two are rather closer than the average work colleagues?' she asked, obviously amused by Emily's greeting to me.

'Good morning, Mrs Smyth-Jones. I'm terribly sorry – I didn't think you'd be ensconced quite so soon…'

'Cressida, please. Don't be daft. Don't expect me to flirt with you though!'

Emily and I didn't quite know how to react to Cressida's previously hidden sense of humour, but her smile was an invitation for us to take her comment light-heartedly, and we all began to share the joke. The mood became instantly more relaxed and I thought that if this were the shape of things to come, we'd all get on famously.

'Right, I must zip!' said my new head of department, making for the door having already picked up her large briefcase containing, no doubt, her equally large briefs. 'See you this afternoon, and if not, on the morrow! Cheerio!'

And she was off.

Emily and I looked at each other in disbelief.

'She's either a hell of a lot easier to work with than against, or she's making a big effort to fit in!'

'Or both,' pointed out Emily.

'I can't believe how many books she has,' I said, wandering over to peruse her shelves. 'I had no idea that there was so much to write about matrimonial law!'

'Coffee?' asked Emily.

'Yes please!'

As Emily left for the kitchen, my attentions turned to the morning's post which contained a letter from John Hunt thanking me for my assistance with his shipping claim, and enclosing a cheque in full settlement of my fees for his sister's case. He went on to say that he had already instructed Teddy in some new shipping contracts that his firm were hoping to conclude over the next few weeks, and that the settlement we had achieved meant that his firm would be able to expand significantly as a result. This of course would mean more work for Bugle & Yarrington. I made appointments for both Cressida's new clients that week: the autumn surge of divorces had finally arrived, and two new cases in one morning augured well for my billing figures, now significantly boosted by the Hunt cheque in any case. My final piece of post was a postcard of Valetta Harbour. It was from Patricia Heath, the wife of the fellow who had driven off with Teddy's boat, thus ensuring the old boy's safe return to the office at the beginning of the Hunt case, and in a way, therefore, the saviour of his career. After the short, sharp advice I had given her in order to save her marriage, my expectations were that she needed instructions as to how to sail her husband's yacht back from Malta to Blighty in the absence of its captain, he having walked the plank on the orders of a mutinous crew. It read:

Dear Mr James,

Thank you for bringing me to my senses. As you see, Dennis and I are now sunning ourselves on Malta and have been having a great time of it. You offered quite the best matrimonial advice anyone has ever given me! If I ever need marriage counselling again, I'll be in touch!

Yours,
Patricia Heath.

I wondered how often I'd ever be thanked for using the same approach again.

Emily returned with our coffees and declared that Cressida must have been working since the small hours because she'd dictated so much. It wasn't until lunchtime that she had finished Cressida's work and had begun mine. I wondered how she would find the time to work for us when we were both busy, but she didn't seem to have addressed the question as she sat working, oblivious to my thoughts.

I had mused much about her paintings over the weekend. Never before had I thought it possible to see an artist's emotions in a painting, nor to glean an insight into an artist's mind, but now, Emily's emotions were laid bare to me, and became vivid in my imagination. I watched her beautifully formed fingers rattling the keyboard, thinking it extraordinary that these hands, this person, could create such provocative paintings. I noticed her pretty rings, one of which I had brought back from Damascus for her, and had remained on the ring finger of her right hand ever since. My eyes followed her slender arms up to her bare neck where her collarbone provided a resting place for them for a moment before they caught the lines of neck rising from her shirt, but slightly obscured by her dangling earring. As I moved my head to a position where the earring no longer obfuscated the shape of her neck, she stopped typing and we found ourselves looking at other.

'What on earth are you looking at?' she said, seemingly embarrassed.

'Your earrings,' I lied. 'They're very pretty.'

'Thank you,' she replied, whilst continuing to look at me in a perplexed manner as I felt my colour rise hotly.

I couldn't cope with these unprecedented feelings, and I grabbed a file and left the room in the pretence of requiring a photocopier. And since I had this thought, I decided to go to the photocopier room in the hope that there would be someone to chat with to distract my thoughts. Indeed there was: it was Matthew who had red eyes and grubby cheeks.

'What on earth is the matter?'

'Hi James. Oh, nothing. I just don't seem to be able to do anything right for Paul and Martin.'

'Well, you're hardly a day into your seat with them. You're not expected to in the first couple of weeks!'

'I suppose. It's just like Tom said: one of them tells me to do something one way, and the other examines it and tells me I've done exactly the wrong thing. I think they were even laughing with each other over it.'

'That's not on.'

'No, but don't tell anyone.'

'I think I should.'

'They said if I told anyone how they work, they'd get me sacked.'

'Did they now?'

'Yes. I'll be all right.'

'I'm sure you will. But you can always come and chat if need be. Keep me updated, will you? You'd better clean up your face.'

'Thanks, James.'

'Pleasure.'

Such was my worry for Matthew, and, after the almost identical experience that Tom had suffered earlier in the year, any other trainees unfortunate enough to find themselves in the office of Paul and Martin, that when I returned to my office, I had quite forgotten about the embarrassment that had caused me to leave in the first place. Emily too expressed worry for Matthew at the hands of the company bullies, and we concluded that despite what they had told Matthew about not divulging the exactitudes of their behaviour, if anyone was going to be sacked, it would be them, rather than a powerless trainee. I therefore resolved to talk to Bugle about it, and duly did so that afternoon.

Cressida did not return that day, and I was delighted to accept Emily's invitation to accompany her to Marylebone High Street for a drink after work.

We ordered a couple of drinks and settled comfortably round a table in the corner of the bar. But all was not well: Emily's normally relaxed manner was being distracted by something.

'What's the matter?' I asked.

'Nothing.'

'Emily, if you don't want to tell me, that's fine, but don't pretend there's nothing wrong!'

'Damn you! Why do you know me so well?!'

I shrugged, smiling at her.

'James, I have something to tell you.'

She looked worried. I was worried: what could this be? My imagination started running riot. Selfish and jealous thoughts raced through my neurones; my heart beat noticeably quicker in the few seconds that it took her to summon up the courage to speak again.

'It's the partner's meeting tomorrow, and I wanted to be the first to tell you.'

'What?!' I said, the thoughts rushing through my head now beginning to get wilder and more grave, sending me into somewhat of a panic.

'I have resigned from Bugle & Yarrington.'

Her words struck me like daggers in my heart.

I couldn't believe she had just dropped this on me, with no prior discussion, warning, or even tiny hint that she was thinking of leaving the Firm. She had never once discussed leaving. What had I done to drive her away?

'Why?' I said automatically.

She smiled kindly and rubbed my arm in a motherly kind of way. 'Don't worry, it's not you!' she said. 'Far from it, really. It's just that I have lots of things that I want to do, and now that my painting is taking off, I want to be able to concentrate on that.'

'But you've always had time to do that as well,' I said, somewhat in desperation, 'Couldn't you do it the weekends? You seem to be so quick at it!'

'No, James, not now that I have galleries interested. If I want to succeed at this I have to keep creating new material and keeping people interested. I simply can't do that with a full time job, and now I have *some* money coming in from my paintings, I can just about afford it, with savings.'

I had no idea what to say.

'I'm sorry,' she continued, 'I've made up my mind. I told a Bugle a fortnight ago. It's official. I leave at the end of next week.'

I was stunned, and must have looked it.

But she hadn't finished:

'And besides, there are other things I have should done a long time ago that I can't do if I'm working with you.'

'Like what?!' I exclaimed, rather indignant that working with me should stop her doing anything.

'This...' she said, looking momentarily into my eyes and then dropping her gaze down, her long eyelashes hiding her eyes as she drew nearer; she wore a scarcely perceptible smile, and with the tips of her ring and middle fingers of her left hand she brushed my neck very lightly making her intentions clear a moment before they were realised. As her face drew alongside mine I could smell her perfume which had mingled inextricably with her own scent, and she breathed warm, faintly alcoholic breath over my cheek sending a shiver down the entire length of my spine. And then her lips touched the corners of mine, and then they were kissing me properly, and then we were kissing each other.

It lasted for some time.

She stopped, almost pushing me away, and sank back into the seat away from me, looking at me with an expression of shock and embarrassment, but overwhelmingly sad.

'Fuck. I'm sorry,' she said.

I wanted to tell her that I wasn't sorry: it had been the most exciting moment of my life. But the feelings of confusion that had engulfed my mind silenced me. This was Emily. She had kissed me. She wasn't drunk. Had she planned it? Had my feelings for her changed? Had she sensed my feelings for her had changed? I looked at her. She was looking at her glass, pained. I hated seeing her anguish, but I could think of nothing to say. Did she think this had destroyed our friendship? Had it destroyed our friendship? Was it still a friendship? Could it be more? Did she want it to be more? Did I want it to be more? And before the vestiges of these thoughts had disappeared, I realised that our feelings for each other were so deep, and on my part at least, so unchecked, that whatever now happened between us, this evening, this moment, her kissing me, would change everything, perhaps not forever, but profoundly.

'I want to leave, but I know it won't help,' she said, still looking at her glass. 'If it hadn't been you, I would have left.'

Silence.

'If it hadn't been you, I wouldn't have kissed you,' she said, looking earnestly at me.

I stared at her, still mute. Despite the torment on her face she was beautiful. Had I been such a fool as to not realise she had feelings for me deeper than I had previously ever imagined? Had the great James James been looking all over London in search of a girl worthy enough for him when in fact his best friend was a girl far more worthy of him than he of her? Did she love me? I loved her, certainly, but did I *love* her? A week ago, I could not have imagined entertaining these thoughts: but something changed the moment I saw Antonio and Anna-Maria by the window. And with that realisation, I knew that it didn't matter if she'd planned to kiss me. She had kissed me because at that moment, it had seemed the right thing to do.

So I did the same.

She reciprocated, and again kissing her was an extraordinary feeling; but the second kiss didn't last as long.

'James, stop. What are you doing?'

'I don't know, but it felt like the only thing I could do.'

'I don't want you to kiss me because you couldn't think what else to do.'

'Perhaps I meant it was the only thing I *should* do.'

Silence.

'Don't say what you don't mean, James.'

I couldn't protest, because I wasn't sure what I had meant or if I had meant it.

We sat there in silence, the first time since I had known her that I was trying desperately to think of something sensible to say. Eventually Emily broke the silence:

'Well, I think I should go. You've got a lot to think about.'

'Me? What about you?'

'I've thought about you so much, James, I haven't got the energy to do it any longer.' And with that she got up. 'I hope I haven't buggered everything up,' she said, smiling sadly. 'See you in the morning.'

And I let her go. I did have a lot to think about.

I spent the night tossing and turning, thinking of Emily when I was awake, and dreaming of her in the short spells of sleep that I did achieve. Lustful thoughts about her physical perfection kept me awake, while thoughts about her, her character, though less immediately potent, did little to induce sleep. In my short dreams, I always woke up before the critical moment.

The next morning, Emily was late into work. She hadn't been late into work all year, and I wondered if it had been deliberate to ensure that Cressida was also in the room when she arrived. If so, her plan had been successful.

'Morning all,' she said, without looking at either of us. She was clearly embarrassed.

'There's only two of us,' I said.

'Morning both,' she said, rolling her eyes at me. 'Who'd like a coffee?'

'Yes please,' I said.

'No, thanks, but I'd love a cup of lemon and ginger tea. I have a box. Bag in, please. I can't stand instant coffee, I'm afraid,' said Cressida. Her choice of hot beverage surprised me: was this the brew fit for a fierce old harridan? She handed the box to Emily, who disappeared to the kitchen.

Once we had our steaming drinks on our desk, the three of us settled down to work. It was odd, because Emily and I weren't trying to behave ourselves as we suspected we would have to do once Cressida had started to work with us; we were trying to ignore each other. I was certainly worried about what she might be thinking about our relationship. What had an evening of sober thought done to her opinion of how things stood between us? Judging by her eyes, she hadn't slept much either. As she typed, I found myself staring at her, wanting to kiss her again. I found myself wanting her to leave the office immediately so she wouldn't be my secretary. I even began to be irked that she was still my secretary. And then the cycle repeated itself as my doubtful side concluded that last night's kiss had been a mistake, and that our friendship would be forever different, forever less pure.

'Are you two always this quiet?' asked Cressida, jerking me back into reality.

'Oh, well, when we're working.'

'I find my concentration span far inferior to yours, Mr James... I need to have a chat about something at least every half an hour in order to keep the day interesting. I know time is money, but it's important to keep the mind active and interested in order that it concentrates to its fullest capacity when it really matters. Anyone who thinks one's brain can think about nothing but law for eight hours a day is unstable. So, what did we all do last night?'

Silence.

'Perhaps the question was too mundane; I apologise. Chitchat never did me much good either.'

Of course, under normal circumstances, the question would have been a good icebreaker, but telling Cressida on day two of our combined careers that my secretary had kissed me didn't seem the wisest of moves.

'Well, actually, last night I did do something interesting,' continued Cressida, re-evaluating her last point, 'I went to Daunt Books on Marylebone High Street. Do you know it? Wonderful place...' she continued, without pausing to see if we did know it, 'I listened to a fantastic talk there by the chap who has written the authoritative text on why God exists. Even Canterbury thinks he's so way off beam as to be dangerous...'

And so began the first of many such chats between us and we soon learned that these interludes ended as quickly as they began, as Cressida's mind wanted to turn its attention back to law.

Once the atmosphere had returned to a learned silence, broken only by Emily's fingers on her keyboard, my eyes naturally fell on her, but they averted her gaze quickly – although not quick enough to avoid her noticing I had been looking at her – whenever she looked at me.

After a few times trying to avoid each other's gaze in this manner, there came from Emily a wonderful smile – so slight that anyone who did not know her intimately might have assumed it was merely her expression changing – but so beautiful, I knew then that she had ensnared me totally.

I wrote on the back of a file 'Lunch?' and pushed it across to her. She nodded, almost imperceptibly, and my excitement levels rose. What would she say to me? Would she say anything, or let me begin? How would I begin?

At the appointed hour, I announced that Emily and I were going for lunch.

Emily departed, saying she'd she see me in reception in a minute, and Cressida peered at me over her half-moon glasses, with such an enquiring look it made me ask, almost impertinently given the immaturity of our new relationship, 'What?'

She smiled.

'Do I gather all this tension is because Emily is soon to be your ex-secretary?' she asked.

The question took me quite by surprise, but my involuntary smile gave her the answer.

'I hope you know what you're doing, Mr James,' she said, but still with an element of amusement about her.

'For about the first time in my life, I believe I do.'

I met Emily in reception and we left the office without a word, arriving in agreement, without needing to agree it, at our favourite lunchtime café.

'Well, Miss Lewis…' I said.

'Yes, Mr James?'

I felt foolish at having no idea what to say next, and a few moments passed in rather awkward silence as we sat opposite each other, staring at the table.

'I don't think we have an option,' I said finally. 'Emily, I've been having a lot of odd thoughts about you recently. You've actually been messing with my head rather a lot.'

She opened her mouth to speak, but I silenced her with a look.

'I've been trying to stifle my own thoughts,' I said, 'and to ignore them, but they keep happening more and more often, and they get stronger. Something odd happened at your exhibition. Your pictures spoke to me as you would.' I shook my head as if thinking about something deeper that I didn't have time to explain. 'I felt guilty for thinking about you as more than a friend, but you're leaving the office, damn you, and you are more than a friend. I know we run the risk of buggering up our friendship, as you so delicately put it, but what about if we bugger up something better by being too scared to try it?'

'James!' said Emily, rising from her chair and collapsing on my knee, and kissing me whilst wrapping her hands around the back of my head. After a couple of seconds I felt her cheeks become damp and then I tasted the salt in her tears.

'Damn you! James!' she said, wiping her streaming eyes. 'Why the hell didn't we do this a year ago?'

'I couldn't possibly kiss my secretary!'

'You just did.'

'It's different – you're leaving.'

'No it isn't, James!' she said, and kissed me again.

'Moneypenny! Not in public!'

'Shut up, James! you bloody idiot!'

That afternoon was the October partners' meeting, and I begrudgingly left the company of Emily for that of my esteemed colleagues.

Bugle seemed to be in a good mood.

'Afternoon all! Firstly, I'd like to welcome Cressida Smyth-Jones, our new head of the family department. James tells me she's a fierce adversary, so we're very pleased to have her on board. Isn't that right, James?'

I smiled ever so slightly sourly, not wishing to let Cressida know that I had been singing her praises. Despite her friendly approach, I was still proud of my recent victory over her, and wanted the feigned rivalry to continue.

She smiled sarcastically back, but her sarcasm extricated itself from her smile as she held my eyes for a moment. Damn woman knew my game.

'Secondly, I am delighted that Teddy's practice seems to have kick-started itself again. Do you know, Teddy,' said Bugle to Teddy, who was for once at the partner's meeting, 'that your victory over Priest and Parsons has already been mentioned in the legal press?'

'No, I don't read the legal press,' said Teddy, a little too honestly.

'Well, it's not every day that that happens! Good work, George!' Bugle never called Teddy by his Christian name. 'Let's hope this exposure means the department gets some new instructions. By the department, I mean you Teddy.'

'That is what I had understood.'

'Next on the agenda is staff changes, which Yarrington will brief us on.'

'Thank you Frank. I'd also like to extend my welcome to Cressida.' They exchanged rather formal smiles. 'And to propose that Tim is made partner. Do we have any objections?'

'Who is Tim?' asked Cressida.

Everyone looked round at her. I felt sorry for her; it had been a perfectly reasonable question, but she was new and I felt she needed an explanation.

'When Yarrington proposes something,' I said, 'it is not customary to object.'

Yarrington looked amused at this, while Bugle looked at me furiously. Neither said anything, knowing that if my comment were construed as defamatory, I would have the total defence of justification on my side. Besides, since the evening that Bugle had spilled his soul to me, my power over him had grown somewhat.

I think poor Cressida wanted to be amused, but she hadn't the measure of either of the Founding Fathers, let alone the rest of the partners, and so remained silent.

'Excellent. Since we all seem to agree, I will discuss the matter with him and hope he accepts,' concluded Yarrington.

So this was how they decided whether to make someone up to partner! This was how easy it was! It made my acceptance of partnership seem somewhat diluted. Nevertheless, it wasn't often that a partner's meeting contained nothing more than good news, and just as this thought popped into my head, Yarrington announced:

'Next week, James and Cressida will be moving to Margaret's room.'

Cressida and I glanced at each other: it looked as if our fortnight together would become a more permanent set up, but at least there were the beginnings of a smile about her lips: perhaps things wouldn't be so bad. Yarrington continued: 'But sadly, the family department is suffering its second recent and most sad loss. Emily is departing to further her career in other fields. She's been a fantastic secretary to Margaret, and then James, and she'll be sorely missed. Nevertheless, her replacement, my very own Lynn, will no doubt provide the support the department needs.'

And Yarrington looked at me, not quite angrily, but imploring me not to say anything in light of his last words.

But Lynn! This was no joke; everyone knew that Lynn was not my favourite person, but so serious and profound were my objections of having to work with the ghastly woman, that voicing my concern or worse still blurting out something rude at this juncture may have been counter-productive. No, I must wait until I had formulated my thoughts and devised a plan of attack. The first query that had been deliberately glossed over and needed answering was why Yarrington was getting rid of his own secretary, and why he was able to do so.

'Thank you David,' said Bugle rising. 'Well, that's all. May I see Paul and Martin afterwards please?'

At least the company duo were in for a talking to over their treatment of the trainees.

'A word, David, if you please?' I said, entering Yarrington's office later that day.

'Ah, James. I thought you might be showing your face. I must say you were very calm in that meeting. I take it you knew about Emily?'

'Yes, she told me last night.'

'You don't seem very upset about it.'

'We discussed a number of things. But as you know, we're good friends. I shall miss working with her, certainly.'

'But I suppose the relationship doesn't need to be hush hush any longer, though, eh?!'

'If you are referring to an amorous relationship, I'm afraid you are entirely mistaken.'

'What twaddle!'

'David. She kissed me yesterday for the first time ever. There, I've said it, and I don't want to hear another word about it.'

'Right you are,' he said, clearly in disbelief and mock seriousness. I let the matter drop; clearly I could not convince him of the truth.

'Lynn. What the hell is going on?' I asked. 'Why are you getting rid of her?'

'Well, the problem is, James, that I am not getting any younger, and to be truthful I'm getting a little tired of all this law. So I'm throwing in the towel.'

'No!'

'Yes. Afraid so – only as a partner. I'm coming in as a consultant three days a week to keep the old grey cells ticking over, but therein lies the problem: I shall need a part-time secretary and it's daft to split the role of a full-time secretary, which leaves Lynn redundant.'

'Redundant! Exactly! Redundancy is the easy way to get rid of employees.'

'Yes, but not if you're hiring a new secretary at the same time – and you and Cressida will need one, James!'

'Bugger. See your point.'

'Look James, I know she's a bitch…'

He paused to allow me to get over the shock of him using such language and the subsequent humour that this caused.

'…I know she's a bitch, but it's bloody hard to dispose of employees these days. There's so much crass legislation that keeps useless bastards employed all over the country, I'm surprised our entire economy hasn't gone down the pan.'

'I thought it had.'

'Well, yes, in the sense that no-one does anything useful any more.' I could sense a Yarrington lecture on the state of the world coming on, and settled myself further into the chair. 'Damn it, James, we were once a nation of industrialists and engineers: now we can't even manufacture toasters; we didn't colour in pink most of the land mass of this planet and win two world wars by complaining that our bosses hadn't given us a twenty minute break for a few hours; we used to have good laws – when I was at school we had a wonderful master who used to tell us we should be proud of our legal system – and we were, but now after years of left-wing rule by an executive who have hardly a legal training between them, let alone any actual legal experience, what do you expect but a mass of badly contrived, badly drafted and barely interpretable laws. And that's because the calibre of politicians has fallen dramatically: the opposition is equally at fault: they should have been jumping up and down wildly to bring the public's attention to some of these daft laws that simply slip through the net. Damn them all! And damn Lynn!'

'You and Frank aren't so different after all,' I said, recalling Bugle's thoughts aired not so long ago.

'What do you mean?' he asked.

'Never mind,' I said, wanting to return to the topic of Lynn. 'It might not be so hard to damn Lynn,' I said, handing Yarrington a piece of paper.

'What's this?'

'That is a chart of Lynn's sick days for the last year.'

'Good heavens,' he said, after examining it for a moment. 'They're all on Mondays!'

CHAPTER 52

Emily

Since Emily had first kissed me on that Monday evening, it had taken me five minutes to realise our relationship would never be quite the same again, sixteen hours to realise that I didn't want our relationship to be the same again, seventeen hours until she agreed and kissed me again, ninety-seven hours until we first made love, and ninety-eight hours until the following conversation:

'Fuck me, James, that was quite incredible.'

'Yes.'

'I love you.'

'I love you too.'

Emily sat bolt upright and looked at me. She looked shocked, and disbelieving, but tried to hide both with the happiness that evidently wanted to shine through.

'Don't say that, James. You can't mean it.'

I didn't reply, because I wasn't sure if I did either. But I came rapidly to the conclusion that my brain was so delirious that this must be love, in some form: perhaps not the enduring tie left in the relationship once the lust has been satisfied; perhaps not the wish to remain as best friends forever; and perhaps not the conscious thought that our lives were so entwined that I could not function without her.

Yet as I thought this, I realised that these elements of what love has been defined as had been part of our relationship for some time anyway.

'I do love you, Emily. It just took me a while to realise it.'

She shook her head, happily, and kissed me, her breasts pressing on my chest.

'How long have you loved me?' I asked.

'I think it was when we took Ben to the races.'

'That long?'

'When was it you realised you liked me as more than a friend?'

'In hindsight, at your exhibition – when I saw the picture of Antonio and Anna-Maria in the window. It's us, isn't it?'

'I think it might be. I had no idea it was when I painted it. Or I pretended not to. I'm still fascinated as to how clever my subconscious is, and how daft I am for not realising. But you said in hindsight. When did you *actually* know?'

'Your kiss helped!'

She smiled.

'But it wasn't then either. I was terrified of losing you totally.'

'I think...' I said, 'it was when Cressida told me she hoped that I knew what I was doing, when we went out for lunch the day after.'

'Cressida?'

'She knew.'

'On *Tuesday*?'

'She could feel the tension between us, apparently.'

Emily nodded. 'Must have been obvious, I suppose.'

'I knew when I told her that I did know what I was doing that we couldn't go back.'

Twelve hours after that, we had made love several more times, and it then being Saturday, we spent the morning in bed, where the following discourse took place:

'So can I call you my girlfriend now?' I asked, immediately thinking it odd that these words, probably uttered by me for the first time more than twenty years ago on the school playground, should still have relevance to my life now.

'I should bloody well hope so!' she said, kissing me.

'Splendid.'

She looked at me fondly, but still said: 'God alone knows why I fell for you!'

'So does this mean we can tell people?'

'Not in the office, until I leave, but yes, otherwise.'

Things in the office were odd for the rest of the time that Emily worked at Bugle & Yarrington. Since Cressida's remark, we tried our utmost to hide our feelings in the workplace, we hoped with some success, since Cressida made no more similar comments.

On the Thursday of Emily's last week, I arranged to go out with Charlie Somers. The dear fellow had been so tied up with Felicity, that he seemed to have forgotten the existence of his friends, so I was relived to find he was finally keen for some male company.

He had agreed to come to the Vaults, not frequented for some months by me, it being a place primarily suitable for the dark autumnal evenings that were now closing in.

Our respective greetings of 'Charlie!' and 'James!' were followed by a manly hug and a seat at the bar where you could see most of the individual vaults occupied by surreptitious couples; we had no reason to hide our relationship.

'How's things?'

'Tip-top!' he said. 'I went out for dinner with Felicity's folks last night. We went in his vintage Rolls – must be worth a fortune – and he was totally pissed when we were driving back to theirs. The old man hit the curb a few times, and when we stopped at some traffic lights, Mrs Warburton-Lee jumped out and tried to extricate the jiggered judge from the driver's seat by opening his door. He drove off without her, straight through the red lights, did a lap of the block, picked her up again, and she sat quiet as a mouse after that! Poor Felicity just wanted the ground to open up for her, but I assured her my parents had been just as loving.'

'Had they?'

'Oh, yes! Anyway, we went back to their house and continued to drink until the small hours. Mrs Warburton-Lee insisted I stayed.'

'I still can't believe you are frequenting the abode of a member of the judiciary!' I said.

'Well, I had something important to ask him when we got back,' said Charlie, smiling.

'You didn't?'

'I did!'

'And?'

'He said: "My boy! I can't think of anyone else I'd rather employ for the job!" and gave me half a pint of whisky and a cigar!'

'Congratulations!'

But Charlie wanted to finish his story: '"It's not a job," I said, and he said, "You may think that, my boy! but I can guarantee in less than a year, you'll be wanting a salary from me to keep the girl in clothes and handbags! You'll find that marrying my daughter is more stressful than advocacy in the Court of Appeal, and you'll want to be properly remunerated for the undertaking!" He's such a hoot!'

'Well, Charlie, many congratulations,' I said, wanting him to acknowledge them. 'Here's to you and Felicity! But what did she say?'

'Oh, good Lord! I haven't asked her yet,' he said. 'I'm taking her to Paris this weekend, and I'll going to ask her then. I'm rather nervous,' he said, reaching into a pocket and producing a box.

'I bet you are!' I said. 'I've never contemplated such a move.'

'Nor have I, until now. What do you think?' he asked, opening the box to reveal a wonderfully endowed engagement ring.

'It's beautiful, Charlie. She'll love it.'

'I hope so.'

'She will.'

'If she'll have me.'

'She'd be daft not to.'

'You have to say that.'

'I do, but you know very well, that aside from me, you are the most eligible bachelor in London Town!'

'Aside from you?!' he asked, and we laughed.

'So what news with you?'

'Well, I have a girlfriend.'

'Who?' asked Charlie, expectantly. 'Do I know her?'

'Emily.'

'No!'

'Yes!'

'Bloody hell, James. Took you long enough.'

'Meaning?'

'She's been in love with you for months: no, years!'

'How do you know?'

'She told me.'

'Why the hell didn't you tell me?'

'She told me not to!'

'That's no excuse!'

'That's why she wouldn't have me. She thought she should try and get you out of her system, but couldn't. When I saw you together, it was obvious. In fact, I didn't even have to see you together: just the mention of your name was enough.'

'Obvious from the outside, maybe.'

'James, it was obvious. Well, look! That's such splendid news. Well done! Another drink? We need to toast this news!'

Friday arrived with a well-deserved hangover, and so began my last working day with Emily. It was an odd feeling, but exciting, in more ways than one, to know that she was no longer destined to be my secretary.

This being the second Friday with Cressida, we soon came to realise that her attention span would be even lower on Fridays than any other day. She worked in bursts: she dictated letters feverishly, or researched some point to include in a brief, and then sat back and talked about herbaceous borders, the best way to cook a duck, or lamented that not enough young men were family lawyers these days, or that the Principal Registry of the Family Division had a higher rate of staff turnover than the Anzac Divisions at Passchendaele.

Lunch came after more interludes than actual work between them, and after taking Emily out for a large and boozey lunch, the afternoon slipped by between the odd phone call rudely awakening me from a number of small snoozes.

Angela came round at four o'clock to make sure we had packed all our personal effects into boxes so that the contents of our office could be moved over the weekend into Margaret's old office – apparently the Firm was now large enough to afford professional removal men, as opposed to forced trainee labour such as I had been used to in that stage of my career. Our belongings duly packed, Cressida decided enough was enough and that today, gin could be taken an hour earlier than the prescribed six o'clock. She left, saying to Emily that she was sorry to lose her, but (with a wink, no less) that she was sure she'd see her again socially.

And so the time came for Emily to depart the grand door of Number 22 for the last time as an employee of Bugle & Yarrington. It was an odd sensation, knowing I'd never walk down these steps after work with her again; knowing that her smiling face and hot coffee would never again greet me in the office.

Having passed through the door and gone down the limestone steps, she turned round and looked up at the Firm's prestigious buildings.

'I sha'n't miss the work, but I'll miss working here, and I'll miss working with you.'

Then I realised I had the most splendid deal in the world. I had lost the best colleague a man could ask for, but had gained the most splendid girlfriend a man could dream of. I realised that the smile and coffee would be much more welcome in bed than in the office, and it

surprised me that the thought had never crossed my mind before.
   'Drink?'
   'Drink.'

CHAPTER 53

Alexander

Michael telephoned late that evening to say that Sarah had given birth to their second son, Alexander, the day before. He'd just driven them home from hospital, and asked if I'd like to help him cook their Sunday lunch again.

I said I knew a girl who would be much more efficient in the kitchen than I; Emily was duly invited, and at the appointed hour, we arrived on their doorstep.

'Emileeeeee!' squealed Ben when he saw her, and rushing past his uncle, hugged her as she dropped to her knees to allow him to do so.

'Hello, Ben, how are you?'

'Hungry!' he said, and then, turning to me, with a cheeky grin, said: 'Hello Uncle James.'

'Oh, hello. I'm pleased to see you're so pleased to see me!'

'Hello, Michael,' I said, once Ben had dashed inside again, 'How are they doing?'

'Not bad at all,' he said, having greeted Emily. 'They're downstairs, and the mother has a large glass of sherry, which the baby is also taking, though indirectly. Come through. Sherry?'

'Sherry.'

We went through to the drawing room where Sarah sat breast-feeding the new sprog. She looked wonderfully well and happy, as did the little Alexander. She tucked herself away and we all crowded round the baby, which, though I hated admitting it, was rather sweet. I declined holding him, learning from my previous mistake of holding Ben a couple of years ago who promptly emptied the contents of his stomach over my shoulder. Emily however, seemed to take great delight in dandling him.

Ben came in, and noticing all the attention was on the new arrival did his best to look unimpressed while driving his toy train along the carpet, not yet having had engineering assistance from his uncle in laying the required train-track.

'Can we fly Terry in the Satterbee Park?' he asked.

'After lunch, I think, if there's enough wind,' said his mother.

'Who is Terry?' asked Emily.

'He's a pterosaur,' I said, catching on.

'He's a *Pteranodon*,' clarified Ben.

And Ben ran off upstairs.

'A kite,' I said to the perplexed Emily.

'Oh, brilliant! I haven't flown a kite in years!'

And in came Terry, Ben concealed behind the expanse of reptilian wing so that he couldn't have seen anything in front of him: indeed he evidently did not remember leaving his train in the doorway moments before. Over he went, landing on Terry. One of them – Terry or Ben – gave out a loud snapping sound: at first I hoped it was the former, and then after further consideration hoped it might be the latter. But either way I knew there would be tears, and when Ben had picked himself up, and then Terry, it was evident that Terry's left wing was in a state of considerable limpness. Then came the tears, which only subsided when I said that I'd buy a new spar from the kite shop to mend Terry's wing.

Thankfully Alexander remained in a contented mood throughout his brother's outburst; mother's milk laced with sherry, I thought, must have been good for the child. Michael, Emily and I took it in turns being head chef, drink distributor and nurse of mother and child, and soon lunch was ready without disaster, thanks to Emily's leadership in the kitchen.

'So, what news?' asked Sarah, once we had all sat down around the table, large plates of delicious looking beef and Yorkshire puds in front of us.

Emily and I looked at each other: this was the moment we'd have to tell them our news, but although conveying a simple fact should have been easy, actually finding the words was rather difficult. Thankfully Emily stepped in:

'James has finally realised he's in love with me,' she said, breaking into a brilliant smile. 'We are officially boyfriend and girlfriend!'

'Thank God for that!' said Michael, and Sarah just smiled. 'Congratulations to you both!' said Michael. Glasses were duly raised, but not clinked, and then we all fell silent.

'Are you having a baby too?' asked Ben, peering at the thankfully flat stomach of Emily.

Emily and I managed to stifle our looks of horror for the benefit of

Ben, but they didn't go unnoticed by his parents, and we all laughed.

'I think it's a bit early for that, Ben,' said Emily, blushing.

Silence returned round the table, and I saw Emily and Michael exchanging a glance, and then Michael wink at Ben. This aroused my suspicions.

'Don't tell me you all knew too?'

'Knew what?' asked Michael, ever so innocently.

'We all knew you liked Emily!' piped up Ben. 'You're so silly for not telling us before! She's liked you forever!'

I looked at Emily who was now very red. Neither of us could contain our smiles.

'Not only that,' I said, 'But Charlie Somers has had the all clear from Judge Warburton-Lee, and is in Paris as we speak with a ring, a rock, a bottle of bubbly and an important question. In fact, he's probably already asked her.'

'Well, chin chin to Charlie!' said Sarah. 'I never thought I'd see the day! This Felicity must be a pretty special young lady – we should have you all to dinner to celebrate!'

'Here, here!' said Michael. 'To blossoming relationships!' he said, raising his glass.

'And to the new member of the family!' I said, catching Emily's eye just at the wrong moment, causing her to choke on the wine she sipped.

'Don't worry, sweetheart, I meant Alexander.'

'James!' said Sarah, slapping the back of my head.

'I'm pleased to hear it!' said Emily, trying to be indignant, but unable to stop herself smiling.

The rain that lasted for the rest of the afternoon didn't foul up proceedings too badly since Terry's accident had precluded his flight in any case, and we spent the afternoon inside, chatting, building railways and trying not to wake the sleepy Alexander. Eventually Emily and I left, exhausted after all the food and drink and having been worn out by Ben, but with an invite to come to dinner with Charlie and Felicity in early December.

CHAPTER 54

A Room With A View

The next morning, the rain still hadn't stopped and I arrived in the office with soggy feet and in a mood as inclement as the weather.

The door of my office swung open to reveal a bare room: not wishing to think about life in the office without Emily, and the unfortunate repositioning of Lynn as secretary, I had forgotten that my office was no longer mine and that I was to move into Margaret's old office, with Cressida.

My mood worsened as I climbed the stairs to the front of Number 22 where this new room was. I entered to find an equally damp Cressida standing with her arms folded surveying the scene. All the filing cabinets stood in the centre of the room with the bookcases. Files, books and stationary littered every available surface, including the floor, and only the desks appeared to be in situ.

'Oh dear,' I said, reading Cressida's expression. 'I'll call Angela, and try and get this mess sorted out.'

'Angela?'

'Head of human resources. Have you met her?'

'Not that I know of.'

'Short woman, greasy hair, greasier glasses.'

'Oh, yes, I've met her.'

I went to a desk, not yet designated to an owner, and picked up the phone.

It wasn't plugged in.

I exhaled deeply, something that I'm not accustomed to doing, and just then I heard the door creak open, and Angela's whiskers appeared round it as if she'd heard my sigh.

'Good morning, Angela!'

'Morning James.'

'What the devil is going on? I thought you were overseeing the office move over the weekend?'

'Don't you speak to me like that.'

'The point is, Angela,' I said, getting cross, 'How on earth are we meant to do a day's work in this mess?'

'I am trying to sort it out as soon as possible.'

'As soon as possible would have been Saturday afternoon.'

Yarrington entered.

'What are all these raised voices?' he asked, before he'd taken in the scene, and once he had surveyed the carnage he asked, raising his voice: 'Angela, what's going on? We paid people to sort this bloody lot out over the weekend!'

'I'm sorry Mr Yarrington, we only had them for a few hours, and it took longer than we thought.'

'How many bloody tea-breaks did you have?' he asked, causing Cressida and I to exchange smiles. 'Get a couple of trainees in here to help clear up!'

And Angela sneezed violently in the direction of Yarrington, with no attempt to intercept the rapidly shifting contents of her nose before they reached him.

'Health and safety,' she said between snuffles, 'the trainees shouldn't be moving heavy furniture.'

'The only major risk to anyone's health or safety, Angela, is you. Buy yourself a pocket-handkerchief and use the bloody thing. Now listen here: I employ you, and I want you to get two trainees in here – now! – to move this furniture and get all the rest of this rubbish into it.'

'Yes, Mr Yarrington,' and she scuttled off crabwise as if not wanting to show her back to him in case he booted up the backside as she left. Another three large sneezes echoed from the staircase outside as Angela spread her cold throughout the entire confines of Number 22.

'Ghastly woman,' said Yarrington. 'I'm sorry, Cressida, that things are such a mess just after you start; it's really not on.'

'That's quite all right. I'm sure with a bit of help, we can get it ship-shape by lunchtime.'

'Where's Lynn?'

'It's Monday,' I reminded him.

'Oh, yes,' he said, pondering. 'Well, let me know if you need more help! Cheerio!'

Matthew and Tom arrived a few minutes later, and we spent the morning arranging the room. By lunchtime it looked like an office, Matthew and Tom departed with our thanks, and Lynn still hadn't arrived which meant one less day in the same room as her.

Cressida and I sat in our chairs in front of our new desks, each by one of the two huge sash windows and opposite each other. We both reclined as we surveyed our new surroundings with delight: the ceiling was high, and the light, even on a gloomy day such as this, was so good that electric light wasn't necessary, and there was at least ten feet of floor space between the desks. The vastness of the room swallowed up the filing cabinets and made the bookcases look small. My gaze wandered towards my window. Rain tumbled down the panes and it rattled in the wind; through the deluge I could see the handsome Georgian buildings opposite, and, leaning towards the window slightly, a good portion of the Mayfair street in which our buildings lay. I saw a woman on the street below battling with an inside-out umbrella, but despite the forlorn scene, it cheered me up: at last I had a room with a view.

CHAPTER 55

Anger Management

The next morning, Lynn's presence in our new office was obvious from the amount of purple chattels that had been imported into the area surrounding her desk, and shortly after I arrived, she announced her presence with her bottom, pushing open the door with it as she reversed into the room carrying two cups of coffee, one with a plate of biscuits balanced on top, and the other a plate of toast. Having opened the door wide enough to get through, she turned round and tottered into the room bosom first, wearing purple high heels far too high for legs with such a substantial weight perched upon them. Her centre of gravity was further raised by her bosom (contained only by a brassiere which must have had a pound of lead sewn into the back to counterbalance the weight of the huge orbs) and I was relieved when both coffees reached her desk without a major spillage.

'Morning Lynn.'

'Morning James. Where's the head of department?' she asked. Office hierarchy was of paramount import in Lynn's world, and no doubt she'd use the proper chain of command exhaustively to exhaust Cressida and I.

'No idea. Shall I relieve you of one of those coffees?' I asked.

'Oh no, they're both for me. I can't do a thing until I've had my two cups and two plates.'

I watched Lynn eat the pile of toast, crumbs going everywhere, and begin a cup of coffee. The sight and sound were both rather off-putting, so I turned my attention to the view outside, which was much brighter today. When my eyes tired of the view, I again glanced at Lynn who had thankfully finished eating, but was now applying some form of makeup with the help of a purple-edged mirror that sat on her desk. Sue rang to say that Cressida was ill and wouldn't be coming in. Irked by Lynn's very presence, I began working. An hour later, she had churned out my first piece of dictation and gave it back. Not only was it not on the Firm's headed notepaper, there was no punctuation at all. The text ran nearly two pages from 'Dear Sirs' to 'Yours faithfully' without a comma, full-stop or paragraph.

'Lynn, what is this?' I said.

'It's the letter you just dictated,' she said, as if I was a sandwich short of a picnic.

'Yes, I can see that.'

'Well, don't ask stupid questions,' she said.

'Are you trying to annoy me?'

'No,' she said, and I think I believed her, 'but I really don't understand what you're getting at.'

Fuck me. She was serious.

'Do you think I wanted to send this letter out like this?'

'You solicit. I type. Simple as that. Nothing you dictate registers with me. I couldn't tell you what's in that letter, I just type it, so I have no idea whether you want to send it like that or not.'

'Firstly, I tend to send my letters out on headed notepaper.'

'Oh I never use that for the first draft.'

'My first draft is my last draft, so kindly do in future.'

'Mr Yarrington always did a first draft…'

'Well, as you see, I am not he, and I do *not* do drafts. I haven't time. All right?'

'Yes, I'll try and remember,' she said, without the slightest hint of sincerity.

'And secondly, did you really think I'd write a two page letter in one sentence?'

'I have no idea.'

'Well look at it!' I said, thrusting it at her. 'Is this something you'd expect to receive from a solicitor?!'

'I wouldn't necessarily expect to receive anything from a solicitor.'

!

'Lynn. There is not a single fucking comma or full-stop in the entire letter.'

'Don't swear at me, Mr James! And don't you think I'm the stupid one. You didn't dictate a single piece of punctuation.'

'Listen to the intonation in my voice! I haven't dictated a comma for years! Emily managed to get it right.'

'Yes, well…' she said, looking sarcastically at me, 'not every secretary performs her duties as diligently as no doubt Emily did!'

'And what exactly do you mean by that?' I asked, through sheer exasperation. We both knew the answer of course, and her raised eyebrows as a response were enough to make me leave the room to cool off before I said something I knew I'd regret.

The next day, Cressida was back in the office.

'Lynn, could I have a cup of coffee, please?' she asked.

'Yes, I should think so. Do you know where the kitchen is?'

'No, not yet.'

'Well, it's all the way downstairs, left at the bottom, past the photocopier room on your right.' And she carried on typing.

'Lynn?' I said.

Her fingers kept rattling at the keyboard.

'Lynn. Coffee, now, or I shall phone Angela.'

At the mention of Angela, Lynn shot me a glare so sour that it was comical, but she hopped up, grabbed a pile of letters that she had just typed, threw them on Cressida's desk so they glided from one side to the other and fell off at Cressida's feet, and stormed out.

'God alone knows how anyone could have employed her,' Cressida sighed, and bent down to pick up her pile of letters. I watched her flick through them. At the first one, her face looked mildly bemused; the expression turned into one of incredulousness after two or three and once she had finished going through the pile she said: 'There's no punctuation at all! I can no longer work with that deliberately obnoxious purple-shaded bitch!'

Later that day, Cressida and I were called to Bugle's office by the man himself.

'James, Cressida. I'm sorry to have to haul you over the coals so soon in your career with us, Cressida.' Pause. 'James.' He said, looking at me with a tired look. It went without saying that he didn't mind hauling me across the coals.

'Lynn has been complaining that you are abusing your authority over her. What do you have to say?'

Cressida and I looked at each other.

Bugle shifted his pose, as if he was about to score over us.

But I had ammunition.

'Frank. You know I get on with most people. I rarely get angry.

But Lynn is impossible. For starters, she consistently takes Mondays off. Look at the figures. Here is a letter she typed for me, and the day after, having had a bollocking from me, one she did for Cressida. Her complaint about our so called abuse of authority stems from Cressida asking her to make a cup of coffee.'

Bugle looked at the letters I handed him, an expression of extreme surprise crossing his face as he took in their severe lack of punctuation.

'Christ!' he said. 'Bad typing is one thing, but I've never seen anything like this – how in God's name did Yarrington cope when she was his secretary? – and furthermore, if you can't rely on your secretary for a good cup of coffee, what in the blazes can you rely on them for?! This is bloody ridiculous! I'll speak to Lynn. Sorry about this. It's a bloody tedious affair, and no doubt you have more important things to worry about. Thanks for popping in though; I know there are always two sides to a story,' he added as an afterthought to reverse his initially caustic approach to the matter.

'Morning, James. Hello, Cressida!' said Yarrington the next morning. 'Just thought I'd drop by and see how things were going with Lynn? I gather from Frank that things have been rather fraught.'

'The woman's bloody useless!' said Cressida, catching Yarrington by surprise.

'Even Frank wondered how the hell you put up with her for so long!' I said.

'I wondered that on many occasions,' said Yarrington, wearily. 'Where is she?'

Just then Lynn's right buttock appeared in the doorway as she steered herself into the room carrying her usual breakfast accoutrements.

'I gather you've had some teething problems in your new position, Lynn?' said Yarrington

'None to speak of,' she replied indignantly.

'I've seen your typing efforts. I should say there was some kind of problem.'

'I would have thought that two partners would have learned how to dictate properly by this stage in their careers!' shooting us a triumphantly evil look.

'One might say that a secretary of your experience wouldn't necessarily require every piece of punctuation dictated for them,' said

Yarrington.

'Rubbish! I type what you dictate. That's my job. And my job does *not* bloody well include satisfying the partner's ridiculously high caffeine demands.'

'You used to make me coffee,' pointed out Yarrington.

At which moment Bugle entered. 'I've got a bloody client next door! Keep this noise down! What's going on anyway?'

'Lynn's typing,' said Cressida bluntly.

'Good, I need to see you later about all that, Lynn. I'm not particularly impressed, to be blunt,' said Bugle.

'Oh I see!' said Lynn. 'All the lawyers ganging up on me?'

'To type a letter with *no* punctuation is the most ridiculous thing I've ever heard,' said Bugle, brows already deeply knit, 'I'll see you about it later.'

Lynn looked imploringly at Yarrington, presumably wanting some support from her old and long-standing boss.

'I must admit,' began Yarrington, 'that I am having some difficulty deciding whether you are being bloody-minded or whether you are just plain stupid!' he said, standing up for himself against this sour old sow at last.

'That's it, David! I'm off! You've really done it this time! I'm not coming back! I don't care what you say! And I don't give a damn if you don't pay me this month's salary!' And with that she gathered up her purple scarf and purple handbag, thrust her purple umbrella into a purple carrier bag and marched to the door which she opened more forcefully than Bugle in a bad mood. She turned briefly to give us all an evil look through narrowed purpled eyes, and then slammed the door after her.

Lynn had left.

It was as if the orchestra and choir had just reached the most bombastic part of Handel's *Messiah* and had both opened up in full voice: *Hallelujah*! And a few bars of that particular chorus echoed through my imagination for a few moments.

'Thank Christ she's gone!' declared Bugle. 'Are we all in agreement that she just resigned in case she tries to claim unfair dismissal or something?' We all nodded. 'Good. These damn socialists think they draw up their statutes to keep their minions employed indefinitely! Nothing like a good, old fashioned resignation to get the buggers out! I'd better get back to my client. I'll say the commotion was a matrimonial dispute between two unruly clients!' he said, chuckling to himself as he marched for the door.

'I honestly don't know how you put up with the old bat,' I said to Yarrington. 'What we need is another Emily! And I'm just the man to find you one. Stick an advert in the Gazette, and I'll help you interview – just don't tell Angela – we can't have her human resources managerial take on things when deciding on a new secretary; Angela doesn't understand the front-line needs of lawyers in action; she'll just cloud the issue with trivialities such as exam results, previous employment, knowledge of computers, typing speeds and the lowest possible salary that the applicant might accept. And, David,' I said with mock seriousness that was in fact deadly serious, 'you can be damn sure if Angela does any interviewing, the successful applicant will not be pretty.'

At this Yarrington began to take note. 'You know Angela is insanely jealous of everyone who is better looking than her, which means... which means she must be the most jealous woman in the entire world!'

'Why do we need a glamorous secretary?' asked Cressida, putting a slight dampener on my little speech.

Yarrington checked himself, considered a thought for a moment, and said: 'Yes, James, why do we need a glamorous secretary?' which made me feel rather foolish. I did not at first understand his reaction because he was usually the first to ask what a new female member of staff looked like, and appreciated his better looking female colleagues like a man should. Only the slight rise of colour to his cheeks raised my suspicions.

CHAPTER 56

Warburton-Lee

Emily had been busy all week painting. I had been rather miffed that she had had enough self-control to be able to resist me for a whole working week, refusing both my invites to tempt her out of her studio and into restaurants, and offers to come over and make tea for her while she painted. It would take some adjusting to become used to Emily's independent and headstrong ways, but my admiration for her simply increased when I thought about her like this.

Since Emily was thus engaged until Sunday, I was delighted when Charlie Somers asked me (through his clerk Philip) if I could join him in the Reform Club on Pall Mall for dinner that Saturday. I tried to elicit from Philip whether there had been a closening of relationships between certain members of 7 Queen's Bench Row, but as usual, his affected professionalism prevailed.

Pall Mall's proximity to my office meant I arrived rather early and was able to wander around the magnificent rooms of the Reform before Charlie's appointed arrival time. Despite a number of visits, I always forget how many books there are lining the walls of the place. Time passed quickly as I perused some of the tomes, and I wandered downstairs to see Charlie just coming in.

'Charlie!'

'James!'

We hugged, and received a couple of raised eyebrows from the older members of the club who happened to be in the hall.

'So, what did she say?!' I asked.

His smile said it all. 'Yes,' he said, 'what else could she have said?!'

'Quite! Well, congratulations!'

'Thanks.'

'So I suppose that makes me the most eligible bachelor in London Town?' I asked.

'I'm not so sure about that!' said Charlie. 'I'm not married yet!'

'Can you be an eligible bachelor if you're engaged?'

'I can!' said Charlie.

'You'd better not hear my daughter say that!' said a booming voice from behind.

'Ah! Judge!' said Charlie. 'Splendid to see you! This is James James Esquire, finest solicitor in the West-End. James, this is Mr Justice Warburton-Lee, sleepiest old bugger in the High Court!'

We shook hands, and the old boy seemed delighted at his introduction: it was evident that Charlie and his father-in-law-to-be got on famously.

'As you no doubt heard,' said Charlie, 'we were just discussing whether it is possible to remain an eligible bachelor if you're engaged. Your thoughts?'

'My dear fellow,' said the judge, 'I've been married over thirty years and have three children. If the right woman came along, I'd introduce myself as a bachelor! As, no doubt you would, Mr James? Are you not the chap who sacked his secretary to get her in the sack?'

I looked at Charlie who gave me the classic Somers 'never let truth get in the way of a good story' smirk.

'She resigned to get me in the sack, actually...'

'Splendid! Well, my boy, I hope she's up to scratch! You never can tell with these secretarial types. Do anything to get a leg up in life!'

Old Warburton-Lee, like his peers, strongly believed in the English classes.

'James has no need to worry there: she has a Cambridge degree and her father is Maurice Lewis,' said Charlie, explaining to the judge that my secretary had a better social standing than any of us.

'Old Maurice Lewis. Bugger me. Useless lawyer, but a charming fellow. I loved his advocacy. He projected his arguments with such logic and such eloquence, and with such brilliant interjections agin his adversary, that as a judge one couldn't help coming down on his side, despite his arguments being somewhat dubious from a legal perspective. That's the beauty of the English legal system. Denning never let law get in the way of his judgements, and I try to be as equitable myself. Of course, sometimes it rather backfires, which is no doubt why I haven't yet been elevated to the peerage.'

His short monologue having come an end, the judge looked around, and concluded: 'Well, let's stop standing around here and go and find a drink.'

Drinks in hand, the conversation continued: 'I've been seeing a lot in the legal press about that old duffer in your shipping department,' said Charlie.

'You don't mean George Teddy who took on Priest and Parsons?' asked the judge.

'That's him,' said Charlie.

'That firm *never* settles out of court,' continued the judge, 'Biggest bunch of litigious bastards I've ever seen. I'd never heard of George Teddy ten days ago, but he's quite the talk at the moment. Best kind of advertising you can get. Big shipping department, then, at your firm?'

I smiled, 'No, just him, and me, when he needs help!'

'I thought you were a matrimonial lawyer?'

'Indeed I am!'

The judge looked surprised. 'This Teddy must be a cracking lawyer,' he concluded. More lucky than anything else, I thought.

After we had been sufficiently lubricated to work up quite a hunger, we adjourned to the dining room. Once we had sat down, the judge looked at Charlie, quizzically.

'I knew there was something I meant to ask,' he said. 'Did my daughter ever give you an answer to your proposal of marriage?'

My jaw almost hit the table: I had assumed that Charlie had already told him, and it was quite beyond me how they could have spent an hour and half in each other's company without a mention of what was, in my opinion, one of the most dramatic pieces of news in a man's life.

'Oh, yes, she did, without hesitation.'

'Good. Glad to have another man round the table at Christmas. Now, what would we all like to drink? They do a magnificent claret here, but of course the fish is also top notch, and you may want to consider the white...' and the judge went down the wine list, giving commentary on the various whites, and which fish they went best with, without giving another moment's thought to his daughter's future husband.

CHAPTER 57

Painting

And so came Sunday morning, and with it, a claret induced headache.

I set off for Emily's flat, the grey overcast late October morning only made slightly better in the knowledge that an extra hour in bed had been blissfully spent asleep as England had returned overnight to Greenwich Mean Time, ready for the dark days of winter, which were now upon us. And of course, my excitement in seeing Emily was building with every step.

'Hi gorgeous!' I said as she opened her door, and revealed herself standing in one of my shirts, mostly unbuttoned, and apparently nothing else.

'Hi darling,' she said, immediately extending her arms and pulling me towards her. As her kissing got more passionate, she started manoeuvring backwards, me in her arms, and soon we had reached her bedroom, whereupon a horizontal posture was assumed post-haste.

'I'd like to paint,' she said afterwards.

'Me?'

'No! Don't flatter yourself, sweetheart!' said Emily. 'Would you mind?'

'Not in the least. Got any books I haven't read, that I'd like to?'

'You know where the bookcase is.'

And so we settled down, me reading on the sofa, Emily painting at her easel (facing me so as not to show me an unfinished work), and spent a contented afternoon passing the time in our respective ways, whilst chatting in between. She looked incredibly sexy, still wearing my shirt, although sadly she'd managed to find some jeans. I told her Charlie's news, about meeting Felicity's father and Lynn's resignation. Emily told me the wonderful news that she had another exhibition in her own name in a prestigious gallery in Cork Street, Mayfair, not too far from the office. The opening night was in late November, and she made me memorise the date so I would not double book myself. After that news, she announced that she would be going off on another painting jolly with her father for a fortnight in the following week.

'Emily!' I said, pained.

'What?'

'It seems that since we… since I finally realised that you were the most splendid girl in the world, you have been so busy you've hardly had time to see me!'

'Poor, poor, James,' she said sarcastically. 'Look, darling, I've had to wait years for you, so you can bloody well wait a fortnight for me! It'll be worth it!'

I shrugged. There was an infallible logic to her argument, and I smiled, shaking my head in defeat. She, having caught my eye, smiled, put down her paintbrush, crossed over to where I lay half recumbent on the sofa, and then climbed on top. A little later she leant me her sewing kit so I could sew the buttons back on my shirt.

CHAPTER 58

Alone Again

And so Emily departed with her father for warmer climes, painting materials duly packed, leaving me alone again.

But it was a tremendous sense of aloneness: I knew that it was a temporary period only, and I knew she'd miss me as much I would miss her. And I was pleased that Emily had the drive and fortitude to decide to do these things without me; that she was independent enough to want to leave me behind, and I loved her for it.

The next Monday, I arrived in the office in a buoyant mood, knowing that temporarily Cressida and I were without a secretary, but mightily pleased to be so: Lynn had gone! Cressida herself commented that this was the first time in her life she had enjoyed typing her own letters.

Not long into the morning, my phone rang.

'Mrs Ricketts is in reception to see you,' said Sue.

'Hello, Mrs Ricketts!' I said, genuinely pleased to see her.

We adjourned to a meeting room, and coffee was taken. We sat opposite each other, and for the first time, largely because thoughts about Sara prevented me from doing so, I could think of nothing to say. Thankfully, Mrs Ricketts broke the silence.

'James, I have just heard from Sara. I'm so sorry things didn't work out. I don't want to hear what happened – I've heard her side of the story – and frankly find it unbelievable – but she's still my granddaughter – I hope you understand?'

'Of course. It's best not to dwell on it,' I agreed. For a moment, my mind wondered what might have been, but Emily's smiling face quashed the thought almost as quickly as it had begun.

'I hope she didn't hurt you too much?'

I didn't reply on purpose: she had hurt me, and I wanted her grandmother to know.

'I'm sorry, James. Well, look! From all evil comes good: now you have no claim upon the Ricketts gold, I want you to be my lawyer again!'

'I should be delighted.'

'I'm sorry it's been such a while. I think the last time you saw me was when I had a contretemps with the pillar-box! Have you any idea how much that cost me to erect again? To say nothing of paying the fellow whose car I squished?'

'I'd rather not know, I think!'

'I think so, too. Have they painted the damn thing again? When the Royal Mail sent me the bill I suggested they should paint it – it had started to rust – no way at all to present such a fine piece of heritage.'

'I have moved offices, and can see it from my desk,' I said. 'I believe they have. It looks very red.'

'Good. I'm glad they've put you in an office with a view. Makes it so much more conducive to work.' I doubted her logic somewhat. Much of my day was now spent gazing out of the window, daydreaming, just like at prep school when the teacher made me sit on my own looking out of the window. It only served to fuel my restless imagination, to the cost of learning trigonometry and other vital mathematical theorems.

'Well, do you need legal advice at the moment, Mrs Ricketts?' I asked, knowing full well this might be a purely social call.

'As a matter of fact I do,' she said, seeming to surprise herself. 'I was thinking of letting some of the grandchildren have some of the assets from their trusts, and I need advice on tax. Capital gains, inheritance tax, and the taxation of trusts. Tim wrote me a letter about it and I don't understand a word of it. It's all about things like exit charges, relevant property and related trusts.'

'Mrs Ricketts, the complex taxation laws of England keep hundreds of lawyers, accountants and statute draftsmen unnecessarily employed: the law is so complex one can spend a lifetime getting bogged down in detail and never understanding the whole. Taxation on trusts is particularly tricky: it is designed thus so that the ordinary citizen is bamboozled into not making trusts so stopping him using them to avoid inheritance tax. Inheritance tax itself now applies to more citizens than ever, now that property is so valuable, but still only accounts for less than one percent of the Revenue's annual income. But the brilliant thing about the whole system is that if you happen to be very wealthy, you can pay people like me to arrange avoidance measures.'

'It's a good job I can afford you, then, isn't it?!'

'Yes, quite. But it's the middle classes who suffer. They have enough money to be comfortable homeowners, but not enough free capital to shaft the system or to pay expensive lawyers. I'd be shooting myself in the foot if I were to suggest it, but inheritance tax needs a serious and fundamental overhaul. Job losses in firms like mine, in accountants firms, and in government statute drafting and advisory departments would be catastrophic, which is why no government will simplify it: complex tax laws keep too many people employed.'

'Well, James, why aren't you lobbying the government?'

'Oh, no! I'll leave that to greater persons than myself.'

And we both fell silent, thinking perhaps that this was not a sufficient answer.

'Well,' I continued, 'when I start my legal crusade, I'll attack income tax too. It's far too complicated and a flat rate would make life infinitely fairer and more simple for virtually everyone. But again, many would lose their unnecessary jobs, so it simply won't happen.'

'Too many people,' she lamented.

'Yes,' I agreed, 'but I'm sure you'll agree that while paying me is something you'd rather avoid, it'll give you an enormous sense of satisfaction knowing that my fees will be a tiny percentage of the money that the government would have levied had you not instructed me!'

'Yes, definitely,' said the old bird, smiling.

'And of course this, in the eyes of the government, oils society further: you must pay me, which keeps me in a job, and since I'm a higher rate taxpayer, I give a big proportion to the government anyway. Everyone's happy!'

'Yes, but it's a daft way of running things.'

'Totally stupid,' I agreed. 'Now, let's discuss your options.'

And then she started asking me about the details of the taxation, her sharp mind missing little. She wanted to know definitions of all the terms and to understand how the sums were calculated. I promised that I would send her the calculations when I'd worked them out. Through bitter experience I quickly learned that carrying out arithmetic in the presence of a client is a dangerous move, especially when the sums are more complicated than working out the angles at the corners of a triangle.

After much explanation, our discussion concluded with Mrs Ricketts smiling at me.

'Thank you, James. I'm glad to have you back.'

'And you, Mrs Ricketts! And you.'

I subsequently spent several days, amongst other trifling pieces of work, grappling with Mrs Ricketts' tax calculations, thanking the legislature for keeping me employed, but all the while thinking what a waste of brainpower the whole thing was. I finished just in time to attend the November partners' meeting, another exercise in restraining anger in respect of wasted neurological function.

Everyone was present, including Tim, who had of course accepted partnership, and was duly welcomed by Bugle. Only Paul, head of company commercial, was conspicuously absent. Martin sat, looking quite edgy without his usual partner in crime, away from everyone else at one end of the Dining Room table.

Bugle rose to his feet, and the chatter subsided.

'Now, it is with regret that I have to announce that Paul has been asked to leave.'

A look of surprise crossed the faces of all present, with the exception of Martin, who simply looked uncomfortable.

'It has come to my attention that trainees in the company commercial department have not been receiving the training they should have been, and furthermore...' Bugle glowered at Martin. '...Furthermore,' he repeated, 'that the senior members of staff in that department have been less than fair to the trainees serving them. And that is putting it mildly. But that is all in the past. I have had words with the members of staff who have been involved, and I want no more discussion on the matter. Is everyone quite clear? Good. Paul will not be replaced immediately, as Yarrington and I believe that there are sufficient lawyers to deal with the current workload. But I would like Martin to voice his official opinion on the matter, if he would like?'

'It's outrageous that Paul had to go in the first place, and I strongly think the senior partner should reconsider his decision to ask him to leave,' said Martin, looking remarkably angry. 'The department will fail without his expertise.'

'I'll tell you what is outrageous,' hissed Bugle, 'and that is your horrid treatment of younger members of staff who are not in a position to fight back. You're bloody lucky not to have been booted out yourself! And no one, *no* one, in the legal profession is indispensable! Why haven't *you* got the necessary experience to run the department?'

Martin shrank back into himself, unable to think of a response, or unwilling to voice it if he had.

'I have nothing more to say on this matter!' said Bugle. 'We are not hiring new lawyers in the department, and Martin will be acting head of department for the moment, until a more permanent solution can be found.'

Martin said nothing.

My admiration for Bugle rose, for although he himself was no angel, it must have been a tough commercial decision to oust Paul, to say nothing of the friction it would doubtless cause with Martin and the rest of the company department.

'And now to more pleasant news!' said Bugle, obviously wanting to improve the atmosphere as quickly as possible. He cast an eye at Yarrington, who then rose to his feet to address the assembled partners.

'Lynn has resigned!' he said gleefully, to a rapturous response of laughter and applause.

'And thank Christ for it!' said Bugle, knowing full well that no one liked her. 'James and Cressida have spent a fortnight – probably quite a relief after having Lynn in their office – without a secretary. But I'm pleased to announce that Kate starts with them on Monday.'

'Who interviewed her?' asked Tim, with a cheeky smile.

'James and I,' said Yarrington.

'She's sure to be a fox then!' said Tim, 'Now old Emily's gone, and all!'

'Don't be so juvenile, Tim,' said Bugle, 'I'm sure James and David interviewed all the candidates on their professional attributes and not anything else.'

Yarrington and I caught each other's eyes, and somehow managed not to break into laughter.

'And they also interviewed David's new secretary, who begins on the same day.'

'Two new corkers!' said Tim.

'Mine's a cracker!' said Yarrington, intending only to tell Tim who was sitting next to him, but audible to all.

'But most importantly,' said Bugle, trying to bring some sense back into the proceedings, 'due to Teddy's recent victory over Priest and Parsons, the notoriously efficient and bloodthirsty city boys, the demand for the services of the shipping department has actually reached an all-time high.'

Teddy reclined in his chair, looking frightfully pleased with the situation.

'Teddy?'

Bugle sat, and Teddy, with some effort, rose. I wondered if his penchant for whisky had necessitated the extra effort he'd obviously needed to exert to stand on his own two pins.

'Thank you Frank. Yes, well, as you know, it was only a few short months ago that my days with the Firm seemed to be limited. And now, thanks largely to James, who found my major new client...'

'It was luck, really...'

'Well, thanks to James, I now have large and ongoing instructions from that client, and also a number of new clients from the coverage of my case in the legal press. This has been particularly gratifying to see, and I'm thankful to Angela, who had the forethought to ask if she could work with me to release details to one particularly widely read legal rag. The rest of the coverage was largely due to that initial article.'

'Christ, have we found a use for Angela at last?' muttered Bugle.

'Don't be ridiculous,' said Yarrington. 'The only thing she's good for is spreading colds.'

A few smiles went round the table.

'Anyway,' continued Teddy, 'I am most obliged to her.'

'Quite right!' I said, not in agreement with thanking Angela for anything, but to encourage Teddy.

'And so, the senior partner decided it would be wise to appoint a new member of staff to assist me, and I'm delighted that the decision has been made to employ Mr Andrew Wainwright as my assistant. He starts next week, and I hope we'll all make him feel very welcome.'

Nods of approval could be glimpsed from the partners.

'Frank also wants me to announce...' said Teddy 'although I do it only under duress...' he continued, smiling, 'that I have been offered the chance to be the editor-in-chief for the next edition of *Shipping Law*. It seems they were so impressed by my recent monograph on the limitations of the current edition, and possibly my press coverage, that they hired me immediately.'

Teddy paused to lap up the respect going round the room.

'And,' he continued, 'the last editor just died!'

Everyone laughed, but the respect for Teddy remained most conspicuous.

'And since I'm on my feet,' said Teddy, looking rather nervously at Bugle, who in turn looked sharply at Teddy, wondering what on earth he was going to say next, 'Since I'm on my feet...'

'Yes?' queried Bugle, a little too sharply to be polite.

'...I would also like to announce something else. Some of you may have met my lady friend, Miss Pound...' he looked embarrassed, and fumbled with the edge of his jacket, before resolutely clasping his hands behind his back and continuing, '...and some of you may have heard me mention that a bachelor I would always be...' and now he broke into a smile '...but last night, she agreed to marry me!'

Claps, 'bravos', 'congratulations', smiles and hand shaking ensued for the next few minutes as everyone gathered around Teddy wanting to know the details. Bugle and Yarrington were conspicuously absent from the throng that gathered round Teddy as they perused the minutes of the meeting, and after a few words exchanged between them, they looked at each other as if having made a decision, and Bugle clapped his enormous hands a couple of times.

Everyone fell silent.

'I'd just like to congratulate Teddy on behalf of the Firm,' he said a little pompously and as if Teddy wanted corporate congratulations, 'but we are in the middle of a partner's monthly meeting, and this is no time to celebrate.'

Everyone looked grumpily at Bugle, and started returning to their chairs. I wondered how Bugle had the inhumanity to be so mean to poor old Teddy, who looked quite deflated after Bugle's words.

Having left a sufficient gap for dramatic effect, Bugle continued: 'And the board room is no place for celebrations, so I suggest we bugger "any other business" until next month and go post haste to The Pub for a celebratory piss up on the Firm! Lead the way, George!'

I smiled. Again, Bugle had surprised me.

CHAPTER 59

Fireworks

On the fifth of November Emily returned to London and on that day I vacated my office earlier than usual to depart for her flat.

She opened the door, we kissed, and very soon ended up in bed.

After that, and after I'd poured a couple of stiff gins, she demanded to be taken to the fireworks on the Thames, which, this year, were on the very day that Guido's plan had come unstuck. Unfortunately, the weather was grim: it hadn't stopped raining since October and the wind was almost off the Beaufort scale. But I knew Emily had a childlike love of fireworks, and my duty was obvious.

We soon left, and despite the squally conditions, my mood was buoyant. Emily was brown from her second sojourn under the Italian sun, and looked quite gorgeous in her woolly hat and scarf. We headed through the empty streets and squares, she kicking the restless plane leaves that had somehow managed to ground themselves despite the wind, and me wanting to sing *The Man Who Broke The Bank At Monte Carlo* simply because I was so happy.

It being so horrid out of doors, there weren't too many people around, so we had the pick of where to stand. We stood watching the fireworks, Emily in front of me, and me with my arms around her. The fireworks were tremendous, and the rain did little to dampen my mood, nor Emily's. Her happy smiling face would turn round and look at me every few minutes, sometimes kissing mine.

We went home wet, but contented.

After undressing, we discovered that we'd both been soaked to the skin despite the number of layers, hats, and waterproofs. We shared a bath to warm up and ended up in bed again.

We hadn't seen each other for what had seemed like months, and chatted into the early hours. She was excited about her forthcoming exhibition, and I was looking forward to seeing her new work, which she assured me, was as different as her last lot was from her previous art. But she refused point-blank to let me see it before the opening day.

CHAPTER 60

Private View

Emily and I enjoyed a few wintry but glorious evenings in the warmth of her flat, spending our time in a very mundane but beautifully content manner. Then, towards the opening night of the exhibition in the gallery in Cork Street, she became very busy and I was banished to the lonely confines of my own flat, spending my evenings enjoying a bottle and a book, until the contents of the bottle made it impossible to readily comprehend the contents of the book. After which point my time was mostly spent missing Emily: but not in a miserable way, which is why when my head finally hit the pillow, I was utterly content. And thus the tail end of November passed.

The great evening arrived. I left the office, dressed impeccably in my best suit and my artiest shirt and tie combination, which admittedly was more City than arty, but looking rather dashing nevertheless.

Arriving at the gallery exactly on the appointed hour, it was pleasing to see that my arrival was unfashionably on time and that there was hardly a soul there. Pleasing because I wanted Emily to myself for a moment before she had perform her role as the exhibiting artist, and pleasing because I wanted to study the paintings before the gallery became too full of milling admirers obscuring the art.

Thankfully, the champagne bearers were on time, and a full tray of the stuff lay in the hands of one of them as I entered. Seeing Emily sans booze, looking quite magnificent in a smart, but casual and definitely arty outfit, I took two glasses and headed over to her, for the moment deliberately ignoring her paintings which adorned the walls.

'Hello darling,' she said, breaking the conversation she was having with the fellow she had been chatting to. She kissed me. The combination of her calling me darling and the kiss rendered me speechless, and I stood there smiling at her, possibly rather vacantly.

'Hello, James, how are you?'

It was only then that I noticed the magnificently large and curled moustache of Hugh Daley upon the face of Emily's partner in conversation.

'Hugh! Good evening. I'm well thank you. Yourself?'

'Couldn't be better. I'm so thrilled to have Emily in the Mayfair gallery – I'm expecting big things this evening. Let's see if there's unsold paintings by the end of the evening!'

'Don't be daft!' said Emily. 'I'll be pleased if we sell one!'

'Well, I won't be!' said Hugh.

'So you own this gallery too?' I asked, perhaps superfluously, but wanting to satisfy my curiosity conclusively.

'Yes, yes. This is the bigger one.'

I looked around. It appeared considerably smaller than the South Ken gallery.

'Not in size,' said Emily, seeing me.

'No, no, in importance!' said Hugh, proudly, again puffing himself up like a cockerel and putting his thumbs behind his overly bright braces. 'We get a good crowd in South Ken, but this is where it's at! No doubt that's why your firm is in Mayfair, not South Ken?' asked Hugh, kindly attempting to show some interest in my life.

'Yes, I suppose so,' I said, not wishing to talk law.

'Excuse me for a moment,' said Emily, seeing someone enter whom she obviously wished to speak to. Hugh and I were left standing alone.

'Well, my boy! I must say you are damn lucky to have this girl. These paintings are simply wonderful. She was being modest just now, but I'll wager that we sell more than half this evening!'

'Can one wager against someone wishing the same result?' I asked, smiling.

'Good point! I think the answer must be no, but in any event, they'll sell like hot cakes!'

'I'm pleased you think so.'

'Do you mind awfully if I have a look round before it gets too busy?'

'No, no, absolutely not!' said Hugh. 'Gawp away! I must play host anyway!'

And with a quick curl of the ends of his moustache, he turned on his heel in the direction of the door, saying to those who had just entered in a loud theatrical voice: 'Welcome! welcome!'

And so I was left to examine Emily's new work.

Emily's *Canvas Adulterated By Unremarkable Daub* paintings were not in evidence, and I wondered if they'd all been sold to unwitting punters. Her technique had now developed into a more *Canvas*

Splattered With Paint style, in what a member of the art world would possibly describe as neo-Pollockesque: they weren't quite the same as Jackson's so-called masterpieces because the subject matter remained identifiable, but there were obvious similarities, and the end result was post-post-modern rubbish.

Upstairs, however, hung some of the paintings that remained unsold from Emily's first exhibition, and some new ones of a more classical bent. These were, in my humble opinion, so much better than the dross that hung downstairs, that it was beyond me why Hugh hadn't hung these in the more obviously accessible and prominent ground floor.

By the time I had seen all the paintings and returned downstairs, the place was getting busy. From my vantage point a couple of stairs up the staircase, I could see the whole ground floor. Hugh Daley was enthusing his guests, gesticulating wildly at one of the *Canvas Splattered With Paint* series. Bugle, Yarrington, Cressida and even Bugle's mistress Jenny were there, standing in a little circle chatting. Bugle must have decided that his marriage was a lost cause, and that his liaison with Jenny should be made public. Emily was smiling and nodding to yet another admirer, and Charlie Somers with his fiancée, Felicity Warburton-Lee, had just entered. I crossed the floor rapidly to where they were, relieving a champagne-bearer of three more glasses.

'Charlie!'

'James!'

'Hello Felicity!'

'Hello James!'

'Congratulations to you both!'

'Thank you!'

The champagne was distributed.

'Cheers!'

I politely kissed Felicity and a manly hug with Charlie followed.

'How are you both?'

'Wonderful!' said Charlie. 'Couldn't be better!'

'Very well, thanks,' said Felicity, smiling fondly at her betrothed.

'Busy at the bar?' I enquired.

'Frightfully!' said Felicity. 'I haven't had a moment for weeks. Poor old Charlie can't understand why I work so hard!'

Charlie and I exchanged quizzical looks, and smiled in agreement.

'Cressida is here. I gather you've been instructed on one of her big divorces,' I said.

'Yes, yes. Cressida and I still work closely. This one has been a bitch.'
'Husband or wife?'
'We're for the wife. She's a bitch, and so's the case,' concluded Felicity.
'Typical!' quipped Charlie.
'It's a shame Cressida and I work together now,' I said, 'because if Cressida and I were still adversaries, I'd instruct Charlie, and then there would be more than one matrimonial slanging match on in the same court simultaneously!'
'Oh, what fun!' said Charlie, revelling in the idea.
'We've done it before,' smiled Felicity, 'and I rather enjoyed it. I seem to remember coming out with a significantly better result for my client than Charlie did!'
Charlie looked rather disgruntled having been made to remember the unfortunate incident.
'I seem to remember our client being suitably pleased with the settlement we achieved... isn't that right Charlie?'
'Quite right James. She was very pleased indeed.'
'Pleased only because you both bamboozled her with bullshit!' said Felicity, who unfortunately seemed to be very intuitive.
'That may be,' said Charlie, 'but it was rather biased: we had a very cavalier judge who was into equality of the sexes and that kind of thing. Very unfair for the lawyers who had briefed their client that most judges are wife-friendly.'
'The point is, Charlie dearest, that if I had been instructed by James, and you by Cressida, James' client would have fared considerably better!' Felicity concluded the argument decisively, much to the annoyance of Charlie who wasn't used to losing verbal sparrings.
'Hoot toot!' exclaimed the voice of Bugle behind me. I turned round to see his unnaturally white teeth gleaming at me. 'A Mr Hugh Daley has just pointed you out to be the boyfriend of the artist! Shame on you, James!'
I knew that I may chance to have some odd quirks and remnants of wit broken on me because I'd railed so long against having thoughts of love for Emily, but does not the appetite for love alter? In any event, I thought it odd that Bugle should raise the subject given that Jenny was hanging off his arm. I reflected that my relationship with Emily was entirely moral compared to his with Jenny.
'I must point immediately that our relationship deviated from the professional only after Emily left the Firm!' I explained.

'What rot!' said Yarrington, sidling up to the senior partner.

'Damn you, David!' I said. It seemed nothing said in confidence was treated as confidential, but in the knowledge that Emily was indeed mine, my temperament had become so vivacious that I concluded that a college of wit-crackers could not flout me out of my humour.

'Ha!' said Bugle. 'My esteemed partner seems to know something I do not! Mr Yarrington, I cannot believe you hid this from me!'

'It was only *a* kiss, so I'm told!' said Yarrington, landing me in it.

'Hello everyone! Thanks so much for coming!' said Emily joining us, perhaps drawn in by mention of a kiss.

'Wouldn't have missed it!' said Yarrington. 'You kept this little talent quiet, didn't you?' he asked.

'It wouldn't have done telling everyone while she was still my secretary!'

'Shut up, James!' said Emily, 'Well, you know, it wasn't so much keeping it quiet – it's just you don't want to tell everyone in case nothing comes of it.'

'How wise you are!' said Yarrington. 'But I really must say, it's a tremendous effort!'

'Here, here!' piped up Bugle.

'Thank you.'

Since the gallery was now rather busy, the large group formed by members of the Firm and acquaintances thereof became rather unwieldy, and it soon dispersed, the members forming several smaller groups. Yarrington ended up with Cressida and Emily, and although my position in the circle meant that I'd been left rather on my own, I was pleased to hear him say to the artist, 'I'm so glad you left the Firm.'

'Thanks!' she said, laughing.

'Yes. Quite the best thing for you. Couldn't possibly have left all this artistic brilliance untapped inside you. Well done!'

'Thank you David. It means a lot.'

At which point my attention was brought to a voice coming from quite the other direction which said: 'Is that you?' and upon turning round, my initial recognition of the voice was confirmed as I beheld Martha.

'Yes, it's me! We seem to be good at bumping into each other!'

'Fate, perhaps.'

'Perhaps,' I said, somewhat more dubiously than she had meant it.

'Well, what on earth are you doing here?' she asked.

'As you see!' I said, looking at my glass and around the gallery.

'I simply love the artist,' said Martha, 'she's *so* talented and full of vision of inspiration.'

'I love her too.'

'I was thinking of buying one of her paintings, but they have become so expensive so quickly. I saw her exhibition in South Ken in September.'

'I almost bought the first picture that was available commercially in London, but was pipped at the post by the moustachioed fellow who owns the place,' I boasted.

'Goodness, you are a fan! I had no idea you were so interested in art.'

'I'm more into the artist on this occasion,' I admitted.

'What do you think of it?' asked Martha, turning toward one of Emily's more hideous pieces of art that hung on the wall nearest us. It was a simple nude but with so many shades of purple and lilacs forming the poor model's bruised body, and with such splashings of paint about the place that one might have been forgiven for thinking that the offspring of a union between Lynn and Pollock had painted it.

'I think it's ghastly,' I said.

'James! Not so loud! The artist herself is here!'

'Good Lord! Is she?! Know her well do you?'

'Yes, as I said, I've seen her exhibiting many times before.'

I always thought that 'many' was used when describing the plural of a number greater than two, and my raised eyebrow was noted by Martha, who sank back, weight on one leg, and put her hand on the weight-bearing hip.

'You know her, don't you?' she asked, reading me remarkably well.

I smiled.

'You really piss me off!' she said, and turned to leave me.

'Sorry, I couldn't resist. Shall I introduce you?' I asked, in a desperate leap from the frying pan, without really thinking what lay ahead.

'Yes, I'd like to meet her,' said Martha, mollified by my apparent offer of amends.

And so Martha and I manoeuvred across the room to where Emily was engaged in conversation with a couple of her adoring admirers. When she saw me, she extracted herself from them looking somewhat relieved.

'Emily, I'd like you to meet Martha,' I said.

'*The* Martha?' asked Emily immediately, much to Martha's surprise.

I nodded.

'Pleased to meet you!' said Emily, and they shook hands.

'Likewise,' said Martha, and then turning to me, 'you do know each other well!'

And then perhaps noting the slight look of apprehension that must have appeared on my face, Martha said: 'You're not *the* Emily are you?'

'I think I must be.'

'Well fancy that! I must say, your paintings are really something...' and Martha enthused about Emily's art, rendering my part in the conversation over.

Thankfully Charlie slid up to me, a full glass of bubbly in hand.

'Gets a bit much when even London becomes too small to escape one's previous lovers!' he chuckled in my ear.

'Too true, Charlie. But I should imagine it's more of a problem for you than me!'

He winked. 'Damn right. It does become a serious problem, especially when one's hedging one's bets! Still, that's all in the past now I'm engaged. Pretty damn pleased too, to have caught such a splendid girl!'

'I should think so! When's the big day?'

'Not sure exactly. June, we think. Largely depends on when the best man is available.'

'Well let me know – wouldn't want to miss out!'

'No, you let me know – you're the best man!'

'Charlie!'

'Of course! Who else?!'

I was pleased to see Martha disengage herself from Emily and turn again toward me. Charlie, bless him, turned immediately to find Felicity.

'Well, James, I must be off. I owe you an apology. Emily's very sweet and if I'd met her a few months ago, I'm sure we'd have been friends. Still, as things stand, I don't suppose that's the best idea...'

I felt a twinge of guilt for having equivocated, but she wasn't part of life any more, and I didn't want her to be. But from the way she had finished her last sentence, I got the distinct impression that her statement was really a question, and that perhaps she wanted something further from me. The silence that ensued was enough to tell her the answer without letting it be known for certain whether I had guessed she had asked a question.

'No hard feelings?' she said, having received her reply.

'Of course not,' I smiled.

How odd it was that Martha had disliked Emily when it mattered to me and not now.

'Good. Well, bye then.'

'Bye, Martha.'

And she gave me one last smile, which was admittedly pretty sexy, and left.

After a while, the other guests began dispersing: Bugle left arm in arm with Jenny, probably for the Ritz, followed shortly afterwards by Yarrington and Cressida. Charlie and Felicity, though, agreed to join Emily and me for a well-deserved dinner at a nearby eatery.

As the opening evening drew to a close, I wandered round, looking with astonishment at the number of little red sale stickers on the paintings. Hugh Daley caught my eye and winked, clearly pleased with business. Incredibly, the post-post-modern paintings downstairs were virtually all sold, and the beautiful portraits, pencil drawings and watercolours upstairs had largely been overlooked, despite their lesser price tags. Was this an indication of where Emily's real talent lay, or an indication of where the art buyers thought it lay? Or perhaps even where they thought other buyers would think it lay? It was beyond me, and I resigned myself to never buying a painting as an investment.

I did consider buying the beautiful nude of Anna-Maria, but concluded that I'd much rather have a self-portrait of the artist in a similar state of undress, and decided to commission her to produce such a piece at the first possible opportunity.

CHAPTER 61

The Last Supper

And so to dinner. We were seated, and the waiter, perhaps sensing where the expertise in wine lay, gave me the wine list. In my slightly over refreshed state, I was pleased to be able to quash my strong Withnailian desire to order the finest wine available to humanity, and instead plumped for a crisp Muscadet. The waiter returned with the bottle which had already collected condensation, and in my enthusiasm to taste the wine, I drank it rather too quickly with the unusual consequence that the wine travelled not over my tongue, but around the roof of my mouth and straight down my oesophagus, circumventing my sensory organs entirely. Anxious to avoid defeat, it fell upon me to proclaim the wine excellent.

The four glasses having been charged, and the sweating bottle deposited in the centre of the table, my duty became obvious.

'Well, I think we should drink to Emily: on a splendid exhibition, and to future success!'

My words echoed round the table from the lips of Charlie and Felicity, followed by a 'Cheers!' in unison.

Having toasted Charlie and Felicity for their engagement and having discussed Emily's paintings and her plans for more paintings, we ordered our food.

'So, how's it going at work, with Cressida and without Emily?' asked Felicity.

'Well, of course I miss her in the office,' I said, looking at Emily, 'But the advantages in the changed nature of our relationship are unparalleled!'

'So are the disadvantages!' said Emily.

'Shut up, dear!' I said. 'Working with Cressida is fun – we get on well – but I'm lost without Emily.'

'What do you mean?' asked Felicity.

'Well, I had to draft a divorce petition on my own the other day. After hearing the general background and the rough reasons for divorce, Emily would have always drafted them. She was a dab hand at petitions for unreasonable behaviour, which most cases seem be. When I came to draft one, I could hardly remember what to write to convince a judge that the behaviour *had* been unreasonable!'

'You mean Emily drafted *all* your divorce petitions?' asked Felicity, with a surprising tone of surprise in her voice.

'Of course!' I said. Why would I want to do it myself?

'That's one of the reasons why I love James,' said Emily. 'He doesn't pretend he's any good at the law!'

Despite my fond smile at Emily, I was somewhat troubled at her thoughts regarding my legal skills. Although I had an inkling that I wasn't perhaps the hottest legal talent in London, there's a big difference between thinking that, and that I wasn't *any* good at my profession. I concluded that she couldn't have actually meant the latter, and thus my spirits rose, and joining in the fun, said: 'I've said it before, but the key to being a great divorce lawyer is to have a great barrister!'

'That may be,' said Charlie, 'but the key for a barrister to being able to win cases, is to have a great team instructing him. And that, James, is why I win so many cases.'

'Listen to them!' said Emily to Felicity. 'This mutual flattery will go on for hours if we don't stop it!'

So Charlie and I stopped talking, but neither of the girls said anything further to berate us in our arrogance, because, I fancied, they knew that what we had said was true.

A delicious meal and a good time was had by all, and we left, very content with what had been a thoroughly satisfactory evening. It was cold outside, and the warmth given to us by the snug surroundings, the wine, food and coffee quickly dissipated.

'Well, the next time we'll all see each other will be at my sister's next Friday.' I said.

'Yes, indeed. We're looking forward to it!' said Charlie, waving down a taxi. 'I insist that the artist and her beau take this cab!'

'Are you sure?' asked Emily.

'Quite sure,' affirmed Felicity. 'You must be tired after chatting to all your devotees!'

Emily did look a little tired, and she didn't argue any further. I kissed Felicity, hugged Charlie, took Emily by the hand and escorted her into the waiting taxi, the door of which Charlie had already opened.

'Thanks for a lovely evening!' said Emily 'Cheerio!'

'Thank *you* for a lovely evening!' said Charlie. 'And congratulations again on the exhibition. It was wonderful.'

The door slammed and the taxi drew away.

'Sweetheart?' said Emily. 'Sometimes your jokes are a little too much, even for me.'

'Oh?'

'That's the last time you and Charlie are to publicly flatter each other!' she said.

And indeed it was.

CHAPTER 62

Christmas Lights

The weekend slipped by, Emily and I completing our Christmas shopping by Saturday lunchtime, having managed to avoid the centre of town, and having only crossed the hideously busy Oxford Street once. We did most of it on Marylebone High Street, and subsequently ventured south down through St Christopher's Place, thankfully salvaged from destruction in the sixties when wrecking balls were so much in vogue, and then down the beautifully illuminated Bond Street, through the Burlington Arcade and across Piccadilly to Jermyn Street for a shirt or two, and some port and cheese from Paxton & Whitfield, the finest cheesemongers in London. On our return we risked Piccadilly Circus and Regent Street, whereon lay Hamleys, the only shop in London Ben thought worth visiting. We spent the rest of the time in happy slothfulness at her flat.

It was now December, the skies had been overcast and monotonous for a week, and on return to the office the next day, it was pleasing to see the Christmas tree in the hall of the office, fully decorated and lit beautifully by understated but pretty white lights.

'Morning Sue,' I said, passing reception.

Sue was grinning at me. Sue never smiled in the morning. The poor woman had to say 'good morning' nearly a hundred times as the staff of Bugle & Yarrington arrived at the office. It could only mean one thing: that the news that Emily and I were boyfriend and girlfriend had reached the office. My suspicions were confirmed when I met Cressida who was ascending the stairs towards our office.

'Kate's terribly upset, James. She wants to know how long it'll be before you get bored with your old secretary! Haven't you noticed the dreamy look in her eyes?'

'I just thought she was dreamy!' I said, smiling at Cressida, who reciprocated.

'I've known for ages,' she said, 'but so does everyone else. Bugle's been doing the rounds to ensure everyone knows.'

'Great. How did you know?'

'I'm a woman, with considerably more experience in life than you,' said Cressida, smiling mysteriously.

Everyone who greeted me in the office that day either attempted a humorous dig in my direction, or smiled knowingly, but as with all secrets, once released, interest quickly dwindled. By that Monday afternoon, despite some ongoing mockery from the more juvenile members of the Firm, everyone in the office knew about Emily and me, and by Tuesday it was old news.

The week passed without further memorable incident, and soon it was Friday, the evening of Sarah's dinner party. It would involve three thirtysomething couples: one married, one to be married, and one unmarried. I suddenly felt for the first time in my life, old, and in need of that security that the others had. But as quickly as that thought had formed, so my senses returned: yes, I admitted that I was in love with Emily, and despite this state – into which a man of a more solid disposition would never have let himself fall – it was with a triumphant flash in my mind that I realised that despite Emily, I was James James, the most eligible bachelor in London Town! James James, the married man?! The thought seemed so absurd it amused me tremendously, until for the second time in a minute, I again felt old.

But I thought how pleasant the company of Sarah and Michael, Charlie and Felicity, and of course, my Emily, would be, and that I would not want to be anywhere else or with anyone else. I even had fleeting thoughts into the not-so-distant future, and imagined middle-aged versions of us sitting round the same table, nothing much having changed.

I arrived at Sarah's straight after work to help her cook. The troublesome Ben had been dispatched to a friend's house for the evening, and baby Alexander was sleeping soundly, no doubt having imbibed a certain amount of alcohol from his mother.

After some messy preparation (cooking and me are not known for their combined tidiness), the pheasants and accompanying vegetables and sauces had been safely stowed in the Aga to cook, and Sarah poured us a well-deserved drink. It was pleasant to cook with her, something we hadn't done since before her marriage to Michael. We chatted about recent events, about Emily ('Was she *the one*?' asked Sarah), and about Ben and his new brother Alexander.

'Evening both!' said Michael, coming into the kitchen and throwing his keys onto the table whilst removing his shoes.

'Good day at work, dear?' asked Sarah.

'No, shocking,' said Michael.

'Good,' said Sarah, 'can you pour us a gin?'

'I got fired,' said Michael with a wink in my direction.

'We can talk about your day later, dear,' said Sarah impatiently, 'the gin... the gin!' she said, pointing at the bottle.

'Glad you're taking it so well, dear!' said Michael.

'Taking what so well?' asked Sarah.

Michael thankfully found his wife's lack of attention amusing and she soon abandoned any hope of a sensible answer having seen our smiles. I wondered how long after entering the state of holy matrimony it took for such a state of bliss to exist between the parties. After some more chatter, some stirring of things in pots from the oven and some screaming by the now apparently hungry Alexander, Emily arrived. Michael duly poured us all more drinks, Alexander's hunger was satisfied by a nasty substance originating from a glass jar in the fridge, cooking was apparently completed for the moment as the dinner went back into the Aga, and we all adjourned to the drawing room to await the arrival of Charlie and Felicity.

Just as our bottoms had hit the sofas, the doorbell rang.

'That'll be them!' I said, 'I'll get it!' And I departed for the hall.

I opened the door to find an officer from the Constabulary looking sternly at me.

'Good evening,' I said, feeling strangely guilty.

'Evening, sir. I believe you are expecting a Mister Charles Somers about now? Is that correct, sir?'

My immediate thought was that dear old Charlie had been caught with his hand in the petty cash tin of 7 Queen's Bench Row Chambers, or that he'd done something daft whilst inebriated, and then I realised that in all probability the two propositions were not mutually exclusive. Then it struck me that he'd sent the officer of the law here so that I could represent him at the Police station. Had Charlie forgotten that my last triflings with criminal law ended when I'd written 'out of time' at the end of my criminal law exam paper to make it look as if my answer would have been longer had there been more time? I couldn't even remember the difference between the *actus reus* and *mens rea*, though I was pretty certain that down the Old Bailey, any jury would find Charlie to have a guilty mind.

'Yes, that's right. Is there a problem?' I said.

Clearly there was.

Silly question.

'Are you family, sir?'

'Well, best man, if that counts?'

'I see, sir. I'm afraid Mister Somers was killed a short while ago in a road traffic accident, sir.'

Never had words had such a physical effect on me, and I recoiled from them as if the officer had just shot me with both barrels, and was now reloading.

He'd told me, simply, curtly, and with no emotion, and such was the shock that, initially at least, I too was emotionless.

'Where?'

'I believe he was on his way here, sir. His passenger, a Miss Warburton-Lee, gave me the address.'

'Felicity! Is she all right?'

'Superficial injuries only, sir. She's on her way to hospital for a check up. She said she'd telephone you.'

'What happened?'

'Mr Somers' car was hit at speed on Fulham Palace Road.'

'How did he die?'

'I believe he died when the paramedics cut the seatbelt, sir. They said it had been so tight after the crash that is must have been restricting a massive internal haemorrhage which his body simply couldn't cope with once the pressure had been released.'

'And who hit him?'

'Drunk joyriders, sir.'

'Are they dead?'

'No.'

The enormity of what happened had not yet struck me. It was only now that I noticed the blinking blue lights of the Police car parked outside, oddly quiet without their usual concomitant sirens, lighting up Michael and Sarah's front steps and hallway, and shooting blue streaks across the ceiling, ghostly in their silence.

There not being much more he could do except offer sympathy, the policeman departed, and as his car rolled quietly away, the blue lights gradually got less bright, and finally, when the car turned a corner, they disappeared.

I sat down on the top step of the stairs leading from the street up to my sister's porch.

'James!' What on earth are you doing? You've been ages!' said Emily, opening wide the already partially opened door. 'James! What's the matter?' Her slightly impatient tone turned to one of worry as I turned to her, my face streaming with previously unnoticed tears. 'James?!' she repeated.

I didn't know for how long I'd been sitting there. I had been trying to think of the best way to tell the others the dreadful tidings. Now Emily had interrupted my thoughts without my mind having come to a conclusion, so I just said it, plain and simple: 'Charlie's been killed.' She came and sat next to me, all the colour draining from her face.

'How?'

'Car crash. On the way here.'

'Felicity?'

'In hospital. Minor injuries, apparently. Hopefully.'

We sat in silence, her arm around my shoulders.

'I'm sorry James,' she Emily eventually.

I tried to smile.

'Poor Felicity. I can't bear it. Does she know he's...?'

I didn't know.

'Come in, James? It's cold out here. Come on.'

And she pulled me to feet and we went in.

I desperately wanted to be on my own, to let Emily tell Sarah and Michael, but I could not allow this. He was my friend, and this was my responsibility. My sister and her husband hadn't known Charlie well – they'd met him on a few occasions only – but they knew how well we got on. They offered me kind words of sympathy, but they were empty words, and I got angry, on the face of it with them, but in reality at the situation which was entirely devoid of any hope.

Felicity telephoned. Sarah spoke very briefly with her, and the news was that she'd been discharged from hospital with no physical damage other than bruising from her own seatbelt. She knew Charlie's fate, but didn't know how she felt, and was going to stay with her parents. She didn't want visitors.

We ate Sarah's beautiful meal so as not leave our appetites wanting, but I had to force it down, having no stomach for anything other than wine. Sarah and Michael offered us a bed with them, which we readily accepted, me not wanting to go anywhere.

That night, I woke sweating and sat bolt upright in bed, having dreamt that the flashing blue police lights were shining on the ceiling, and that a policeman had come to tell me Emily was dead.

'Ssh, you were dreaming,' she said, finding my hand in the dark and squeezing it.

'I really loved him,' I murmured, not quite realising if I was awake.

'I know. I think most people who knew him did,' said Emily. 'And at least you had the privilege of knowing him well.'

I sat up, now wide awake, and turned on the bedside light.

'Did I? Sometimes I wonder: there was a lot I didn't know about him.'

'Yes,' agreed Emily.

'And there was a lot he didn't know about me.'

'There's a lot I don't know about you.'

'I should tell you,' I said.

'Yes.'

'I'll tell you one thing right away, then. Every morning, when I wake up, I think about the contents of the books on the shelves at the end of bed, one by one, remembering their words and facts, and wondering how to write my own.'

Her kiss stopped any more foolish words escaping from my lips.

Eventually, I dozed off, but woke on more than one occasion from the sickening, recurring dream of blue flashing lights on the bedroom ceiling, and a knocking at the door.

CHAPTER 63

Six Foot Long Six Inches Short

That week at the office was ghastly.

Of course bad news travels quicker than gossip, so now instead of being mocked by the whole office about Emily, I had to listen to them all offering sympathy, which was kind of them, but the end result was tiresome. Only Cressida seemed to know how to cope with me, and did her best to not exactly cheer me up, but to get on with things. It worked; a wise woman indeed.

A couple of days passed, and then, unusually for the office, a handwritten envelope arrived in my post. I recognised it to be written in the hand of Sara. Inside was a Christmas card, containing a letter, which read:

Dear James,

I'm so dreadfully sorry to hear of Charlie's death. I'm sorry for what I said about him...

The words 'obnoxious oaf' rang in my ears, and I wondered if that's how she viewed me. I continued reading.

...It was unkind and unfair of me to judge him as I did. There is little in life more important than being a good friend, and I know he was the best of friends to you, and you to him.

I'm sorry too that things didn't work out between us. It was cruel of me to have leapt headlong into it in the first instance. I know that deep down you are a good man, and you deserve someone better than me, who will love you for who you are. In truth, after all I said at the time – which I then believed to be true – I wonder whether I am really over Simon's death.

I hope you are happy, despite everything.
Love, Sara.

It was odd receiving these words from Sara: I had largely forgotten her since Emily had unexpectedly stolen my heart. As I read them, I heard her voice saying them, and sad though they were, I knew her voice would have sounded playful if she had spoken them to me. But saying I deserved someone better than her was an untruth, and I felt this backhanded form of self depreciation was designed entirely to make me acknowledge its falsity. It left the letter slightly soured in its conclusion. In a way, though, Sara's words seemed to be true: Emily did love me for who I was. And I was happy, despite everything.

On the day of Charlie's funeral, I woke feeling unusual. I think I knew this day would've been better postponed by forty years, and I didn't want to live it today. Even dressing came with problems: wearing a suit to the office wouldn't have troubled me in the least, but having to wear one to one's best friend's funeral really angered me. Such are emotions, and I wished I could control them.

Emily was patient with me beyond need, and after a silent morning, we drove, again in virtual silence, to the church. We arrived just as Charlie was leaving the hearse, carried by six men, one of whom was instantly recognisable as Charlie's father, and another as Mr Justice Warburton-Lee. Felicity and her whom I presumed to be her mother followed the coffin as the unhappy troupe went up the damp, mossy path, beneath a monotonously dark grey sky, into the little church in the Surrey village where Charlie Somers had grown up.

We followed a couple of minutes later, and entered the church.

Charlie lay at the front of the church and the Somers and Warburton-Lee families had already taken up position in the front pews. A few minutes later, the Church was full; all the pews were packed, and many guests had to stand at the back of the church. The service began with *Hills of the North, Rejoice!* which Charlie had said was a favourite since prep school.

As the organ boomed out the opening notes, I wondered whether Charlie would have been happy with his funeral arrangements. He was rather morbid at times, and on more than one occasion he'd said to me he thought he'd die a young man. This pleased him, he said, because it'd mean that everyone would remember him in the prime of his life, but I could see that when he said this, he only half believed it. Indeed he had expressed to me that his one ambition in life was to be remembered after his death, not by his friends and family, but by a wider audience. He was worried he might not have enough time to do this in the way he envisaged. He never said what he did envisage, probably in case it didn't happen, and I never asked, probably for the same reason. But it seemed a silly reason now.

But his (probably somewhat casual) belief that he'd die young did mean that when I visited the Bugle & Yarrington will safe to retrieve his will, I found a long letter of wishes accompanying the will which detailed the funeral arrangements. I'd half expected the will to read: 'I desire that my body should be buried in Westminster Abbey'. Only Charlie could be so audacious in death, and he'd said to me once that he'd like to be buried there so that his ghost might have some interesting peers to chat to during the long winter nights. Mr Justice Warburton-Lee, upon finding out Charlie's actual burial wishes from me, commented: 'Blimey! That does surprise me. He told me he wanted his ashes scattered on a beach so that he could still get into girls' pants when he was dead!'

The hymn finished, with me smiling broadly at the memory of this.

Charlie's eulogy was by the head of 7 Queen's Bench Row Chambers, none other than Terence Philip, Queen's Counsel. I say none other than Terence Philip, Queen's Counsel as if Terence Philip is famed for his life's work in the legal sphere. In fact, he's one of these sensible lawyers who does it for the money, and rumours are that he's shortly to achieve his lifelong ambition: to retire and leave the world of pens and wigs firmly behind him.

He was a damn good speaker though, and began thus:

'It has been some years since Charlie's name first came to my attention, and I'll still never forget the first letter I received from him. It read, "Dear Sir, You'd better take me on, because I'm good, and there is no-one more suitable for a tenancy in your Chambers than I. If you refuse me, my estimations of the legal profession will fall so far and so fast, I will no longer want to be part of it." A week later he moved in, and I'm glad to say he was right.'

Terence then went on to say that Charlie was indeed one of the best juniors who had graced his chambers, and had had so many instructions, that the clerks could never keep all the instructors happy in their first choice of counsel.

We learned that dear Charlie had been a champion of legal aid, fighting for the rights of those who could not afford legal representation, and tirelessly lobbying the government to keep the legal aid budget from dropping even further. I knew that Charlie had been keen on legal aid work, but I hadn't realised how many committees he'd been on, how many articles he'd written in the legal press, and in the broadsheets, or how well known he was in ministerial circles. Terence went on to declare that Charlie's doctorate on the provision of legal services as a basic human right had just been accepted by the University of London, and Terence confirmed that they would be awarding it to him posthumously. I had never known he'd even begun a Ph.D.

By the time I discovered that his ambition to stand for the Conservatives as a Member of Parliament was in the process of coming to fruition, my surprise had diminished somewhat, because surprises, though one doesn't know their exact form, are never as surprising when one expects them.

What did strike me though, was that this had been one of my closest friends, and he'd never said a word about any of these aspects of his life that must have taken enormous quantities of time, and therefore drive, to accomplish. Selfishly, I felt belittled next to my deceased friend, and wondered whether he hadn't talked to me about these things because he thought I was intellectually beneath all that.

Most of the rest of the service to me remains forgotten. My lucid memory of it begins again when the pallbearers, Mr Justice Warburton-Lee remaining one of their number, hoisted the coffin and marched solemnly down the aisle to the tune of Siegfried's Funeral March, chosen by Charlie himself in his last gesture to his love of Germanic pomp. The other mourners followed row by row.

Charlie left his church for the final time.

He was to be buried in the churchyard, and the congregation followed the vicar and pallbearers to the empty grave, with dark green carpets draped around the edge to save the muddying of feet and to stop high heels disappearing into the mud. The number of young ladies gently weeping around the edge of the grave, next to which Charlie's coffin had now been placed, was astounding, and testament to his social success. Perhaps cynically, I wondered how many of them would at some point brag that they had been the once-girlfriend of the late Charlie Somers.

The funeral service was brief, and the vicar, knowing full well that Charlie was more fearful of house spiders than of God, kept talk of the afterlife to a minimum. But unbeknown to him, Charlie had always

taken a mild interest in what happens to individuals after death: he had
once told me that he had found it fascinating how quickly bone – the
very substance that carries our bodies through life – decays, but how
hair – in life, so unnecessary – remains intact for so long after death.
Musings on more theologically biased theorems failed to interest
Charlie: his knowledge of science was good enough for him to conclude
that when you're dead you're dead, and that's that. End of story. It didn't
bother him, or me. I didn't want to meet him again in the afterlife; I just
wanted to go to the pub with him this Friday.

But as the pallbearers stooped to pick up the coffin for the final time,
it struck me that never again would I have such fine male company; my
throat stuck, my eyes welled, and I wept.

The pallbearers lifted the coffin to their waists, and in readiness
to lower it, they straddled the pit where it was soon to lie. Once the
ropes that were to be used for lowering were in place, the coffin began
its slow descent, only to stop firmly at ground level. It soon became
apparent that in measuring the length of the hole, the grave-digger
had clearly not considered the proportions of the coffin that was to
fill it and, unfortunately for the gathered mourners, the longitudinal
dimension of the coffin exceeded that of the hole. Each end of the coffin
was lodged firmly in the carpet covering the parapet.

Several gasps and worried looks went round once people began to
realise what was wrong. Had I not seen Charlie's funeral wishes, I would
have concluded that the gravedigger had been deliberately instructed to
dig the hole too short, and the thought of this made me smile through
my tears at this most inappropriate juncture. Even Emily, whose sense
of humour is well honed to mine, dug me in the ribs. Of course, when
one shouldn't laugh, the situation only becomes more humorous, and
my smile broadened. I looked around to see how many dirty looks I was
receiving, and my eyes met those of Felicity. She too was smiling, and
for a moment we shared a wonderful moment of sad understanding:
we both knew Charlie would have found this enormous fun, and we
both wished he'd been there to share in the amusement his coffin was
causing.

Everyone else, of course, was frightfully serious. The coffin was
replaced on the side of the grave, and two of the pallbearers quickly
volunteered to make the grave a couple of inches longer at each end.
Everyone else stood round pretending to be patient and dignified while
the brave men and their shovels did their work. The awkward silence

broken only by steel working the sides of the grave did not last for as long as one might expect, and very soon the grave was sufficiently long.

Again Charlie was lifted over his grave, and slowly lowered. This time, the coffin slid into the grave, the ropes bearing it sliding through the pallbearer's hands as they lowered it. This was final. Charlie wouldn't come up again. The vicar spoke, but I remember none of his words. When the first handful of earth was thrown on top of coffin, I blinked, and my closing eyelids caused the tears that had again been building in my eyes to stream down my cheeks.

Strangely, through the emotional turmoil that my mind then underwent, it somehow concluded that burials are so much more satisfactory than cremations.

The party left the graveside and wandered towards the churchyard gate. Emily's tears were almost as abundant as mine, and we squeezed each other's hands in the hope of offering a little piece of comfort. Emily went off to talk to Felicity, and I found myself walking next to Felicity's father, Mr Justice Warburton-Lee.

'Hello, James,'

'Hello, Mr Just...'

'Arthur, please. Bloody awful, this business.'

'Yes.'

'You know, I've lost count of the number of ill-suited suitors that Felicity has presented to Margery and I over the years, and frankly Charlie was the only one I'd have proudly called my son-in-law. He really was a splendid fellow.'

'Yes, he was.'

'Poor Felicity. I'm not sure how she's coping.'

'Nor am I.' I meant myself, not her, and after a moment's thought I really had no idea how Felicity was coping. I couldn't imagine losing the person you so recently decided to spend the rest of your life with; I couldn't imagine losing Emily. Then the judge looked at me curiously.

'Mind you, you're not such a bad chap yourself,' he said. 'Are you still in with old Lewis' daughter, the artist?'

'Yes, Emily,' I said, looking fondly over at her.

'Shame. You'd have been a good son-in-law too,' said the judge, shaking his head, and apparently being entirely sincere. 'Still, I must admit, I had always imagined Felicity marrying a member of the bar,' he concluded.

'Yes, I'm afraid my interest in and ambition for life the bar is probably insufficient for me to become a successful member of it!'

'I quite understand,' said the judge with a chuckle. 'Given my time again, I'd teach physics at Cambridge. I discouraged my children from the law, and what did I end up with? A son as a solicitor and daughter as a barrister! But, hush! We must not speak ill of our learned friends, since one doth approach! Here, I'll let you two chat,' said the judge, slipping away from me as his daughter arrived.

Felicity had been one of the few women at the graveside who had held back her tears; I admired her fortitude. But as she now came nearer, I noticed that she looked quite different from the norm. The glint in her dark bright eyes had gone, and her confident, bordering on arrogant countenance had been replaced with one of tiredness and sadness.

'Hello James.'

'Hello Felicity. How are you?'

'Coping, I think. Thank you for asking – no one else has. I think everyone thinks that if they ask me, they'll tip me over the edge. How are you?'

'I'm all right.' If she could cope, I must. We smiled at each other, acknowledging that neither of us were coping, and that we were far from all right. This was the second instance that Felicity and I had exchanged thoughts without speaking during the course of the funeral, and there seemed now to be a marked understanding, a deepening of our friendship, and I liked it. I offered her my arm as we slowly followed the other guests round the low wall of the churchyard.

'What are you doing for Christmas?' she asked.

'I'm with my sister and her family. Emily is coming too. What will you do?'

'Just a quiet one with mother and father, and my brother. It was going to be the first ever Christmas I would have spent with my man.'

'It would have been good. I spent Christmas last year with Emily, but I hadn't realised that I loved her then.' I felt foolish; I could not have chosen my words more unsympathetically, but again a moment of understanding passed between us, and Felicity smiled in acknowledgement. She said nothing.

'What will you do afterwards?' I asked, partly in a slightly cowardly attempt to extricate myself from the embarrassment I had just landed myself in, but mainly because I wanted to know how this apparently strong woman did plan to recommence her life.

'I think I must put my all into my work. Philip – you know Philip at 7 Queen's Bench Row – yes of course you do – Philip has promised me all Charlie's instructions as well as my own – which is a fantastic opportunity, and it also means I'll be frightfully busy.'

I wondered how many other women in the country would view being able to take her dead fiancé's work as a fantastic opportunity.

'Well, I shall certainly instruct you!' I said.

'And so will Cressida, no doubt,' she added.

'No doubt.'

We shared one more smile, as if both remembering the past times we'd enjoyed together professionally and socially, but mainly because we recognised that this conversation had sealed our continued friendship.

'Well, Felicity, it looks like you should be off,' I said, nodding in the direction of her parents, who were jointly trying erect an umbrella to combat the drizzle, which was just beginning to become unbearable. 'Take care.'

'You too, James,' she said, embracing me strongly, and kissing me as she withdrew. 'See you in court!'

'See you in court!' I smiled, nodding in acknowledgement of what had passed between us. She turned to join her parents, and they made their way under a small, half erected umbrella to the judge's car.

By God! What a woman!

CHAPTER 64

The Last Week At Work

Christmas fell on a Tuesday, and the partners of Bugle & Yarrington had adopted an excellent plan (at the request of a certain junior matrimonial partner) to give the employees Christmas Eve off, thus ensuring, as last year, the greatest period away from the office while using the least amount of holiday. New Year's Eve was a Monday, and since Yarrington had no intention of messing up his annual escape from the office, he persuaded Bugle to close the office then too. Oddly, but happily, the Christmas party was planned for the coming Friday – the twenty-first – and there were only five working days between then and eleven days out of the office.

On the day of the Christmas party, my mind was totally beyond work. By this stage, Kate, our new secretary, had settled in well. Cressida and I were mightily pleased; although she couldn't draft my divorce petitions, she was highly efficient, did not require punctuation to be dictated, and though not quite as gorgeous as Emily was still voted the foxiest secretary in the Firm in the November poll.

It pleased me when just after Kate had bought up our mid-afternoon coffee, Cressida declared:

'Well, James, I for one don't intend to do any more work this year!'

'Well, if the head of my department isn't going to, then I'm buggered if I am!'

Kate looked aghast.

'Sorry for the profanity.'

'It's okay. No, I was thinking that if you both stop work, I won't have anything to do.'

'And why is that a problem?' asked Cressida. Even she was genuinely intrigued.

'It's so boring when there's nothing to do!'

'Well, Kate, Bond Street isn't a million miles away!'

'Good idea!' said Kate, springing into life. 'That is okay, isn't it?'

'Yes!' chorused Cressida and I.

'See you tonight at the party!' she said, and left. Since Kate usually began getting ready to leave half an hour before the appointed time, we were surprised how quickly she managed to extricate herself from the office when given leave to depart early.

Once she had left, Cressida and I reclined in our respective chairs and looked at each other contentedly. After a few moments of cogitation, my first thought was that it was odd how quickly we had become so close; but my second thought was it wasn't odd, because even though when we had been acting against each other, seemingly sparring and fighting, we actually enjoyed it, while respecting one another simultaneously.

'I do miss you ringing up with another half-baked idea that you think I'll actually believe!' said Cressida, reading my mind.

'Most of them were true!' I foolishly insisted. 'You couldn't make it up if you wanted to…' Cressida looked at me incredulously. 'Well, half true, anyway!' I had to add when Cressida's look of increasing disbelief became too much to handle. 'I miss those phone calls, too. I used to love it when you were acting against me… but damn it, Cressida, despite the arguments and wit-cracking, it's actually very pleasant to work *with* you!'

'*Pleasant*?! Is that all?'

'Yes, you're right,' I said, 'it's a privilege to work with you.'

'And the honour of working with you, my boy, is mine!'

'*Honour*?! Which is higher praise: privilege or honour?'

'Let's be satisfied with both!'

'Yes, let's. And look forward to next year,' I said.

'That's going a bit too far, don't you think?!'

We smiled at each other. I couldn't have asked for a better colleague, and had one of those rare moments when one actually realises how lucky one is for something at the time, and not with the advantage of hindsight or sentiment.

My telephone rudely interrupted my train of thought.

It was Sue to announce those ever recurrent but nonetheless dreaded words: 'Mrs Ricketts is in reception for you, James. She says she's glad you're not in a meeting because she saw you at your desk on the way in.'

Damn!

The previously unthought-of disadvantage of having such an excellent view of the street was that clients would also have an excellent view of me. But at least I thought I knew what her visit was about: Mrs Ricketts and I had been in close correspondence with each other in relation to the monies she wished to distribute from her various trusts to her family in time for Christmas.

The funds had been released from trust and were now sitting in the Bugle & Yarrington client account for distribution to various members of the Ricketts family. The inheritance tax had been paid on the trust money, my bill had been issued to Mrs Ricketts, and was for just shy of three times the amount of inheritance tax payable. Of course, I told her my fees were worth it because I'd manage to save her untold fortunes in tax, which was true, in a way, but didn't stop me coming to the conclusion that a government should not be treating its citizens in such a manner: should people really have to worry about what happens to their hard earned (and already hard-taxed) income when they die? And should someone like Mrs Ricketts be taxed simply because she had wealthy parents?

'Hello, Mrs Ricketts!'

'Hello, James, and Happy Christmas!'

'Thank you, and to you.'

'I know it's the last Friday of term and you probably groaned when Sue told you I was here, so we'll make it quick. I just wanted to say thank you ever so much for sorting out all that trust business in time for Christmas. Sterling job, and of course, you need feeding, so here's a cheque for your bill.'

'Thank you.' One could always count on Mrs Ricketts for paying promptly.

'Rather you have it than the tax man, dear!'

A wise woman, indeed.

'And here's a bottle of port. No doubt you're partial to a spot of the stuff over Christmas.'

'Mrs Ricketts, you really must stop bringing bottles. It's quite unnecessary.'

'Many things are unnecessary, dear, but it doesn't stop them being pleasurable!'

I could not argue with her impeccable logic, and so smiled instead.

Her expression changed as she said, 'I saw Sara last week. I asked her about you.'

She paused, as if waiting for a reaction from me to allow her to judge how interested in the beginning of her story I really was.

The pause became so long that I was obliged to say: 'Oh, yes?'

'She says she rather misses you. I think she rather regrets it, James.

But I won't mention her again. I'm sorry, I've said too much, or I haven't said enough...'

Her words did not make immediate sense with me, and I left it at that, not wishing to make sense of them. She understood.

'Well, my most exciting news is that I've just got two kittens in time for Christmas.'

'Oh, how lovely!' I said, not really caring for cats at all. 'Does that mean that poor old... your elderly gentleman tomcat has snuffed it?'

'No, he's still around. Bit miffed at the kittens. They're terrible. Shredding all my furniture, and very fussy eaters. They refuse to eat anything other than smoked salmon.'

I wondered if this was because they were offered nothing other than smoked salmon.

'Well, James, I must dash – I must pop into Fortnum's before the rush hour. I'll be popping into see you in January – got a few alterations to my will that need implementing. Do you remember my brother's slightly wayward son? He's gone and married some foreign girl almost young enough to be his daughter. I'll be damned if that little harlot will see a penny of my money! Anyway off to the country tomorrow, and back in Town in the New Year.'

'Splendid! Well, have a very Happy Christmas.'

'And you, dear.'

I walked her to the door and opened it to see a very muddy Land Rover parked right in front of the now upright and very red pillar-box.

She saw me note the proximity of bumper to box, and we both smiled.

'Not a word!' she said.

'I'm upset that you hold such a low opinion of me!' I said. 'Thanks for the port, and for paying my bill so promptly!'

'Pleasure, dear. Good-bye!'

'Good-bye, Mrs Ricketts.'

And I watched her cross the road, mount her steed, and, this time, drive safely off, waving as she did so.

Returning to my office briefly to sort things out before departing for Christmas, I noted that the files in the pile mentally labelled 'to do before Christmas' were as numerous as when the pile had been created, and that the pile would now have to be dubbed: 'to do in the first week after Christmas'. Such mental renaming was a constant source of satisfaction, and it was with a certain sense of achievement that I quit my office for the Christmas party, which was this year (as always) to be held at The Vaults.

CHAPTER 65

A Christmas Party & Some Mistletoe

The Christmas party was guaranteed to send Bugle wild with rage. Every year he watched as his employees got pissed at his own expense. Yarrington had long learned that getting pissed too was the only way to enjoy it, but Bugle wouldn't hear of it. Tim's theory is that he daren't get too drunk in case he lost his faculties and in this state allowed his incredibly long arms to venture to posteriors prohibited.

In any event, when I arrived at The Vaults, Bugle was already there, looking distracted and nervous, probably thinking only about the hole that satisfying his entire staff in both food and drink would leave in his wallet. He didn't seem to care that the other partners thought nothing of spending a few bob on an annual party; he only cared about his share of the expense.

The Vaults was decorated with a necessarily short Christmas tree and streamers all over the ceiling. They were rather annoying for those of us standing taller than five foot six. The Firm had again booked out the whole place, having two large dining tables down the centre of the main bar, with the individual vaults to each side reserved for more private mischiefs later on in the evening. Once a number of people had migrated towards the bar, drinks were served, and I was pleased to see Bugle throwing one down the hatch in short order, and taking another. Perhaps he was finally loosening up.

After a few minutes, most of the staff had migrated from the offices to The Vaults, and only the workaholics remained behind, pretending to be too busy for such frivolities as the Christmas party, the only time in the year that the whole firm went out as one. Everyone present seemed to be in good cheer, which soon became very good cheer after a drink or two. I made an effort to chat to those whose offices were geographically separated from mine: indeed I hadn't seen some of the more shy inhabitants of Number 20 since this time last year.

After some minutes of chitchat, I saw Tom and Matthew propping up the bar and discussing something, heads together, and very earnestly.

An investigation was required.

'Hello boys!'

'Hi, James,' they said in unison.

'What are you gossiping about?'

'Nothing!' they said in unison, immediately looking at each other embarrassedly for having fouled up their response so comprehensively.

'I see! So, are you going to let me join in? It's been a while since I heard any decent gossip!'

'Oh, no gossip, we were just talking about what department we would work in next,' lied Matthew. The days of James James the office intelligence officer had been replaced by James James the partner. The next generation of gossipmongers were usurping my position. The strange thing was, it bothered me not in the least, and I even found myself thinking that these two were worthy candidates to take my place.

'I'd really like to come and work with you,' said Tom. 'Matthew said you were a good teacher.'

'You think flattery will stop me enquiring what you were actually talking about?!' I asked, not expecting answer. 'Well, that's kind, and I hope you can too. Once Matthew got to grips with things – which frankly shouldn't – and didn't in his case – take too long, he was a great help to me.'

'So,' said Matthew, 'How's life without Emily?'

'The question should be, "how's life *with* Emily?" And the answer is splendid!'

'I can't believe you took so bloody long. The tension in there was incredible!'

'Matthew. Is this the first time you've been to a party where the booze is free?!' I asked.

He nodded, as a guilty schoolboy might in the headmaster's office. It made me smile. 'Don't worry, I'm not even going to say it – you won't listen. You'll find that even in ten years time, the concept of free drink is enough to instil excitement into a lawyer's blood! Cheers!'

We three clinked glasses, and I left the trainees to their gossip, overhearing Matthew say: 'He's a legend!' which comment, coming from a man, albeit a young man, made my head swell considerably more than when had I heard an attractive girl whisper to her girlfriend 'He's cute'.

I already knew I was cute, but now I was a legend to boot.

When it came to sit down to dinner, it was no surprise that one table was largely filled with those of Number 20, and one with those of Number 22. The staff common to both – the trainees, float secretaries, and management dispersed themselves as best they could. The end of the tables nearest the bar generally had the older, more senior solicitors while the more junior members of the Firm stuck together at the opposite ends. As a now responsible partner, I found myself nearer the bar end than the other, next to Yarrington who sat with Cressida on his other hand, and opposite Bugle. Kate, being rather shy, and not yet really knowing anyone else, sat next to me, and opposite her Tom had positioned himself boldly next to Bugle, with Matthew drawing up a chair next to him. This anomalous mix of senior partners, junior partners, trainees and secretaries meant that the conversation was centred on our common ground: law.

Law is intrinsically tedious in a social setting, and thinking on it, any setting. I therefore attempted to take the conversation in other directions, but it soon swung back. Nevertheless, we all seemed to have a jolly time, aided by the surprisingly good wine and food to go with it.

After a splendid dinner, Bugle stood up and began hitting his full glass of wine with a knife. Some members of the Firm on our table ceased their conversations and looked expectantly at him, but the hubbub from the second table meant that his glass-tapping was inaudible to those sitting on it; he therefore began hitting the glass with increased vigour, but it was only when he wielded the blade with a force too great for the brittle wine glass causing him to issue a loud 'Fuck!' as wine dribbled from his hand and splintered glass hit his empty dinner plate that the attention of the whole Firm was his.

'Right. Sorry,' he said, as titters went round the table. 'Not the way I wanted to begin, but I've never yet made a decent speech, so I suppose I've started as I mean to go on.'

No one laughed, so he proceeded.

'Well, we've had another splendid year at Bugle & Yarrington. The Firm continues to flourish and expand, and long may it last. There of course have been changes. Some welcome, and some not. Many of you will have been sad to see David step down as senior partner. Partly of course because we all know how well he managed the Firm...'

Bugle paused for a chorus of acknowledgement.

'...and partly of course, because none of you thought I'd be any good.'

He paused again for a second chorus of more amused acknowledgement.

'Well, frankly, I don't like blowing my own trumpet…' he continued, leaving a dramatic pause which he evidently would be filled with laughter, but was in fact filled with several people groaning at his favourite and overused double pun on his own his name.

'…but I hope I have exceeded your expectations…'

And he made an exaggeratedly affected pause for acknowledgement, which he knew wouldn't come. But the joke went down well, and laughter began to erupt as the Firm's employees recognised his self-depreciating sense of humour.

'…and I will continue to try my best next year,' he said, sincerely, at which there was a muted but nonetheless obvious assent from the employees. 'There have been other changes. Sadly, and most seriously, Paul was asked to leave due a difference in working styles. It came as a blow to the company department, but reinforces the stance that the Firm takes in working as a team, and treating each other as equals.'

Matthew and Tom looked at each other, and everyone else tried not to look at them.

'But on a happier note, the shipping department has gone from strength to strength: Teddy's practice has increased to such an extent that we had to employ a new solicitor to assist him. I hope we're doing all we can to welcome Andrew Wainwright into the Firm, and I welcome him now, to his first Christmas party. May it not be his last!'

'I'm sure it won't be!' said Teddy. 'His shipping law knowledge is bang up to date! Twenty-first century stuff!'

'He's *two* hundred years ahead of you?' asked Yarrington, causing much merriment.

'Yes, indeed,' admitted Teddy. 'He, not I, should be the editor-in-chief of the new edition of *Shipping Law.*'

Much merry dissent from Teddy's assembled colleagues ensued.

'Most importantly,' continued Bugle, 'Teddy – and these are his words not mine – the confirmed bachelor – has become engaged!'

A chorus of congratulations and claps ensued followed by a more formal toast.

Everyone was smiling simply because Teddy looked so chuffed.

'The family department has seen two excellent members of staff depart,' said Bugle. 'Margaret had been at the Firm for more years than I care to remember, and I'm sure we all wish her well in her retirement.

And, of course, Emily, James' much loved secretary…'

Laughter ensued, causing my face to turn the colour of my red Christmas tie.

'…Emily, has also departed to pursue a career in the art world… and of course, to pursue James!'

The laughter continued, and I joined in, knowing at this stage that there was no chance of remission.

'But with every sad departure, there of course comes a welcome addition to the Firm. Cressida, who I have recently discovered was James' nemesis in the courtroom, joined us as head of the department, and no doubt, satisfactorily for her, James' direct senior. I hope the arrangement is working out well, James?'

'We tolerate each other,' I said, not quite managing to hide my smile.

'But of course the department wouldn't function without Kate, James and Cressida's new secretary. I hope they're treating you well?' asked Bugle of the shy Kate.

She smiled in assent.

'And I hope, James, that you manage to keep your relationship with your new secretary much more professional than your previous one!' said Bugle. I looked at Kate, and she at me, and neither of us knew what to say as everyone else roared with laughter.

'I'm sure,' said Cressida rather crossly having seen Kate's understandably somewhat nervous reaction, 'that the relationship between Emily and James had nothing to do with their professional relationship.'

'That's right!' I said. 'I'd only kissed her once while she worked for the Firm!'

'Methinks he doth protest too much!' said Yarrington to more laughs.

'Must have been a bloody long kiss!' said Tim, at which point I gave up any further attempts at defending my honour.

Bugle waited for what seemed like an age, deliberately making me squirm.

'And of course,' he eventually continued, 'the Firm is always looking to the future, and recognises that home grown talent needs to be nurtured, encouraged and given every opportunity to flourish. Two more trainees have become solicitors this year, and we trust that they will continue to add to the Firm's expertise. We also hope that the new trainees, Matthew and Tom are enjoying their careers with us, and will want to be solicitors here when the time comes.'

A ripple of laughter went round the table, as all the solicitors exchanged jokes about the foolhardiness of harbouring any form of ambition to become a lawyer.

'That will of course depend on who the senior partner is at the time!' I said. 'I'd be happy to accept the position, if it were offered to me!'

'That will never happen while I'm alive!' exclaimed Bugle.

'Don't tempt me!' I said, finally achieving a laugh at Bugle's expense.

Once quietness again prevailed, Bugle began his conclusion.

'Well, that's all from me. Thank you all for working hard. You are all what makes the Firm what it is. Thank you for coming tonight, enjoy the evening, and let's work together for the continued success of the Firm in the coming year. Happy Christmas!' he said raising a new glass, and making way for tipsy applause and a chorus of 'Happy Christmas!' among the entire staff of Bugle & Yarrington.

The conclusion of the dinner and speech meant that everyone shifted seats to chat to someone new. My chair was vacated swiftly with the intent of draining one of the bottles that had thus far been out of my reach. I successfully manoeuvred around the table, recharged my glass and noticed Tim was heading in my direction.

'That's my cue. Cheers, James. I'm off,' said Tim in as casual a manner as possible in a vain attempt at trying to make it look like leaving the Christmas party before ten o'clock was normal.

'Already?!' I said. 'You can't possibly be leaving this early!'

'I promised Charlotte I'd be home by half ten. I made the mistake of telling her I was sitting next to Kate, who she knows is almost as good looking as Emily. It's ironic – Charlotte didn't give a damn about Kate until she discovered you weren't interested in her. But sadly Kate has no interest in me anyway, so I must curtail my evening and salvage something from it – to keep my darling wife happy.'

'She's your wife, not your bloody mother, Tim. She should be happy you're having fun at your firm's Christmas party.'

'Charlotte, happy?!' and he gave a little grunt coupled with a wry grin to himself, and made no effort to hide his emotions from me. 'You're right though, it is a shame – I want to be able to flirt with the secretaries *one* night a year! But even worse, I'm off to the Midlands tomorrow – and not returning 'til Boxing Day. This evening is going to be the last Charlotte-free evening for days! God alone knows how I'm going to cope. I'll have to listen to the women of the family all squawking together in their hideous singey-songey Birm-ming-gum ack-sents. I won't get a proper meal unless I take Charlotte out, and there won't even be turkey sandwiches after the big day itself: last time we went there for Christmas the turkey was the size of a large quail – and it was supposed to feed twelve! Then I'll have to be pleased that Charlotte's parents have bought me yet another bottle of some creamy and foul-tasting liquor which they seem to think I like. The problem is, they've bought me so much of it, I couldn't possibly admit that I detest the stuff and always leave it out for the milkman as a Christmas treat.'

I couldn't work out whether Tim was being intentionally humorous in a grumpy way, or whether the humour was a wry attempt at making the best of a bad situation that he really was dreading. It was only when his sadly amused expression lost all sense of joy that I realised it had been the latter.

Tim's marriage to Charlotte was a mystery: despite the romantic beginnings, of late he never seemed to be happy with her, nor she with him. He actively disliked her family, and this must have shown. And she kept him on such a short reign, revolt on his part was inevitable, whether it was the odd cigarette at work, or something much more serious a little further down the line, or indeed, now. Which made me wonder how long their marriage would last. How did they view their marriage from the inside? Would they bumble on for years and only see that they were so entirely unsuitable for each other after their as yet unborn kids had become teenagers, or did they know now they should never have married but were too scared to be alone? Or was the marriage different behind closed doors? Did their mutual love and affection manifest itself only when they were alone? There was a possibility of this, of course, but I quickly reflected that I couldn't imagine Charlotte being *more* reasonable away from the public domain, and that although less probable theories have doubtless been proven, substantiation of this theory was beyond the realms of the realistic.

'I don't envy you,' I said.

'No.'

The pause that followed was slightly longer than it was comfortable to bear.

'What are you doing for Christmas?' asked Tim.

'Going to my sister's with Emily.'

'Lucky you, it sounds lovely!' he said, with a sad smile. 'I must fly! Happy Christmas!' he said, with the same expression.

'And you, Tim.'

'Bye, James.'

'Bye.'

And he slipped out, unnoticed by the rest of the revellers. Moments after Tim had departed, I saw Teddy wandering amiably in my direction.

'Hello George!' I said. He was wearing his magnificent party suit: a three-piece affair, and flamboyant in every manner possible: the material so thick that it might have kept one quite warm all day had one's office had no heating, the chalk stripes so bold that no clerk could wear them, it had enormous lapels, double outside hip pockets, working cuffs and a waistcoat which had become a little too small for Teddy's expanding girth, the bottom button of which was correctly but also necessarily undone, and from under which bright red braces could be seen reaching down into the trousers. The braces were certainly superfluous to needs given that he must have had to breath in very deeply to button the trousers, which themselves were deeply pleated and carried enormous turn-ups. He looked wonderful!

'Evening, James!' he said. 'How goes it?'

'Splendid! And you?

'Never better! It's been an interesting year though, hasn't it?'

'It certainly has!'

'Bugle's speech was all right.'

'Surprisingly good for him, yes,' I agreed. 'And just about the right length!'

'When I listened to it, James, I again realised that my success at work and therefore in love has been down entirely down to you. I tried to thank you publicly at the November partner's meeting, but it didn't quite work. So I want to thank you properly now. You know I couldn't have done it without you, so thank you.'

'Thanks, George,' I said, graciously accepting, 'but I'm not sure I deserve it. It was good fortune more than me, I'm sure.'

'Well, be that as it may, you and Matthew worked bloody hard for me for a while, and I certainly couldn't have beaten Priest and Parsons without that input. Thank you.'

'It was a pleasure. I'm not sure I got fully to grips with the law, but then I couldn't claim to be totally au fait with my own area of expertise either!'

We laughed.

'How are you enjoying editing *Shipping Law*?' I asked.

'You see!' he said, 'I must thank you for that idea too! Oh, it's brilliant! I've always wanted to write a book, but I've never really had an idea that I simply couldn't contain, so this is perfect. Being an editor is really criticising other people's work, which is easier than starting the damn thing from scratch! It's given me a new lease of life. I haven't even read December's *Yachting Monthly* I've been so busy, but you know what? I'm enjoying it! I haven't enjoyed law for years!'

'I'm glad,' I said smiling at Teddy's newfound enthusiasm.

'And of course, Miss Pound thinks I'm frightfully important! I suppose the book does have an authoritative title!'

'And an authoritative editor!'

'I wouldn't go that far...' said Teddy, stopping without saying more, knowing full well that with some motivation behind his intelligence he could be as authoritative as he wished.

'Well, James, I must be off, I'm too old for this type of thing! Have you seen David and Cressida?'

'Not since dinner, I'm afraid. Well, have a very Happy Christmas!'

'Oh, I will, James!" he beamed. 'I'm actually looking forward to it for once, now I've got someone to enjoy it with.'

'Send my best to Miss Pound.'

'Will do! Cheers, James, and Happy Christmas!'

'Cheers.'

And he departed, no doubt to say his goodbyes to Yarrington and Cressida. It was then that Angela clocked me on my own, and began her usual crab-like scuttle towards me. What could she possibly chastise me for? Perhaps she'd come to tell me about the health and safety problems associated with drinking too much. If so, I doubted whether she'd have nearly as much practical experience as me, and my intention was to tell her so should she deign to raise the subject. But first and foremost, my plan was to avoid conversation at all costs. In terror, I looked around for another body to make conversation with, but alas, I was alone, and due to the surprising speed of her scurrying scuttle, she was upon me!

'You're looking very handsome this evening, James!'

'Why, thank you, Angela.'

My answer came automatically, but her comment nevertheless left me in a state of surprise: Angela was flirting with someone from the office! Not just someone, but me! How much had she drunk? Her eyes, enormous through the beautifully shiny lenses of her glasses, looked up at me, as if waiting for a response.

'Your hair looks nice,' I said, just to stop her gazing at me so intently, but which was in fact true, relatively speaking. She must have had her December hair wash recently.

'Thanks, I've just washed it,' she said.

Claiming to have just washed one's hair was not normally something one brings to the attention of colleagues, I thought. But she hadn't finished: she shook her clean, but nevertheless scruffy, head of hair as if promoting her particular brand of sheep-dip.

'Do you like my new glasses?' she asked.

'Yes, much better than the old ones,' I said, truthfully. I then began wondering why she was talking to me in this odd manner.

'I don't think we've ever really seen eye to eye, have we James?'

Due the grime on her previous glasses, I wondered if I'd ever seen her eyes before.

'Well, I wouldn't put it like that...'

'I'm not sure how you'd put it, put that's how I'd put it. You find me very annoying don't you?'

'Are you drunk, Angela?' I asked, avoiding the question, which we both knew had only one answer.

'Very!' she said, lurching toward me in the most alarming manner. I held my arm out in front of me to balance her, and to ensure that she couldn't attempt a hug.

'I thought so.'

'I'm surprised to see you sober.'

'I can take it.'

'Well, since I am very drunk,' she said, 'I just thought it'd be a good idea... Much as it may surprise you, I have a lot of respect for you... I think you're great, actually... I really do hope we can get on better next year. One of my revolations is to bring happyarse into the orifice... sorry, came out wrong, but you mow what I knean.'

'Well, Angela! Good luck with your revolution!'

'Thank you, Mister James. And a Merry Christmas to you!'

And with that she detached herself from my arm and stumbled off to harass someone else. It gave me an insight into what it must be like having to do a job which one knows annoys everyone else. It made me feel momentarily sorry for Angela, until the realisation struck me that if her job was forced upon me, I could accomplish the necessary evils of managing the human resource needs of a group of lawyers, who would in those circumstances be my seniors, with significantly more humour and much less bitterness and annoyingness than her.

'So, James, how are things?' asked Bugle, sidling up to me and enquiring in a suspiciously caring manner.

'Tip top!' I said, in an unsuspicious manner.

'Chatting up Angela?' he grinned.

'I think more the other way round. She's drunk. But more importantly, how are things with you? Are you enjoying the party?'

'Actually, I am enjoying it. Yarrington told me the only way to enjoy it is to get drunk along with everyone else, which is now my plan of action. I've always been rather worried that my drunken self will try it on with one of the secretaries, but Kate's an ice-maiden, and all the others are as ugly as my daughters. You bagged the only decent looking one left!'

He paused, as if he thought he'd said too much.

'Kate's just shy,' I said, mainly to fill an awkward gap.

His expression became more thoughtful, and then slightly pained.

'How is everything?' I asked again, this time more sincerely, and leaving a pause for him to answer.

'You don't want to know,' said Bugle, looking at me directly in the eye, eyebrows ever so slightly knitted. His expression was hard to read: did he mean that he really didn't want me to know and that no further questioning should be undertaken, or did it mean that like once before, he simply wanted someone to talk to, to release his pent-up thoughts.

'I do now,' I said, as ambiguously as possible.

He shot me another look, this time possibly wondering whether or not he should open up.

There was pause, which I filled by taking a drink, not necessarily wishing to move the conversation on at this particular juncture. Bugle looked behind me, and then behind himself to see if there was anyone in earshot. His glances were suspicious, and carried out as if he was used to doing it, which no doubt, he was, having been leading an affair for goodness knows how long. Having established that eavesdropping by another was improbable, if not impossible, Bugle announced:

'Jenny's pregnant.'

'Christ!'

'I doubt it; I'm not nearly as gullible as Joseph.'

I smiled, despite the expression on his face.

'What on earth will you do? Is Cathy still refusing to divorce you?' I asked.

'Yes, but that isn't really the main problem.'

'What is?!'

'I've had the snip.'

'Christ!'

'You seem to be keen on this idea,' said Bugle, this time with a smirk. 'I'm flattered that you think Jenny may have been chosen by God, and I agree that the Second Coming may be one hypothesis, but the more *likely* answer is that she's slept with another man.'

He had a point.

'She doesn't know I've had the snip,' he said, almost sadly, but with more of an air of weariness than anything else.

'What has she said?'

'Nothing about sleeping with anyone else. Bitch.'

'I'm so sorry, Frank.'

'I'm not. Makes things much easier.'

'Will Cathy have you back?' I asked, presuming that Jenny's indiscretion had prompted Bugle to attempt a reconciliation with his wife.

'No, but in any case, I don't want her to have me back. That would make things complicated. I don't want either of them. I sometimes wonder if I've ever been in love with either of them. Certainly, I've been in love with the *idea* of both of them, but is that the same thing?'

'No.'

'Oh? You seem very sure...?'

'For me it was the other way round: I realise now that I was in love with Emily for years; it was shutting out the idea of being in love with her that stopped me from realising that I did love her. Therefore, they can each exist without the other, and if you *are* in love with someone, you needn't be in love with the idea of them because that would be superfluous, but neither should you pretend that you don't love them. For Yarrington, it was different again: he was undoubtedly in love with his wife, but also in love with the idea of remaining in love with her after her death.'

Bugle smiled. 'I think the idea of someone is often more attractive than the reality,' he said.

'That is almost universally true,' I agreed.

'Except Emily?'

'Except Emily.'

'I'm not an envious man,' said Bugle, 'but in this respect alone, I envy you.'

I smiled, partly through happiness, and partly, I admit, through smugness.

'Well, there's my conclusion,' continued Bugle. 'Strangely, I've never felt so at peace with myself. And I feel liberated. For the first time in my life since I was married, I am my own master! I could retire tomorrow and do whatever the hell I wanted. It's a good feeling!' he beamed, thinking about it.

'A satisfactory conclusion, then.'

'Yes, indeed. But I won't retire.'

'I know.'

'But it's nice to know I could.'

'Yes, it must be,' I said.

We paused for a drink.

'But I fear I'll never know the feeling,' I said, 'because if I was ever in a position to retire, I would have already done so!'

'And with any luck, when that happens, I'll be long past caring!'

We paused to drink again.

'I've enjoyed these little chats with you, James.'

I smiled, he catching my glance. But I could not bring myself to verbally agree.

'Good.' He said, 'Well, if I don't see you again, have a Happy Christmas, and see you next year.'

'Thank you, Frank. You have a good Christmas, too.'

'I will. For the first time in years, I know I will.'

And then, as if we'd been lifelong friends, he extended his hand for me to shake, which I did, thinking it'd feel very odd, given that the last time I'd shaken his hand was when we'd first met, all those long years ago when I had been a young, green trainee. But it didn't feel odd, and I found that this physical connection between Bugle and I had reinforced the growing sense of respect between us.

'Cheers, James,' he said, releasing my hand, and departing towards the bar.

'Cheers, Frank,' I said to his back.

I felt I needed a breather to get back into the swing of things after my chat with Bugle, and headed for the vault to the left side of the bar, which was always the last one to be filled, and the furthest from the rest of the Firm's employees. I sat on the edge of the seat which went round the vault, circling the table that lay in the middle, looking out at the rest of the Firm.

Within seconds, Kate had seen me, and began making her way over. She seemed very relieved to see a familiar face. She was very attractive, and I was surprised that she was so shy.

'Hi,' I said.

'Hi,' she said, sitting opposite me. The candle on the table made it difficult in the gloom of the vault to see anything other than what parts of her face were illuminated by it from below.

'You miss Emily, don't you?'

It sounded an obvious question to ask, but it was, in fact, very perceptive.

'Yes, I do.'

She smiled.

'Do you have another half?'

I'd never asked before – our relationship hadn't really progressed from professional to friendship – largely, I thought, because of her shyness.

'No, my heart was broken badly some time ago, and I've not been interested since,' she said, quite plainly.

'It won't always be that way,' said Cressida's voice from the back of the vault, almost causing us to suffer cranial injuries from the low roof as we jumped with fright.

We peered into the darkness to see her sitting with David Yarrington at the rear of the vault.

'Sorry,' she said. 'I thought I had to say something at that juncture!'

The deep chuckle of Yarrington resonated through the vault.

'Hello, James. Kate,' he said.

'Hello,' said Kate. There was little else to say, I suppose.

The two older solicitors shuffled round from the back of vault, Cressida next to me, and Yarrington next to Kate. Now they were nearer the slightly brighter lights coming from the bar, we could see them more clearly, although the candle flickering up from the table top still played eerily with the contours of our faces.

'I meant what I said, Kate,' said Cressida. 'Your heart does heal. It took years for it to happen to me, but happen it did.'

Kate smiled. Even I couldn't think what to say. Neither of us expected to be having such a conversation with Cressida, with Yarrington listening in. 'Come on Kate, I'll get you a drink,' said Cressida. Either she was genuinely concerned that she and Kate had run dangerously low of their respective drinks, or it was a convenient ploy to extract herself from the situation. Kate didn't argue, and slid off the seat. I stood up to allow Cressida to shuffle round the seat to the entrance of the vault, and off they went in the direction of the bar.

'Didn't take you long to begin chatting up the new secretary!' said Yarrington.

'I wasn't chatting her up. I was just getting to know her better. You know, to try and make us friends, rather than colleagues.'

'Sorry. I know. Just kidding.'

'I should really be asking what you were doing in there with Cressida. Chatting her up?!'

'Good God, no!' said Yarrington. 'That, my boy, has already been accomplished!'

'What on earth do you mean?'

Yarrington leaned over the table toward me, the candle's light making his eyes into black holes as his face drew nearer the flame, shining up from the tabletop.

'This goes no further, James. Understand?'

I nodded.

'We've just been discussing when to tell everyone at the Firm that we're engaged.'

The amazement that must have crossed my face made Yarrington smile broadly.

'You had no idea?' he asked.

'None at all! But congratulations!'

'Thank you!'

My amazement was total. There hadn't, on the face of it, been one shred of evidence to suggest such a union was possible, let alone contemplated or even effected. But as my mind considered this point with the advantage of hindsight, it remembered one or two instances when it had seen Yarrington and Cressida together and not within office hours. But of course at the time, these sightings had not been considered with a questioning mind.

'You're a bit of a dark horse, David.'

'Nonsense, I just know when I see something I like.'

'So when are you going to tell everyone?'

'Not yet, and she'd kill me if she knew I'd told you, but it's so hard to keep these things quiet!' he said, with a mischievous smile. 'But mum's the word, yes?'

'Indeed.'

'Cressida was quite right in what she said to Kate. Before I met her, I had resigned myself to never finding love again, and I think Cressida felt the same before she met me.'

Yarrington paused.

'Forgive me, James. Ever told you about the sailing trip after Oxford – leading up to the Cairo incident?'

'Everyone knows that story!' I said.

'Everyone knows I ended up in Cairo, totally pissed aboard a burning yacht, but no-one knows *why* I was pissed.'

'But you're about to tell me?'

'I've not spoken about it for years. Teddy is the only one who knows what happened.'

He paused.

'Mum's the word?' I asked, to encourage him.

Yarrington nodded.

I nodded.

He continued.

'You probably know I sailed from Scarborough to Murmansk, and then from there to Oslo?'

'You've never mentioned Oslo before.'

'No. I usually say the Baltic to keep it more vague. Oslo is where I met my wife, you see.'

He paused, and frowned, which eventually turned into a wry smile.

'Don't remember much about the day itself, except sailing north up Olsofjord past the guns that sank the *Blücher* during Weserubung, which even then were ancient, but still manned.'

I always thought it odd how Blücher himself had helped win Waterloo for Wellington, but that a hundred years later, and then a score beyond that, the Prussian hero had leant his name to cruisers of the High Seas Fleet and then the Kriegsmarine, which ships had been deployed against the very nation whose union with Blücher had made him famous in the first instance.

'Don't remember much about the day itself,' continued Yarrington, 'but I remember every detail of the evening. Oslo was warm then, and I remember thinking it was strange that the almost perpetual light made me an insomniac, when usually sleep came to me more easily than winking. Remember the door handle of the restaurant – once painted a beautiful blue colour, but by my visit was mostly a dull ferric red – come off in my hand, and a boy in the street run off laughing as I wondered what to do with it. Remember the acrid smoke emanating from a stove in some corner of the room. Remember seeing her parents, and being pleased that there were some English to talk to. Remember seeing her sister, and being pleased that their daughter was good-looking. But seeing *her* for the first time is a memory so vivid, that in comparison, the others seem dull and unreal, as if they had entered my memory from reading a piece of poor literary description. Even remembering her face as she first saw me makes my heart miss a beat thirty-odd years on. It's a peculiar feeling, seeing for the first time someone you know you must marry.'

If I married Emily, I'd never know this feeling. I felt I loved her now, but Yarrington's story made me feel, for a moment, inferior: why had I not realised I loved her the moment I'd clapped eyes on her? But Yarrington was about to continue, and my thoughts could not formulate themselves into a conclusion before he did so.

'They were sailing on, and marry her I knew I must, so the day after, when they sailed, I sailed in their wake. Sailed south to Copenhagen, by which time I'd become friendly with the whole family: her father had warmed to me when he'd discovered that I'd been at Exeter, Oxford. We sailed on, this time, north. By the time we reached the north of the Baltic – which was some weeks later – and after, due to a moment's lull in concentration, almost sinking my yacht under a huge iron ore barge in Lulea harbour, her father had proclaimed I was the son he'd never had; and him discovering that my father had also been at Exeter as almost his contemporary I think clinched it: the night after he agreed to let me have his daughter. We were married in Stockholm on the way south again, and for the first time, she was allowed on my yacht unattended. But romantic nuptial bliss was necessarily postponed as the yachts sailed back to Oslo through a terrific storm. Unkind weather!'

And Yarrington paused to drink. He was again talking quickly and excitedly, quite unlike his usual, more thoughtful manner of delivery, and his eyes were shining.

'It was at Oslo – the second time we'd been there – that she packed her trunk and boarded my yacht permanently, us heading south for Dunkirk, Calais and so on, and her parents and sister heading north, bound eventually for Bergen. Quite odd, her leaving her parents, and the first time it felt like we were really married. Terrific feeling!

'Soon, we got tired of the cold North Sea winds, and decided that some Mediterranean sun was needed. It was then we decided to head for Cairo, which we eventually did, visiting most of the countries on each side of the Med first. Except that *we* didn't visit Cairo, only I did. Been to Sicily – last leg of the trip – Teddy had flown out to Cairo to help crew the yacht back to England – bit of a jaunt for him too – and we were meeting him there. Lovely day. Blue skies, fair wind, terribly loved-up. Perfect. I'd gone forward to change the jib. When I got back, I thought she'd gone below, and I smoked a few cigs to while away the afternoon.'

Yarrington leaned further forward, his face right up to close to mine. His voice slowed down, and he spoke quietly.

'We were making good progress – ten knots I remember thinking. After a bit I called down for a cuppa, which didn't come. I went below, but she'd gone. Must've been sailing for a good hour before I realised. Of course I tried to retrace my course, but nothing. Nothing was missing. Think she just slipped off the back end, and I didn't hear her cry since I was on the prow. Maybe she hit her head and didn't call out. After sailing back and forth for two days without sleep, I couldn't find her.'

Yarrington blinked and a tear trickled down his face, lit up by the flickering candle. He didn't seem to notice and continued.

'Which is why when I got to Cairo I got tremendously pissed, and eventually fell asleep while smoking. Bloody fag fell into a coil of rope or something, and set the whole damn thing on fire. It's amazing how flammable boat varnish seems to be! All gone: her, our marital home as we'd known it, our life together. Memories, burned in an evening. Probably best the ship did go up, really. Teddy arrived, punctual as ever, and managed to disembark me, ungraciously, into the sea, which, as you can imagine, woke me up in fairly short order! Pretty amazing wake up call, really: despite the booze, was pretty sober once in the drink, which was pretty damn cold, even though it was the Med. Saw the mast ablaze, and the cabin red and orange through the windows. Reminded me of the boiler of a steam train, I remember. Sails had gone up long before I'd got out. Flames, reflections dancing on the water. Dreamt about it for months. No, for years.'

And Yarrington sat back, away from the candlelight. His black holes once more became eyes as the candlelight filled the shadows. His eyes blinked, and fresh streams of water streaked his cheeks.

'And the point of all this rambling, James, as I'm sure you have guessed, is that since that day, I've never thought it possible that this world could possibly have two love affairs of this nature lined up for me. And of course, Cressida has proved me wrong!'

He eyes shone bright, the tears having vacated them.

'Yes, James! When I saw Cressida, I knew again that I would love, and I thought I could see it in her too. Didn't take long to establish that I was indeed in love with her, and that she was rather fond of me, too!'

'When was that?'

'Her second interview.'

'How on earth did you do that? Didn't you interview her with Bugle?!'

'Indeed, sir! But Bugle is about as romantic as a dozen red roses picked too long ago, and the subtext of the interview went quite unnoticed by him!'

I shook my head in (almost mock) amazement, which tickled Yarrington pink. And it amazed me. Here was a man not afraid to live life. A tragedy – in the proper sense of the word – had befallen him, and instead of complaining, instead of remaining bitter, he had lived out his life as best he could – not expecting love, but embracing it when it finally arrived.

'And you knew she… loved? you? Right from then?'

'Oh yes. The first time I asked her out was the most natural thing in the world. She knew I'd ask, and I knew she'd say yes. Knew where we'd go, and knew she'd like it; knew our relationship would immediately escalate beyond the professional. Funny how it happened, when you think of it. Top girl, Cressida. Speaks very highly of you, I might add, James!'

'Under any other circumstances, I'd speak highly of her, but I won't now, because you'll just assume I'm trying deliberately flatter you both!'

'Quite right, James.'

And he looked at me, kindly, in almost a fatherly way, before concluding.

'Well, James, I think I'd better find the betrothed before her suspicions are aroused. We've been in here some time now!'

'Quite right, David. Mum's the word!'

Before he quit the vault, Yarrington reached up to the roof and plucked, from a previously unnoticed branch of mistletoe, a small sprig which he put in his breast pocket. Seeing my questioning expression he declared: 'I've never kissed anyone under mistletoe before.'

'Nor have I.'

'Plenty of mistletoe here last year!' said Yarrington with a smile.

Protesting would have simply fuelled his wit, so I just smiled.

'Well, James,' said Yarrington raising his glass, 'Happy Christmas!'

'Cheers, and to you! And many congratulations, David.'

We clinked glasses, and drained the depleted drinks they held.

We left the cocooned comfort of the vault, and Yarrington headed over to where Cressida stood talking to Kate. I stood watching them. Kate was smiling and animated in her discussion with Cressida which pleased me. It made work so much more pleasant when individual members of a particular office got on well, and it looked like Kate would be a very satisfactory replacement for Emily. Teddy and Bugle were laughing and slapping each other over the shoulder. Now Teddy was a financially viable member of the Firm once more, Bugle was now his best friend, and it looked like Teddy had forgiven Bugle for attempting to give him the boot. This was possibly because Teddy knew that if he'd been in Bugle's place, prior to his newfound onslaught of work, he would have found it difficult to find reasons not to make himself redundant.

After that, I looked at my watch, something previously unheard of at a Christmas party, and realised that I'd done so because it just wasn't the same without Emily. I had chatted to everyone I had wanted to, and decided that, despite it being Saturday the next day, it was almost Christmas and I wanted to enjoy my weekend without a hangover. I wanted to enjoy my weekend with Emily.

I departed.

CHAPTER 66

Newtonian Theory

I woke up on Christmas Eve again having dreamt that blue flashing lights flicked across the bedroom ceiling and that bad news was almost upon me. My relief was great when I opened my eyes to find nothing more threatening than a shaft of sunlight entering the room via a chink in the curtains.

Shortly after, Emily arrived. Sarah and Michael had invited us for Christmas day, and because of this, Emily and I had (admittedly at my insistence) decided to have our own turkey and all the trimmings on Christmas Eve; it is hard to do without turkey sandwiches in the first long and depressing week of work in January. Being a lovely morning, we embarked on a long walk up through the Regent's Park and to Primrose Hill. It was good to get out. I began to wish for the countryside: for a dog to walk, and for frozen cowpats that make such excellent frisbees if you can successfully peel them from the grass.

After that, Emily wanted to paint, and so got changed into her paint-covered denim dungarees with only one strap over her left shoulder and tight white painting t-shirt underneath. She must have known she looked sexy. She probably bought the outfit with the express intention of making it her sexy painting gear.

Her breasts were looking wonderful and I wanted to undress her then and there, but realised she should be left in peace to paint. Soon, my thoughts drifted to whether if, on the Moon, or Mars, where the gravitational pulls are respectively sixteen and thirty-eight percent of the Earth's, various parts of human anatomy would be less prone to the effects of gravity that are so common on our own sublunary sphere, and whether, once humanity has colonised these new celestial orbs, there would be a scientific paper written on the subject. This thought made me smile, and Emily asked what was going through my head. It was unusual for her to ask that because she had become used to me smiling to myself years ago, and I didn't tell her: some things are best left unsaid, even to those you love most.

I began reading, and thus we spent the afternoon in contended bliss: painting, reading and generally being in love.

After tea I popped the stuffed bird in the oven and began preparing the rest of the feast. At six we had a gin, and I continued cooking, Emily joining me in the kitchen, for company and the occasional word of advice in matters culinary. She was such an excellent cook, and such an entirely useless delegator, that she ended up assisting in the preparation of our food to such an extent that my position of head chef was under some threat of being usurped. Still, she was more content to command than watch, but my wry smile when thinking about the role reversal didn't go unnoticed.

'James!' What are you smirking about?'

'I'm meant to be cooking for you!'

'Don't be daft, James! You know I can't not be in control in the kitchen!'

'Yes, it was foolish of me to think my authority could last more than five minutes!'

She poked me in the ribs, causing a wave of sticky tonic to break out of my glass and splatter across the floor.

'James! You're so careless! Get out of the kitchen!'

I duly obeyed, and tactically retreated to the living room and to the relative safety of the sofa, picking up a book and pretending to be deeply engrossed in it.

Emily's face soon appeared around the kitchen door, and the rest of her followed, one of her hands bearing a fresh glass of gin and tonic. I read deeply, ignoring her apparently amorous advances.

'I'm sorry, darling!' she said, kissing my forehead and sliding the glass from her hand to mine.

Still I read, furrowing my brow in mild irritation that she had interrupted the fascinating page that held my attention so deeply.

Her concern was increasing from the casual to the real, but unfortunately the cheeky smile that had already spread itself across my mind was now beginning to find its way onto the contours of my face.

'James! You bugger! You're not even reading, are you?' she exclaimed, having noticed the same. Then she rolled over the back of the sofa on top of me; the gin glass found its way safely onto the coffee table before she started kissing me passionately.

After a brief interlude in the bedroom, we found ourselves again in the kitchen rescuing the temporarily forgotten food. Emily finished the cooking and the end result was therefore most splendid. We dined at first in contended silence, and latterly in animated conversation. After we had eaten, we decamped to the comfort of the sofa, each sitting at one end with legs uncivilly but comfortably entwined across it, her little feet on my lap.

'Emily, you really are gorgeous,' I found myself admitting. 'I can't believe it took me so long to fall for you.'

'Nor me. Still, men are slow learners!'

We smiled, but there were more serious questions on my mind.

'Seriously, Em. I love you.'

'I love you too. I always have.'

'I'm sorry.'

'For what?'

'Taking so long. Asking your advice about my disastrous relationships with other girls when I knew you loved me.'

'Did you know?'

'I'm not sure. I think so. Anyway, I'm sorry.'

'Don't be daft,' she smiled.

Later, I filled a stocking for Emily with the little presents I'd been diligently collecting over the last few weeks. Neither of us could sleep, both wanting the other to nod off first to effect a successfully secret visit from Father Christmas. Eventually, tiredness won, and we agreed with a nod (and a smile because not a word was said) to place the stockings simultaneously.

Once done, we fell asleep in each other's arms.

CHAPTER 67

Christmas Day

Waking up in my flat on Christmas Day with Emily in bed was frankly the best Christmas present I'd ever had.

After I'd unwrapped and played with this perfect present several times, and the present herself had emptied her stocking, and me mine, we had breakfast of scrambled eggs, smoked salmon and Champagne. This was Emily's favourite form of breakfast, and a long, hot bath rounded off the first part of the morning beautifully.

We then departed for Sarah's house.

She opened the front door as I rang the bell.

'What a beautiful wreath!' said Emily, looking at Sarah's imperfectly perfect creation.

'Thank you, Emily! Well, welcome! Happy Christmas! Come in!'

Christmas chaos was evident everywhere: Ben scampered round in great excitement, toys littered the floor, food preparation rendered every kitchen surface full, Sarah chastised Michael for using the tea towel to dry his hands, and then for offering us drinks at eleven in the morning. Thankfully she capitulated shortly afterwards and drinks and nibbles were served in the drawing room. It looked splendid: the tree was, as always, only six inches shorter than the room's fourteen feet, and there were Christmassy touches everywhere: the pile of presents beneath the tree extended further out than its lowest branches, a gloriously red poinsettia sat on the mantelpiece, holly and ivy adorned every picture, including Emily's, proudly hanging in the prime position over the mantelpiece, and Christmas cards covered every other available surface in the room. Baby Alexander was sitting in an ever-so-comfortable-looking chair facing the room looking earnestly around; he appeared to be satisfied about the situation, and was very pleased when Emily knelt down beside him and began talking to him in a language that clearly only women and babies (and possibly dogs) can understand.

Presents were opened, much to Ben's delight, especially as he was also allowed to help open his baby brother's, and the day drifted past as

Christmases should. The only sadness in the proceedings came when only four presents remained under the tree, and Emily asked:

'Who are they for, Ben?'

Ben looked at the labels in turn, and turned to the room, wide-eyed.

'Two are for Flickety and two are for Charlie,' he said.

Thoughts of Charlie were always in the back of my mind, but having his name brought so suddenly into the middle of the conversation stumped us all, and no one seemed sure what to say. Charlie and Felicity had been invited to come to Sarah's for Boxing Day, and in the rush after the accident and before Christmas, their presents had been forgotten under the tree. Sarah, universally acknowledged to be in charge of Christmas, looked mortified at having made such a mistake, but it was Ben who broke the silence:

'Can we send them to him in heaven?'

As his parents looked at each other wondering who would, or how to respond to his question, Ben had already given up waiting for an answer. It was clear from this quick dismissal of expectancy for an answer that even at his young age, he was beginning to realise that what he'd learned thus far about God and heaven was perhaps the watered down version, or the child's version, or not quite the whole truth, and that the answer his parents would give wouldn't satisfy his curious mind in any event.

Ben's apparent lack of interest for an answer made his parents believe they were off the hook, and Sarah said: 'We must cook!'. So then all our attentions turned to the kitchen, and all hands were called on deck, Michael basting half cooked roast spuds, Emily making bacon rolls, Ben pricking the sausages, and with a loud yelp, himself. My deployment was in the vegetable corps and my first tactical objective was to 'do' the sprouts. Sarah stood by issuing orders and everyone seemed to have forgotten Alexander.

Finally the turkey emerged from the oven, and Ben stood gazing at it in awe.

'It's big!' he summarised, concisely. 'Is a turkey bigger than an emu?' he asked.

A discussion between the other adults ensued as they discussed the morphology of the turkey. Ben listened in fascination as he discovered that turkeys must be very special birds indeed if even the grown-ups couldn't decide between them how they appeared when not plucked, depedalised and decapitated.

Again, his interest had waned by the time his seniors had come to a conclusion, but was rekindled when I showed him a picture of a turkey from *Birds of the World* which I happened to know was the only non-cookery book that resided on Sarah's cook book shelves next to the dresser.

Emily smiled at me.

A year ago I would have instantly concluded that she was observing my excellent paternal and pedagogical instincts coming to the fore, but now I wasn't sure: her look seemed deeper and more complex than that, and the only thing to do was smile back.

Eventually, all was ready and we all adjourned to the dining room. The dining table looked wonderful: it had been polished and the table cloth removed to show off the deep mahogany; all the best flatware and crockery had been laid, red Christmas napkins and crackers adorned each place, and I could almost hear the table groaning under the weight of food and wine. But it was silent, no doubt not wanting to complain too much for doing the job it was supposed to.

Once the magnificent Christmas dinner had been served, Ben told us about his presents; Emily talked of her plans for future exhibitions; I kept the family updated with news of the Firm, and the respective fortunes of Bugle and Yarrington themselves in the arena of love; Alexander tried to join in by vocalising his need for yet more sustenance and Michael ranted about the economic climate.

By the time we'd all finished, only Sarah and Emily seemed to be capable of bipedal movement, the boys having somewhat overindulged themselves. The girls agreed to do the inter-course clearing and bringing in of pudding so long as the boys washed up. We readily agreed, all being proponents of the adage that has served the male dimorph for eons: never do now what can be put off until later. And so on came the Christmas pudding, mince pies, and a huge round of stilton. Michael produced a bottle of port, and eating again commenced.

Alexander, and then Ben, were put to bed, and once Michael had returned from the latter task, he looked at Sarah with a questioning look, to which she gave a nod.

'We thought we'd tell you,' said Sarah, 'once Ben was asleep, that we're moving to the country.'

I was shocked. Michael was a Londoner through and through and Sarah has become one. I had assumed they would remain in Town forever.

'Why?'

'The kids, mainly,' said Michael. 'Whenever Sarah talks about it, I envy your childhoods. But I've had it with the City. It has become too much.'

'Well!' I said. 'I don't know what to say!'

'How lovely!' said Emily, 'I *am* envious.'

I looked at her and she smiled; we would talk about it later.

Sarah enthused about leaving London and Michael explained his reasons for leaving his City job. I understood their reasoning whilst acknowledging that I would miss them enormously. Another chapter of my life had come to an end, but how the next would open remained unclear.

Going to bed with the first Christmas present I'd unwrapped that morning drew the day to a perfect conclusion, and as our arms wrapped sleepily around each other and I smiled at Emily's gorgeousness, I realised that because of her, because of Emily, this was the happiest Christmas I'd ever had. Finding the words to convey this to her took longer than it took her to fall fast asleep, and my thoughts turned again to Emily, and our combined pasts.

Emily, whose beauty had struck me on our first acquaintance and whose friendship had been given shortly thereafter; Emily who'd loved me for years, and whom I'd loved in friendship for as long; Emily, the thought of whose laugh made me smile and Emily, Emily...

My Emily.

I did not lament that it had taken so long for me to fall for her. The lessons learned from my mistakes in love had indeed made my love for her stronger. And now, I turned to the beautiful face of this Emily, contentedly asleep next to me on the pillow.

And as I lay there watching her sleep, I knew – if one can establish such a definitive moment on such a thought – that I must marry her.